BETHANY WITTE-KRANTZ

The Mountains of Ebbon

First published by Bethany Witte-Krantz 2024

Copyright © 2024 by Bethany Witte-Krantz

All rights reserved. No part of this publication may be reproduced, stored or transmitted in any form or by any means, electronic, mechanical, photocopying, recording, scanning, or otherwise without written permission from the publisher. It is illegal to copy this book, post it to a website, or distribute it by any other means without permission.

This novel is entirely a work of fiction. The names, characters and incidents portrayed in it are the work of the author's imagination. Any resemblance to actual persons, living or dead, events or localities is entirely coincidental.

Bethany Witte-Krantz asserts the moral right to be identified as the author of this work.

Bethany Witte-Krantz has no responsibility for the persistence or accuracy of URLs for external or third-party Internet Websites referred to in this publication and does not guarantee that any content on such Websites is, or will remain, accurate or appropriate.

Designations used by companies to distinguish their products are often claimed as trademarks. All brand names and product names used in this book and on its cover are trade names, service marks, trademarks and registered trademarks of their respective owners. The publishers and the book are not associated with any product or vendor mentioned in this book. None of the companies referenced within the book have endorsed the book.

First edition

ISBN (paperback): 9798991145114
ISBN (hardcover): 9798991145107

Editing by Susan Gaigher
Editing by Chris Barcellona
Cover art by Bethany Witte-Krantz
Illustration by Bethany Witte-Krantz

This book was professionally typeset on Reedsy.
Find out more at reedsy.com

To younger me, when you wanted to read this book, it didn't exist. Now you can expand the minds of readers to your own little universe.

Contents

Prologue		1
1	The Wind Whispered	2
2	Meeting Lilja	21
3	Falling In	41
4	The Tree Whispered to Me	52
5	The Girl who Became a Tree	62
6	Haunted Past	72
7	Revealed	81
8	Secret City	90
9	Ossory Wolf	103
10	Murder	109
11	The Path Down	118
12	Ebbon City	123
13	Damsel in Distress	128
14	Belle & the Sea Shanty	137
15	Valdis News	144
16	Newlyweds	152
17	The Beginning of What?	159
18	Morally Grey	166
19	Scrambled	175
20	Sald Forest	181
21	Murder?	188
22	A Deal with a Nymph	196
23	The Past Held in a Rock	204

24	Disobeying a Direct Order	213
25	Just a Little Chat	220
26	Body Dump	227
27	Telling a Secret	233
28	Fated?	239
29	Child-like Glee	244
30	The Mother of All	249
31	Before the Seasons Change	254
32	For a Favor	259
33	Found Family	270
34	The Skin Weaver	276
35	The Enemy	282
36	You Will Always Be Enough	293
37	Attack, Explode, Kidnap	312
38	Just a Toy	318
39	Suspected Dead	327
40	Resolved Feelings	332
Afterword		341
God's and Goddesses		342

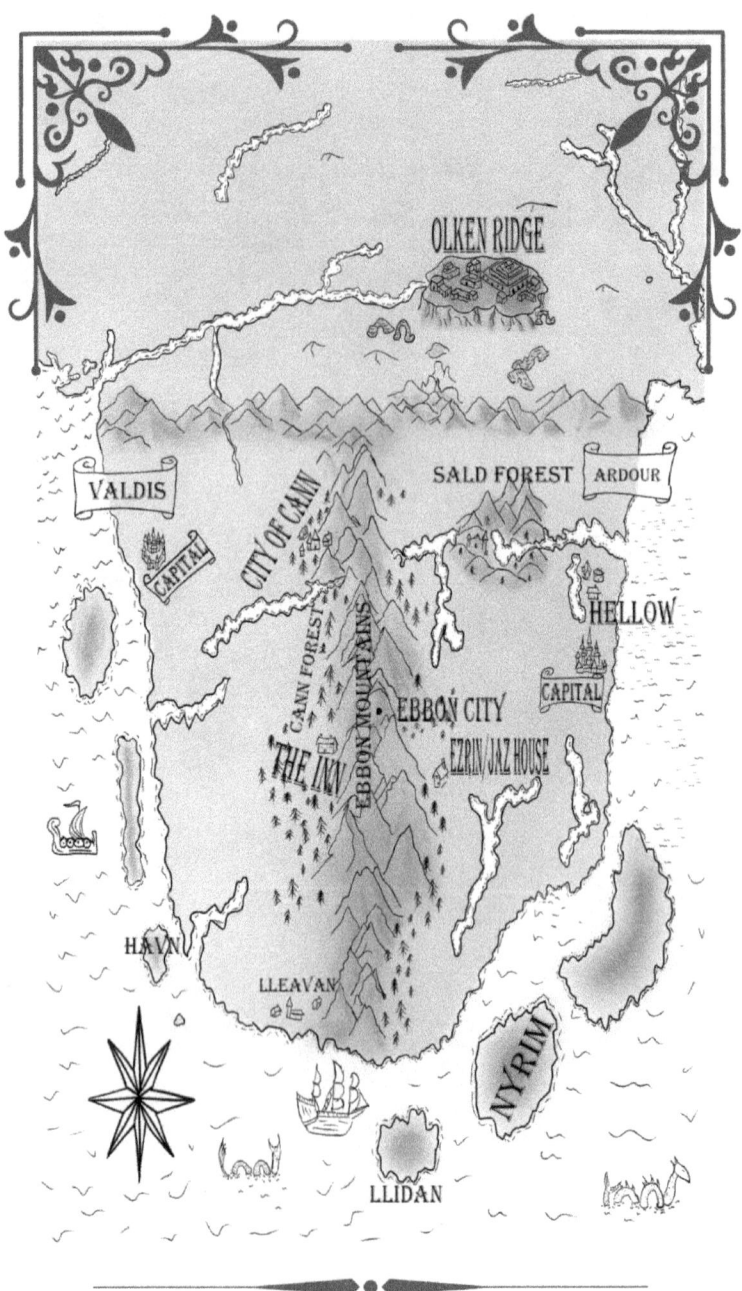

Prologue

A long time ago, I was a prominent member of the upper circle in town. My life was laid out for me, guaranteed. As long as I spent my time studying the path my Father wanted me to take. At least, my life was supposed to be guaranteed. They have turned away from me from the life I once knew. My lifestyle came into the light after talking to someone with a loose tongue. High society deemed the way I wanted to live as unacceptable. Using the remaining coins to my name, I wandered through the forest frantically until I found a piece of land. Where I could live undiscovered by society in the far stretches of the town's perimeter.

Employing carpenters from the neighboring towns, a cottage was built. As they built a respectable cottage, I found a new life where one was lost.

1

The Wind Whispered

Elowen, the wind seemed to whisper.

I glanced up from the plant laying before me. The forest stilled, as if to say, *that wasn't me.* The silence was unnerving and frightening. *I am too far away from anyone. Nobody is out there,* I tell myself. My hands went back to the medicinal plant in distress. I pulled the last remaining weeds encroaching on its will to live. Brushing myself off as I stood up, giving the forest surrounding my cottage a look over once more. I grabbed my basket, and then—

Elowen, the wind whispered again.

My hand paused for a brief second until I realized my mistake. I needed to act natural if there was actually someone there. I cursed myself in my head. My faltering hands most likely went unnoticed by the potential threat, *but they could have noticed it.* I walked towards the cottage, went inside and shut the door. The latch fell into place with a deafening thud. I tried to be invisible. I threw the basket on the table, and pulling away the curtain, I peered outside.

The forest was once again deathly quiet. I took a deep breath. As I attempted to calm my racing heart, I closed my eyes. *It's nothing, it's nothing, IT'S NOTHING. My* mind screamed at me. I glanced around at a quiet and empty house. Taking another glance out the window, exposing myself to whatever potential threat lurked outside. *See, no one is there. You are overreacting.* Mindlessly, I rub the ugly raised scar on my arm.

The world had been quiet as of late; my existence in the world appeared to be forgotten as I let the forest consume me. I busied my hands by adding the herbs to the stockpot on the flame. Learning the craft of plants was a self-taught ambition, a dangerous one at that. But a necessary one if I wanted to survive on my own. All I knew came from books I traded from travelers, and experimenting on random plants that grew in the forest was dangerous. I shuddered when I thought about it. I felt like I was throwing up my insides after eating a mushroom.

Never again. I trembled at the memory and sighed as I opened my cabinet, the contents of which were dwindling so severely that the spiderweb in the corner stood forgotten and empty. The season switching over was to blame. Society had forced me to my current home at the wrong time, leaving me with not enough time to stock for the impending cold season. If I wanted to survive the winter, I needed to get supplies.

Fuck, the gods must hate me. I needed to find someone to trade from, someone to buy supplies from. I grabbed jars with precisely written labels from the shelf and shoved them into my satchel. I put my cloak on, pulling the hood over my head. The flame in the hearth dwindled to nothing as I smothered it. Little red sparks flew into the air before dissipating into nothing. Wordlessly, I prayed to the gods. *Please let no one recognize me.* As I moved through the overgrown path leading to the main road, the jars clinked in the satchel.

The forest surrounding my newfound home was dense and filled with old growth. As I traipsed through the overgrowth, the chill air stung my nose. It had been two months since the incident, two long, silent months. My heart ached at the memory, and the emotions were still felt fresh in my heart. After being silent for months, I was unsure if my voice would carry.

My exhausted form reached the road as the sun met the earth in a warm embrace after a day apart. I made camp off the road, knowing only the desperate traveled at night. I was desperate, but not *that* desperate. Too afraid to start a fire, I snacked on cold jerky.

Stealth was important; I didn't want to call attention to myself. As hazardous as it was for a woman to travel, it was extra dangerous to be a woman traveling by herself. I piled weeds together, attempting to make a layer between my body and the ground, knowing if I didn't, the earth would sap away the heat in my body. I huddled down, pulling the cloak around me, and I resigned myself to a cold and fire-less night.

My mind raced as I closed my eyes, thinking about the potential outcomes for tomorrow.

Why was I born this way?
Why can't I be like everyone else?
Would anyone try anything?
Would the lower circle recognize me?
Would they know what I was?

I tried to calm my erratic breath caused by the runaway thoughts in my head by listening to the sounds of the night. *In, out, in, out,* I commanded. My hands shaking, I pulled myself up into a sitting position, trying to level my breathing.

The jerky in my system rolled around in my stomach, threatening to come up with the unwelcome motion. I put my head in my hands as if trying to stop the sway of the earth, which was giving my unruly stomach ideas. But I couldn't waste food. *It's okay, it's okay.* My hand rubbed my leg. My breath soon slowed and my stomach stopped swaying. I laid back, my head pounding, looking through the treetops to the welcoming stars in the sky.

The sounds of birds woke me. I looked around, surveying my soundings. The sun pulled away from its long embrace with the earth as I gathered my supplies to begin the long walk to the nearest town. The road was empty, other than a few wild animals crossing the forest. I thanked the gods for this, and then they laughed at me.

Forty minutes down the road, I saw my first traveler. He was a rough-looking man, his hair speckled with gray and his face tanned and weathered from seeing many seasons. His disheveled clothing clung to his thin form. His tunic was torn and dirty, and the bag he carried appeared to be mostly empty, save for some insignificant items.

My inner voice debated with the logical part of my brain. On one hand, this man could just ignore me on my path. On the other hand, desperate people did desperate things. I shuddered, making my decision, squaring my shoulders. I tried to make myself seem bigger and more confident than I was.

I cursed myself. I had no weapon save for a small dagger attached to my hip. Keeping my normal pace, my senses hyper aware of the figure, I quickly outwalked the aging traveler. I took a deep breath, my shoulders relaxing back into their normal position. *I have to stop overreacting,* I told myself. *Everyone is not out to get you.*

The sounds of life assaulted my eardrums as I inched closer to the town's perimeter. The clangs of the blacksmith's hammer, the laughter of children, and the voices of sales clerks filled my ear. I was happy to hear the sounds of others, but terrified their actions towards me. I pulled my sleeve over my scar, the only visual reminder of my previous life. The large wooden gates were open as I reached the outskirts of the town. I held my satchel close to my body as I entered, not wanting my pockets to be picked by some desperate souls.

The noise everyone made as they went along with their daily life astounded me, after my months of being in relative silence. I followed a path with other travelers, who seemed eager to find their way like a herd of cattle. I set up shop in a small space between a jar merchant and a rug seller, setting a worn blanket on the ground and laying out my jars filled with medicinal properties. They were all made of herbs found growing wild in the forest surrounding my cottage. I was confident that the properties of the jars could benefit people ailing within the town's limits.

The day passed by slowly. Jars exchanged hands and directions of use explained to paying customers. No one looked at my face more than a second. My customers only wanted relief for their ailments. As the jars sold, the sun got lower and lower in the sky. With the last remaining light, I picked up the leftover jars and my blanket.

Other sellers were doing the same. Shoppers from earlier had dissipated, leaving only a few stragglers in the courtyard. Once I cleaned up my space, I stood up, cursing myself for sitting so long. As my youthful body groaned in protest, as if I was an elderly lady who had seen many summers. Worry set in as I wondered where I would sleep tonight. I walked farther into the town.

My eyes set on the Black Beard Tavern, I heard the sounds of rowdy, intoxicated people already inside. With my coin purse clutched in my hand, I took a deep breath and walked in. A band played in the corner. Ladies of the night speckled the crowd, identified by the lack of clothing covering their bosoms. No one paid me any mind as I walked to the bar. The person at the counter was older than me.

"Hello, I'd like a room for the night, please," I said, my voice cracking. The man looked at me up and down, grinning. Probably mistaking my stutter as nervousness about him. In reality, I wanted out of the crowded common area as soon as possible.

A lazy grin spread across the employee's face. "Sure thing, dumplin', two silvers please."

I already regret choosing this tavern, I thought cynically. We exchanged for the keys and I trudged up the steps, feeling his eyes on me the entire way. I shut the door, pulling the chest from the edge of the bed to the door, blocking any entry or exit from this room.

I opened my satchel and took an inventory of the jars I had left and the coins I gained throughout the day. I threw myself on the bed in a huff and moaned. It'd been a while since I had a bed that wasn't hay. I slid underneath the blankets, blowing out the flame flickering on my nightstand, and allowed the dark to overcome me.

It was dark when I opened my eyes. As they adjusted to the dark, I gave my surroundings a once-over. My breath caught in my throat when I realized there was a human-sized form in my room. A chill set in.

"Hello, dumplin', you weren't supposed to wake up quite just yet," he said as he lunged at me.

I screamed, madly grasping for my satchel. His clammy hand seized my wrist right before I could reach it.

"No, no, we are just getting started dumplin'," he grinned, showing his white teeth. "We aren't even to the good part yet."

I rolled over, kicking as I met the soft spot in between his legs. He grunted, releasing his hold on me for a fraction of a second. Just long enough for me to grab my satchel and dagger. I unsheathed it in one fluid movement. I stared at him. My chest rose and fell fast because of my rapid breathing. My heartbeat pulsed behind my eyes.

I glanced back at the chest in front of the door, my body tense. "How did you get in here?" He smirked and pointed towards the window.

"It was quite the surprise when I tried the door to find it barricaded. Clearly, it wasn't enough to stop me," he said. Like it was some stupid game.

With the blade still pointed towards him, I struck a match and lit the candle next to me. The flame illuminated the room with a soft, ominous glow. The shadows danced on the wall next to him.

I gritted my teeth vehemently, "Get out."

The wind howled through the room, a distant storm finally meeting the town. He lunged towards, as if I was a wild animal. Missing me by a fraction of a inch towards the door landing on the chest.

He drummed his fingers on the lid, staring at me with a brazen smile. "How do you propose that? You did such a good job barricading yourself in."

My anxiety began traveling towards my hands, making them sweaty. The dagger felt slippery. "Out the way you came," I said with disgust, keeping my voice level. He put his hand on his heart, feigning scared.

"I could never do that. What if I fell? It could be fatal."

"That's too bad," I said, my voice betraying my genuine emotion. He stood up, squaring his shoulders and striding towards me, stopping just out of reach of my blade.

"Do you know how to use that?" He gestured to the blade in my hand.

I grinned wildly. False courage filled my body from the adrenaline coursing through my body. "Do you want to find out?"

He lunged at me, and I ducked down a moment too late as he grabbed me by my face, pulling me back up. I screamed again, swiping the blade at him making a shallow cut on his cheek. The blood already swelled to the surface. He grimaced, grabbing my wrist, making the blade fall from my hands. With his sturdy body, he pushed me up against the wall. He grunted.

"Damn, you weigh more than I thought."

"Fuck you," I said, spitting in his face. He pushed my hand against the wall above my head and my sleeve fell down, leaving my scar exposed. Glancing up as I felt the cold air hit it, his gaze followed mine. Recognition lit up his face.

Time stopped as he stared at me in disgust. "You know, maybe you haven't tried someone who was good." I stared at him, repulsed.

Suddenly, the door pushed open and the chest moved.

A guard looked at us as he entered the room. "What's going on here?"

The tavern worker's face contorted into distress, letting go of me. "Officer, she's a sinner and tried to come on to me. When I refused, she attacked me," holding his bleeding face.

My jaw was on the floor I gaped at him as if Leland the Overseerer of Fate had dropped new lore onto the world to explain the act he just gave. I pulled down my sleeve and adjusted my shift and crossed my arms, trying to cover myself as much as possible.

The officer looked at the tavern employee, turning to me. "Do you have any proof to substantiate this claim?"

"Yes, just look at her right arm!" The tavern employee—the *asshole*—said, exasperated.

"Show me your arm," the guard said.

I dragged back the fabric covering my arm, exposing my brand, a symbol of the previous life that society had forced out of. He looked at it and his gaze narrowed as he strode towards me. He pulled chains from his belt and clamped them around my wrist, bruising me further.

"You are under arrest for coming back into town, you wench," he seethed. The kindness in his voice had disappeared, replaced with disgust.

Tears ran down my face, and my heart pounded behind my eyes. "Please, just let me go. I'll leave and never come back."

"You had your chance," he said, pushing me forward.

"Wait! Can I have my bag, please?" I hiccuped as a near-constant stream of tears ran down my face.

The asshole lowered his eyes to look at me, hate gleamed in them. "You won't need the bag where you are going." I glared at him, the tears falling off my chin and down to my neck. I sniffled, snot threatening to explode everywhere. The officer grumbled in agreement but still grabbed my satchel and threw it roughly into my hands.

I scowled at him and lunged, spitting in his face. "I hope whoever you try to do this to next kills you, you bastard." The guard grabbed onto my shoulders.

"That's enough, wench." Officer man pushed me out into the hallway and pushed me down the steps. My body roughly bounced down the steps and I squeaked in surprise, trying to make my body into a ball to avoid hitting anything important. I met the ground floor with an unceremonious thump. I looked up at the officer, dazed, as he thundered down the steps. His large, calloused hands hauled me to my feet and walked me out into the street. The sun has pulled away from the earth's embrace once again.

"Where are you taking me?" I asked, my voice void of emotion. Maybe it was time to give up.

"To the jail so we can try you for your crime."

"I did nothing, just let me go," I said as I pulled against his grip, digging into my arm.

"You being alive is crime enough. Your kind disgust me," he said, spitting to the side as if saying "your kind" left a foul taste in his mouth. The guard led me down the winding streets and soon we walked in streets I recognized from my childhood. A few moments later, we were standing in front of the prison. The building was imposing on the outside, made of white rock, the windows barred.

"Let's go," he said as he pushed me into the building.

The inside looked even less inviting than the outside. The hardened criminals behind bars looked at me with confusion for a second—just long enough to remember how men acted—and then the whistling and obscene yells commenced. The language was sure to make even the ladies of the night blush. The guard shoved me forward again, ripping the satchel out of my hands, unlocking an empty cell, and closing me in it.

The lock clanged back into place, sounding eerily final. "The judge will arrive later," the officer said. He flicked his hands dismissively as he spoke and walked back down the hall.

I took a breath and sighed, sliding down the wall. The jagged stone wall dug into my back uncomfortably. Putting my head in between my knees, I dozed off. I awoke to the lock opening with a resounding clank.

I looked up quickly to see who was entering. A man in clergy robes holding a cane was in the front. The white piece of fabric on the top of the black robe glared at me. Two men behind him wore decorative armor, complete with swords on their hips. The one to the right looked mean. Brown shaggy hair poked off the top of his head, unruly, and his eyes, almost black, seemed to pierce my soul. I looked away from him, focusing on the man on the left. My eyes met his, and I glanced away as recognition settled in my mind.

Jasper. What is he doing here? I wondered. Not willing to look at the left man anymore, I looked down.

"What is your given name, child?" the clergyman stated.

I looked at my interlocked hands and mumbled, "Elowen Alwyn."

"Speak clearly," the clergy stated, using his cane to force my face up to look at him. The left guard looked at the clergy member, seeming surprised at his boldness.

"Elowen Alwyn," I enunciated, glaring at the clergyman.

"Do you deny the claims on which we brought you in? It is clear someone has already banished you from the town," he states as he gestured to my branded arm.

"No, I don't," I said, glaring at him. His cane moved from underneath my chin, rapping me in the head, catching me right above my eyebrow.

"No, what?" he seethed, staring at me.

"That's enough," Jasper stated. "She already answered you; you don't need to hurt her." I looked up at him in surprise. He wouldn't look me in the eye. Instead, he glared at the clergyman.

"She's an abomination," the clergyman said, exasperated.

"Yes, and she will answer for her crimes before the gods. A human, even a holy one, should not lay the god's punishment, even you," Jasper said, his face empty of any type of emotion.

The clergyman mumbled to himself and looked back at me, pulling a roll of paper from his large sleeve. As he unrolled it, a little stream of blood ran down my face and into my eye, blurring my vision into a pink swirl. "You, Elowen Alwyn, were charged with Same-Sex Desire and now you are charged with disregarding your banishment. Banishment was given to you for your earlier crime," he said, his upper lip curled in disgust. "Because of your previous status, the crown declares Elowen Alwyn to be put to death by hanging." He grinned. "They should never have allowed you to live. Your kind is what's wrong with the world today, against the god's plan."

I opened my mouth to give a smart reply, but nothing came out. Jasper made a sound of surprise and then closed his mouth. He looked at me sadly. The clergyman glanced at him, narrowing his eyes, but said nothing. "We shall put you to death at first light tomorrow. May the gods punish you in the afterlife," he said as he turned and walked out. Jasper glanced back at me one last time, throwing his handkerchief at me. He said nothing as they walked away.

I brought the handkerchief up to my head and winced. *That'll leave a scar,* I thought to myself. *No, it won't,* a voice in my head replied dryly. I scoffed. Coming into town to buy supplies might have been a mistake. *No duh,* the little voice said again. Even my inner monologue was going to bother me, it seemed. With the back of my hand, I wiped the blood away from my eye. Was there any way out of this mess? Picking myself up off the floor, I started pacing. My mind swirled with worry. My breath became erratic, my chest heaved up and down, tightening as my heart beat irregularly.

I stared out the window, trying to distract myself from the literal impending doom approaching me in the morning.

"You're still struggling with that?" a voice from behind me asked.

I whirled around, and the world tilted side to side with the movement. I went down with an ungraceful thump.

"Hey it's okay," Jasper said, his voice barely above a whisper, "just breathe with me." He took one dramatic breath in through his nose and blew it out through his mouth.

I listened, begrudgingly rolling my eyes in response. As I tried to match my irregular breath with his steady one. Eventually, my breathing matched his, and I stared at him glumly. "What, are you here to yell at me some more?" I said. He looked at me with surprise.

"No, I came here to help you escape," he said, grinning.

"Why?"

"Because I don't think you should die because of who you love," Jasper stated.

I looked at him in surprise. "What do you mean, you don't think I should die because of who I love?" I seethed. "You're the one who sold me out!"

Jasper looked at me with surprise and hurt. "That was a mistake! I told Elfric, and he is the one who sold you out, not me."

"*You* told him!" I said, my voice rising from a whisper to a normal level. Jasper glared at me, telling me to shut up with his eyes.

"Do you want my help or not?" Jasper asked. I nodded reluctantly, knowing I didn't have a choice if I wanted to survive the next twenty-four hours. "I don't have long before somebody wonders where I've gone, so listen to me. After midnight, I will come get you. The guard change will happen then. I'll arrange for a boat."

I looked up at him sharply. "I can't swim! Why can't I go back to the cottage?"

He turned away from me for a second, attempting trying to compose himself. He must have failed, because when he turned back to me, he had tears in his eyes. "I know, but you don't have a choice. You need to get out of this region and go somewhere else. If they catch you again, they will kill you on the spot." The wind howled through the bars in the window, bringing the harsh reality down upon me.

"Where will I go?" I asked him.

He shrugged. "Anywhere is better than here." I looked at him numbly and nodded in agreement. "It's settled. I'll arrange for a boat and you'll get away from here and build a new life." Without another word, he walked away.

My mind raced once again.

I waited for him. The moon rose. It was full tonight, my favorite time each month. Its beauty always left me in awe. Each minute passing felt like hours. The current guards slid a tray of food under the bars. The tray contained a bowl of mush and a slice of bread; I mixed the mysterious sludge. It was so thick it held the path the spoon made. I pushed the extra thick porridge and grabbed the bread. I chewed it absentmindedly, trying to ignore the random green growths on it. Wondering if Jasper was really going to show up. Time ticked by as the moon rose higher. Slowly, the voices of the other inmates turned into snores and quiet mumbles.

My nerves were on edge as the jail got quieter and quieter. I glanced out the window, and the storm was still howling through the bars. I could see the sea if I stood on my tiptoes. The sound of footsteps started at the end of the hall. I glanced back at the bars of my cell. The space beyond it was black with shadows. I held my breath as the footsteps got louder.

"You awake?" Jasper asked in a hushed tone.

"Yes," I said as I grabbed at the bars.

"Good," Jasper said, "let's get you out of here." He put the key in the lock, and we both held our breath as he turned it to unlock the door. The clank of the lock turning seemed deafening in an otherwise quiet jail. I waited, half expecting alarms to be sounded, but nothing happened. He handed me my satchel. I looked down at it dumbly.

"You got it back for me?" I asked.

"Of course I did. That's the last thing your mother gave to you. I know how much it means to you," he said, his voice soft. "Now let's go, before we get caught and the upper circle have us hanged," he said as he grabbed my hand.

His once-soft hands were calloused with training. I didn't pull away from the physical touch. Instead, I welcomed it and looped my fingers with his, like we did when we were kids. There was no love behind it, at least not the type of love my father had wanted. We slipped out into the streets; they were empty and dark, rain pelted down on us as we ran through them. The only sounds were our feet hitting the cobblestone.

My mind thought back to our childhood. We were always together when we were younger, running around and constantly getting into trouble. Things changed when we hit puberty. They suddenly expected me to be a lady. Immediately, my father sent me to a girls' boarding school, and Jasper's family sent him to train for the military, to be a knight. The clock tower suddenly forced out of my daydream as a bell sounded.

"Shit," Jasper said, his voice low. Even though we were several blocks away, we quickened our pace. We made it to the dock. On most nights, sailors filled each nook and cranny. However, with the storm tonight, it was fairly empty save for a few drunken sailors awaiting their next job.

The salty air filled my nostrils as my anxiety rose from my stomach. Jasper pulled me over to a small boat with a sail. I looked at him. "This must have cost a fortune."

He shrugged. "It's the least I could do." He helped me into the boat and I stared at him. Rain plastered his usually curly brown hair to his face. His typically shining brown eyes looked unbelievably tired. We stood there looking at each other for a second.

"You could come with me," I said, almost yelling because of the storm.

He looked at me, surprised, and then looked at the town. "I belong here. This is my place in life. You are the one that needs to leave so you can find your place." I cringed at the wording but nodded.

He was right. I don't belong here, and I probably never did.

"I hear there's a small island northwest of here, a few miles. Restock and buy a better map than the one I put in your satchel. It's outdated," he said with a shrug. "Then find somewhere that accepts you," he said as he leaned in and hugged me. My head rested on his chest. I breathed in his familiar scent, now mixed with salt water.

"Thank you," I said, my voice cracking with emotion.

"Now get going, before somebody sees you," he said as he untied the sailboat from the dock, giving it a push. "And Elle," I looked at him, surprised by the usage of my old pet name.

"I'm sorry; please be safe," he shouted, his voice filled with sorrow as my little boat got farther and farther away, his face disappearing into the storm.

I sat down on the boat as it rocked. With no lit lamp on the boat, it was pitch black. I didn't want to risk being seen by the shore. The lights from town got smaller as the tide pulled the boat. I shivered as I pulled my cloak closer together, its cloth soaked through from the unforgiving rain. I opened my satchel, grabbing at the compass I had stashed away.

The worn letters on it were nearly illegible, trying to find what direction I was going. Waves hit the boat, and the compass went overboard. "No," I yelped as I tried to reach for it; watching it sink with despair. *Why me?* I groaned. I tried to position the sailboat in the right direction, unsure if it was correct. The lights from town were no longer visible when I looked at where my childhood home should have been.

I turned my head up at the clouded sky. I yelled. "Why? What did I do that was so bad, that I angered the Gods, to deserve this!" No one answered. The rain and waves continued to assault the little sailboat. I looked back ahead, and fear crept up my throat. How was I supposed to know what direction I headed?

Minutes passed, turning into hours. The sun embraced the earth; it didn't seem like it wanted to let go. I shivered in the little boat and held on as the waves hit the boat furiously. With one hand, I gripped the rope that was attached to the sail, hoping to keep it going where I originally intended. My stomach flipped with each wave. Soon enough, bile reached my mouth, and I threw up overboard. Rain and tears ran down my face, washing away the evidence of the clergyman hitting me. The storm was getting worse by the minute. I took a deep breath, trying to stay calm. It seemed like I was getting farther out to sea than I intended.

Muttering every curse in my arsenal, I tried to readjust my course with the sail, grabbing the rope. The line rubbed my hands raw as the wind blew the sail the opposite direction, ripping it out of my hands. I screamed, clutching my hands at the flash of pain, opening them tentatively. An ugly welt appeared in streaks on my fingers and palms. A sob escaped my throat as I laid down on the floor of the sailboat, clutching them, giving up as sobs wretched through my body.

"Please," I said, whimpering to no one in particular, "I just want an opportunity to be me." The sun seemed to hear me as it rose in the distance. A bright pink line lit the edge of the horizon. I sat up, looking back at the shore I once called home. With the land behind me, I knew what way to go. Wrapping my hands in my cloak to protect them, I pulled the sail rope again and then hissed with pain.

I looked in the direction I headed. It was still gray with rain and the ocean unruly.

The waves grew higher. I pulled my satchel closer to my body. An enormous swell billowed towards my sailboat as I glanced at the horizon. I screamed at the gods again, closing my eyes just as the wave hit me. Water filled my nostrils as the wall of water swept my body off the boat. I struggled to make it to the surface of the water, cursing myself for never learning how to swim. As I reached the open air, I gasped for breath and watched in horror as the boat capsized with the next wave.

Desperately, I attempted to swim towards it; the waves making it more impossible than it already was. Miraculously, I made it, grabbing onto what had been the bottom of the boat as I tried to haul myself up. The weight of my cloak made it impossible. I let go of the boat with one hand and unbuckled the clasp. The cloak untangled itself from my body and sank. I stared as it disappeared under the waves. *Shouldn't it float?* I turned my attention back to the boat, heaving myself up with my satchel, which scraped against the boat as I reached its highest point.

The rain appeared to lessen up, and I breathed a sigh of relief. I looked around, definitely far away from the coast, farther than I intended. I could see a dark line on the horizon—land. Luckily, the tide was pushing the boat in the right direction. I glanced up at the sky. The clouds dissipated. I sat on the top of the boat, shivering. I wore only the shift I had slept in. The white material had essentially become see through because of the rain. *At least I don't have to worry about my modesty,* I thought grimly. I was utterly alone.

By now, the sun was high above me, and I could discern shapes on the incoming land. My skin was red from the sun, my hair and clothes crunchy from all the salt. I licked my lips, feeling the dry skin flake off as the salt coated my tongue. I opened my satchel, and my heart sunk a little as I realized the contents were waterlogged.

I pulled out the soaked map Jasper placed in there the day before. Gently, I unrolled it. What used to be words were now streaked throughout the page. The landmasses were still legible. I glanced at the growing land mass before me and then back to the ruined map. I sighed, as none of them quite fit the look of this mass of land before me. *Out of date, my ass. Incorrect all the way,* I thought.

My mind drifted as I waited. I thought about the events from the last couple of days and shuddered to think of what the future might hold for me. *Obviously, I'm cursed.* The sun slowly set again, turning the sky into oranges and dark blue hues. I thanked Hesper the god of night, as my skin was painfully red.

The land mass was so close. I sighed, but instead of heading towards a nice sandy beach, I was approaching the cold shoulder of a cliff. By the end of the night, the boat lurched as I ran aground. As I slid off the boat into the frigid water, I held my breath. When I resurfaced, I gasped as once again, I was drenched. *I hate water.* After a few moments of struggling, I finally made it close enough to land where my feet could touch the bottom.

On my hands and knees, I crawled up on the rough land, kissing the nearest salty rock I could find. I surveyed the cliff area, looking around, trying to pick the best possible place to start my climb. I turned towards the cliff side and took my first step up. My body screamed in protest as I lifted myself up to another ledge. My fingers curled into the sharp rock face. The welts on my hands seemed to say *please stop*.

Ignoring my body's protest, I whispered, "One more step, one more step." I was so close. I was unsure how much time had passed. The sun was gone.

The stars and the moon were my light. As I reached a landing large enough for my frame, I paused, catching my breath. I looked up, so close. *You need your rest*, my inner voice seemed to say. Pushing myself as far away from the ledge as possible, I shut my eyes. The cliff face dug into my sunburnt back. Quickly, I fell into an exhausted slumber.

I awoke to the sounds of birds. The sun was rising once again. My mind raced as my current predicament crashed back into me. I swallowed the sobs that threatened to come up and began my climb up again. I focused on the rock right in front of my face, not wanting to discourage myself further.

"One more step, one more step," I repeated my mantra from yesterday; instinctually, I reached for the next rock ledge to hold on to. My hand met with something soft and wet. *Grass!*

I reached to pull myself up and over the ledge, finally arriving at the top. I stood and looked up, taking a step forward closer inland. As the events of the last few days finally caught up to me, I swayed.

My eyes meet someone else's as the world fades. Just before I lose consciousness, I think, *Wow, she's beautiful.*

2

Meeting Lilja

Lilja POV

I stood out near the edge of the cliff, overlooking the brightening sky. It was nearly time for breakfast. The ground felt odd; vibrating, calling to me.

Is someone else here?

A hand grappled over the lip of the cliff. I crossed my arms, watching as the partner to that arm popped up as well, pulling the connected body up with it.

Who the fuck is that? I really don't have time for this shit.

A mess of a girl pulls herself up, standing shakily. She was well built, her body was covered in bruises and cuts.

I raised my eyebrow, surprised anyone could climb that cliff in one piece. Well, sort of in one piece. The girl stood dazed, her lips cracked and dry, her hair matted to the sides of her face. A satchel in poor condition hung limply to her side; its contents almost spilling out.

"Who are you?" I called to her.

Her eyes glanced up at me, glazed and unfocused. I could see a moment of realization and then nothing as her eyes rolled back. She slumped to the ground.

"What kind of spy is that?" Kallan, my second-in-command, remarked, coming up behind me.

"We don't know if she is a spy, dumbass, don't assume." *Plus, what kind of spy looked like that?* I thought. Even as this girl was crumpled on the ground, I could tell she wasn't spy material. She looked soft and well fed. She looked beautiful.

Kallan approached the heap on the cold, wet ground outside my tent and rolled her over. He grabbed the satchel. The strap finally surrendered, separating from the bag. Kallan grumbled something about shoddy workmanship under his breath as his nimble hands went through the contents.

"There is nothing incriminating in here, just a notebook and random junk," he noted, almost to himself, as he handed me the book. "All soaked through."

I flipped through the pages, half expecting information about the military forces camped behind me. Unexpectedly, it was filled with drawings of plants and descriptions of their applications.

"Grab the physician." *Probably shipwrecked.*

Kallan looked up from the girl, surprised. "Why not just kill her? We'll just roll her off the cliff or slit her throat. In the state she's in, it will be quiet and quick."

"We need to find out who she is and what she knows, plus she might not be a spy. I'm not in the mood to kill a helpless girl tonight."

Kallan nodded, knowing he wouldn't be able to change my mind. I felt strange. Anger simmered in the pit of my stomach. Why did his comment make me so mad?

He walked in the physician's tent direction. "Kallan," I said. He glanced back at me. "Keep this under wraps until we know who she is."

He turned and gave me a mock solute. "Yes, ma'am."

I rolled my eyes as I squatted next to her, not being able to resist the urge. I brushed the hair out of her face and tucked it behind her ear. A gentle shock ran through me as I did so. Sucking in a breath, I realized instead of her ears being pointed; they were rounded.

"Fuck, she's human," I announced to myself. I slipped an arm underneath her shoulder, picking her up. Her head rolled into the space between my shoulder and neck, perfectly.

I opened the flap to my tent and laid her down on the mattress. Nimbly, I slipped off what appeared to be a nightgown off of her. She grumbled once and then became quiet. I took up the other side of the tent, pacing, my thoughts racing as I thought about the possibilities. *Why the fuck is there a human in Valdis? Has Ardour employed the humans to do their dirty work? Does Ardour know of our plans to attack?*

My thoughts were interrupted as a voice called out from the outside of the tent. "Your highness, you needed me?"

"Enter, Grayen, and be quiet about it. We don't want to wake the camp," I said, pinching my nose. *It's too early for this; I haven't even had my coffee yet.*

Kallan entered the tent holding a mug. His stance was stiff, as if he was on alert for this girl to suddenly wake up out of deep sleep and try to kill me. I sighed. The aroma of the contents of the mug drifted towards me. I frowned, knowing full well the bastard only grabbed some for himself, and swiped the mug out of his hands. As I pulled away, the hot liquid sloshed over his hand. He hissed, bringing his singed hand to his lips.

"Thanks for the coffee," I said as I brought the mug to my lips.

He glared at me, and I moaned as the hot coffee entered my mouth and slid down into my belly. Grayen cleared his throat, bringing Kallan's and my attention back onto the forgotten girl currently passed out in my bed.

"She's a human, your highness. She's dehydrated, but she appears to be healthy despite being exhausted from whatever ordeal she endured.

Who is she?" he asked quizzically.

"Wish I knew. You may take your leave, Grayen, but keep this quiet. We don't know anything yet, and I don't want whatever this is," I gestured with my arms, "to be circulating the camp, yet."

Grayen nodded in understanding and left.

Kallan grunted in agreement, crossing his arms. "What do you want to do with her?"

"We'll wait till she wakes up and question her to find the truth. If she turns out to be a spy, you can kill her. If she isn't, we will let her decide what she wants to do. For right now, let her sleep and get back to your duties. I need to read through the correspondence from yesterday's messengers."

Elowen POV

My eyes were unwilling to open as I came to. I was warm; a soft fabric covered my bruised and battered body. Groaning, I reached up and rubbed my eyes, rubbing away the salt crusties covering my eyelids. As I opened my eyes, I met a view of a tent ceiling.

"Look who woke up," a monotonous voice announced.

I looked in the voice's direction, sitting up quickly. Sitting on a stool was a woman. She had short hair, longer on the top, with it shaved on the sides of her head. Her body turned towards me, hands clasped together and her head resting on them. Her gaze seemed to pierce into my soul. She glanced down and then back into my eyes. A slight smirk took shape on her face. I followed her gaze, to realize the soft blanket covering me earlier was the only thing I had on. Yelping, I pulled up the blanket, my cheeks burning.

"Where are my clothes?" I croaked; my voice, hoarse.

"I took them off," she said in a matter-of-fact way. My mouth opened in surprise. Nobody had ever done that. My cheeks reddened further, making her laugh.

"Well, I wasn't about to leave you in soaking wet clothes, especially when you are laying in my bed."

"Who are you?" I held the blanket closer to my chest, my mind racing.

"I am the one who should ask you that." She moved off the stool and walked towards me. She squatted down so that our eyes were nearly level with one another's. The thin women reached off to the side, grabbing a pitcher and a cup, pouring water into it, keeping eye contact with me. Suddenly I realized how dry my mouth felt. The salt from the sea water seemed to coat every inch of me, including my mouth.

She brought the cup to her lips, taking a sip, still staring at me. I squirmed, uncomfortable with this much eye contact with a stranger. She extended the cup to me. My hands clasped around it so fast I nearly spilled the contents before they made it to my mouth. I gulped the water. I stared at the pitcher, unsure if I could get more. She nodded and grabbed the pitcher, pouring me another glass to the rim.

"Are you going to give me your name?" she asked, still squatting before me.

I glanced at her, trying to keep my focus on the water in my hand. Could I trust her? *She saved me.* "I'm Elowen."

Her gaze followed my movements hungrily, as if she wanted to know everything about me. "Why did you come to Valdis?"

"Valdis," the vowels rolling off my tongue tentatively. "Where's that?"

She looked at me, surprised. Silence stretched a few seconds more than what was normal. "Why did you come to Elven Country?" she asked, this time slower, like saying it slower would change the answer.

She's crazy. "Is this a joke?" I asked, looking down at my hands, trying to keep my hands steady.

"No," she said.

I looked up again, trying to search her eyes for the truth. They were hard and emotionless.

"Why would I lie? How do you explain my ears, then?" she stated, pulling away the hair hiding the tips of her ears. I stared, my mind seemed to pause all logical explanations as I stared at this beautiful woman's ears, seemed to leave me. My mouth was agape, as my brain struggled to catch up, racing with information I learned from my years at school, and I laughed. She stared at me, confused, until my giggles subsided and I could form words.

"You're crazy," I said.

"You are in Elven Country," a male voice boomed from behind the woman. He drew his sword and pointed it in my direction. "And how dare you insult my queen?"

They are both crazy.

"Calm down, Kallan. It's not like she knows who I am. She wasn't aware she was in Elven Country until a few minutes ago." She glared at the crazy man behind her, who was brandishing his sword. "What did I say about entering my tent unannounced?" Her eyes narrowing at him in annoyance. I scooted away, trying to distance myself from both of them. *I have to get out of here.* His sword faltered, surprised at her response.

"She insulted you," he said his eyebrow raised. "My queen," he added, giving a bow.

"She doesn't know any better, you dumbass," she said, looking at him. "Put your sword away. You're scaring her." She looked back at me, glancing down again. I realized I was still naked before them both now. My cheeks reddened again.

Noticing my growing discomfort, the woman frowned. "Get out," she said to him.

He stared at her. "She could be lying."

"I can take care of myself, especially against a sick human. Oh,

Kallan," she said as he headed towards the exit, pausing as he looked at her. "Get Grayen again, please."

He stepped out. It was just us two, again. She motioned in front of me, "How did you get here?"

"I don't know," I said, not fully trusting her. "I just meant to sail to a small island off the coast."

The queen brought the stool over, sitting on it. She grabbed a paper without looking up at me. She nodded at me as if to say, *tell me*. So I started rambling, telling her needing food, going into town to sell medicine. Her eyes hardened as I got to the part where the asshole assaulted me.

There was almost a familiarity with her. I had never met her before, but I felt like I could trust her. I continued, taking a deep breath. As I neared the part where they threw me in jail, I pulled my arms closer. Careful to omit the exact reason, I just admitted to the part of being banished. She didn't ask why the crown exiled me, but I could tell she wanted to. I sucked in a breath, going on with the story. How Jasper saved me by getting me on a sailboat.

Her pen wrote furiously writing everything down with amazing speed, as I continued on with the story. By the time I was done with my tale, tears streamed in silent sadness over my cheeks. She opened her mouth as if to say something, but Kallan entered with someone I assumed was Grayen.

"My queen," the older gentleman said as he bowed.

I took this interaction as time to survey the tent. It looked posh, certainly fit for a queen. *If she is a queen*, a voice whispered from the back of my head. I looked at the people before me. Their ears were pointed. *They must all be deformed, some type of birth defect.*

"Kallan, come with me," the supposed queen said, gesturing as she walked towards the front of the tent.

"You're leaving?" I said, panic clear in my voice.

She looked back at me, surprised at my outburst. "Yes, we need to find you some practical attire, unless you want to wear that blanket for the rest of the day."

I looked back down at the blanket that was barely covering my important bits, and Kallan laughed. I turned my head to the side, my face reddened once more, and internally I cursed my pale complexion. The queen turned, hitting Kallan's head with a loud thump.

"Hey! What was that for?" Kallan grumbled. Unsuccessfully, I tried to stifle the giggle that erupted from my mouth.

The queen gave me a lazy smile and turned back to Kallan. "You know exactly what that was for," she said, rubbing the hand she'd smacked him with. I looked at the man before me; his eyes made me want to trust him.

I pulled the blanket up higher on my chest. "I'm not decent."

He held a red bag. "I've seen plenty of naked bodies, madam. Yours will not surprise me," he said. "Elven or not."

"Somehow that doesn't make me feel better," I said.

He chuckled, checking me over, clicking his tongue and taking down notes.

"Are we really in Elven Country, or has everyone lost their minds?" I asked as Grayen checked my pulse.

"Yes, my dear," he enunciated each word, as if not wanting to scare me.

"How did I get here?" My voice cracked as I took in a deep breath.

"Well, it's been years since anyone has made it across," he said, deep in thought, rubbing the stubble on his chin. "The gods have a track record of transporting humans here. The full moon has been known to have enough power to transport humans across the barrier, but there aren't many accounts of humans coming here. It's not safe for people like you. Humans who end up here do so on purpose. They stay or cannot go back."

I felt my stomach flip. Bile climbed its way up my throat. I looked around, desperate for a spot to throw up. Grayen grabbed the pitcher that contained water and handed it to me, sensing my panic. Tears pricked the corner of my eyes as the bile emptied into the pitcher. I coughed as the last bit of the bile projectiled into the pitcher. Grayen placed his hand on my back. I flinched at his contact.

"Please don't touch me," I whimpered. There was no bite behind my words.

"Sorry," Grayen said, removing his hand.

"Elowen," the queen said in a sing-songy voice as she entered the tent. Her peppy demeanor changed as she paused at the entrance, observing the situation at hand. She rushed over to me, dropping the bundle of clothes she held.

"She's fine," Kallan said as he sauntered in after, grabbing the clothes forgotten on the ground.

The queen glared up at the physician. "Does she look fine to you?"

I dry heaved, nothing left in my stomach. Her hands grabbed the hair that was clinging to my face and pulled it into a twist behind my head. I dry heaved again, and a sob escaped my mouth.

"Make it stop." My heart beat erratically, and my quick breathing tried to match my pulse.

The queen looked at Grayen for advice.

"She's having an anxiety attack. If she wants to control it, she must be calm."

I looked at the queen as she grabbed my face. Fully hyperventilating, my eyes began to un-focus, and the edges of my vision grew black.

"Come on, Elowen, you need to calm down," she said. "You're working yourself up too much. Leave us, Grayen, you've done quite enough."

He gathered his items stiffly and shuffled out of the tent. Her eyes, still level with mine, seemed to break through their stoic cage and emotion shone through as she stared at me. I took a deep breath, trying to breathe it out. I did this repeatedly until my heart stopped pounding.

"Adequate," Kallan said.

I looked up, surprised at his compliment. *Was it a compliment?* He threw the clothes at me and then walked out of the tent, shrugging his shoulders.

"These clothes should fit you," the queen said as she stood up, grabbing the pitcher and setting it outside her tent. "If they don't, tell me and I can find you some new ones." She turned back, staring at me.

"Could you stop looking at me, please?" I squeaked, holding the clothes in my hand. She sighed, rolling her eyes and twisting her body to face the entrance to the tent. Quickly, I put the pants and tunic on. Both fit. *Thank the heavens.* "Done."

Turning to look at me, she cracked her mouth open as if to say something, and then closed it. "Let's go," she said, walking towards the exit.

"Wait!" I said. She looked at me sharply. "I don't even know your name…and…you've done a lot for me already. You don't know who I am. I could be a spy."

The queen looked at me and sniggered. "Elowen, it's my duty to take care of the subjects on my land. You are obviously not a spy." She paused, as if she was trying to find the right words to say, and continued, "You're too soft, not muscular at all."

My mouth stood agape as I stared at her. *Did she just call me fat?*

"Which is not a bad thing." She ran a hand through her short hair, seeming uncomfortable with the conversation happening in her tent. "I am Queen Lilja of Valdis, but you may call me, 'your highness,'" she said as she straightened her black tunic.

"Okay," I said. "Your highness."

"Let's go to the mess tent. It's dinnertime." She opened the flap of the tent and allowed me to walk through. The sun had indeed made its embrace with the earth. They had set green tents up in neat rows, with enough walkway between them for four bodies to walk side by side. Fires burned at every other tent, allowing the heat from the flame to reach the tents and lighting the way.

Each person seemed to have walk with purpose, and the camp was lively. I could hear shouts and laughter in the distance, glasses clanging. As we walked through the camp, people bowed to her highness, trying not to pay much attention to me. But I could tell they were curious. *Curious about the human in Elven Country,* I thought to myself. The sounds of voices got louder as we got closer to a large tent. Smoke billowed out of a pipe that exited at the top.

Her highness strode through the crowd of men and women, all of them seeming to make a path for her imposing stride. I fell behind her, murmuring, "excuse me," to the people surrounding me. She stopped at a round table with six chairs, including her own, placed neatly around it.

She cocked her head to the side, motioning to the chair. "Sit."

Politely, I nodded, sitting in the chair farthest away, unsure of where I should sit.

She stared at me, sighing loudly, and then glanced at the chair beside her. "Sit here," pointing to the chair to her left. "Trust me, you're going to want to sit as close to me as possible. You'll thank me when you see the ruffians that sit in those chairs."

"Ruffians! I'll have you know I am wounded by your comment, your highness," Kallan stated as he took the seat to her right.

"You don't even have table manners, Kallan," a girl wearing a green cloak and sporting a thick head of curly red hair said, coming up to sit next to him. She paused, staring at me. "Who's this?" She said, motioning to me as she stared at the queen.

"A human," a broad-shouldered man said as he plopped next to her.

"I can *see* that, Aidan" she said, punching his arm. "Why is she here in Elven Country?"

I stared at my fingers underneath the table.

"So she could grace us with her good looks. You guys are oblivious," a black-haired man said as he seemed to appear out of nowhere. Kallan coughed, nearly choking on whatever was in his cup. I smiled at him shyly, a tinge of red hitting my cheeks. "Wouldn't you agree, Keres?" I followed his gaze to a black-haired woman who looked like the black-haired man next to me.

"Of course, brother." She stared at me. "You're in my spot."

"Oh! Sorry—" I said as I began getting up, but her highness placed a hand on my thigh, pushing me back down in my seat.

"Pull up a chair, Keres." her highness said.

"You can sit next to me, Keres," the redhead girl grabbed a chair from behind her. Keres trudged over to the other side of the table, flicking her hair.

"Thank you, Cassia," she said as she sat down.

"This is Elowen," the queen gestured towards me, "Elowen, this is my team."

Each of them rattled off their names, offering no hints as to what they did and why they were a team. The tent area quieted and Armand, the black-haired man next to me, stood up, looking around, and snapped his fingers. Plates appeared around the table from his slight gesture. The crowd whooped in appreciation.

My mouth hung open as he settled back down. "How did you do that?"

"Magic." Armand extended his hands, wiggling his fingers, making a show of it.

"Magic?" I asked. "For hundreds of years, magic has been absent. We lost it in the great war."

"You mean they irradiated it in the Human Realm? It was a genocide caused by power hungry people," Aidan squared his already-broad shoulders, ready to give me a much-needed history lesson. "The magic genocide caused by the humans never made it here. Elves are a part of the earth; magic is a part of our being. Humans used to manifest magic too, usually with the help of the gods. The old kings and queens grew greedy for the power the human witches possessed and hunted them, one by one. Collecting them for their own special magic team. If they refused, the knights of the kingdom would kill their family members until they submitted and came with them."

The energy at the table turned somber. Slowly, I nodded my head. Turning to face him directly, I asked, "So does everyone have magic here?"

He shook his head, "No, not every elf develops magic; most develop their powers and awaken when they go through puberty. More than half of the population never does. Those who do can choose to join special forces of the government to help grow their communities."

"We can continue this history lesson later," Kallan said. "My food is getting cold."

The food was not unlike the food back home, except it mainly contained meat and very little vegetables. "You guys must really like meat," I said as I swallowed a large piece of fish from my fork.

Her highness' fork faltered. I'd unintentionally struck a nerve.

"Well," Cassia said.

Her highness' eyes were in slits, glaring at her. "No, Cassia," she said, bringing her fork to her mouth. She slowly chewed. With each bite, I could tell she was fighting with the voices in her head. "We will talk about this later, Elowen." She seemed so small as the words exited her mouth.

"I'm sorry," I said, "I didn't mean to offend you, your highness."

"Don't be," she said. She was smiling, but it didn't quite reaching her eyes. "Just a sensitive subject."

"So Elowen, what are your plans?" Cassia said brightly. "Are you coming with us to Cann Forest?"

"Well, I don't know. I suppose I should find a way home," I said. *Where is home? Do I have one?* The table quieted. I glanced around, staring at their somber faces. "What?"

"It's just that you won't be able to make it back," her highness articulated slowly, as if she was unsure of how the conversation would go over, "at least not right away."

"What do you mean, not right away?" I said, my voice rising an octave.

"Not until the next full moon," Cassia said.

"Oh, so I just have to wait another month?" I said, exhaling a sigh of relief.

Her highness cocked her head to the side, interjecting, "Yes." Kallan looked at her quizzically, but said nothing.

"I'll go with you to the Cann Forest. I will just come back before the month is up," I said brightly, my earlier discomfort gone.

"Okay!" Cassia said. "Finally another girl in the group!" Keres rolled her eyes.

Keres stood, stretching, and gave a dramatic yawn. "Well, I'm heading to bed."

Everyone used Keres' departure as an excuse to leave the table. They all said their goodbyes, departing for their tents. Her highness got up silently, however, deep in thought as she walked away from the table, leaving just me. The air had set a chill into my exposed arms and I shivered. Where was I supposed to go?

I stood up, glancing around. A few stragglers sprinkled throughout the mess tent. Some congregated and were playing a heated yet hushed game of cards. I walked and followed the path of worn down grass, letting my feet take me. My thoughts swam with the newfound information I gathered today. *Elven Country? Magic still existing in this realm? Elves have a weird thing about meat?*

I found myself in front of the queen's tent. My cheeks burned. *How did I end up here?*

I crossed my arms, sighing, trying to rub some warmth into them, turning I meandered towards the fire in the walkway, wanting its heat. "Elowen," a soft voice called in the dark. My eyes met with the darkness as I turned.

I stilled, waiting for the voice to call out again, but silence filled the air. I began the walk to the fire again.

"Elowen," the voice called once more. I turned sharply, expecting someone there. The dark behind me seemed to grow, its lack of light making it seem incomplete.

"Screw this," I said to myself, annoyed, as I stalked over to the fire and plopped myself down. The flames crackled and popped, releasing its heat to me. With my eyes closed, I breathed contently. My stiff arms and fingers immediately welcomed the heat.

"What are you doing?" her highness called out from behind me.

I stared up at her, twisting around. This angle only made her seem more imposing.

"I...well...um, I wasn't sure where I was supposed to go." My pulse quickened with anxiety.

She raised her eyebrows, staring at me. "To my tent," she said flatly. My mouth opened slightly, the other parts of my body freezing in place. *Does she know what I am?* I wondered to myself. *Does she know what this scar means?* I thought, as I grabbed my brand absentmindedly.

"I wanted to elaborate on the conversation we had at dinner, plus I have to monitor you. You could still very well be a spy for the Human Realm instead of being a spy for Ardour."

Ardour?

"Oh! Of course!" I brushed off my pant legs, following her to the tent, mumbling thanks as she held the flap aside.

"Elowen, the information I am about to give you is strictly between you and the Elven Country. If you get back home to your own realm, you may not disclose the information to anyone, not even family," she said firmly. "Do you understand?"

I don't even have a family, I thought as I nodded. *At least, not anymore.*

"This information could make the Human Realm think they could take advantage of my kingdom. I don't want them to think they could overthrow me." I nodded, keeping silent, not wanting to make the energy in the tent worse.

"There has been a blight infecting our crops for a hundred years. We have scientists working around the clock for a remedy to destroy the fungus that is killing our food, but we haven't found a solution yet. That is the reason for the decreased number of vegetables on your plate."

"Has it really been a hundred years?" I tapped my foot on the dirt floor, awaiting her answer.

"One hundred and four long years," she said as she sat at the table she was at earlier when I woke up.

I stood awkwardly in the middle of her tent, unsure of where I should exist in her space. "Is that all you wanted to tell me?"

"Why," she cocked her head to the side, "do you have somewhere to go?"

"You need to get some sleep," I said. "You had a long day." *Taking care of me.*

"*And* where will you sleep?" A smirk was plastered on her face.

"I'm not sure," I said, trying to think of a suitable response to give her. "I was going to sit by the fire and think about it." Meeting her tone with attitude, I stuck my chin out.

"Oh look, the little human has spirit. All I had to do was put some food in you," she said in a sarcastic tone. Absent-mindedly,

MEETING LILJA

she grabbed her quill and sat at her desk, turning her attention to the paper laying on it. "Elowen, you will sleep here tonight, until I can be sure I can trust you, that is. You are a human, after all." Her voice was light, but the meaning behind them was solid.

"I'm supposed to sleep in here?" I squeaked with discomfort. I looked at my hands, clutching them. My cheeks burned. *Why am I so embarrassed by this situation?* I scolded myself in my head. *You hardly know this woman. Am I supposed to sleep in her bed?*

As if she read my thoughts, she pointed to a cot in the corner. My bag was placed on top. I scrambled towards the satchel and opened it. The contents were dry. I looked up at her in surprise. "How?"

"I had them dried out with Armand's help." She shrugged. "If you brought it this far, it had to be important."

I nodded, unable to articulate the words swimming around in my brain.

"Now go to bed, Elowen. We leave tomorrow for the Cann Forest," she said.

"What about you?"

"I have paperwork to finish and then I will also head to bed. Do you have questions before I start my work?" she asked.

"No, goodnight."

"Goodnight, Elowen, sleep well," she said as I turned towards the cot, my cheeks burning with embarrassment. I quickly changed out of the clothes given to me that morning, trying to ignore her highness's stare as I slipped under the warm, fuzzy animal pelt that covered the cot. I closed my eyes, letting myself succumb to sleep, wrapping me in its warm embrace.

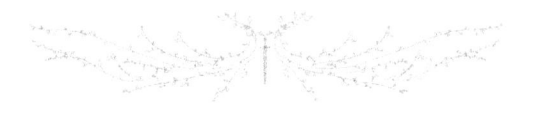

Sweat covered my brow, dripping into my eyes, making them burn. Why was it so hot in here? I opened my eyes. Slowly, they adjusted to the room's darkness. A large fire burned in the middle of the room. I attempted to move, but a rope restrained my body. I glanced down. My forearms faced up, awkwardly strapped to the arms of a splintered wooden chair. My legs were tied to the chair as well. I opened my mouth to say something, but all that came out was a low gargle.

"Please help!" I tried to say. I scooted the chair, hitting something metal on the floor next to me. As I realized it was the brand that had marked my skin, I groaned. My scar, a reminder of my past life. *How did I get here? How was I supposed to get out?* My thoughts were interrupted as the door on the other side of the room slammed open, and a round, red-faced man stepped through. My father, a man well respected in the high circle, stared at me with disgust.

"Everything I've ever done for you, Elowen, has been for the best. I raised you after your mother died, so you could be a well-respected young lady. A young lady any father could be proud of. A young lady who was supposed to get married and have babies, my grandchildren," he seethed. He grabbed my forearms, his rough hands bruising me as he stared at me uncomfortably close to my face. "You were *supposed* to be normal, Elowen," he said, spitting in my face with each word. He bent down, releasing my now-bruised arms, and grabbed the brand.

"No, Papa!" I screeched, tears falling down my cheeks. "I can be an obedient daughter. No one has to know!"

The brand glowed in the flames. My father's face was grim as he stalked towards me. He stared at me for a moment. For a split second, it looked as if he didn't want to do it, but then his face contorted into a grim, disapproving frown and he brought the hot iron on my forearm. The smell of burning flesh filled my nostrils and made my stomach do a somersault.

"*Elowen!*" her highness's voice yelled.

My eyes sprung open. My breath was coming in quick; my chest heaved up and down. Her highness was above me, her right hand grabbing my wrists and her left one covered my mouth.

She looked scared and confused as she stared down at me. Her brown eyes scanned my face for clues about my dream, and her short hair framed her face. I focused on my breathing, slowing it down as I watched her. My body burned with shame; a tear fell down the side of cheek.

"I'm sorry," I blubbered as more tears fell.

She pulled me up with her as she sat up. "Shh, don't be." She pulled me into an embrace, wiping my tears, her warm arms wrapped around me. My head rested in the crook of her neck. "Do you want to talk about it?"

I shook my head, sniffling, croaking out a "no."

She picked me up, carrying my large frame to her bed. I froze in her arms. Gently, she laid me down and slipped into the covers beside me.

"Your highness," my voice cracked, "what are you doing?"

She yawned and opened her eyes to slits. "I don't think I'm going to get proper sleep unless you are in this bed with me. Now go to sleep."

I closed my eyes, crying, as the memory nightmare played behind them. Then I twisted around to stare at the queen, who had fallen asleep. She seemed younger. A stray hair had fallen into her face, and I resisted the urge to move it behind her ear. She slightly grumbled in her sleep and moved her leg over mine.

I froze in place, embarrassed. *Why does she make me feel like this, whatever this was?*

Accepting my fate to be her highness' body pillow, I closed my eyes and let sleep take me.

The sound of horns awoke me. I sat up in bed abruptly and turned to the side she was sleeping on last night, only to find a space that had already gone cold. *Did I dream last night? Is that truly what happened?*

3

Falling In

Sunlight filtered through the thin cloth making up my shelter as I hurriedly dressed and made my way out of the tent. People—not soldiers—were packing up their tents, each with determination. *Why do they look so somber?* I continued to walk through the quickly disappearing camp, unsure of the role I was supposed to play.

I found her highness and her team in the mess tent around the table we all sat at last night. The only difference was my currently occupied seat.

Her highness projected her voice, clear and concise. "Now, it's settled. We'll follow the road till we hit the forest and then disperse our team and travel light to the village. The rest—" Glancing up, she paused her conversation with the group. "Well, good morning, Elowen, nice of you to join us, finally. It's nearly noon."

Some snickered, while others looked at the map.

I gave a small curtsy. "Good morning, your highness."

The snickering turned into full-blown laughter. I stood my ground, staring at them. Her highness raised an eyebrow at me.

"I see someone trained you in etiquette. Not everyone can bow correctly. How did someone banished learn how to do that?" she probed, clearly interested in the answer. The rest of the table eyes had turned to me, waiting.

"Well." My heart beat quickly in my chest, *how do I tell them without lying?* "I used to be in the upper circle. It just didn't work out." *What am I saying? A story about a nasty breakup?*

Cassia flamboyantly clapped her hands in excitement. "Oooh, a dramatic back story."

"It's not that exciting," I said hurriedly. "I just didn't like the drama behind it."

"Isn't that the truth?" Kallan nodded his head in agreement. "Everyone knows everybody, and everyone talks to everybody."

They looked at me, trying to decipher my words. I internally screamed. *Why does everyone need to know about me? If they discovered the truth, they wouldn't care about me.* The team glanced back down at the map, clearly not satisfied by my answer.

"The team will depart from the other soldiers; while we go to the village, they will continue to the mountain pass." The queen pointed down at the map.

Unable to keep my curiosity to myself, I asked, "Why are you going to the village?"

"Not us, we're going to the village together. You too." Armand shoveled a forkful of food in his mouth, speaking with it full.

"We have to monitor you," Keres quipped.

"Oh, right," I cringed.

"She's a human, Keres. It's not like she'd really be able to hurt us." Aidan flashed me a grin.

"She could be gathering information from us." Keres rolled her eyes in Aidan's direction.

"True." Kallan looked at the queen for an answer.

"If she wanted to do something nefarious, she would have done it last night." Her highness stared Keres down, folding her arms, leaning back in her chair.

"How do you know that?" Keres slammed her hand on the table.

"After all, she slept in my tent," her highness challenged.

Mouths opened around the table, agape and shocked. My face turned red, and I stared at my hands. "I thought you said she was going to get a tent supplied to her," Kallan said, clearly surprised.

"It doesn't matter what I said, Kallan, I changed my mind, and until she shows us otherwise on why she can't be trusted, we shall treat her with respect. Is that clear?" She folded her hands and placing them on the table. Collectively they nodded, agreeing—well, maybe not *agreeing,* but listening to her. I gave her a smile, thankful that they were not questioning my trustworthiness. *Am I trustworthy? After all, I am lying.*

"Anyway," Aidan said, "I've got to explain the plan to the soldiers and divvy up the duties."

"Elowen, go with him. It'll do you well to get to know the soldiers," her highness said. I quickly agreed, scrambling over to the already moving Aidan, thankful for any reason to get out of being interrogated further. His strides were long as he walked over to the growing line of soldiers.

I gave her highness a small bow as I struggled to meet his stride. "Thank you."

Aidan glanced at me from the side. "For what?"

"For defusing the conversation," I said as we reached the other men and women.

He just nodded, not saying anything back to me.

"Attention!" he bellowed, and the soldiers quickly turned to face him. Most wore the same uniform, a few wore a different garb, probably indicating their ranks. Some carried a bow, and others wore a sword on their hip, and others brandished two curved swords.

Aidan rambled off information to the soldiers. Not really paying attention to what he was saying, I continued to look around a few figures that caught my eye, cloaked with a green cloth like Cassia's. I glanced back at Aidan, who pointed at the figures as I moved over to them. Soldiers came up when I walked away.

Shyly, I approached the figures. "Hi." One whirled around. A girl, who seemed about my age, met my eyes. Her hair was short, shaved on the sides with longer strands framing her face, her dark complexion complimented by jewelry pierced through the bridge of her nose. A gold band wrapping around the outside, hooking either side.

I held out my hand. "I'm Elowen." *Why am I drawn to these figures?*

"Greetings, traveler." Her voice was low. She grabbed my forearm and embraced me in a welcome.

Her hand brushed my scar underneath the fabric of my tunic. I flinched. I pulled away from her as she held onto my arm. She said nothing as she pulled up my sleeve in one fluid movement, revealing my ugly scar. "Someone hurt you, traveler?"

I nodded numbly, not wanting to talk about it. Her hand released my forearm and grabbed my palm. Her finger followed the lines. "You have a traveling spirit." She said that was unique. "I am Keira. Where do you hail from, Elowen, the traveling spirit?"

"I am from the Human Realm, far away from here," I said. "What do the cloaks signify?"

"The cloaks signify the earth, Elowen," Cassia interrupted, her green cloak covering her head, not enough of it covering her hair as it spilled out from the sides.

"We listen to the earth, and find what it wants to teach us. We are healers," Keira said.

"Correct, Kiera, good job." Cassia nodded, approving of the explanation.

"You guys use plants to make elixirs." I excitedly grabbed my book from my satchel. Its pages water damaged from the salt water, but the words were still mostly intact. "I make elixirs too! At least I did when I was in the Human Realm. Are plants the same in the magic realm?"

Cassia nodded. Taking that as a sign, I plowed on, showing them the drawings from my book and talking to them about the plants' properties. Keira interjected a few times, adding to my medicinal purposes.

A horn blew and Cassia pointed in the direction we came. "You better get back to Lilja."

I nodded, surprised at how informally she mentioned her queen. I made my way through the mass of soldiers, carts, and horses. Each person I passed peered at me, as if wondering why I was there. I soon spotted the queen, who was on horseback. A smaller horse, adorned with an elegant saddle, was empty next to her.

"How was your outing, Elowen?" she asked.

"It was nice. I met this really pretty girl that was a part of the healer group. I talked to her and Cassia and we conversed about plants and their healing properties," I said, excitedly. The queen stalled slightly at the explanation of Kiera, and then pointed to the smaller horse.

"Can you ride?" She asked.

"Yes, my mother taught me," I said, thinking back to the early years of my life riding in the forest near our manor while father was away at business.

"Good, it'll be a long ride." She watched as I mounted the small horse. It neighed quietly.

"What's her name?" I asked.

"Lady," Kallan said as he rode up next to me on his own brown horse.

"She's still young, but she's well trained. She will answer to her name and a distinct whistle. Can you whistle?" After I nodded, he went on, demonstrating a loud, shrill whistle ending with a short tweet at the end resembling a bird. "Most horses of this breed will only return to their owner, so please be careful. She will follow you to the end. They're one of the best breeds out there." He puffed out his chest proudly.

I mounted Lady, looking back at Kallan. "You seem to know a lot about horses."

"The horses for the Royal Army are raised by my family, including Lady. Lady is just small because she's not fully grown, as you were an unexpected addition to the group," he said.

"Your family must be very reputable to have such esteemed horses," I said.

He squared his shoulders and puffed his chest out a little. The queen said nothing as the group pushed forward.

The sound of everyone made it nearly impossible to communicate with anyone, even the people right next to me. The day was filled with movement as we traveled through the countryside. I could see everything. The land seemed remarkably similar to the Human Realm, yet different at the same time.

This world seemed to hold magic in every inch. I opened my journal and sketched. Not anything in particular, sketching a solid page of art. *If you could call it that.* I shut the book with a resounding thud and glanced at the surroundings that I had overlooked so far. The scenery we had passed had changed from the flatland surrounding the island to patches of greenery. Shrubs had sprung up everywhere, and trees had sprinkled the land. Each tree we passed looked larger than the next.

"Elowen," a voice whispered around me.

I glanced around, searching for the call of the voice. *Am I going crazy?* People did not suggest that they had heard my name being called.

I looked for the queen. She had gotten behind me somehow. I stalled

Lady slightly, allowing the queen's horse to catch up. She nodded at me, still in the middle of a discussion with Kallan. We continued to ride as the sun had begun its descent to give the earth a long embrace, giving the land a soft orange glow.

"You know, the world looks beautiful this way," the queen said as she rode closer to me, almost yelling at me because of the noise. I nodded, disregarding the idea of yelling across to her. "This is where we will pull off from the group. Follow me," she said, veering left and away from the group.

I followed behind Kallan. Keres, Armand, Aidan, and Cassia also pulled away from the spots in the mass of people traveling with us. They quickened the pace, nearly galloping at full speed as we traveled into the imposing forest growing in front us. Soon we were far enough from the group, and the foliage surrounding us deafened that the sound of them. I looked around, appreciating the silence.

"Alright," her highness held her hand in the air, signifying us to listen to her. "We will travel through the forest until we reach Cann Village. Please keep an eye out for anything unusual, and stay together." We dismounted, as the ground had been too uneven for the horses to continue. Bird sounds and rustling filled the air as we moved. I noticed the silence of the group.

"So, why are we going to the Cann Village? Why did we separate from the rest of the soldiers?" I said, slightly above a whisper. We continued to walk, and the others gave no sign that they had heard me, until her highness spoke up.

"The army will move to the mountains, gaining bodies along the way. I have instructed them to go town to town. We will need strong, trained soldiers to fight in the possible war between Ardour and Valdis. The Cann Village people aren't known for their etiquette towards outsiders. They are an extremely religious group, focused on keeping to themselves one with the earth. It is said that each one of their inhabitants possesses some sort of magic. All types, whether it be earth, water, fire, or air. There is also a rumor of a rare subdivision of magic being created here: the power to see what's happening many miles away. It's said that people who harness this magic can also see into the future."

"It comes at a cost though, people who possess such magic become horribly disfigured and consumed back into the earth," Cassia said bitterly.

"If it comes at such a cost, then why would anyone want such a power?" I said, alarmed at this newfound information.

"People will always try to gain power, no matter the cost," Armand said.

I glanced at the people before me. Each one seemed disgusted by the information. *Then why are we going to them?* Keres seemed to read my thoughts as she said, "The only reason we are going to the Cann people is because we need help."

"We need to save our people from the blight infecting our crops, and if it means that we have to go to this village for help, then we will." The queen said, angrily kicking a rock in the direction we headed towards.

"Elowen," the voice whispered. My head flew up, looking around. *Where is this voice coming from? Why do I keep hearing my name being called?*

Aidan glanced at me, surprised by my sudden movement. "Are you okay?" He raised his eyebrow at me.

"Yeah, I just thought I heard my name, that's all. Must be because I got very little sleep last night," I said hurriedly, trying to play off my awkwardness.

He stared at me sympathetically and nodded.

"Nightmares," I said sheepishly.

"I too used to suffer from nightmares," he said, his eyes full of emotion.

"How did you get over them?"

"I found that talking to someone or even writing it down helped me get past my demons. Sometimes I still write in a journal, when I feel like I need to." His body language was tense, the veins on his neck more prominent than before.

"Let's settle for tonight, with only a small fire. We don't want to get ourselves any unwanted attention," the queen announced.

To give our horses some relief from the weight they carried, we unpacked them. We set out on laying down tents in a circle, each one facing another. Kallan began making a small fire while Aidan and Armand began pulling food from their packs. Keres tended to the horses. I stood, unsure of what my task should be. I glanced at the queen. She was prepping a small bag of arrows and a bow. She looked up at me as if she felt my gaze.

"Do you want to come and hunt with me for dinner, Elowen?" she said, my name rolling off her tongue with ease.

"I have nothing to hunt with," I said, shrugging my shoulders.

"Here, take mine," Kallan said as he threw his bow at me.

I nodded to him, giving a silent *thank you*. I followed her highness deeper into the woods till we could hear only our footsteps from the rest of the group. We walked slowly, avoiding any extra sounds, trying not to spook any potential dinner. I set snares every few hundred feet, hoping to catch small game. Her highness, noticing me do so, gave me an encouraging look, making my heart flutter. *Shut up*, I thought to myself. *I can not let myself fall into another trap. Look what happened last time.*

A twig snapped to our left. Slowly, I turned my head, not wanting to spook our unsuspecting dinner. A small doe was grazing, content with the world, until now. Slowly the queen drew her bow, letting go of the bowstring. It gave out a *thwap* as the arrow let go. Seemingly in slow motion, the arrow flew, striking the target. The doe fell and instinctively I looked at the queen and grinned. She looked back at me and smiled at me. It was a genuine smile that reached her eyes.

I looked back at the fallen doe and trudged forward; twigs snapped under my feet. The queen on my heels, I looked around at the calm forest. A normal person, unaware of the danger of the forest, would have felt safe in the quiet forest. However, it was too quiet.

My arm hairs stood up, and a tightness filled my chest. Our dinner, the doe, was still alive, but its breathing labored as it neared death, I forced myself to move forward. The arrow was sticking out of its side, just missing the killing shot. Blood poured freely from the wound as we kneeled before it.

"*Elowen!*" the voice screamed at me. I looked up sharply at the greenery of the forest.

We were being watched.

The queen seemed unaware of my paranoia and grabbed her dagger from her belt. "May the air carry your spirit far and may the earth find happiness with your absence," her highness prayed as she delivered the final blow to the suffering animal. "Blessed be the gods." She planted a small kiss on the animal's head.

I looked at her, her somber face still stared at the deer, saddened by its necessary death. My inner voice screamed, *Hey! We're being watched!* Her eyes stayed on the deer for what seemed like hours rather than a few seconds. She finally looked at me, searching my face, looking for the reasoning behind my stare.

I stood up slowly, trying not to do so abruptly as she tied the legs of the doe together and swung its carcass over her shoulders, grunting as she stood up. *She understood what I was trying to say, right!?*

"Elowen," the queen said quietly next to me. "What is wrong?"

"I feel like someone is watching us, your highness," I said hurriedly. The forest was silent, not even the birds chirped. There was no sound

FALLING IN

until the ground swallowed me.

4

The Tree Whispered to Me

I groaned as my body connected with the cold ground below the surface. I gasped as it knocked out the air of me; my ears rang and the world seemed to change from shades of green to shades of pink as blood dripped into my eye.

"*Elowen*," someone called. "Are you okay?" the feminine voice called out again.

Where is this place?

Roots seemed to hiss and rustle as something moved around. I tried to open my mouth to say something, but all that came out was another gasp of breath. I wiggled my fingers and curled my toes. Nothing seemed to be broken, just battered and bruised. I prayed to the gods that the cut on my head was nothing serious. I turned my head to the side as another rustle erupted from my right.

"For someone who cursed the gods, you seem to pray to them a lot," a familiar voice seemed to whisper as if the roots were the one talking to me.

I attempted to sit up. The earth seemed to sway as if it was a spinning top. I opted to prop myself on my elbows.

"Your highness," I could finally croak out.

"Elowen, thank the gods." She breathed a sigh of relief. "Are you okay? Is anything broken?"

"I don't think so, but I don't think I'm alone. I heard someone talking," I whimpered out as I fully sat myself up.

"You hit your head. No one could be down there," she said, trying to reassure me.

"That is where you are wrong, your highness, my dear Elowen is not alone down here." the mysterious voice seemed to materialize out of nowhere. Roots moved suddenly and aggressively, taking shape into a woman.

Startled, I yelped, trying to crawl backwards from the figure.

"Elowen, hold on, I'm coming!" the queen shouted.

The gnarled, rooted woman stalked over to me as if I were her dinner. At *this point, I probably am.* She crouched down before me. We were now eye to eye. "Well hello Elowen, it's nice to meet you, finally," her voice seemed to bounce off the inside of head. I screeched, clutching my head in my hands. "It was difficult to get you here," she said.

I glared at her, my eyes in slits. "What are you talking about?"

The rooted lady clapped her hands gleefully. "Elowen, darling, I know you heard my call, a girl connected to the human and elf realm. How exciting."

A rumble seemed to shake the room. The woman looked at the crouching figure of the queen. Her tunic was bloodied from the doe, and the arrows on her back gleamed with the want for blood. Her short black hair hung slightly in her eyes, but otherwise, she seemed perfect.

The queen nocked an arrow, pointing it at the lady. "Get away from her."

"Now, Lilja, is that any way to talk to me," the rooted woman said. I stared at her, aghast that she would talk to the queen in such a way.

"I don't care who you are. If you hurt Elowen, you'll have to answer to me. I'll ask you once to step back away. She might be human, but she is one of my subjects now. We don't want any trouble. Let us be on our way. Unless you want to be the firewood to cook my dinner," the queen said.

The rooted lady stared at her blankly and then began a high-pitched laugh. The cavern we were in seemed to grumble with disagreement. Rocks crumbled from the ceiling, further cracking the ruined floor.

"Connection already seems to be taking hold, my dear Queen Lilja of Valdis. A helping hand in bringing the prophecy to fruition is you. Elowen, the path before you will not be easy, filled with heartbreak and death. Do you accept your fate?" the rooted woman asked.

She made me fall through that hole and now wants me to accept my fate. It was my turn to laugh. The queen gave me a crazed look, the arrow she had pointed at the woman wavering slightly. Heat traveled up my neck to my face as anger boiled through me. "I will follow my own fate." *Why is it always me?*

"It will always be you, Elowen," the woman said, as if she could read my mind. "I can indeed read your mind. It has been rather easy to get into. The gods have fated you to live this life for millennia. *You* do not get a choice at your own fate." The woman held out her hands. The surrounding roots wiggled alive, coming to attention. She motioned towards the queen and the roots listening slithered over, ready to strike.

I lunged for the queen, trying to get her to safety. "Wait, don't hurt her!" The roots stopped. Inches away from her body. I didn't know why I felt compelled to help this woman. *I can't let anyone else get hurt because of me.*

"Will you accept your fate?" the rooted woman called out.

"Yes!" I sobbed out, unsure of what I just accepted as my life. Roots changed direction and charged at me. The roots grabbing onto my wrists and ankles, making me stationary. The queen screamed my name. Why did she sound so distant?

The rooted woman stalked towards me like a hungry animal. I knew I was the prey. The roots of her fingers slithered and unraveled, reaching for my face. Another scream sounded from behind the women. The queen was tied to the ground like me.

The roots clawed their way to my face, entering my nose, mouth, and ears. I tried to scream, to pull away, my heart beating faster and faster.

Air, I *needed* air. I tried to flail around, to dislodge the roots, and tears sprang from my eyes. I was dying. The world went black.

I opened my eyes. *Did I die?*

As I tried to move, the scene changed from black to a tree, *no*, a house made from a tree. Smoke billowed out of the chimney off to the side and a fire lit the windows. My body seemed to teleport inside of the house. It was quaint, a classic older home. Antiques filled it to the brim, books stacked haphazardly on the ground next to a shelf already bursting at the seams with tomes and scrolls. An elderly man sat in a rocking chair, sleeping, his glasses almost sliding off the tip of his nose.

Why am I seeing this? I wondered. I stepped forward. The wind whistled through a crack in the window. The old man snored himself awake and pushed his glasses up, looking around. His gaze focused on me.

"Well hello, who are you?" the sleep-heavy older man inquired.

I curtsied out of instinct. "Elowen."

"Ah yes, Elowen. I've been expecting you for quite some time. You are just not quite what I expected." The older man peered down at me through his glasses. *What was he expecting?*

"Who are you?" I managed.

He stuck out his hand for me to shake. "Who? Me? It's been so long without people to talk to. I have seemed to have forgotten my manners, my apologies. My name is Leland. I am the overseer of fate."

Instinctively, I grabbed his hand to shake, my mind racing. *I must be dead.* "Of fate?" Realization crashed down on me: my fall, the cave, Lilja. Tears sprung to my eyes. I caused her death. The rooted woman must have killed her by now. Lilja died because of me. *I caused someone else's death again.*

"Don't cry, young one. Lilja is still very much alive, as are you. You're in the in-between right now so you can talk to me. You can't expect me to visit you. That would be preposterous," he said. "The Elven Realm is changing. The blight caused famine, more than expected, and you need to stop it."

"Why am I needed to save a kingdom? I can barely take care of myself. I couldn't save *her*. What can I do?"

Fear crept up my throat as he continued. "You are Elowen, a human connected to the Elven Realm and the Human Realm. If you want the Elven Realm to survive, you need to get rid of the blight." The older man leaned back in his chair as if it was the easiest thing to do.

"How am I supposed to get rid of the blight? How is that supposed to save the Elven Realm? What do you mean, I am a human connected to both realms?"

"The Elven Realm is sensitive to change. The blight is going to spread, it's going to develop a new strain. The two kingdoms will lose their magic if it isn't stopped. We cannot allow that to happen. The gods cannot change things directly; there is a grand plan in place. Change the course the kingdoms have set themselves on." His voice seemed to get farther away, the house fading out and into nothingness.

Gasping, I sat straight up with my hand flying to my face, checking for roots. The world was bright; the trees swayed slightly in the wind.

"She's awake!" Cassia called out from beside me, her face portraying worry.

The queen rushed over, grabbing my face, her forehead creased with concern.

"Are you okay?" I burst out.

Lilja raised an eyebrow. "That demigod hurt you, Elowen. You saved me and now you are asking if I am okay? I should ask you that. What happened?"

I stared at the woman before me, her eyes, her short hair parted through the middle. *Should I tell her about the dream? Was it a dream? Should I tell her everything? Do I know enough information?* I needed to mull the information over more.

"What happened to me?"

The queen looked at me, as if she wasn't sure how much to divulge. "I thought she killed you." Her emotion was clear in her voice. "As soon as she attacked you, the roots disappeared from my body and yours. I was unharmed, thanks to you. But you—you were so pale the whites of your eyes showed. Your breath was so shallow that I could barely detect it. You were grey. Elowen, you looked dead."

"She forced me into the in-between—" I said as Aidan interjected.

"The shadowrealm? How fascinating. What did you see?" Aidan pulled out his journal from his bag and began furiously scribbling notes down.

"Now is not the time to write a history book, Aidan," the queen said, her hand grasping his shoulder and pulling him back behind her. "Continue, Elowen. Please explain everything."

I began the story, describing everything in as much detail as I could remember. As I continued with the details of the previous hours, their mouths hung agape and shock was clear in their faces. Poor Cassia had turned two shades lighter, making her look like a ghost. I spilled almost everything, even about me "accepting my fate." The only thing I did not divulge is that I couldn't save Belle, so what makes the gods think I can save a realm.

"You met Leland, the overseer of fate. *You* met the *gods'* secretary," Keres said in disbelief.

I nodded, not able to form any other words.

"Can you believe that?" she said, scoffing, her body language changing from relaxed to on guard.

"How can you say that, like you don't believe her?" Armand shouted. I winced at the sudden noise. "We have no reason to not believe her, Keres."

Keres's hands curled into fists, and her face flushed. "How can a human possibly save the Elven Realm? If the blight has really transformed into a new strain, we are better off dead."

"Leland said I'm connected to both realms. I don't know how it's possible, but the gods think *I* can help save everyone. But—" I glanced at the queen; her brows furrowed together. She absentmindedly tapped her fingers on her leg as if playing an instrument. Her face portrayed someone thinking of any reality where her struggling kingdom survives.

"The rooted lady and Leland said you need to help me in order to be successful. Will you help?" I said, unaware for a moment that the group had all turned their complete attention to me. "What?" I asked, suddenly self-conscious of what I could have done wrong.

The queen had admiration shining through her brown eyes. "You sounded very brave, Elowen."

She held her hand out to me, allowing me to clasp it.

"Can you stand?" Her fingertips were warm against my cold stubby ones as she pulled me up. She grasped my forearm. "I, Lilja, the Queen of Valdis, accept your help against the blight."

"And I, Elowen Alwyn, lend my hand to you in any way possible." My voice carried high through the trees and they seemed to rustle in reply. My scar tingled.

We all looked up as the trees appeared to dance, agreeing with our newfound bond.

"Well that answers that, doesn't Keres?" Aidan nudged her with his shoulder. Keres looked at Aidan with distaste, but said nothing.

"What's the plan?" I asked as the queen and I let go of each other. My cheeks were red. The team glanced at the queen, awaiting an answer. She looked at us with determination.

"We stay on course; we need to find the Cann Village. We are already off our schedule by a few days, thanks to a rooted demigod."

"A few days?" I raised my eyebrow, alarmed. "I've been out for a few days?"

"Don't worry, we took care of you," Cassia said.

"We were bound to be pushed behind schedule anyway," Kallan said. "At least this gives us motivation to go harder."

Armand gave a whoop of excitement and pumped his fists in the air. I smirked, looking at the crew before me. They all looked happy together. *Was this what having a family felt like?* Then I frowned. No, it wasn't. *If they knew what I really was, they would push me aside... like everyone else.* No one noticed my change in mood, or maybe they thought it was because of what had happened. But we cleaned up camp, each of us mounted our horses, and we started towards the direction of Cann Village.

Nightfall befell us easily. I felt apprehensive of our previous few days, when we traveled in the dark. We didn't speak, afraid to draw too much attention to ourselves. The only sounds were of nighttime creatures, some squawking and some almost screaming. Riding so close together, we could almost touch one another.

The path we followed became more overgrown. I feared we had strayed too far off course. Lanterns began appearing, quickly replacing my second thoughts with anxiety. Unlike normal lanterns, they were round glass orbs with a blue flame. The flame overcast the forest with an eerie light. As we followed down the overgrown path, the blue lanterns grew close together, and soon our ears filled with life. People talking and laughing. We glanced at each other, clearly nervous.

The village wasn't a village at all; it was a city. Shiny, pearl-like stones lined the streets. Houses and shops were whitewashed, reflecting the light with ease. The elves inhabiting this beautiful city stared at us entering; disgust and surprise covered their faces. *They must really not like outsiders,* I thought. The building at the end of the street we were on was clearly the main council building. It was larger than the rest, with a tall, spindly tower and arches covering the windows and doors. Stained glass decorated the windows.

The ornate door, made of a single panel of wood, opened slowly, and three jaw-dropping ladies exited. They each wore a white dress and were adorned with jewelry resembling plants. They wrapped their hair up in large, sheer fabric. The woman in the middle was clearly the monarch of the city. She carried a wooden staff embellished with a carved owl on top. Yellow stones adorned the owl's eyes. I shivered, unnerved.

The middle lady pounded the staff on the stone road. "What a pleasure to see you, my queen. What can I help you with, my highness?" Her loud voice drew the attention of the townspeople, who unabashedly stared at us.

We dismounted from our horses; the queen was the first to talk. "We wish to speak in private."

"We do not hide secrets here. Anything you wish to say, you can say in front of my people." The monarch gestured to the crowd of people.

The queen paused for a minute, taking in the faces surrounding us. "Very well. The blight is changing. It will soon affect things other than the crops we used to feed our families." Nervous murmurs filled the air. The monarch held up her staff to silence the crowd's uneasiness.

"We wish to speak to the person who harnesses the rare subdivision of magic that allows them to see the future, for guidance." Another nervous mumble erupted through the crowd like a wave. This time the monarch let the crowd rumble longer than before.

"Please come into the cathedral," the monarch spoke as she gestured to what I assumed was the main council building.

The queen nodded. We followed as the door opened. The colorful streams of light from the glass washed over us. I glanced around as the door shut with a thud.

"We have known about the blight changing for many months. How did you come to find out about the change?"

My mouth opened with surprise. *For months?!*

"We have our own sources," the queen said. "What may I call you?"

"I am Lady Aluma. I have looked over this city for three hundred years. Longer than your human friend can fathom." Lady Aluma gestured to me. The queen stepped closer to me. The proximity of our bodies made my stomach do little flips.

"This is Elowen," the queen said, speaking for me. "She is our companion, and you will treat her with respect." I looked at her as she finished her statement. My face burned; I once again cursed my fair skin.

"I know who she is, my queen. I meant no disrespect by my statement. She is fated to be here. She is the only one the oracle would like to see." Lady Aluma stared at me, as if sizing me up.

I looked at her, aghast. "Me?"

"Yes, Lady Alwyn, my daughter only wishes to speak to you," she said, as if it irritated her. "She turns away anyone else, even me."

5

The Girl who Became a Tree

"I'll bring you to her tomorrow. You look travel weary, and I do say you could all use a bath."

I wanted to protest, I really did, but I *was* travel weary. Surely the oracle could wait one more day.

The cathedral also doubled as the permanent residence of the upper circle council members. "I shall have food delivered to your rooms for the night. Once you are done, just place the empty platters in the hall. Servants shall be by to clean them up." Lady Aluma showed us to a hall full of doors. "The first door will be the queen's. You can divide the rest up; breakfast is at 7. Please be punctual. Good night," she said as she walked away. Her hips seemed to sway for dramatic effect. *Well, she seems uptight.*

I looked at the queen. She must have thought the same thing; her mouth turned upward into a smirk. We all bid each other goodnight and chose rooms. My feet shuffled to the door across from the queen and pushed it open. My jaw hit the floor. It was prettier than any room I've ever had. Fabric draped over an elegant iron bed frame. A large window covered the wall opposite to the door. A tub was off to the right. I shut the door, sighing, content to stay in this sanctuary forever. I turned the water on and slipped into the tub. The hot steam welcomed my body with open arms.

It washed the events of the day away. The water got cold as I sat in it, my fingers resembling dried prunes. When I got out, I flopped down on the bed, not bothering with the food that had been delivered.

Slipping under the blankets, I allowed sleep to take me.

"Get off of me," I giggled as the taller girl pinned my hands above my head.

Belle leaned down and kissed me. "Never." She started at my chin and made her way to my earlobe, nibbling. My knees buckled at the sensation. Dear gods, she'd be the death of me. I groaned, allowing her mouth to get deep towards my chest; my dress barely covered any of my cleavage. She pulled away to look at me. My face flushed. I pouted. *That's all?* I asked myself.

Her long curly hair, pinned up, was slightly messy. She took a deep breath. "I'll never tire of you."

I stood on my tiptoes, giving her a small peck on the lips. "And I'll never tire of you."

A gasp called out from the end of the hall. Our heads flew to the sound. Katherine stood at the end of the hall, her mouth covering her mouth in shock.

"I always knew you were freaks." She moved her hand to display a look of disgust.

"Shit," Belle said under her breath. She pulled away from me, running towards Katherine. Her heels clicked on the stone flooring. Our intruder yelped and ran away from the hallway we inhabited. I followed behind Belle, towards Katherine's quickly disappearing form. My thoughts ran wild as we chased her. What was she going to do? We turned the corner, nearly running into a clergy member who was talking with Katherine. Unsure of the situation we just interrupted, we halted.

She gave the clergy member her best pouting eyes. "Jasper was right. I saw them, they were kissing! It's not natural; she's betrothed!" I stared at her, the interaction between them giving me heart palpitations.

The clergyman looked up at us with disgust. "Is this allegation true, girls?"

We shook our heads furiously, denying any suggestion of what we were doing earlier. The clergyman looked from us to Katherine. His old, wrinkled face almost hooded his eyes with sagging skin.

"My kind sir," Belle started out, nervousness clear in her voice, "we would never do such a thing. Elowen and I were trading secrets, gossip, if you will. While gossiping is a sin, I can assure you we'd never be caught disobeying the gods' words. Katherine is just jealous. She's never had a friend as close as we are."

The clergyman brought his hand up to his chin, rubbing his stubble, while looking at Katherine. "It is a pretty severe allegation to announce because of jealousy, my dear." It was apparent that he was trying to see the lie that wasn't there.

"Very well, please try to include Katherine in any further get togethers." He narrowed his eyes while looking at us. "You should discourage such allegations again." We glared at the back of Katherine as she stomped away. The clergyman followed shortly after.

Belle looked into my eyes, grabbing into my arms. "We cannot see each other for a while, Elowen; the risk is too great. You could lose your spot in the upper circle and I could lose my place in the library."

I wanted her; I wanted a chance of life, a normal one.

I woke up, tears streaming down my face, the moon shining through the window and creating shadows on the ground. The room was silent. I sighed, wiping away the tears. I tried to get comfortable in bed again and willed sleep to take me over. Every time I closed my eyes, her face plagued me. The past seemed to haunt me.

I sat up—sleep was avoiding me—and stretched. Curiosity filled me as I looked out the large window. Moonlight lit the courtyard, hauntingly giving it a cold glow.

Throwing the sheet haphazardly on the floor, I allowed my feet to take me, and I found myself in the courtyard. The music from the bugs filled the air, creating a sense of peace.

"Hello Alwyn, I see you finally came to visit," a voice called out from somewhere in the courtyard. I whipped around to face my nighttime companion.

Even with the moonlight, I could not see my visitor. "Don't be alarmed, young one. I'm not here to hurt you. Quite the opposite, in fact. Please sit with me."

"Where are you?" I asked into the dark. *Am I going crazy?*

A giggled erupted, a childlike laugh, which emanated from a small tree whose base was disproportionately large to the rest of it.

"I am the tree you are staring at, silly," the voice said.

I gazed at the tree more, letting the moon's glow highlight the shape at the bottom. I gasped, realizing there was a child growing into the tree. Magic textured her dark skin much like the tree she was transforming into. She sat cross-legged in a meditation pose.

"Don't be alarmed Alwyn, it doesn't hurt," the tree said again.

"How did this happen?" I stumbled over to the tree in shock. She giggled as I touched the leaves instinctively. They rustled in response.

"Sto-o-op, that tickles."

I backed away from her quickly. "Oh, sorry. You know my name, yet I don't know yours."

"I am known by different names, but the latest one is Oracle. Please sit, I get lonely at this time of night," Oracle said.

I complied, sitting cross-legged like she was.

"How do you know my name?" I asked the small form before me.

Her leaves rustled as she spoke. "I know a great many things. My roots travel far. Everything is connected, even the Human Realm to the Elven Realm."

"How am I connected to both?"

"That I can't tell you; plans are already in play. Each result differs from the other."

Frustration boiled inside of me. *Why is everything so vague?* "Are you saying that each choice I make changes the future?"

"While the solution seems like a straightforward path, there are hundreds, each one offering a different way to get there. Some include heartbreak, death, and destruction. You'd do well to follow your heart," she said, closing her eyes. "Meditate, young Alwyn, ease the troubled soul encased in your body. Maybe you can see what I see."

I looked around nervously. "Will I turn into a tree?"

Her leaves rumbled like a belly after a hearty laugh. "Gods no. You are just taking a glimpse, much like with Leland."

My eyes widened at the mention of his name, but I listened. The sounds of the night consumed me; darkness welcomed me. The moon seemed to open up to me, letting me breathe a sigh of relief. I saw nothing at first. It started small, almost like a tiny painting placed on a large, blank wall. It was the team of elves; the one I found myself welcomed into. They were standing over a large table, poring over a map. Quickly, the scene changed to a hazy scene of fire, the table overturned, Kallan holding the queen's body. The view changed again to a phoenix, a flash of brown hair, laughter, and then darkness.

I woke abruptly to the queen shaking my shoulder; my body was damp from the morning dew. I stared at her. The queen's black hair covered her eyes again. "What are you doing out here? Did you sleepwalk?"

Kallan stood next to her; a frown seemed to be set in stone on his face.

"No, I couldn't sleep—" I began.

"Well, you seem to do a good job of sleeping in the grass, in your nightclothes," Kallan scoffed at me.

"I was meditating with the oracle." I glanced back at the tree. With her eyes closed, her body seemed more tree-like than yesterday. She seemed to sense our eyes on her as she flung hers open. Her blue eyes were the same color as the sky. A gasp erupted from Kallan. The queen seemed stoic as ever.

The oracle peered at the queen and Kallan, a grin growing on her face. "My apologies for stealing away your human partner. Her troubled soul seemed to wake us both with the dream she had." Kallan's frown deepened at her wording.

"We meditated to see what the earth wished to show us. Did you find the right path?" Her leaves rustled again.

I looked at her, frustrated. "No, it made little to no sense. All I saw was us, an explosion, and a phoenix."

The queen stilled next to me, grabbing my exposed forearm, touching my scar. I shivered. "What?"

"The phoenix," she said through gritted teeth, her sharp nails digging into my arm, almost breaking skin.

"What else did you see of her?"

Who was this woman?

"All I saw was brown hair and a phoenix, nothing else, I swear. Please let go of me. You're hurting me." My chest tightened, my heart beating faster. My father flashed before my vision.

She released my arm instantly, her anger gone, now replaced with worry. "Shit, sorry." Queen Lilja glanced over to Kallan. "It's Alieta."

"It's fine," I wheezed, trying to ignore the flashbacks. It was hot suddenly, so hot. Sweat pricked the sides of my eyes, making them water.

"Alwyn," the oracle said sharply. I glanced at her, trying to take a breath in. Everyone seemed so far away. "The past is in the past. It can no longer hurt you. Try to calm yourself. Your energy is affecting me."

I looked at her; the shadows in the corner of my eyes nearly took over my vision. Her leaves seemed to shake with each quick breath I took. The queen stared at me with pity. *I hate how people see me.*

Kallan stood off to the side, staring at a plant as if it was the most interesting thing in the world. I closed my eyes, trying to force my breathing to normal. *Breathe Elowen, breathe,* my voice commanded in my head. I allowed the rustling leaves to fill my ears. The pounding heartbeat threatened to come out of my chest. Somebody grabbed my arm. I flinched at the contact, instinctually.

Visions flooded my closed eyes, glimpses of what could be. A hand, obviously male with copious amounts of hair, grew upon it. *Why am I seeing a hand?* The sword shaped nails held onto something. What? What is he holding onto? The vision hazed out. Nothing was making sense. I opened my eyes once again. The oracle's blue eyes pierced my soul, clearly just as confused as I was.

Kallan and the queen stared at the oracle and me, confusion and concern plastered on their faces. I moved to stand up; the earth protested. Little blades of grass had grown into my nightgown. Looking down, I glanced back up at the Oracle, surprised.

"The view to the future is not always free. Glimpses are allowed, but the earth protests, young Alwyn."

"What did you see?" the queen asked as we walked away from the oracle.

"A hand." I shivered as the morning dew chilled me.

"You looked into the future and saw a hand?" Kallan asked.

"Hey, I don't know how to look in the future perfectly. I didn't even know elves existed until I washed up on shore," I argued.

"This will all make sense soon, we just have to keep going," the queen said. "Now Elowen, please refrain from any more nighttime adventures, unless someone is with you. Go change and find us in the dining area. It's time for breakfast. I'm sure you're famished." She pinched the bridge of her nose and scrunched her eyes.

I nodded, staying silent. *Is she mad at me?*

I walked up to my room, taking my time, allowing myself to take in the art on the walls. Each one a different portrait of different women, all beautiful in their own right. Making it to my room, I threw on clothes, eager to go eat. I found my way to the dining room, which was full of life. Each one of my companions appeared replenished from sleep; now they were eager to eat everything in sight. The queen, however, was sitting at the head, her fingers crossed, her food untouched. Lost in thought. My entrance went unnoticed as I slipped into an empty seat next to Keres. I piled food onto my plate, a small amount.

Keres glanced at me, rolling her eyes, scoffing.

Suddenly, I was self-conscious about the food on my plate. "What?" *Is it too much?*

"You need to think of people other than yourself," she said, stabbing at the remaining food on her plate.

"What is that supposed to mean?" I said, squaring my shoulders up.

"Lilja couldn't find you. She was worried sick. Plus, when you did your whole heroic bit with that rooted demigod, she was beside herself until you woke."

I looked down at my plate. "I-I didn't think."

"That's right, you didn't think. Sometimes you should just close your trap and not say anything or do anything. Be seen and not heard. The world doesn't revolve around you, Elowen Alwyn," she huffed, roughly grabbing her plate, leaving at the same time Lady Aluma entered.

She took the head of the table at the other end. "So Ms. Elowen, I heard you visited my daughter last night." Her voice projected to where I was sitting.

"Indeed, madam, she's splendid company," I said, taking a bite of my food. The room was quiet other than the sound of people chewing.

"I hope you found what you are looking for, as each time she sees into the future, the earth consumes her bit by bit." Her eyes filled with anger as she glared at me.

"I assure you, Lady Aluma, I never asked her to look into the future. I just couldn't sleep. She suggested we meditate when I found her in the courtyard." I looked at her, stunned.

"We meant no harm," the queen announced. "Elowen is innocent in this situation. I can say that the suffering of your daughter saddens the Kingdom of Valdis. I hope a solution is found soon. Now, I can see we have overstayed our welcome. Once we are done with our meal, we will pack up and be on our way. Thank you for the hospitality." Her head was high as she spoke. An air of superiority surrounded her.

I looked at the queen and then back at Lady Aluma. *This is my fault.* I stood, bowing my head to the queen and Lady Aluma. "Please excuse me, I need some air," I walked out of the room with all of their eyes burning holes into my back.

They hate me, I thought. Somehow, I found myself back in the courtyard, next to the oracle.

"That bad, huh?" she said as I sat down. I nodded, upset. "Don't feel too bad. This is my fate, and it's set in stone as yours is."

"We will leave once the rest of the team finishes eating breakfast. I should pack."

She slowly lifted her stiff arm towards me. "Be strong, Alwyn, the world isn't as harsh as your mind makes it out to be."

I grabbed hold of her hand, with a grim realization of how tree-like she felt. I stooped my head down, giving her a light peck on her hand. Making my way upstairs, I packed my meager supplies into my bag.

Where were we going next?

6

Haunted Past

A knock rapped on the door, the sound startling me. "Elowen, it's time to go, are you ready?" Cassia called out from the other side.

"Yes," I said as I pushed myself off the bed, starting for the door.

She peered in, her long curly red hair seemed to be in a perpetual explosion as it protruded from her cloak. I flung my own cloak over my body; its blue color complimented my fair skin. In the hall it was quiet other than the taps of our feet. "Where are we heading now?" I finally questioned, breaking the silence.

She sighed. "We are going to the mountains, a reconnaissance mission."

"For what?" My thoughts swirled in my head. *What's going on? Are we in danger?*

"I think it would be better if you asked Lilja that. I've probably already said too much." She said quickly, making it evident she wanted to end the conversation as fast as possible.

"Okay," I said slowly. *Why is this such a sensitive subject?*

We found ourselves in front of the cathedral once again. The daylight made the city look even more magnificent than it did in the dark. The streets were still full; perhaps the city never went quiet. Armand and Kallan bickered about how to pack the bags on the sides of their horses. Keres looked as disinterested in the world as normal, not making eye contact with anyone. Aidan wrote in his journal, his blond hair falling into his eyes, making him appear younger. The queen stood next to her horse and my own. She stared at me as I walked up. I gave her a small smile, she didn't return it.

"Alright, team," she said. Everyone turned to her in attention. "Let's get going. I will give further information when it becomes pertinent. Please be patient as I try to organize what we do next." I mounted Lady, giving her a few affectionate pats.

Lady reminded me of the times with my mother, before she got sick. Every morning she would allow me to ride with her. It was one of the few nice memories with her. We would get breakfast and have tea after the ride. Our conversations would be filled with heated discussion over the poem we read the night before together. Tears sprung to my eyes at the memory; I allowed them to fall as we rode out of the city. It was important to heal from the memories that could never happen again. The world existed and ended with life and death, and sometimes it left people behind to learn how to live without the other.

The scenery changed around us as we traveled through the city; the buildings became more condensed, making it evident that we had entered the residential part. The houses were not unlike the houses in the Human Realm. All of them seemed to be occupied; in fact, the city appeared to be bursting at the seams with life. Almost as if they were at full capacity. Soon the houses began to appear farther and farther apart, and we entered the forest once again.

Aidan and Kallan were still discussing the logistics of traveling with just the packs on our horses versus having a donkey pulling a cart. I looked at the queen again. She stared ahead, as if lost in thought.

"My queen."

She turned towards me, startled out of her train of thought.

"I apologize for the inconvenience of having to leave the Cann Village. I truly did not mean to cause Lady Aluma any offense," I rambled on.

"Elowen, Lady Aluma is upset with the grief of losing her child. Nothing you did or said would have caused us to be thrown out of that place. In addition, it was a nice surprise to be able to see the village. In all my two hundred and thirty years of life, I've never seen it, I was actually quite surprised to see it look so grand. Reminds me of home."

"You're two hundred and thirty years old?" My jaw nearly fell on the ground. *That's impossible. How can she look that good? Good? I mean young.* She chuckled at me as if it was normal for people to live to two hundred and thirty years old.

"Well yes, Elowen, I am two hundred and thirty years old. Why, do I look old?" She mocked being offended by bringing her hand to her chest dramatically.

"What? No! You look great for being two hundred and thirty," my cheeks burned, "I just mean that I'm only twenty-three, and we look the same age."

"Thank you for the compliment, most people think I'm quite limber for my elderly age too," she said, leaning over on her horse slightly to wink at me. "Wait, what did you say? Did you just say you are twenty-three years old?"

"Did you just say twenty-three?" Kallan said, nearly falling off his horse.

"Holy gods, you're literally a child," Armand exclaimed, nearly spitting out the water he was trying to drink out of his canteen.

"I am not a child," I said stubbornly. "I might be young by your standards. But in the Human Realm, I am past the age of when young women get married and start bearing children." I crossed my arms. *Why are they acting like this?* "Why do you act so surprised? I know the humans have forgotten about the magic realm, but you all seem quite aware about the Human Realm."

They all quieted down at my statement, until Cassia spoke up. "Actually, knowledge about the Human Realm is extremely limited. There have only been a few humans to make it across to our realm. Many find themselves killed shortly after coming."

Aidan looked up from his journal, his glasses nearly on the tip of his nose. "Wait, if you are past the age of when normal humans get married and have children—" I flinched at the word *normal* as it rolled off his tongue. "Why aren't you married? Why don't you have kids?" They all looked at me, awaiting my answer. The queen's eyes were staring at me intently.

"I-It was once arranged for me to be engaged to a young childhood friend of mine. His name was Jasper, he was kind and a gentleman—"

"If he was so great, then what happened? Did he die?" Keres interjected, suddenly interested in the drama unfolding.

"No, he didn't die, something happened, and I called off the marriage," I said, looking down at my hands.

"Is that why you got banished, because you called off the marriage?" Cassia said gently, as if I was close to breaking. Was I close to breaking?

I nodded slowly. It *was* part of the reason, and partial truth was still truth, right?

"Well, the Human Realm sounds archaic. In most regions in the Elven Realm, women are allowed to marry when they want, bear children when they want, it's up to them," Aidan said as he scribbled something in his journal.

"Women are picky here, if you ask me," Armand said, rubbing the back of his neck.

"You only think that because not a single one wants to sleep with you," Kallan said, chuckling. The group roared with laughter, while Armand turned red, making everyone laugh more.

"Hey, I'll have you know I'm quite the ladies' man back in Valdis," Armand said to me, wiggling his eyebrows at me and winking.

"I'm sure there are plenty of women waiting in line for a piece of you," I said, placing a hand on his arm, smiling.

"Maybe manifest that with some meditating," the queen said. I could hear the smile in her voice without having to look at her. "Just don't fall off your horse, again."

"Again?" I asked incredulously.

"It was *one* time, guys," Armand huffed and whined. "You had us riding all day, I needed to meditate sometime."

I stifled a giggle; the queen rolled her eyes. The sun had embraced the earth and the moon had come out. Stars glittered in the sky, there were so many. Millions of lights seemed to shine upon us, lighting the path. "Let's make camp, tomorrow we will reach the inn and we can make a plan for the next few weeks," the queen announced.

The next few weeks? The full moon will be back by then. Should I part ways with the group when we reach the inn? How long will it take for me to travel back to the sea by myself? Wait. I shook my head to shake the thoughts away. *I'm stuck here. My fate is tied here. I have to help these people. Do I want to?*

I dismounted from my horse. *Why do I have to think about these things that make me doubt myself. I* do *want to help these people. I'm a good person. Right?*

"Let's set up tents and get to bed, I'm exhausted," Kallan complained.

We made quick work of making camp, all of us tired from the day's ride. I fed the horses before plopping down beside Kallan next to the fire. Cassia heating up some rabbit that Armand caught. I yawned, too exhausted to eat, and my eyes fluttered closed. I was warm; the fire kept me toasty.

"Why can't we just leave her here, she's the one that fell asleep next to the fire?" someone whispered, probably Keres.

"She'll roll in if we leave her here," huffed someone else, a male voice.

"Just put her in my tent, she doesn't sleep well," a commanding voice resonated in my ears.

I tried to will myself to open my eyes, but sleep conquered. I felt myself being picked up, someone's arms under my legs and holding my back. My head curled into the nook of their neck. I felt myself being laid down, before sleep took me over completely once again.

"Elowen," Belle whispered out. I opened my eyes, blinking slowly as my eyes adjusted to the darkness in my room. I walked over to my balcony and peered down.

Belle stood in her nightgown with her hair tied back, lantern in hand. "Come down here," she said from the garden below.

I placed my finger on my lips to shush her and ran through my empty house. Papa was always away; other than the servants, I was the only one residing in the manor. As I exited the house, I slowly shut the door, trying to silence the click of it shutting with my desire to go undetected.

"Belle, we can't keep doing this. We are going to get caught," I whispered fervently.

"That's the thrilling part," she said back grinning as we ran to the barn in the back. We climbed up the rickety old ladder to the hayloft. The animals below us were still sleeping, unbothered by our almost nightly escapade. A giggle escaped my lips as she kissed and nibbled at my neck; she groaned in return.

I let her have her way with me.

Even with nearly every night being together, I could never get tired of coexisting in this space with her. I sighed, content with the night, even with the hay poking me uncomfortably. The air was quiet around us as we held each other, and the only audible sounds were of the frogs and insects. I must have dozed off, because I awoke to the clatter of footsteps. A flames' light illuminated the barn, making the shadows dance on the walls and the stacked hay. *Flame?* Sleep dulled my senses as I sat up; Belle grumbled in her sleep. I shook her awake. *What is going on?*

"They are here somewhere, men, keep looking," a gruff voice commanded.

I turned to Belle startled. Who were they looking for? Criminals? Her she put a finger to her lips, silencing the questions rising from my throat. Her eyes hardened as she grabbed my hand and we ran to the opening at the wall, peering out. Twenty or so men surrounded the barn, each with torches.

"Belle and Elowen, come out now," my father's voice commanded. I glanced down at him; he was as perfect looking as normal. Always showing everyone else how impeccable he was, and how perfect he wanted me to be.

They weren't looking for criminals; they were looking for us. We were the criminals in this situation.

My father glanced up at the open hay door and saw me; his eyes glistened with anger. "There they are, guards! Get them so they can answer to their crimes!"

"What crimes? We haven't done anything. There must be some miscommunication," I cried out, desperate to get this confusion settled.

"Jasper and his little whore friend told me all about the secret relationship that Belle forced you in! No daughter of mine will be gay!

Now get down here, you *will* marry Jasper tomorrow. That will end the rumors going on in town," he seethed his voice thick with anger.

A sob escaped my chest. How were we supposed to get out of this mess? Hands grabbed me from behind. I screamed.

"Let go of her, you asshole," Belle yelled, reaching for the hands grabbing me by the waist.

Another guard came from behind me, brandishing a sword, its polished form reflecting the light from the torches. Belle lunged for him, attempting to grab the sword away from him, blinded by anger. I continued to struggle against the man holding me, but his grip only seemed to tighten against my body.

He grunted. "Gods, you're heavy."

I watched as the guard slid his knife's blade into Belle with a sickening crunch as it went in between ribs.

"*Belle!*" I screamed out. My voice seemed to carry. I sobbed as another scream erupted from my mouth. She looked up at me in shock, her face pale, blood dribbling from the side of her mouth.

"Elowen," a voice called out.

"Elowen," it called again, and the world began to shake, my vision blurring.

"Wake up!" the queen called out. I sat up, sobbing, tears streaming down.

I put my face in my hands. "It's all my fault." I wept as she held me, her warm arms circled around me. "She's dead. It's my fault." I cried harder, my breathing ragged.

"Who's dead," the queen asked softly. Noise was coming from the outside of the tent.

"Belle," I cried, heaving slightly, my chest tightening. "She loved me, and my father had her killed!"

The queen stopped the rocking motion. Pulling away from me slightly, she looked at me, her eyes searching for the meaning behind my words. "What do you mean, darling, why would he have her killed?" she asked.

"I ruined the perfect image he had," I sobbed out, another wave of tears wreaking havoc on my short frame. *She doesn't understand, nobody does.* I cried harder, gagging as my heaves pushed the food I ate up towards my throat.

"Calm down, Elowen, you'll make yourself throw up if you don't," the queen warned, rubbing my back.

"No, you don't understand," I wailed out. "I was banished because I'm gay. She died trying to save *me*!"

The queen stilled the rocking motion to look at me once again. This time, however, confusion coated her face. "Why would you be banished because of that?"

7

Revealed

I stared at the queen, dumbfounded. *What does she mean? Why would I be banished because I was gay?* "Because being gay is a 'sin' and unlawful." The tears had stopped running down my face. The salt from my tears made my face feel dry.

She stared at me for a moment, digesting the words I just said. Her jaw clenched, and her mouth began curling up in disgust. She grabbed my arm and pointed at the iron brand mark on it. "Being gay in the Human Realm gets you branded and thrown out?" Her skin turned a darker shade of red by a second, and the large vein on her forehead grew more prominent. The ground rumbled, the tent shook with it. Was it an earthquake?

I nodded, staying silent, scared to make the current situation worse. *Does she hate me now? Is that why she is so mad?* I clutched the pelt I was covered with. She stood up, pacing the length of the tent. *Maybe she wants me to leave.* I struggled to get up, still shaking from the dream. The pelt fell off of me. She stopped and stared at me.

"I'm sorry," I said, my voice cracking from my earlier sobs.

"What are you sorry for, Elowen?" The queen asked, pinching the bridge of her nose.

"I-I guess for being like this." I shrugged sadly. "I can leave, I'm sorry." I headed for the tent's exit and she grabbed my arm. Flinching, I turned around.

She pulled away slightly, as if not trying to scare me. "Why would you need to leave?"

"Because…you presumably—" I hiccuped, tears streaming down my face. "—you possibly find me repulsive." I chastised myself. *Elowen, you found a path in life and you ruined it by being you. Again.*

She stared at me, scrutinizing me, and grabbed me, pulling me into a hug. In the tent, her usual stoic appearance melted into warmth and gentleness. She murmured something to herself, something I couldn't make out. She pulled away; her head bent down so our foreheads were practically touching.

"Elowen, I now realize that our realms are very different, something I didn't realize sooner. While being gay in your realm is a 'sin' and means banishment or worse. In our realm, we accept it." Her eyes burned with such passion as she talked, "After all, the Kingdom of Valdis is ruled by a gay person."

"It is? But I thought you were the queen," I said, not understanding what she was saying.

She laughed and swiftly regained her composure. "I am the Queen of Valdis, and I am also gay."

I stared at her. She was gay? "Oh."

"Come on, Elowen, did you think this attractive woman in front of you could fend off every female who threw themselves at me?" she said, giving me a flirtatious smile. She pulled away from me, leaving me cold. "Now, let me look at this brand." Her flirtatious smile was gone, replaced by hard eyes.

I sniffled and held out my arm, the skin around my scar covered in goosebumps from the cold air. The original brand was nearly unrecognizable, as I had tried to cut it out of me on one of the dark days shortly after my banishment. I shivered at the dark memory.

"Why does it look like this? What was the brand originally?"

"It was a triangle with lines protruding from the sides, a line for each god," I said. *By gods, I sound so weak.* She traced the symbol I described into my arm absentmindedly.

"Why does it look like this now?" She gestured to the raised scar, now replacing the brand. The scar's color was typically red, but now was a slight tint of purple as a chilly breeze from the night seeped into the tent, leaving me cold.

"I-I tried to cut it out, to hide it. To hide it from me and others who might cross my path. The Human Realm doesn't take kindly to my—I mean our—kind," I said, my voice cracking.

"There is no *our kind*, Elowen. We are all people. There isn't one of us who's more important than the other because of their sexual preference." The queen said firmly, crossing her arms.

"I nearly bled out, I passed out, I awoke the next morning covered in blood," I said, ashamed of the past.

Her eyes darkened, maybe with hate or maybe with sadness. "Please don't try that again. Once this is over, we can get it healed. The palace healers are quite skilled, using medicinal plants to create salves imbued with magical essence. This is a reminder of your past and they will get rid of it. They weren't able to find the cure of the blight, but they sure as hell can heal a scar from abhorrent people."

I didn't want to try again. *I might as well live out of spite. So that Belle didn't die for nothing.*

"Let's get you something to eat. You must be starving."

I nodded and my stomach started growling at that very moment. She walked towards the tent flap and opened it, revealing the mostly died-down fire. Kallan was sitting on a rock by it, his sword placed on his lap, his hand on the hilt. As he kept watch over the other sleeping forms in nearby tents. He looked up, his face did not appear to be startled. In fact, he appeared sad as he gazed upon us.

My face heated, realizing he probably could hear the entire ordeal. *Fuck, what if he knows? Wait, the queen said that people like us were accepted. "Us" has a nice ring to it, less lonely, less alone.*

We sat by the fire, and she handed me a piece of meat. It was cold but still tasted good. My stomach relished the protein entering my system. I swallowed. "Thank you, my queen," I said as I finished the last of the rabbit.

She stared at the fire, not making eye contact with me. The flames' reflection danced in her eyes. "You can call me Lilja when we are amongst friends."

Kallan let out a noise that sounded something like a dying animal. Lilja turned to glare at him.

"What?"

"I was wondering when you were gonna let her call you by your name. My queen was getting annoying to listen to. I was worried about it getting to your head." He grinned at me, giving me a wink. "You know, when Lilja and I first begun to hang out, my father made me call her your highness. Until finally she told him it wasn't needed. Such a mouthful," Kallan said.

"How did you guys start hanging out? I thought you just raised horses." I sniffled, my curiosity piqued despite my tired brain telling me the best thing was to go back to bed.

"My family did just raise horses, but Lilja used to sneak off to the stables almost every day. She would always claim that her parents, the king and queen, knew she was there. Of course they didn't know and my father was just charmed by her manners. He used to say, 'Kal! You need to be more like Lilja.' I used to hate to see her come in everyday, because he'd always make me go riding with her. Even if she was a royal, hanging out with a girl everyday was lame." Kallan chuckled, to himself lost in thought.

"He and I only really began to be friends after I saved his scrawny butt from falling into a river, and we've been inseparable ever since." Lilja said as she looked up at the sky. It had just transformed from shades of blue to yellow, orange, and hints of red. "We should wake the others. Today will be a long day. At the base of the mountain is the inn. The plan is to recover from our journey there and find a way up the mountain without being seen. I want to find out what Ardour knows. I want to know how they are protecting themselves against it."

Kallan and I both nodded and woke the others. We broke down tents and stomped out the fire. The sunrise was brilliant. The added light showcased the beautiful countryside before us. Tall firs and cypress trees spotted the countryside, the mountain ridge became more and more visible. It made the surrounding land seem miniature in comparison. Passing a few towns, we stopped at the third for lunch. It was small, a few houses littered a few side streets, and a large shop sat next to a jail. I shivered at the sight. *I do not want to end up back in one of those.* It was not as nice as anything back home, nor did it compare to the Cann Village we were just thrown out of.

Voices emanated from the surrounding buildings. Lunchtime was in full swing at the bar. As we entered, we were met with a plethora of people, apparently disregarding the time, as they appeared drunk. It quieted down as we walked through the doorway, but the conversation picked back up as we ordered our food. "Do people know who you are?" I asked Lilja.

"Yes. Why?" she said, raising an eyebrow.

"Well, it's just that in the Human Realm, many royals can't even get out of the castle because of how people act when they see them."

"In my younger years, I used to go gallivanting throughout the countryside, looking for a purpose. My kingdom has been in hard times since I was little. I used to go out and fix things, small things like fences. Carry heavy things for old ladies, anything to prove my worth to my citizens. They became numb to my frequent appearance in their town. Now if you get farther north, it'll be a different story. The previous rulers of Valdis, my parents, banned me from ever going there. Bandits and criminals used to roam the countryside. A few years ago, I made the boys go up and break the hold the criminals had on the towns."

I glanced at the guys sitting across from us. They grinned like children getting a new puppy. Aidan crossed his arms. "Hey, all we did was do what you asked."

"If I remember correctly, all I asked you to do was rough them up, not set fire to their whole hideout." Lilja laughed.

"That explosion made each one of you lose your eyebrows. It took months for Armand's to grow back," Cassia said, giggling at the memory.

Keres took a large gulp of the soup the server placed in front of her. "At least they finally had a good excuse for why they couldn't get any ladies." We all giggled at her remark.

"We will make it to the inn in the late afternoon. There, we will regroup with the rest of the formation," Lilja said in a low voice, trying to make it so no one other than the people at her table could hear. The giggly mood was extinguished as she explained the plan she had in store for the next few weeks. She wanted to cross the mountain and separate. *Wait? Separate?* My pulse quickened at the idea. Kallan sensed my discomfort and added, "It would look really suspicious if all of us warriors entered towns together. Because if recognized, we could unintentionally start the war."

War?

Lilja sipped at the mead in her cup. "There could very well be no war. We could find the answer we yearn for. We will all use personas, keep our eyes and ears open for anything suspicious. Cassia, you will infiltrate the court. I don't care how you do it. But get on the inside and listen to the chatter between the lords and ladies. Aidan, I need you to go to the university in the city, try to read everything you can about the blight. See what they know about it and see if they have any treatments for it. Armand, I need you and Kallan to be buddies with the military personnel. I hear that many of them go out on the town during their break season. That is in a few months. By the time we get through the mountain, it might be upon us. Keres, be sneaky and be invisible. I need you with Cassia. You need to relay any life-threatening information between all of us."

"Elowen, you're going to be with me. We are traveling together, as a couple of wandering upper circle ladies," she said with a smirk growing on her lips.

Are we acting as a couple of upper circle ladies or a couple? I nearly fainted at the thought of acting as a couple with Lilja.

With the plan laid out before us, we headed out of town and towards the inn once again. I patted Lady on her neck, quickly picking up speed. All of us were eager to put the plan into play. I found myself excited about the future, something I hadn't felt in a very long time.

The air got colder as we slowly traveled uphill; the ground losing the vibrant green color, transforming into shades of brown foliage. I shivered, pulling my cloak up and around my body more. My breath created a fog around me as I leaned towards Lady's body more, hoping to get some of her body heat.

I hate the cold.

I glanced at the rest of the group. They were reacting the same as me. "Aidan, do elves have a different tolerance for heat and cold than humans?"

He looked up at me as if it surprised him that someone would ask him a question. I made a mental note to ask more later. Pushing his glasses off the tip of his nose, he grabbed his journal from his satchel.

He flipped through it to find whatever he was looking for. Some pages stuck out oddly, as if someone had pulled them out and roughly put back in again.

"Depending on whether elves have powers or not, they can either react the same as humans or have more tolerance towards such things. For instance, someone with air powers like Armand can move the surrounding air, keeping their body temperatures warmer than someone with water abilities. People with earth magic can keep themselves warmer if they are in connection with the ground as they can shift the earth beneath them, finding heat sources. People born with fire can obviously keep themselves warm. They struggle with the cold only because it saps away their energy faster than in normal temperatures."

I nodded, trying to absorb all the information being thrown at me into my slightly frozen brain. "Do all of you guys have some sort of magical ability or is the all-powerful Armand the only one?"

Armand turned a few shades redder than his normal dark skin color, as the rest of the group cackled.

"Lilja and I have earth abilities," Aidan said with his teeth chattering.

"I have water abilities," Cassia said from underneath her cloak, which she had wrapped herself in almost completely. How could she even see where she was riding?

I looked at Keres expectantly, awaiting her answer. Out of all of us, she was the only one without a cloak. Her pale complexion seemed completely void of any discomfort from the cold. She rolled her eyes, staring at her nails. "I have the ability of fire."

I raised my eyebrow at Kallan, awaiting his answer. Kallan shrugged. "My power is good looks."

Lilja barked a laugh. "While Kallan doesn't have a power, he is indispensable to our team. In both battle tactics and, I suppose, his good looks. Or at least that's what the ladies tell me."

The farther we trekked up the road, the windier it got. I cursed myself silently for not being more warm-blooded like Keres. Soon a large building came into view, the only one we had seen in hours. There was a stable next to it. The wind had blown snow into piles, making it look like a gingerbread house on a mountain of icing. Lights flickered in the windows, giving it a warm and inviting look. *Gods know I could use a warm bath.* Wearily, I grinned at my travel companions, happy to make it in one piece.

8

Secret City

"Thank the gods, we've finally made it. Keres, since you are the only one of us not frozen, please put the horses in the stables. The rest of us will regroup in the inn. Please join us once you are done," Lilja asked in a non-negotiable tone.

"Ope, you just got volun-told," Armand laughed at Keres, who just glared at him in response.

Lilja rolled her eyes as she dismounted from her horse. "Ope, it looks like Armand can help you now."

We all followed shortly behind her, shivering as I did so. *I'm pretty sure the cold froze my cloak to my ass from my butt sweat.*

Cassia threw her arm around my shoulder, making me jump at the unexpected physical contact. She grinned at me, unaware of the reaction she caused in me. A plump, short man stepped out of the inn's front door. His beard was white with age, his cheeks tinted red from the cold.

He waved us inside with a flourish. "Hello travelers! Come in, come in, you're in luck. My husband just finished making cookies! They are quite wonderful!" *Husband?*

We followed him inside hurriedly, eager for the warmth of his business place. He glanced around and gave us one last look, stopping at my unpointed ears. He glanced away, as if ashamed for staring at me.

"If you don't like the cookies, say nothing about it. Or I'll have to listen to it for years."

Cassia grinned at his response, and all but pulled me deeper into the building. The room was lit by an enormous fireplace. Fur rugs covered the ground haphazardly. Large, mounted animals adorned the walls, some deer and some I didn't recognize. Quick paintings of smiling groups sprinkled throughout the room, on the mantelpiece and on the walls in between the stuffed animals.

"Your establishment is very cozy," I said, trying to find words to describe his style choices.

"Thank you," a skinny man said as he burst through a nearby door with a plate of cookies. He strode over to us, holding the plate out to each of us. As I tried to eat it, the still-melted chocolate got on my fingers.

"I cleaned up the place when I received your letter. They are all ready. We distributed supplies for each of your endeavors in your respective rooms," the short man said as he straightened up his shoulders and back in the attempt to appear taller. I looked at Lilja sharply. When did she send a letter?

My look went ignored as Lilja began replying to the man. She shook his hand. "Thank you, Elbio, your loyalty to the Kingdom of Valdis has not gone unnoticed." His husband beside him puffed out his chest in pride.

"My queen, I'm sure you had already thought of this, but I suggest you cover the ears of your human friend. Humans aren't very common in the area. She's due to cause you unwanted attention." The skinnier man said, quietly. Lilja contemplated me for a second, as if she hadn't thought about the disruption of my lacking anatomy.

"What do you propose, Dumont?"

Dumont fidgeted with his hand. "We could make her false ears from some things around the house, making them appear as real as possible."

She nodded.

"Food will be ready shortly. Why don't you and your team go get washed up? We equipped each room with faucets that have hot and cold water. Please enjoy yourselves."

All of us just about ran up the steps to our rooms. Each room in the corridor had names stapled to the door, but none of them bore my name. I looked at the queen, confused.

"I wrote to them about our rooming arrangements. After all, I can't have you screaming yourself awake and awakening the rest of the inn." She shrugged.

Why do I have to get special treatment? I'm such a hassle to deal with, I thought.

"Plus, I do rather enjoy someone sleeping next to me," she grinned at me, giving me a wink. I felt my face turn red at her remark. She laughed, which just deepened the blush on my cheeks.

She opened the door, revealing a small but spacious room. At the door, the inn attendants had piled our supplies for the next few weeks in a corner. A bath was off to the side, a gigantic bed, *big enough for two*. I squeaked at the thought. Lilja gave me a weird look but said nothing.

"Do you want to take a bath first, or do you want to take one together?" She wiggled her eyebrows at me suggestively, making me squeal with surprise.

"You can take a bath first, your highness." I bowed dramatically low, and all but ran out of the room. I could hear her laugh as I retreated. I found myself in the kitchen, where Dumont and Elbio were giggling and cooking together. They paid little attention to me as they continued to cook our meal. They moved in unison as if dancing, nearly touching, but not quite. A large pot sat on top of the wood stove and a large animal turned on a metal pole, roasting over a fire.

"Did you not wish to take a bath, ma'am?" Dumont said as he chopped the last of an onion and threw it in the pot.

"I do, but Lil—I mean the queen—wished to take one first," I said, stammering, trying to cover the fact that I almost called her by her first name.

Elbio wiped down the counter, not looking up at me. "I'm surprised you didn't just take one together."

"It's not like that," I said, my face turning red again. It seemed to do a lot of that.

Elbio and Dumont gave each other a knowing look but said nothing.

"So, how long have you two been together?" I asked, trying to change the subject off of myself.

"How long has it been, honey?" Elbio asked Dumont. The dark-skinned man looked at him and then down to his fingers, as if doing mental math.

Dumont dramatically leaned down to kiss the shorter man's cheek. "Next month, it'll be 349 years of having to put up with your stinky butt."

My mouth fell open. *349 years?* "How old are you?"

Dumont puffed out his chest proudly, his long, braided hair falling towards his face. "546 years old."

I turned towards Elbio, awaiting his answer.

"654 years old, and I do not have a stinky butt," he said, trying to look disgruntled, as a hint of a smile curved up his lips.

"You definitely have a stinky butt, but only when you eat cheese." Dumont smiled as he hit Elbio's butt slightly.

They continued to make dinner as I watched, wondering if I should offer to make anything. *I'm a terrible cook; I was barely surviving off the meals I cooked when I lived in the forest.* I shuddered at the memory of all of my barely edible meals.

"Do you want me to help?"

Dumont looked at me up and down as if scrutinizing my ability to cook. "No, it's okay, hun. Elbio and I have years of experience of cooking together."

I sighed, contently. "Thank the gods, because I can't cook to save my life." Elbio handed me a hot mug and laughed. "I never learned how to cook," I said as a wet Lilja walked into the kitchen with a towel in hand, drying her hair. She had on a loose long-sleeved shirt and black pants. *Absolutely delectable. Why did I just think that?*

"Even I learned how to cook," she said, grasping the mug from my hand and taking a sip, trading it for the wet towel in her hand.

"Hey that's mine," I said, "well, your highness, I am not as well-rounded as you. I'm gonna take a bath, and since *even you can cook,* you can help them."

I walked up the steps to our floor. It filled our room with steam from her bath. I undressed, refilling the tub, and the water hit all of my muscles, which were sore from riding all day. I wanted to stay in forever, but I knew if I stayed in the tub, I would miss dinner. My stomach protested at the thought of it, gurgling loudly. I got out, braided my hair, and threw on a plain outfit, not caring about my appearance too much.

They decorated the dining room much like the front room; large mounted animals decorated the walls, and an ornate wooden table sat in the middle of the room. Everyone save for me was already present with the food already on the table. My mouth watered. Keres, noticing my entrance, rolled her eyes, muttering to herself.

"Finally," Kallan grumbled, holding a fork in his hand. I stooped my head down and mumbled an apology for taking so long. I sat by Lilja in the only spot available.

Lilja leaned over, whispering in my ear, "I made them wait until you got done, since I hogged the bath earlier." I gave her a grateful smile. Our bodies were impossibly close.

Dumont and Elbio gave each other a look and Elbio picked up Dumont's slender hand, giving it a kiss.

"Let's eat!" Lilja announced. Aidan and Armand all but pounced on the meat that was at the center of the table. I laughed.

"Hm, this reminds me of the meals we used to have at home with ma' and da', before we went to live with Lilja," Armand said as he stuffed a large leg wholly into his mouth.

Keres sat up straighter, shuffling small portions of food onto her plate. "Yeah, right, brother, I think you've romanticized our childhood a bit more than necessary."

"You went to live with Lilja, when you were younger?" I glanced over to Keres, surprised.

"Yeah, our parents died because of blight, leaving me and this grouch to fend for ourselves." Armand jutted the now empty bone in Keres' direction.

"You mean while I formulated carefully crafted plans to steal food with you." Keres crossed her arms, looking pleased with herself.

"You guys used to steal food?" I leaned into the table, more eager to hear the rest of the conversation, my meal forgotten.

"Yes! Keres and I would trick stall owners and snag provisions from them. Until we got caught and thrown into jail. It just so happened that the king and queen were touring the jail, as it was newly renovated. The queen saw us and took pity, taking us in. It's a good thing that she did, because the punishment for stealing is losing a finger. I don't know about you, Keres, but I need every one of these babies, otherwise how else could I do this?" He said sticking out his middle finger.

Keres gaped, throwing a cooked carrot at him.

"Hey now, let's eat. I am sure Dumont and Elbio didn't make this food with the intention of it becoming fuel for a food fight," Lilja said a smile plastered on her face.

After our meal, Dumont pulled out a large map from the cupboard. The map was ancient and weathered—nearly the color of coffee—and the wrinkled edges appeared as if could fall apart at a breath. Elbio quickly cleaned the table as Dumont unrolled it. The map was covered in lines and included a detailed drawing of the mountain. An extensive network of tunnels ran underneath the mountain, and in the middle was a cavity.

"What's that?" I asked, pointing to the empty spot on the map.

Dumont straightened his back, putting his hand on his hip. "That is the City of Ebbon, an ancient city, not known by many topsiders, like ourselves. Hidden by all its occupants. They're a mix of all cultures."

"Then how do you know about it?" Kallan crossed his arms, leaning back, balancing on the back two legs of his chair.

"Well, that would be because I was born there. To pass through it, you will need this letter," Dumont said as he handed a wax sealed paper to Lilja. "It is a written letter to the queen," he said, his voice faltering.

"Queen? I thought you were the queen, your highness," I said, careful not to slip up and call her Lilja.

"The land under the mountain is neither property of Ardour nor of Valdis, which makes the City of Ebbon its own kingdom," Elbio—finished with clearing the table—cut in and laid his hand on his husband's shoulder.

"Thank you for your help, gentlemen. I will reward you once we finish with our quest. We leave at first light." Lilja said, giving the couple a small bow. We departed to our rooms, each of us talking about our expectations of Ebbon. Lilja shut the door as we got into our room. Awkwardness hung thick in the air.

"Where would you like me to sleep?" I asked her as I looked at the only bed in the room.

Lilja pulled her shirt off in one motion. "With me, of course." I twisted around to face the opposite side of the room.

"But—but it isn't proper—" I said, insufficiently keeping the panic out of my voice. *She's gay.*

"You didn't seem to mind when you thought I was straight." The sound of her footsteps moved close to me.

"No, I did, I just—"

"Just what?" she said as she walked in front of me. Her chest was bare. My face turned red as I looked up at the ceiling.

"I just couldn't explain to you why I was uncomfortable with sleeping in the same bed," I mumbled, still looking at the ceiling. "The entire group probably thinks we are something. No wonder why they were so flabbergasted that you made me sleep in your tent the first night."

"Are we something?" she grabbed my chin and pulled it down so I was looking into her eyes.

"What? No! We just met!" Was I ready for something like that? Again?

"Why are you so uncomfortable sleeping in the same bed as me? We are just going to sleep," she whispered, searching my eyes for the answer. I looked down at my hands, which were clasped securely, as if they were trying to hold me together. My knuckles turned white as the circulation left them.

"I-I just think you wouldn't want me to, if you knew I was gay." I ran through the words, afraid of the reply. "You make me nervous. Every time you're near me, it feels like I can't breathe. The surrounding space feels static-y." My voice cracked as I kept talking through my thoughts, not thinking, just spitting out words.

Lilja stared at me in shock as my thoughts spilled out of my mouth, word by word. Silent for a moment, she glanced up at the ceiling as if her usual retort had flown out of her mouth and painted itself on the roof.

"Elowen, it's because we...our paths are...fated together. You heard the rooted demigod women. You are the link between the two known realms." She ran her fingers through her hair. "If you are genuinely that uncomfortable with sleeping in the same bed, I can speak to Elbio and Dumont. I'm sure they can set up a room fast enough."

Was it the fact that our futures were bound? Is that why I felt like this every time I was near her? Did she feel the same way? Was it right to ask her to make Elbio and Dumont do that at this hour? "No," I said, trying to pick the right words, "this will be fine. I just was misinterpreting what I was feeling."

She faltered for a minute, but nodded. "Let me know if you change your mind."

Turning away from her, I slipped off my clothes. I could sense her eyes on my back as I donned the nightgown, which I had accidentally acquired from the Cann Village. It was thin fabric, but I shuddered at the thought of sleeping naked next to Lilja. My face burned at just the idea. I turned around to find her already slipped under the covers, her eyes closed. Gently, I lifted the blanket just enough to get into the bed and under the warmth of the covers, trying to avoid seeing a glimpse of skin.

I flooded the room with darkness as I blew out the candle. My insides churned as I stared at the ceiling. *Why am I feeling this way? I didn't feel this way when I thought she was straight.* Small snores interrupted my train of thought as they started emanating from Liljas' thin frame and I rolled my eyes. *That's going to get old real fast.*

I closed my eyes, allowing sleep to take me, or I at least tried. Lilja turned over in her sleep and wrapped her arm around me. I stilled, not even breathing. *What am I supposed to do now?* Desperately, I tried to ignore the thoughts in my head as her warm arm pulled me closer to her, our bodies touching.

My whole body warmed as my thoughts wandered. I closed my eyes tightly, trying to ignore the world. At some point I succumbed to sleep, as the next thing I saw when I opened my eyes was Lilja poking me awake, thankfully fully clothed.

Light had begun to filter through the windows. "Good morning," she said cheerfully, sleep gone from her voice. *She must have been awake for a while,* I thought as I sat up.

"Good morning," I croaked out as I pushed myself off the bed, going over to the bath's faucet. I splashed water on my face, attempting to wash the sleep out of my eyes.

"What time is it?" I questioned her as she looked to be going through the items in the corner and throwing them on the bed.

"It's nearly six. Now get dressed and grab your pack. Elbio and Dumont have probably finished your ears. I want you to wear them today. It's best if no one else knows you are human. Although, odds are that news of your presence has already spread."

Nodding, I quickly threw on an outfit, grabbing the remaining pack on the bed, struggling with the weight of it as it dug into my shoulders. I grimaced.

"You'll get used to it," Lilja said, as she noticed my discomfort.

We met the team in the room where we ate the previous night; all wore similar packs. Dumont and Elbio were in the corner. Once our presence was noticed, they walked forward holding a small black box. Dumont opened it revealing a pair of almost lifelike ears. The only thing giving away that they weren't genuine was that they weren't attached to an elf.

"They look so real," I said. My hand shook when I moved to grab one, as if they were going to feel real. They were made of a rubber material and felt stiff. "How do I put them on?"

"Well, that's the thing. They are going to get glued on," Elbio said.

I looked at him sharply. "What?"

"Well, to make them look as lifelike as possible, we didn't want to take the risk of someone seeing a wire on your ear so we made this paste out of tree sap and animal grease. It's completely safe and holds up fairly well," Dumont said, his anxiety seeping into his words.

"How long will the glue hold on?" the queen asked.

"I'm not sure, madam, I imagine a few days, maybe a week," Elbio said. "Just be sure to not get them wet as they dry. You don't want them to get crooked."

I sat on the chair as Elbio and Dumont heated the glue up with a nearby candle. It was slightly too hot as it touched the sensitive skin covering my ears. I winced. The queen placed her slender fingers on my shoulder. Her touch sent a wave of tingles through my body.

"Please be careful, Elbio, do not burn her," the queen said, slightly increasing the pressure in her hold on my shoulder and sending another wave of tingles through me.

"It's okay," I said, as Elbio's plump face turned red with the queen's comment. "The heat is bearable, just warm." Another bead of hot glue slid down the back of my ear. I sucked in a breath, trying to avoid making another face. Lilja swatted away Elbios' plump fingers and quickly swiped the hot glue off the back of my ear. I ducked away from her, not wanting to make a scene.

"That's enough," she said, her voice leaving no room for argument.

"My apologies, miss, I meant no offense." Elbio and Dumont bowed low before me.

"It's okay," I said, embarrassed at the situation that had arisen. I rose from the chair; the glue had already dried enough so that I could move around without the ears shifting.

"How long will they take to dry? I don't want the snow to mess them up."

"Just a few minutes. By the time they pull the horses from the stables, the ears should be fully dried," Dumont said, looking at his feet.

Glancing around, I spotted a mirror as the rest of the group seemed to dissipate into the outside world. I stared at myself. My face was still round and soft. My eyes were still the same light blue, my hair was still the same not-quite-blonde-or-brown color. But the ears, which were now seemingly Elven, made me appear different, feel different. From the reflection, I could see the queen approach, her eyes softening as she reached the space just behind me.

"You look beautiful, Elle," she said. She stooped down and gave the back of my head a kiss.

My heart fluttered as she turned and walked away, my back now cold from the lack of her body heat. *Ugh, why does my fate being tied to her make me feel like this?*

I gave both Elbio and Dumont pecks on their cheeks, as a gesture of goodwill. Elbio grabbed my hand almost roughly as I pulled away.

"Please watch over the queen. Do not make her worry so much. The connection between you and her is unique," Elbio said fervently.

I fought the urge to roll my eyes. "Yes, I know it's like this because fate connects us." *This really wasn't a big deal.*

"No, you don't understand. The bond is special. Something that needs to be nurtured to grow," Elbios said, his eyes wide with... fear? "Listen to this." He pulled my hand to his chest, and Dumont grabbed my other hand and did the same. *This is incredibly odd.* The hearts inside their chest beat, each thump felt underneath my fingertips. The thing that struck me as odd was that with each pound, it became almost unnervingly clear that their hearts beat at the same time. As if they were one.

Gasping, I pulled my hands away. "What does *that* mean?"

Elbio's eyes became sad. "It will be clear in time. Please take care of yourself and the queen. All of our futures depend on it."

I nodded, not fully understanding what they were trying to tell me.

The frigid mountain air bit my cheeks as I stepped out of the cozy, warm inn. The military members we had separated from had finally made it to the inn. They had larger wagons in their possession now, and more people. More alarmingly so, they appeared to be ready… ready for war.

9

Ossory Wolf

Military members had sprinkled their way throughout the front and back lawn of the inn, dwarfing it; panic seeped into me.

"What are they doing here? I thought you said that we were doing reconnaissance, not war."

"They are a just-in-case measure. We can't be sure that our mission will succeed." Lilja stared at me, her eyes hard again. Leaving no evidence of the tender moment that I thought we'd shared in the inn just moments before.

"Are they going to the City of Ebbon with us?" I asked. Why was I so upset by this?

She laughed, her voice void of humor. "Gods, no, I do not plan to start a war with a kingdom I've never set foot in; I would like to sign a treaty with the City of Ebbon."

"Where are they going, then?" My voice rose slightly, a mix of anger and confusion seeping into my words.

Lilja put her hand on her hip. "They are going over the mountain to stay unseen. If you must know, Elowen, they are sending out informants into Ardour, finding out things we wouldn't otherwise know. Why does it matter?"

"It just doesn't feel right."

"It doesn't feel right? Elowen, you just got here. You do not know how hard it is to watch your kingdom starve to death. The people I am sworn to protect are dying, because I can't find a fucking cure for this disease. I have to find it. What's the point of being queen if I can't?"

Her voice never rose beyond a normal speaking voice. Somehow that made it worse, because she *was* right. I had no idea of how severe the blight was, let alone what it would look like when it eventually mutated.

Kallan strode up to us on his horse, seeming to sense the negative energy from our interaction. "Are you both ready?" His eyes were unable to hide the questions he had.

Lilja looked at me, her usual stoic mask replaced with a tired expression, nodding to Kallan, turned away from me, and walked towards her horse, avoiding eye contact as she mounted. Kallan stared at me as I got on Lady, but said nothing. The false ears felt heavy as we made our way to the mountain.

The air bit at my exposed skin as we traveled. The snow covered more and more ground as we traveled slightly up the slope. My teeth chattered as I looked around, and more snow covered our footprints as it continued to fall. Every one of us appeared to be frozen—that is, except Keres. She had no jacket on; I rolled my eyes in her direction, jealous.

Lilja huddled in her cloak upon her horse. The thick fur jacket she wore underneath her cloak had little frozen spots as the water from her breath froze to it. She looked grumpy. Regret formed a pit in my stomach. Why did I have to always ruin everything? The sun was shining as we trekked up the mountain. *I thought we were going inside*, I thought miserably.

Cassia, sensing my thoughts, rode closer to me. "The tunnel is farther up, probably another day's ride."

Another day's ride? Fuck me, how am I supposed to not freeze to death in the meantime? Aidan and Armand rode close together, deep in conversation, just far enough that I couldn't discern what they were talking about. Kallan was speaking to Lilja about the cave entrance. "Let's break for lunch. Elowen and Cassia, go find some dry-ish fire wood. Aidan, go catch something, I'm starving," the queen said.

Cassia and I dismounted from our horses, shivering. "Let's stick together. We don't know what is in these trees."

I stayed silent as we trudged through the ever-growing snow covering the mountainside. The snow deafening the sounds around us; the only audible noise was our footsteps.

"How are we going to find dry firewood?" I said.

"Lilja said dry-ish, but you have a point." Her face was unreadable; her cloak nearly covered her cold pink cheeks.

"I kind of messed up my words when I was talking to Lilja. How do I make it up to her?" I rushed out, unable to contain the thoughts swirling in my head.

She sighed, glancing at me quickly, and then turned to face ahead. "Lilja has been through a lot. The past we share follows us because of our duty to the crown. Lilja's childhood was rough. When we were young, the war took a toll on her family. Her parents are sick, and the blight makes it difficult to get food for everyone. We've had to turn to less conventional methods of feeding the subject of Valdis. We had just returned to the mainland when you washed up on shore."

"What do you mean returned to the mainland?" I asked.

"It's not my place to say, Elowen. You'd be better off if you didn't know," she said, her voice having a sense of finality to it.

I groaned. "Just tell me. I can handle it."

"I told you, it isn't my place to say. Lilja is probably just worried about scaring you away. Let's just pick up some firewood and get back to everyone else."

The finality in her tone scared me. What was so bad that she didn't want to tell me? We gathered up firewood in silence until I spotted some animal tracks. They resembled a wolf footprint but were much larger. Its pad impression was nearly the size of my hand. I sucked in a breath, surprised.

"This wolf's print is huge. It's like two of my hands."

Walking over, her face turning stoic, she said, "Let's go, keep the firewood that you have, but don't stop to pick any more up." Cassia grabbed my hand, pulling me back the way we came. I yanked my hand away from hers, nearly dropping the fallen twigs, stumbling a bit.

"Why are we heading back to camp? It's just a wolf. They usually hunt at night. It will be more scared of us than of him even if we come across it."

Cassia gave an exasperated sigh. "You don't get it, Elowen, that is no ordinary wolf track. The size suggests that it's an Ossory wolf. They are vicious. Once they find a scent they like, they hunt it until they find it and kill it."

I tried to push down the fear rising in my throat. "Oh."

"Yeah, *oh*, it's not good, so please stay quiet and follow me."

I hunched over as we rushed out of the forest, my eyes scanning the spaces between the trees, desperate to not make a sound as we nearly ran to the clearing. The wood in our hands clanged together, but other than that, it was silent. Cassia stumbled on a fallen branch almost all the way buried in the snow. She gritted her teeth and let out a groan as she contacted the snow-covered ground.

"Fuck, are you okay?" I dropped the pieces of wood from my arms, kneeling beside her. "Are you okay?"

Cassia shook her head, grabbing her ankle. "Ugh, no, I think I sprained my ankle."

"Elowen," the wind seemed to whisper.

I glanced around quickly. After meeting the crazy tree lady, I'd thought the voice had stopped. I turned my attention back towards the red-headed person before me, seeing nothing.

"Can you walk?" I asked her as she grimaced, trying to move it.

"You're gonna have to help me. I won't be able to walk by myself in this state." She held up her hands for me to grab. I hauled her up into a standing position. Cassia winced as she put pressure on her ankle.

I slung her arm around my shoulder, letting her lean her smaller frame against me. "I could carry you if you wanted me to," I said as we trudged our way.

Cassia scoffed, looking at me. "I can't let a human carry me. If anyone saw us, they'd never let me live it down."

"What's so bad about being carried by a human?" I shot back, holding her a little tighter than necessary.

"Elves live such a long time compared to humans. It's like being taken care of by a baby. Elowen, be quiet. If we get spotted by the wolves, it'll be the end of us."

"Elowen," the wind whispered again.

I glanced around quickly, and the world fell off balance as I was thrown away from Cassia. The wind knocked out of me, I gasped, trying to inflate my lungs with air. A deep growl emanated from next to me. Dazed, I stared at Cassia's crumpled form.

A line of spit filled my vision, reflecting my startled face. I looked up, only to be met with an enormous wolf's face. Its eyes were half crazed, its brown snout curled in hunger and anger as it looked down at me. We stared at each other for a split second before it tried to snap at me.

I let out a scream, rolling away from the hungry wolf. The cold bit at my hands as the snow soaked through my mittens. I half ran and half crawled back to Cassia, who was still unconscious from the wolf's attack. Grabbing a log that I had discarded earlier, I held it like a sword, cursing myself for not having a real one. The wolf circled us, growling low as it looked for an opening to attack.

"You better stay away from us. I'll hit you with this," I said, unable to keep the fear from my voice. It lunged at me, closing my eyes. I swung my arms, jarring from the contact as I hit its muzzle. Its head tilted to its side. He swung back, staring at me as if surprised. I hit it, and it lunged at me again. It bit into the log in my hand, pulling it free from my grasp,

Of course, this is how I die. I make it this far just to die from some oversized wolf.

Cassia groaned behind me, making me leave my self-deprecating thoughts behind.

Shit, I can't die yet. I have to save her, at least, I thought as the ground rumbled beneath me.

An arrow sang past me, narrowly missing both my cheek and its intended target in front of me. The wolf howled as another arrow shot from behind me. This time, the arrow embedded itself in its shoulder. Fully forgetting its original target, the wolf turned towards its more dangerous prey. I crouched hurriedly, looping my arms under Cassia's shoulder and hauling her to a hollowed out tree.

I stood in front of her, searching for the person trying to save us. A whoop came from Kallan as he rode up. The wolf turned towards him and growled. The horse spooked and neighed slightly, but Kallan quickly calmed it with a pat on the shoulder. His sword swung at the wolf, but the brown-colored beast backed up at the last second, narrowly missing the blade. Another arrow shot out from the dense trees, hitting the wolf on the side. It howled again for help, just as another smaller wolf came into the clearing.

10

Murder

The small wolf's white fur almost completely matched what used to be clean snow. Its yellow eyes stared at us, trying to assess the situation.

Aidan and Armand practically flew into the clearing, jumping off their horses in one swoop. They rushed the larger brown wolf, attempting to cover Lilja as she put more arrows into it. Cassia began stirring behind me. I turned to her. She groaned, grabbing her head, looking up at me, and attempting to stand.

"No, just stay down, Cassia. The team has this."

Cassia's eyes widened as I spoke. I spun around. The white wolf was crouched down to look at the prey before them. Unfortunately, Cassia and I were its next meal.

"I have your back, Cassia. I need you to run as fast as you can and hide. I'll hold it off for as long as possible." Not waiting for a reply, I rushed at the wolf, grabbing an arrow from the ground that had missed its original target.

This is a bad idea, right? I pushed the thought to the back of my head as the wolf snapped at me. I launched myself to the side, grabbing its fur and leaping onto its back. Using the arrow, I punched it into the thick fur at the neck. The wolf howled in pain, jumping up on its hind legs, attempting to throw me off like a bull.

I gripped the wolf's greasy fur, closing my eyes out of fear as its body swayed side to side, trying to get me off. The white wolf dropped to all fours. I ignored the sounds of fighting around me, focusing on the arrow still in the beast's neck before me. The fight-or-flight instinct took over as it ran. *It appears, Elowen, that you made a slight miscalculation of your strength here,* I thought.

The wolf bolted through the forest, its body bouncing mine in the air. I grabbed onto the arrow and yanked, pulling it from the embedded flesh it had called its home. The wolf howled again, jumping back on its hind legs, flipping us over and rolling on top of me. The forest looked fuzzy before me; warm liquid rolled down my head.

My shaking fingers went to touch the source. It wasn't until I pulled away my hand that I realized it was blood—*my blood?* Desperately, I looked around for the arrow. The snow now trampled down, pink snow covered the ground. As if it were intermingled macabre art from both me and the wolf before me. It stalked around me, growling. The wolf ran at me. I jumped sideways. Its large body, unable to re-correct its lunge, ran face first, cracking into a large tree. The tree protested the attack by dropping all the snow from the branches, dumping it on the now discombobulated and injured wolf.

I used those seconds of distraction as an opportunity to search for the arrow, my only useful weapon in this attack. With my glove-less hands, I began digging in the trampled snow, where the wolf had rudely thrown me off his back.

My hand contacted something thin. I prayed to the gods and yanked it out from underneath the snow. Breathing a sigh of relief, as my eyes fell on the not broken arrow—well, the head and half of the shaft were still intact. The wolf, freeing itself from the snow mound, crouched, ready to attack. The world stilled; the wolf and I became the only moving parts. It bounded towards me as if in slow motion.

Still sitting, I screamed a war cry. I held up the arrow like a dagger. As the beast tried to bite me, I rammed it into its mouth with my fist. The wolf halted, its eyes turning glassy and rolling back into its head. Its body shook as it fell to the ground, crushing me. Gasping, I tried to push the enormous beast off of me. The ground rumbled beneath the snow.

"Elowen," Liljas' voice bellowed far out from my position.

"*Lilja!*" I said, attempting to yell back, though the wolf made it impossible to get a big breath from my lungs.

It's crushing me. I killed it and now it's going to kill me.

"Elowen." Voices seem to echo around me. I squirmed underneath the quickly chilling wolf's body, trying to free myself. Unable to move it a fraction of an inch, I relented, the cold ground beneath me seeping into my bones.

Find me, find me, FIND ME, LILJA! My inner voice howled. The ground rumbled underneath me again.

"She's this way," Lilja said, her voice faint.

I looked around frantically, trying to find her, the snow obstructing my vision. *She must be able to see the wolf. HELP*, I thought, unable to croak out the words. Each breath I took became more and more labored.

The wolf felt like it was multiplying its weight after death, out of spite. Snow crunched as footsteps made their way into the clearing. *I'm stuck, please find me,* my inner voice pleaded, tears springing to the corner of my eyes. The sounds of footsteps stumbled around me, and the ground shook, shooting out a mass of earth into the dead wolf and pushing off of me.

My hand flew to my chest. I turned myself to the side, gasping, desperate to fill my almost empty lungs. Lilja rushed to my side, rubbing my back. Once I had a sufficient amount of air, I launched myself at her, looping my arms around her.

Lilja faltered, hugging me back, putting her head in the nook of my neck. She pulled away from our hug. "What happened?"

"I'll tell you what happened. Elowen kicked some ass," Aidan whooped out as he walked into the clearing, peering at the dead wolf.

"Not too bad for a human," Keres said, springing up out of nowhere. *Where was she this whole time?*

"I needed to draw the wolf away from Cassia. I didn't want her to get hurt, so I tried to kill it with a jab to the neck. But it wasn't enough, and now here we are," I said, my breathing not yet back to normal. My head pounded as I stared at the queen.

Worry creased her forehead. Her eyes frantically searched my body for something more than cuts and bruises. "You are human, Elowen. You die much easier than the rest of us. Stop doing reckless things. You are going to get yourself killed."

Why is she yelling at me? Shouldn't she be happy that I saved her friend?

"Why are you angry? I was trying to save Cassia!" My voice came out stronger than before.

"Because—because you could put this entire plan in jeopardy! The gods say you are a piece in the fate, that *we* have to complete this quest in order to save the kingdom," she said, her face so close that her warm breath hit my frozen cheeks.

She was right. I was just a pawn. A pawn in a bigger game than I could theorize. Just a tool. Was that all I was?

I stayed silent. The rest of the crew seemed to disappear as she yelled at me.

"I'm sorry." Was I? No, I wasn't sorry that the wolf would have killed Cassia. "You know what, I'm *not* sorry. That wolf would have killed Cassia if I hadn't made it run off. So *sorry* that I saved your friend. Next time, I'll be sure to let her die." My teeth chattered as I tried to put force behind my words. I sneezed, the force making my head throb. I winced at the motion.

Lilja's eyes softened. "I'm sorry." She bowed her head. "That's not how I meant for that to come out. I just—I just don't want to see you get hurt. Not just because you are supposed to help me move my people out of famine, but because—because you are a part of this team."

My heart pounded at her response. I wasn't just a pawn; I had a part in this team. She brought her hand to my head, touching the sore spot from when I was thrown off the wolf. I winced at the contact. "How bad is it?"

"Not too bad, just needs to be washed up. All of you could use a good wash." She crinkled her nose as she looked at me, her eyes held laughter as she looked at me.

I gazed down at myself for the first time. The fight covered my full form in scrapes, blood and mud from the attack. The fat on my body did nothing to keep the cold from getting to me, and my cloak was long gone from the attack. *I keep losing my cloak. Will I ever be able to hold on to one?*

Lilja got up, smiling as she held her hand out to me. Grabbing a hold of her warm hand, I pulled myself up. The earth felt steady under my feet. Lilja whistled a high-pitched shrill. A few moments later, her horse appeared. She pulled herself up and then me, grunting slightly.

"Let's get back to camp and get your head cleaned off. Unfortunately, the rest of you will have to wait till we make it to Ebbon City." She tugged her cloak up, pulling my frame underneath it, draping it over my body. "Sit close so you don't freeze."

We rode quickly to where we had originally stopped. The rest of the team, including Cassia, was already there. Pulling the cloak off, I jumped down from Lilja's horse, wincing as the bruises had settled.

Armand clapped me on the back roughly. "I heard you took down that wolf all by yourself. Good job!"

I grinned at him, his words full of pride and astonishment.

"If you smack her like that again, she might just take you down too." Aidan grinned, laughing.

I looked at Cassia. Other than her swollen ankle and a couple of scrapes and bruises, she appeared fine. "Are you okay?" I asked, walking over.

Giving me a small smile, she nodded. "Thanks to you. Perhaps I should have agreed to let you carry me back to camp originally."

I smiled back. "Probably." The world seemed to sway slightly. I turned back towards the queen just in time for her to rush up to me.

"Why don't you sit down so I can clean your head, preferably, before you fall over?" She gripped my arms, helping me sit.

"How did you know I was going to fall?" I pouted as she dabbed the cut on my hairline; I had to stop hitting my head.

"I can feel your feet drag on the ground. Vibrations can become quite telling when you know how to read them." Her explanation was short and concise. *Does she pay attention to how I walk that much?*

Her fingers seemed to flutter and flit around my wound. She reached down and grabbed a small tin from her pocket and rubbed it on the wound. "What's that for?" I winced; it burned as it contacted my skin.

"Sorry," she watched me squirm uncomfortably at her touch. "It's a salve made from medicinal plants are supposed to aid healing, numb the pain, and keep infection away. Cassia made it when we got attacked in the Cann Forest. Do you feel comfortable enough to keep going?" Lilja's eyes were full of worry as she spoke.

"Yes, the faster we get to Ebbon City, the better." I rubbed my arms for warmth.

The team devoured lunch, silent. Weariness from the earlier fight had settled in all of our bones, making us quiet. I covered myself with my blanket, saddling up, cursing myself for losing my cloak again.

Lady neighed softly as we began our trek once again. I comforted her as I looked around, leaning Lady closer to Lilja.

"Lilja, I'm sorry about before. I know you are just trying to help your people. I'm just confused. I keep feeling like I am missing something about the hatred between Ardour and Valdis. Why do you think it's Ardour's doing?" I said through my chattering teeth, my snot freezing to the inside of my nose with each breath.

Lilja stayed looking ahead, never glancing back in my direction, making me think she didn't hear me, before replying, "Ardour and Valdis have fought many times in the last couple hundred years. The first war was four hundred years ago. From an outside look, it appears asinine. War always is. My parents attack Ardour for rights to trade routes. Ardour was—and is—known for being closed off to the rest of the world."

Lilja sighed before continuing. "When that war ended after a few years, no conclusion was made, people died on both sides for nothing. After that there was another war on the Ebbon Mountains. Honestly, I am not sure who started it. But there was a rock slide due to an explosion killing, Queen Alieta's father. Of course it wasn't intentional, but Ardour still blamed us for his death. The queen at the time went insane with vengeance. Later on she began having Alieta's uncle attack villages in Valdis, even though we were already struggling with the blight. Shortly after, I think her guilt or sadness caught up to her because she killed herself.

"That's around the time my parents passed on the crown, handing me this mess to clean up. All Ardour has wanted since the death of their monarch is revenge. I can't say I blame them, I don't know what I would do if I lost my fated in such a way." She gave me a long look before making her horse pick up the pace, leaving me alone in my thoughts.

The snow had finally stopped; the wind, however, didn't. It bit into us like hungry wolves—no pun intended. Everyone looked frozen, except for Keres. She sat high in the saddle, not hunched over like the rest of us.

"Is there any way you can also make us warm, like you?" I asked Keres.

She glanced at me, rolling her eyes. Everyone looked at her expectantly. "Maybe, I've never tried." She rubbed her chin thoughtfully.

"Well, don't do it if you think you're gonna fry us," Armand grumbled, his body hunched over, trying to preserve warmth. Keres looked at the sky for a moment as if deep in thought, and then sent a small burst of flame in his direction, laughing.

"How's that for warmth?" Keres said in between laughs.

Armand said nothing, but scooted a little farther away from her. Keres took a deep breath, closing her eyes and spreading her hands out, her palms facing downward towards the earth.

Keres opened her eyes abruptly, her usually brown eyes glowing orange. The ground below us began warming, the snow melting away, leaving mud in its wake.

"Wow, that was amazing, Keres," The chill already lifted slightly off my bones.

Lilja grinned. Dirt still plastered on her face from the attack earlier, and her black hair still had little specks of mud in it. "Do you think you can sustain such action until the tunnel?"

"We can try to do it in spurts. I don't want to deplete my magic. We need to think about incidents that could occur." Her voice sounded strained already.

"Wait, I thought you were born with these abilities. What do you mean to deplete your magic?" I asked.

"Magic is like a muscle. It needs to be trained and kept in optimal peak form for it to work well. However, even with your muscles in optimal form, they can still sometimes fail if used too much. Therefore, many elves only use their magic when they absolutely have to. When training to use your magic, it is important to not push yourself too hard. Otherwise, there could be physical consequences to your health," Aidan said.

"Physical consequences?" I asked, my voice laced with confusion.

"Magic can manifest in many ways, especially when you overspend it. Usually it's fainting or a nosebleed. Occasionally, you hear stories of people trying to do something so large they go into a coma, and even face death." Aidan finished his explanation with a shudder, as if there was a story behind his words.

Kallan rubbed his temples. "Please be quiet, guys, my brain got scrambled by that oversized mutt, and my head is killing me."

The sky had changed from shades of day to night, and Keres slowly eased up on the warmth she provided for us. The chill quickly settled back into my bones. Lilja stayed quiet throughout any other conversations that occurred. Her brow set in a *I'm thinking; don't bother me* look.

The almost gentle slope changed to rocky. We dismounted, the ground becoming too unstable to allow the horses to walk over while mounted. I slipped slightly as the ground slid out from under me, Lilja grabbed my arm, hauling me back up into a standing position.

"How can you feel me falling with all these small rocks around?" I said, embarrassed that she had to keep saving my butt.

"Who cares if I can or can't? I just know that you are clumsy," she flaunted, shooting a smile in my direction. "Look," Lilja said, pointing towards a large closed off entrance that appeared to be an abandoned mine. *Great, that looks so safe,* I thought to myself as I stared at the decaying wood blocking the entry into the tunnel.

"Dumont said that this is the only working tunnel to get down. They closed the rest off because of the blight." Lilja pulled the letter and map from her bag. "This is where we go down."

11

The Path Down

Walking closer to the entrance, Armand and Aidan yanked boards off the dark tunnel, throwing them in a stack with a loud thump. Kallan and Lilja stared at the map she had taken from the inn, their faces plastered with different emotions.

Anybody close enough to Lilja could feel the childlike excitement coming from her. Kallan's face was another story. He was pale, sweat gleamed on his brow like morning dew on grass.

"What's up with you?" I asked the tall, pale man before me.

"Mr. Kallan," Aidan said while clamping his hand on Kallan's shoulder, making him jump, "is afraid of tight spaces, and I think I consider the mountain a *pretty* tight space."

"I just don't like the idea of being somewhere where we can't get out if something goes wrong," Kallan said while he crossed his arms.

"Nothing will go wrong, Kallan." Lilja placed her hand lightly on his shoulder.

Kallan shrugged her hand off his shoulder, walking towards the entrance peering into the black void, visibly gulping, his Adam's apple going up and down. "Let's just get going. The sooner we get to the city, the better."

THE PATH DOWN

With our torches lit, we entered the tunnels. Kallan walked to the rear, looking as if he'd rather run back up towards the surface. We locked eyes with each other as I gazed back at him. He gave me a strained smile that didn't quite reach his eyes. Our torch flames appeared to dance on the walls as we walked farther down. The tunnel was in good condition compared to the entrance, just large enough for most of the horses to walk comfortably, except Lilja's enormous horse. Poor thing had to dunk its head down. It looked miserable. I made a mental note to give it extra attention when we finally made it to the city.

"How long will we have to travel this way until we reach the city?" I asked out loud.

"Dumont—he never mentioned how long it was going to take and I—never thought to ask," Liljas' voice ricocheted through the otherwise quiet tunnel.

"You never thought to ask," Keres stumbled over a rock, barely catching herself. Armand grabbed at her elbow, attempting to steady his sister.

"Let go of me, brother, I *can* walk, you know," she said.

"Yeah, about as well as a drunken sailor," Armand said, trying to cover his laugh with a cough.

She harrumphed, but didn't retort back.

"I can't imagine it'll take longer than a day," Lilja said ahead of me.

We stayed silent for a moment. It was impossible to tell how much time had passed. I didn't know if anyone carried a watch on their person. As we traveled farther down, the once frozen air become warmer, so much so that we could shed our heavy coats, cloaks…and my blanket. The tunnel slowly began widening out. We passed larger rooms, all empty besides random forgotten items.

The vibe from the tunnels was spooky, the shadows created from the torches, making it worse. The only sounds were the rocks under our feet and breathing. My heart beat in my chest, the beat pulsing in my ears. I glanced back at Kallan; his usual golden skin with red undertones was replaced with a ghoulish, pale complexion. His hands balled up into fists and his posture was rigid. I paused, allowing Cassia and Aidan to walk in front of me, leaving me next to Kallan.

I knew the look on his face. Anxiety rolled off him in waves. He avoided eye contact with me as I stared at him, reaching for his hand. He flinched but allowed me to hold it.

"You know, it helps to think about something that makes you happy. Think about a thing that will make you laugh. I'd say meditate, but I don't think you want to get a face full of dirt." The words left my mouth before I could think about what I was saying.

Kallan chuckled and looked at me. His eyes were tired.

I let go of his hand and moved my way up to Lilja. "Hey, I'm getting pretty tired. Can we stop for the night?"

Lilja glanced at me. My face must have given away my true feelings. Her eyes softened, nodding as she held her hands up to stop the rest of the team. They all enthusiastically stopped, as if their feet turned into the rock holding the tunnel together.

Camp—if you could call it that—got set up. We sent the horses to the front of the line so we didn't have any unfortunate accidents while we were sleeping. We rolled beds out on the solid ground, food passed out to each hungry, exhausted hand. For whatever reason, the darkness seemed to sap the energy from us. All but one light was extinguished.

"I'll take the first watch. The rest of you guys look dead on your feet," Aidan announced to us. Nobody spoke out to change his decision.

Kallan glanced at me, nodding at me in thanks. Lilja and Cassia rolled their beds out next to me, Lilja's just close enough for me to wonder what her intentions were. *Stop, Elowen,* my inner voice reprimanded me. *She doesn't have any nefarious intentions, maybe she just wants body heat. It is warmer than the surface, but it is still pretty chilly.*

As soon as Cassias' red-headed form fell asleep as soon as she hit the pillow, soft snores quickly followed. Smiling to myself, I rolled away from her sleeping to face Lilja.

Her brown eyes stared at me. "Thank you for what you did for Kallan. He doesn't like to show his weaknesses. He wouldn't have asked to stop. That man would have walked until he dropped." Her lips barely moving as she spoke out the words to me. "We will sleep for a couple hours and then we will carry on to the city. We must be close by now."

"Okay," I said, being careful not to raise my voice to a normal speaking level. When I finished speaking, I realized how close to each other—our bodies were a mere inches away. While Cassia's body was also the same distance apart, with Lilja, it felt different. Was I ready for something like this again? *Wait, what was this?* I wasn't ready. *She's a queen, for gods' sake.*

I closed my eyes, trying to push my runaway thoughts away. I sighed, allowing sleep to take me, the silence of the tunnel lulling me to sleep. A rare night of dreamless sleep welcomed me with open arms.

I awoke to Lilja shaking me awake. I rubbed my eyes to clear the gunk. The rest of the team began collecting their items up and putting them away. Keres was feeding the horses grain from her pocket, whispering to her horse. My heart felt a tinge of guilt, as she cared for her horse and for mine.

We began the trek further down into the mountain; the rock becoming slick and more uneven as we furthered our expedition. A ramp came into sight as we approached it; it became apparent that the ramp was intentional. The mysterious builders had carved the solid rock and polished it smooth. Lilja and I looked at each other, saying nothing as we continued.

The ramp led to a large chamber; large crystals lit it up in each corner, each one giving off a strange white light. With all of them lit up, they lit the space. The end of the room held two large doors. Each ornately made of material similar to the wood found in the Cann Forest. Two oversized men guarded the entrance. Each wore gold color armor with emerald colored fabric accenting it. They looked at us, giving no sign of surprise to see a handful of elves and a human coming to their front door.

No wait, they think I am an elf because of the ears, I remembered. I fought the urge to touch them.

Lilja strode up to the guards. Her whole body gave off *you should let me in* vibes.

"I am the Queen of Valdis. Here is a letter addressed to Queen Zahra that details our mission."

The guards looked at each other, and the one on the right grabbed the letter from Lilja's hand with a nod. He peered at the stamp, and then glanced back at his fellow guard, flashing the wax seal Dumont had placed on it. The other guard's eyes widened, and he opened the doors, revealing the large and magnificent City of Ebbon.

My only question was who the hell was Dumont? Why did the seal garner so much panic from the guards?

12

Ebbon City

As the doors opened, light emanating from streetlights washed us with color. Unlike the lamps in the village of Cann, the Ebbon builders made these of twisted metal; a smaller version of the crystal found in the previous room placed the top. One guard led the way, occasionally looking back at us. Walking at a fast pace—nearly running—my small legs struggled to stay caught up. Each of the buildings we passed was more magnificent than the last, carved into the mountain. All appeared to be spacious and wonderfully decorated. Large green flags hung from the streetlights; all of them had a large golden emblem.

I glanced at Lilja. Her face was passive, her shoulders squared, making her appear confident. Kallan's color had come back, looking more at ease than he was in the closed tunnel we came out of. As we walked to the middle of the city, we passed strange dark green plants growing in garden beds.

Ornate mosaics decorated the path as we entered a large open pavilion, incense burned in a large, decorated pot that hung from the ceiling, giving off a sweet bergamot scent. A tall, curvy, dark-skinned woman, who I assumed was Queen Zahra, sat upon a carved throne. Her hair was braided with golden charms braided in the charms reflected the light from the crystals that were embedded into the pillars next to us.

She glanced up at us, as if she was inspecting rare goods. Lilja bowed, and the rest of us followed suit. Her deference surprised me. It was so submissive. Was that how she did things?

"Hello to you, travelers. I hear you have a letter with a very interesting seal. Can I see it?" She phrased it like a question, a dare to us to defy her.

Lilja said nothing, nor did she seem particularly surprised by the tone the lady on the throne gave off. From her bag, she pulled out the letter, striding towards the lady. Confidence oozed from her as she did so, not giving into the intimidation tactics.

The older lady's face fell as she gazed upon the wax seal, the red wax pressed into a crest—Dumont's crest. She opened the letter almost frantically, in panicked movements. Her eyes skimmed over the paper as she frantically read the words, as if she was worried they were going to fly off the page and disappear into the mountain above us. As if the moment of weakness was forgotten, she looked back at us with a mask on.

"Hello, Queen Lilja of Valdis, I, Queen Zahra, welcome you into my city. Please make yourselves at home for your stay."

Lilja nodded, placing her hand on her chest, and spoke: "Thank you, Queen Zahra, for your hospitality. I understand you do not welcome visitors. I am very thankful you have allowed us to stay in your beautiful city during this difficult time. The threat we are combating is very real. The future has been foretold, and if we do not stop it, this threat will consume us all." Lilja's voice was strained as if it brought immense emotion to say the words out loud, again.

"If the threat is as bad as you say, it would do the other kingdoms well to assist you in any way possible, which is what I wish to do. My brother Dumont would want me to do so. He cares for you deeply." Tears welled in her eyes as she finished speaking. "Please wander about my great city. My people may be wary of you at first, but they will open up."

The team grinned at each other, our once weary bodies now reinvigorated with thoughts of exploring a hidden city, food, and a hot bath. I, for one, did not care about which came first. They quickly showed us an inn where we could stay.

I threw my bags to the floor and bolted out of the inn, eager to eat and explore the hidden city I knew nothing about. Street vendors had built hot holding stands, terracotta pots insulated with brick. Each of them held an assortment of meats and soup. Stands that didn't have hot holding capabilities displayed spices, tiny mountains of flavor.

The residents of the city parted ways for the mysterious new people coming out of nowhere. Many shades of skin colors filled the street I was in. Many had braided long hair, delicately braided in jewelry charms, much like the ones adorning Queen Zahras' head.

I glanced back behind me, finding myself separated from the team. I carried on, shrugging my shoulders. *How much trouble could I possibly get in?* With food on my mind, I pounced on the first street vendor who sold something I vaguely recognized. The vendor grinned at me as I handed over the money, his teeth stamped with stones on each incisor. I rolled my eyes as the coin passed hands. Lilja insisted on paying for each of us, even me.

She had said, "On this mission everyone will get paid. We are risking life and limb and missing the comforts of home." I didn't have the heart to explain to her I didn't have a warm house to go back to. In all honesty, I felt like I had no choice; I was going to take part in the quest either way.

Shaking the thoughts out of my head, I chomped down on the grilled meat, covered in a brown sauce. I moaned as it melted in my mouth.

Good gods, this shit was delicious. I nodded my thanks to the vendor as he laughed at my reaction. People passed by me with a sense of importance. I grabbed a young lady's arm gently, feeling bold, wanting to learn more about the culture of the city.

"Where is everyone going?" Her blond bangs hung almost all the way over her eyes. It would be a surprise if she could even see out of them.

"There is a gladiator match tonight, young maiden," her elegant voice flowed out like thick honey. The way she talked made her sound so much older than me.

"Oh! Where is it at?"

"At the arena, darling, down the way. Would you like to attend with me?" she said; her voice seemed almost hypnotizing.

I nodded. Did I even like gladiator matches? Unfamiliar with the term, I followed her. The crowd multiplied around us. The food I'd bought was forgotten in my hand. She glanced at me, smiling, and my eyes went hazy with excitement. Music filled the air and the sounds of metal clashing. *What did she say her name was? Did she even tell me that? Why am I following her again?*

"Hey, what is your name again?" My voice slurred as if I was drunk. She grabbed my hands, making me drop the food. *Why did she do that?* I thought, frowning.

"My name doesn't matter, my darling. All that matters is we are together." Her hands were soft, with no calluses. Her hazel eyes met mine. My vision swirled, my stomach dropping.

Where are you? Lilja's voice said in my head.

"How did she get in there?" I said, scratching at my head. The women glanced at me, smirking, but pulled me into the extensive building made of stone. Crowds of people sat in the stadium, blending together, making the stadium look like color swirls.

"Why is everything so blurry?" My head pulsed and my ears began ringing. I winced.

Elowen, the voice said again. *Answer me.*

How is the little voice inside my head so demanding? The woman kept my hands in hers as we sat down. The stone was cold against my skin. *Where are we? Maybe if I ask her, I can tell the voice in my head to be quiet.* "Where are we?" My voice slurred again, making it seem like there were no pauses between each word.

Without even looking in my direction, she spoke, "We are at the stadium, darling, where the fight happens, and afterwards I get to eat you."

I don't think I'll taste very good. Why do I want to watch fighting? I slouched and pouted dramatically. The day was supposed to be fun.

Taste good? What do you mean fight, Elowen? Who's fighting? Your queen demands you to tell me where you are, this instant. Liljas' voice boomed in my head.

Why was my voice being like this, presumably because she's so pretty? There was a pause. My voice went quiet for a moment before speaking up. *Elle, are you in the stadium?*

Finally, she understands me, for my own voice in my head she certainly seems kind of slow. *I am not slow Elle, stay put. I'm coming for you.*

13

Damsel in Distress

Ugh, the voice in my head makes me sound like a damsel in distress. I hate feeling like a damsel in distress. Unless it's Lilja coming to save me, she can save me anytime, anyplace. My little voice squealed in my head.

The fight in the arena below us preoccupied the lady. She smelled sweet-sickly sweet. She let go of me, folding her soft hands into her lap.

Why do I feel like this? My thoughts were slowly coming to me. *I need to leave this lady; an Elowen sandwich doesn't sound appetizing.* I scooted away from her, holding my breath, attempting to not alarm the no-name lady next to me. She didn't react. The arena was loud, and the no-name lady seemed enthralled by the entertainment of an animal being slaughtered for no reason other than to fill the stands.

I moved over again, this time farther. She screamed, making me jump. I looked at her in alarm. Instead of yelling at me, however, she was yelling at the gladiator. The unfamiliar animal had bitten down on the arm of the poor gladiator.

I began feeling less sluggish. Slowly, I turned my head, attempting to look for the exit. Stationed guards stood at what I presumed was the exit. I just had to make it there. They would help me. Did I need help? Looking back at the no-name lady, I took a deep breath.

Fuck being a damsel in distress. I was more than that. Sweating from stress, I stood up and bolted towards the exit. The crowds entirely ignored me, but the movements made my breathing labored. *Why was this so hard?* The crowd shrieked with despair as the animal one, giving the elf a killing blow. The mess happening in the arena had enthralled the woman, but apparently she wasn't distracted any longer. I felt her presence before I saw her. She shot up from her stand and began moving towards me, quickly.

Much faster than my current condition would allow. The crowd of people were not taking notice of the situation unfolding before them, too enthralled by the elf's mutilated body below. I was so close. *Why was the exit so far away?*

Exit? I thought I told you to stay put. I'm almost there, Elle, the voice in my head said again.

No, I'm going to save myself. No-name attempted to reach me. I turned away.

The guards were so close. The ones at the exit took notice, slitting their eyes at us. Mere feet away, I pushed myself harder, sweat pricking my eyes and soaking my clothing. I launched myself at the guard closet to me, and he caught me, pushing me to the ground.

"Get away, drunkard. You shouldn't come if you're upset with the show's outcome." His voice was rough.

I coughed while facing the ground, spitting blood. The impact had split my dry bottom lip.

"Get away from the queen's tent," he said, kicking my torso, sending me skidding to a halt a foot away. No-name lady was gone, probably scared off by the guards. Gasping, I sat up, my head swimming. *I haven't felt this bad since I accidentally drank that whole wine bottle.*

Accidentally, my inner voice asked me, their voice light now, as if they laughed. I glared at the guard. *Who does this guy think he is?* My stomach churned.

Queen Zahra peeked her head out of the door I presumed was the exit.

"What is going on here?" Her eyes scanned me. Concern grew on her face. Bile fought its way up my throat. Exhausted and unable to fight against the feeling, I vomited. Puke splattered around the ground. It was a sickly purple color.

Wiping my mouth, disgusted, I glanced back at her, bowing my head in apology to her.

"That doesn't seem right." I stumbled, and the world swayed. "I think I need to sit down."

Queen Zahra rushed me, putting her arm under my shoulder, supporting some of my weight. Queen Zahra pulled me into her private area. She glanced at the guard who kicked me.

"We will talk about your actions later, Devdin," she snapped, narrowing her eyes at him.

Her private area looked cozy. Incense burned, giving the room a calm feeling. She settled me on a cushion next to hers. Her servant poured a cup of tea for both of us. "Here honey, drink this. It will calm your stomach," she said, taking a sip of the tea.

"Thank you. I don't know what happened. The lady I met took me here, saying she wanted to eat me. Or at least that's what I think she said—everything is fuzzy." I sipped the hot tea, relishing the feeling of it going down my throat.

"You've met a scaly, a wicked subspecies of elves. They catch people with their voices and touch, and they give out a drug that makes the person feel lethargic and drunk. I will send the guards out for the lady. You are lucky that you got away. How did you manage that?" She sipped her tea again, her dark skin reflected on the light tea cup.

I paused. *How did I get away?* "I-I-I'm not sure. Everything was so hazy, but I heard this voice in my head. I don't know how to explain it. I'm probably insane," I said, forcing a laugh out. She raised her eyebrow but said nothing. The ground rumbled, clattering the teacups on the small table in front of us together.

"What was that?" Queen Zahra asked.

"Lilja, I-I mean Queen Lilja." I stood up quickly and stumbled over to the doorway, ignoring the protests of the queen. I searched the boisterous crowd for my queen. She stood at the bottom near the arena, looking alarmed as her eyes scanned the crowd.

"Your highness," I screamed, waving my arms trying to get her attention. *Please see me,* I thought to myself. She stilled and then zeroed in on where I was standing. Lilja began bounding up the slope, and making new steps as she went, the rock bending to her will.

How did she hear me over the crowd? I quickly abandoned the thought as Lilja pulled me into a hug, pushing me back into Queen Zahra's private seating area. Lilja began berating me with questions. Her eyes and hands roamed my body, searching for injuries. She grabbed a napkin off the table, wiping the blood from my lip with a light touch.

"A scaly almost got her," Queen Zahra mused, watching the interaction between us.

Lilja pulled away from me and bowed to Queen Zahra. "Thank you for saving her. She is a vital member of my team."

"Oh, don't thank me, Queen Lilja, it is not I who saved your Elowen, she saved herself. She would have come out unscathed, but my guards need sensitivity training." Lilja made a face but said nothing to the queen.

"Are you okay?" she asked me, her brow wrinkled with concern. I nodded silently, thankful she came to the arena.

"Let's go back to the inn so we can rest. We will pick up exploring tomorrow and leave this city after that. Can you walk?" she questioned me. I squeaked out a "yes" and apologized to Queen Zahra profusely, embarrassed that I'd thrown up and caused such a ruckus.

She directed a knowing smile at me, saying nothing.

Lilja led me away from the crowd, which was still cheering for the second Elven soul who was thrown in the arena, by choice or force I didn't know. Once we made it out of the arena, the crowd's noise diminished significantly. We walked in silence. At one point, I might have been uncomfortable with the silence between us. But now it felt like there was no need for words. The market was still busy, but nowhere as busy as before. The man selling the delicious meat was still in operation. My stomach betrayed me by growling. Lilja chuckled, following my eyes to the stand.

"Would you like one?" She asked me.

I walked up to the stall for the second time today, and the merchant recognized me. "I see the scaly didn' get ye.'"

My mouth opened with surprise. He knew that woman was a scaly and didn't tell me. "Why didn't you say anything earlier?" I said, nearly shouting. Lilja placed her hand on my shoulder, calming me.

"I didn't want it to get me, those tings' are nasty lil' buggers," he said, holding his hands up in the air to surrender.

I mean, that statement holds true, I thought to myself.

Lilja, however, did not find that reason acceptable. Her usually pale face was a color of deep red. I could practically see the steam coming out of her ears. She pulled her hand off of me and quickly knocked him in the jaw. His body flew backwards, hitting the full pot behind him, causing the contents to come spilling out, the cooked meat sliding onto the floor. I made a sound of surprise, looking up at Lilja, who was shaking her hand out.

"Was that really necessary?" I said, watching the man struggle to get up from the position.

"Yes, it was, Elle. The man just watched you walk away with someone who he knew was dangerous."

I cringed at her reply. It was true, but I couldn't expect everyone to save me.

Her expression softened. "Look, I just don't want to see you hurt. Come on, let's get back to the inn." We returned to the inn without incident, grabbing food from another stall. Lilja insisted on paying, while grumbling about high prices. The inn we stayed in was clean. The red tones of the rock gave the room's warmth.

As for our usual sleeping arrangements, we were roomed together. An odd red crystal sat in the room's corner, giving off warmth. The rest of the walls were plain, save for a window facing the street, allowing the light to filter through from the streetlights. Lilja slipped off her shirt, her pale skin seeming to glow in the room.

"Oh gods, what are you doing?" I said, turning around to face the door.

"What? I'm going to take a nap, and so are you," she stated simply, as if that was the easiest deduction from her action.

What was the other action? A voice whispered in my head. I blushed at my own thoughts, staying silent.

"I'm not sure why you are so bashful about seeing me naked. You like to snuggle in your sleep." Even though I was facing the other direction, I could feel the smile on her face.

"I do not!" My cheeks turned a darker shade of red.

She walked up behind me. "Can I?"

I nodded. *Wait, what did I just agree to?* She tugged at my shirt, pulling it up and above my head. Her light fingers seemed to flitter over my skin, making me shiver. Lilja grabbed my waist, turning me around. Her eyes lit up as she reached behind me, undoing my undergarments in one swoop. *Show off*, I thought to myself, rolling my eyes, trying to keep my face passive.

She grinned at me, turning away.

Lilja unbuttoned her pants and stepped out of them. "Come on, get into bed."

Is she just trying to get me riled up?

She slipped into bed, which creaked under the movement. I joined her, not wanting to stand out in the open naked. I turned towards Lilja, pulling the blanket up. Her eyes were open, staring at me, searching for an answer that she knew the question to. Lilja pulled me into a hug, my face and hers touching cheek to cheek—among other things touching.

"This is how you snuggle at night, like a monkey wrapped around a tree." She rubbed our faces together.

"Stop it," I said, giggling, trying to pull away from her death grip she had on me. "Also, I refuse to believe I cuddle into you, especially because you sleep like a furnace. I'm already sweating."

"Pft, it's a good thing I sleep like a furnace, especially when you use my royal body heat to warm your cold toes on my legs," she said.

I suppressed another laugh. "More like a royal ass pain in the ass."

Lilja opened her mouth in surprise, growling, rolling on top. Her short hair cascaded down, hiding her face.

"Would you like to retract that statement, Lady Elowen Alwyn?" She grinned at me, her smile spreading throughout her entire face.

I stuck my tongue out at her. "I would not like to retract my statement, Lady Royal Ass."

She closed the space between our two bodies, growling playfully, trying to nibble at my neck dramatically. I squealed, trying to worm my way out of her iron grip. A knock sounded at the door, the doorknob wiggled and opened the door.

"Hey would you like—" Armand's voice died out in shock. *Gods kill me now. What am I doing? I can't do this, not so soon.* My thoughts ran rampant in my head.

"Uh, you guys could have locked the door or something—geez. Like get it, but next time not when I can walk in." He rubbed the back of his neck, and a blush crept up his face. "I was going to ask if you guys wanted to go out for some drinks, but I see you're otherwise occupied, so uh, I'll get going."

"Wait, you guys should go to the bar. I don't want to keep you guys from having fun," I said, the words falling out of my mouth, eager to be alone. Lilja stared down at me, as if trying to read my facial expression.

"Oh, yeah sure, but what about you?" Armand asked.

"I'm okay, I don't—I don't drink," I said. It was true. I tried to avoid drinking, as I didn't like how it made my stomach feel. Lilja sat up, her legs straddling me. She got up and off the bed, silently. *Why isn't she saying anything? Did I make her mad?*

Her breasts perked up with the air. I stared at her forehead, trying to look at anything else.

"Are you sure? You could always come with and not drink," she said, making eye contact with me.

"No, it's okay. I don't want to be a downer. Why don't you go without me? I had a long day and could use a nap," I said, forcing a yawn halfway through, trying to make it look more believable. She nodded.

I did have a long day. Somebody tried to eat me.

"Well, okay—if that's what you want," Lilja said, her voice hollow.

"It is. I'm just exhausted," I said, forcing another yawn.

Armand stood stiffly at the door, his back still turned to us. Lilja looked at him and then at me. I could almost see her thoughts turning in her head.

"Okay, we will be back before too long. Armand here doesn't know how to hold his liquor and neither can the rest of the guys." Liljas grinned as she spoke.

She slipped on the clothes she had on earlier, glancing back at me one last time. Worry coated her features. She grabbed Armand's shoulder, signaling him to leave with her. Leaving me alone in my thoughts.

14

Belle & the Sea Shanty

What was I thinking? *She literally asked for permission and I just gave it to her. What if she wanted more than just a nap, and I said yes. Ugh, Belle died in front of me, she loved me, and I-I.* My inner monologue trailed off, the words dissipating in my head; what had been my relationship with Belle? Had I been in love with her?

Tears streamed down my face as I thought of all my memories of Belle. She was so fond of me, bringing me snacks and comforting me after mama died. A sob wrecked my body. *Was I just using her?* I rubbed my face with my hands, my skin pulling uncomfortably.

No, right? It wasn't just sex; it wasn't just experimenting—but was it love? Belle was in love with me, that much I am certain of. She always talked about running away and living in the forest together. I clutched the blanket to my body, getting off the bed. *Was it right to be with Lilja, mere months after her death? Was I a bad person?*

I stared out into the underground city we occupied from the balcony. The blue crystals illuminated the city, giving the red rock a golden hue. Lights hung between the streets as well, and rowdy laughter emanated from below. I smirked. *Those are probably from my friends,* I thought, sniffling, drying the tear streaks on my face.

I watched the people in the streets dwindle. A bell rang in the distance, signaling the time. Mentally I counted the chimes: one, two, three…all the way to ten. Without the sun, I just assumed it was the evening, which was just further proved by the crystal streetlamps dimmed. *I wonder how late everyone will stay out?* Turning back to face the empty room, I slipped into bed. My mind wandered to the past. It haunted me, my troubled darkened soul creating nightmares.

The wind pulled at my hair; the salty air stung my cheeks. Seagulls shouted out above me, looking for their next meal. People laughed excitedly. Their day was just beginning.

Was mine ending? I had yet to go to bed. The words and the wounds from father still stung. The bruises would fade, but I was unsure if the words would do the same.

The people around me ignored me, save for the few odd glances. My presence disturbed them. They pulled their children away and whispered in their ears. I could only imagine the words they said to them. *Ignore her, she looks deranged.*

"Elowen!" Belle said from behind me. Belle's curled hair bounced in the wind, and her dress was pulled up to avoid the sand and pebble beach. She perched herself in front of me, covering the view of the sea. A beautifully made light blue dress hung on her every curve. Expertly placed ruffles and small bows made her lean figure look larger.

You should look more like your mother; instead, you look like the pig out back. My father's voice echoed from the night before in my head. Tears welled in my eyes. Belle stayed silent as I cried, pulling me up.

She tugging me to the changing shack at the start of the beach. She let me cry out my frustrations, hugging me. Her warm embrace seemed to dissolve the sobs wracking my body. As they subsided, I looked up at her, my tears and snot dampening her blue dress.

"I'm sorry," I blubbered out, wiping my snot with the sleeve of my nightgown.

"Shhhh, it's fine, baby. It's just clothes. Come here." She motioned me to her. I was enough, that's what mattered. Belle made me feel like I mattered.

"Forget what happened with your dad, Elowen. Focus on me. I am more important than him. I can make you feel good. Just stay with me. I can make you perfect." I felt small next to her, even though I could easily be one and a half times her weight. Belle always made me feel tiny, like I was any other girl on this beach—she made me feel wanted. My anxiety jumped as she went to the door.

"Wait."

She glanced back at me, her face calm.

"Can't we just hide away together?" I said, searching her eyes. I felt like I belonged with her. She made me feel like I mattered. No one made me feel like that.

"Elowen, you left me." Her voice was hollow, her eyes glazed over, appearing milky.

"What?" I looked up, startled by her words. The sound of rain hit the shed, and the wind whipped the door open. The door banged against the side of the shed, making my heart jump into my throat.

"I gave you myself, and you left me." Tears dripped down the sides of her cheeks as she spoke. Belle's body was drenched with water as if I pushed her into the sea.

"I-I-I didn't leave you." I backed into the corner of the small shed, splinters ran into my back through the thin cloth of my nightgown. *Why did I leave the house like this?* I cursed myself in my head. Belle's ghastly form stood in front of me, her head cocked to the side, analyzing me.

"You left me for the arms of another." Her voice ricocheted in the shed.

"I didn't—I swear. You—y-you died, I watched you die." Her soaked image blinked in and out of existence. Her blue dress was now replaced with the nightgown from the fateful night that took her life. What used to be an off-white nightshirt was now soaked with blood, starting at the left side of her rib cage. Belle's skin was pale and lifeless, as if she was dead and her soul possessed the body to stand upright. Her head shook from side to side violently, froth coming from her mouth.

"*You* left me to die alone!"

I woke up with the words repeating in my head. My stomach churned with hatred, fear, and exhaustion. I stumbled out of bed, dropping onto my knees, and frantically crawled to the trash can, throwing up into it. My body shook with convulsions as my early dinner emptied from my mouth. The coolness of the rock, chilling my sweaty cheek as I laid my head on the rim. I wondered if everything here in this city was made of stone. I crawled my way back to the bed. The stone floor was cool to the touch. As I reached the bed, a drunk Lilja stumbled in.

She righted herself, swearing, wobbling over, not yet noticing that I was out of bed. She mumbled to herself, what appeared to be an Elven sea shanty.

"Oh, the pretty lil' lady is in my bed tonight
Rocking with the boat, with all her lil' might,

Tomorrow she'll be gone b'fore we leave the port
Rocking with the waves, the wind will help tonight
G'bye my lil' lady
I'll dream of you at night

What are ye' doing out of bed," she hiccuped, still holding a mug of beer.

"I heard you coming," I said, not wanting to make the night about me again. I wiped my mouth with the back of my hand, the remaining vomit now gone. Lilja stumbled into me, her body warm from the effects of the alcohol.

"You're drunk," I said, struggling to hold on to her as she laid her entire body weight on me.

"Nooooo, I'm not drunk, just a lil' tipsy," she slurred, standing up by herself just long enough to motion *a little bit* in a pinching hand signal.

I rolled my eyes, grabbing the mug from her hand and pushed her onto the bed. She fell with an *oof* escaping her mouth. I sniffed the liquid in the mug, cringing, I took a tentative sip, attempting to hide the smell in my mouth. As the liquid hit my tongue, I made a face. I walked over to the patio and threw the rest over the side, praying nobody was down below.

Once back to the bed, I pulled off Lilja's shoes. She stared at the ceiling, her eyes half open. My hands went to her pants next, unbuckling them at the top.

"Hey, taking advantage of my current state is frowned upon, princess," she slurred, her words sounding like one word.

"I am just undressing you for bed, not trying to seduce you." My cheeks burned. "And I'm not a princess."

She leaned over to me, sitting up, her pale cheeks tinged red. "Wanna hear a secret?" Instead of her whispering in my ear like a normal sober person, she whispered in front of my face.

I rolled my eyes. "Sure."

She awkwardly pulled off her shirt. "You're gonna be my princess."

I smirked. *My queen has a crush on me,* my inner voice sang out. *She doesn't mean it,* the more logical side of my head whispered. I nodded in agreement with the more logical side of my brain as I finished tucking her in. Then I walked back to the patio, throwing on a robe, the urge to sleep gone with the nightmare. The city was now dark, besides a few dimly lit crystal streetlamps. *I wonder how they turn them on and off.* The streets were empty save for a few random, passing stragglers. *If I'm gonna stay up, I'm gonna need to find coffee.* With the abandoned mug in hand, I searched for the kitchen.

I wandered the halls, walking down the steps to the first floor. Most of the doors were shut, each of them numbered, indicating that they were rooms for board. *Why do they need these rooms in a hidden city with no visitors?* I asked myself. After a few moments, I found the kitchen; the counters were covered in dust. Which just cemented the fact that the inn was barely, if at all, used. I rummaged through the cabinets for grounds to make coffee. Dust covered the cupboard and its contents.

"You are up really early, or you never went to bed," Aidan's voice chimed out. I whirled around to see a disheveled Aidan, his glasses off center. In his hand, he had his journal and pen. He sauntered to the counter sitting at the tall counter.

"I would say the same to you but with that in your hands, I'm gonna guess you're up early." I gestured towards the journal. "Would you like a cup of coffee as you write?"

He nodded, so I grabbed a dusty mug from the cabinet and dusted it off with the bottom of the robe I still wore. I poured him a glass, which he greedily took from my hands like a child wanting a toy. He sipped it tentatively, his face appearing more awake with each sip.

After a moment, he mumbled a *thanks,* sighing as he opened his journal; each page had neat writing, some with drawings over the top of the words.

"Do you want to talk about it?" he asked, still looking down at his journal.

"No," I said, my tone coming across more harshly than I intended.

He looked at me knowingly, his face full of sympathy. "When you are ready, you can talk to me anytime."

I nodded solemnly. I knew he wanted to help, but I wasn't ready to talk about it. We sat in silence as I drank my coffee and he wrote about his dream. I wondered what he had nightmares about, but like me, he probably wasn't willing to talk about it.

He said, never looking up from his journal, continuing to write as he spoke: "You know, when I was young, my father would punish me for talking about my feelings. His name was Sterk'n, honestly his name should have just been Stoic, since he never wanted to talk about his own feelings. He always wanted me to grow up like him. He was *the* general, the best. He couldn't understand why I'd rather read and learn about history than fight like a brainless idiot. Lilja would always be there for me when I needed to get away from him. She used to let me read in the royal library for hours at night, just so I could get away. Maybe, since you don't want to talk about it to me, you could talk to her about it."

Could I talk to her? Would she understand the guilt I had simmering just beneath my skin?

15

Valdis News

Gradually, the sounds of waking people blessed my ears. For whatever reason, sitting in the kitchen with him gave me feelings reminiscent of the good parts of my childhood. In my younger years, I used to sit in the kitchen with Mama as she read the paper and drank coffee herself.

I smiled at the memory as people began filtering into the kitchen. Keres was the first, her black hair disheveled and her night clothes crinkled.

"Your brother busted into my room last night to take Lilja out for drinks. Do you know if he ever made it home?" I asked, omitting the part where he found Lilja and me in a compromising position.

She rolled her eyes as she grabbed a mug from the cabinet, making a face as she blew the dust off. "Yeah, I know he went out. Everyone went beside you and Aidan."

She sighed as she poured the now cold coffee in her cup. Keres closed her eyes for a second, taking a controlled breath, and then coffee was steaming again.

I wish I could do that, I thought.

"Why would I know if he came back or not? I'm not his babysitter.

I was otherwise preoccupied. Someone warmed my bed for the night. The people of Ebbon are quite skilled in the sheets."

I choked on my coffee, staring at her, surprised at how easily the words slipped from her mouth.

"Yeah, speaking of warming people's beds last night—" Armand said as he walked into the kitchen.

"Not another word, Armand, not unless you want to dig your way out of this kitchen," Lilja warned him.

She looked worse than Keres, like she had also warmed the bed with someone. Even though I knew it wasn't the case. Armand shut his mouth, but wiggled his eyebrows at me—making Aidan give me a questioning look—but said nothing. Lilja walked past me to the coffee, making more, not mentioning her catchy tune last night, nor did she say anything about calling me a princess.

Kallan strode into his usual black attire, the scar on his face appearing more prominent, presumably because of the lack of sunlight. His usual sun-kissed skin was a few shades paler. He gave me a small knowing smile as he grabbed a mug for coffee. *What does he know?*

Cassia was the last to walk in. She looked ready to start the day, giving us all a chirpy "Good morning!"

"We leave today; each of us will split up here in the city, besides Elowen and I. Each of us knows our orders. Spy on the people of Ardour. Find a solution to the blight, be safe, if you find something important—get it to Keres immediately so she can spread the word. Queen Alieta has to be behind this."

The team looked at her solemnly. The severity of the mission was clear. People were going to die if a solution wasn't found. For the first time in a while, I was going to miss people. I was worried; if Ardour caught us spying, my friends could die. These elves were my family, a family I chose.

Once everyone had their fill of coffee, we said our goodbyes. All of our eyes were fearful and wet with unshed tears. Lilja and I walked back up to the room, climbing the stairs in silence until we hit the floor they'd housed us on.

"I'm sorry for last night," I said, while staring at my hands.

"No." Lilja took my face in her hands. "I'm sorry. I shouldn't have tried anything. You'll let me know when you are ready, and even if you are never ready, that will be okay with me, too." She pulled my face forward slightly as if she wanted to kiss my lips, and then changed direction, planting a small kiss on my forehead and sending a wave of warmth down my body. "Spending time together is enough."

A wave of vomit hit our noses as she opened the door. My cheeks burned; I didn't want to tell her I threw up.

I opened my mouth reluctantly when she looked at me sheepishly. "Sorry, I'm pretty sure I threw up once I got back to the room. After the eighth drink, things got pretty fuzzy. I don't even remember getting undressed." She rubbed the back of her neck with her hand.

"I undressed you, and your drunk butt thought I was trying to seduce you."

She raised her eyebrow, looking at me suggestively. "Well, were you?"

"What? No, I figured you wouldn't want to sleep with all of your clothes on," I said as I changed into a pair of trousers and a black linen shirt. "What is the plan for today?"

"You and I will bid goodbye to the queen and head up to the surface. The first city in Ardour's kingdom is only half a day away. That is where we will meet with an old friend of my parents." Lilja slung her pack over her shoulder. With my bag in hand, we went to the pavilion, where we had originally met with Queen Zahra. She was seated on a large cushion, going over farming records with an elderly gentleman. He had a long scraggly looking beard, his face and hands wrinkled with age.

"Queen Lilja, so nice to see you," Zahra said, "and you as well, young Elowen." She nodded at the older gentleman, dismissing him. He quickly packed his papers up and left, bowing low as he did so.

"How are you feeling after the altercation with the scaly?" Zahra asked.

I gave the queen a bow. "I am much better. Thank you for asking. Rest was all I needed."

"Indeed, I have supplies being gathered for you both. Gowns to fit into the upper circle. Please find all the answers you can for the blight. We received grave news from Dumont and a messenger brought a newspaper down from the surface. Each has troubling contents." Zahra handed over the paper.

Lilja grabbed the paper from the queen's hand, skimming over the contents, her already pale skin lightening a few more shades.

"What! What does it say? Let me see," I cried out, grabbing the newspaper from her hands. My heart sank as I read the words.

"It's begun." Her voice strained with emotion. She ran her fingers through her hair nervously.

"What does the letter from Dumont say, your highness?" I asked, almost forgetting to add the proper title at the end. I could almost see my inner voice cringing in my head.

VALDIS NEWS: Blight mutates affecting hundreds.
The illness infecting the vegetation surrounding the Kingdom of Valdis has begun to mutate and infect fellow Elves.
Symptoms include: Loss of Magic, coughing, shaking, fever, and even death.
The queen has refused to comment at this time. It is unclear how this illness has mutated so quickly.

The queen handed the letter to Lilja, her face grave. Her knuckles gripped the paper, looking up at me, her eyes filled with tears. "Elbio has been stricken with the blight. He urges us to hurry."

My heart sank. Poor Elbio. *He has to pull through, right?* "What are we waiting for? We must hurry. Elbio and Dumont are counting on us."

Lilja stared at me for a moment, something shining in her eyes. Pride? Admiration?

"It will be very difficult to deliver information to you when you are on the surface. This will be the last news I will be able to send. You will be in the dark. I will contact my connections from Ardour to gather intelligence from Valdis and Ardour for you both. Please be safe and act hastily. Dumont and Elbio are counting on you." Queen Zahra stood up, grabbing Lilja's forearm and pulling her into a hug. She wrapped her arms around her tightly, pulling away and looking at me.

"Even though you were not born here, I can tell you have a love for this realm, young Elowen." She glanced at Lilja. "And for its people. I hope you may find peace here. When this is over, please come and visit us." She leaned down, grabbing my hand, kissing it, allowing her lips to flutter on my skin.

My cheeks burned. I looked in Lilja's direction. All she did was shrug her shoulders in response.

Lilja and I mounted our horse returned by the stables at the entrance of the city. With Lilja in front, we traveled through the streets. People parted, allowing us to run full speed to the exit that would take us to the surface. I wondered what Ardour would be like. I've never even been to the capital of Valdis. Would they be similar? Would Lilja tell me if it was?

As we neared what I assumed was the exit, the city landscape got less and less urban, buildings being replaced by farmland. Instead of plants from the surface, they grew virtually translucent ones. The veins on the leaves glowed, similar to the glow the crystals gave off. If it were any other day, I would have spent hours looking and trying the plants if I could; I marked it down in my mental calendar. I had to come back. It felt necessary to draw these plants and test out whether they had any medicinal properties.

Lilja said nothing as we rushed through the darkened countryside of Ebbon. The streetlights were gone, save for a few, replaced by the darkness that usually accompanied being underground. The air was moist the farther and farther we went from the city. Soon the only sounds were of the horses' hooves hitting the cavern floor. We slowed to a walk, allowing the horses to take a breath. I pulled alongside Lilja. Her face hardened with her *I'm thinking* expression.

"What will happen when we reach the surface?" I asked.

"We get into contact with my friends, gather supplies and gain our new identities for the time being. From there, we will gather information on what they know about the blight."

"New identities?"

"Yes, new identities. We can't do it as ourselves. A human and Queen of Valdis would gather more attention than we need. Don't you think?" she said with a smirk. I grinned at her, my teeth showing. *It's been a while since I saw her smile.*

I rolled my eyes at her playfully. "I suppose."

The road we followed was getting smaller and smaller, making it impossible to travel side by side. Lilja took the front and I the back. *We must be getting close.* I tossed my hair in a bun. In the process, knocking one of my ear tips loose. Quickly, I grabbed at it, catching it as it attempted to roll off my body. I stared at it, making a face. *I have to put it back on—again.* The memory of hot glue made me cringe.

"We're here." The horses stopped, making me lurch in my saddle. The wall before us was huge, and the crudely carved door stood ominously. Almost as if saying *stay with me*.

Lilja dismounted. "No one must leave once they come down." Her fingers traced the pattern carved beside the door. The door opened with a loud creak. I glanced around nervously as we walked inside.

It was as if light didn't exist here. The light from the city was completely gone and now replaced by complete darkness. Lilja grumbled, rustling in her pack for her flint, striking against the unlit torch from her saddlebag. The sparks danced to life, spreading on the torch's fabric. This tunnel appeared much older than the first tunnel, stalactites and stalagmites grew on the sides. The ground was slick with brown water. Lilja made a face but said nothing.

"This place looks like the caves back in the Human Realm. Jasper and I used to explore them," I said as I traced my finger along the damp wall.

"Jasper? The man they betrothed you to," Lilja said, cocking her head to one side as if hoping to hear more.

"Yes, Jasper and I were good friends. We grew up together. His father and my father were both merchants, that's the reason they promised us to one another. Father always said it was going to grow the trade market. I-I just went along with it because it would make him happy. He-he was scary when he was angry." My voice stuttered as memories of his angry outbursts crossed my vision; absentmindedly, I rubbed the scar on my arm.

Lilja paused, allowing me to walk side by side with her, grabbing my hand with her empty one. Her fingers intertwined with mine as she rubbed my hand with her thumb. As we walked, we talked about each other's childhoods, the light topics. As I didn't want her to focus on negativity; we had enough to worry about with our friends traveling by themselves. The incline became steeper as we hopefully neared the exit. The horses struggled to get up, slipping at some points. I silently prayed the incline would stay the same.

Leland—or at least one of the gods—must have been listening to my prayers as the ground below us leveled. The exit could be at the end of the tunnel. We both looked at each other, grinning and sprinting towards the exit with a newfound energy spurt and into the unknown territory of Ardour.

16

Newlyweds

We squinted as the tunnel ended; spending time underground made our eyes accustomed to the dark. Everything seemed so green and bright. I panted; my lungs strained by the exercise. Lilja didn't even break a sweat. She pulled a shirt and trousers that the queen had given us from her bag. Lilja threw them over her shoulder. She strode over to my pack, pulling out a sophisticated dress.

It was a light blue, finer than the clothes living at father's accustomed me to wear as a teen. It was apparent that whoever made this dress made it for autumn; it was of thicker material than a typical summer dress. However, it wasn't as heavy as a winter gown. The thread was gold colored and looked expensive. I grinned at Lilja as she passed it to me. Finer clothes always made me feel pretty. I loved the way they felt on me.

Lilja looked at me grimly as she stripped, using her old shirt as a rag to clean her dirty face. My face burned with embarrassment as I followed suit, changing out of the practical pair of pants and into the gown. *How in the world did they know my measurements?* I stared down at myself. Seamstresses willing to create clothes in my size were few and fair in between. They always deemed it fit to tell my father and me to starve myself instead.

"You look beautiful Ellie, truly magnificent." Lilja's voice was barely over a whisper. "Let me help you with your ear tips. It's better if we hide your identity from Ezrin and his wife. For your protection and theirs, that way nothing can accidentally be exposed to Queen Alieta and Ardour's defenses."

I handed over the fallen ear tips, peeling off the other, which was barely attached. Lilja quickly got to work peeling off the old glue and reapplying a fresh coat.

She gave me a sympathetic look as she pulled my hair back gently and placed the ear tip in place. I bit my lip to hold in the whimper that threatened to escape. I grabbed onto her nice shirt for support.

"Sorry." She wiped the extra glue off quickly. After finishing the other ear up, she grabbed her royal seal from her bag, as well as the cloak she usually donned on colder nights, stuffing them into a hollow log next to the entrance of the tunnel. "Let's go."

"Wait, what about your things?" I asked her, confusion clear in my voice.

"Ellie, those items are evidence of my heritage. If, for whatever reason, we get caught, they could use those items against us, like sending correspondence in my name. It is easier if we go into this kingdom anonymously," Lilja said, trying to keep her voice light, her brown eyes filled with sorrow.

"I I," my voice died out, and my heart dropped to my feet. *Did she think we were going to fail?* Lilja gave me a sympathetic look, remounting her horse. She reached into her bag, retrieving a map, unrolling it, and examining the routes. She used a finger to trace one specific path with her slender finger. I shivered as I thought about how well those same fingers took off my shirt yesterday. I crinkled my nose as another thought quickly passed nearly simultaneously.

You're not ready yet. It's your fault.

As we rode past the countryside, I took attempted to memorize the way back. The trees and vegetation looked remarkably similar, although more vibrant. The plants on the west side of the mountain appeared more dull. Here, on the east side of the mountain, they looked more alive.

Lilja must have read my thoughts as she piped in, "It's the blight. At one point, the entire continent looked so vibrant, the water and tree nymphs would dance in the open. Now the nymphs have gone into hiding. We haven't spotted them in nearly 400 years." Lilja sighed as she finished her explanation. As if that form of the world was taking shape in her head, a world her 230-year-old self had never seen.

"How did the blight start?"

Her horse faltered for a bit, sensing her hesitation. Or maybe he was just sensing a small animal in the trees as we passed as she began talking again. "No one is certain how the blight originated. The infection began in a small fishing village north of the castle. It showed up in a small, rooted vegetable first. Unbeknownst to the crown, the Valdisians began unintentionally spreading the disease to many of the edible plants in the area. Soon the kingdom was fully infected, by the time the crown knew of the blight it was too late." Her voice cracked towards the end.

She cleared her throat, attempting to hide the emotion prevailing in her voice.

"The smaller towns suffered first, the elder elves and children suffered the most. The infected plants are inedible, and if you do accidentally eat them, you get sick. Many die from dehydration, even with water mages to help, because the infected can't hold anything down."

"What are water mages?" I asked.

"Water mages are individuals who are blessed with the ability to manipulate water. They are a different breed of elf. A rare race, nearly extinct. They manifest their magic differently than the average elf. It's manifested physically in and on their body. Blue tattoo-like impressions cover much of their body and their eyes are milky. They can heal the sick and injured, but for whatever reason, they couldn't help us."

I wracked my brain trying to think about the history of elves my schooling had taught me. Water mages? Blight? None of these topics had ever come up. *Then again, the existence of elves was placed in fairy tale books.* I frowned. *Why wouldn't the mages help if they could?*

The conversation died out, the air around us melancholy. The land before us, however, was transforming from dense trees to fields of wheat and other late-season vegetables. Lilja's eyes widened slightly, yet she said nothing. A few lone farmers were sporadically spaced out in the fields; carts traveled the dirt road, filled with various vegetables. The scene reminded me of the farmland back home, the fields I used to run in and play hide and seek in.

One elderly farmer was pulling a cart in the direction we were headed. Lilja flicked her reins slightly, moving her horse up to a trot to ride over to him with me close on her heels.

"Well hello travelers, can I help ye' with anything? Since you came to bother me this morning," he said, his voice gravelly with age.

"Now Ezrin, you may be an old man, but I am not against pushing you over into your cart." Lilja said.

My eyes widened in surprise at her tone, looking between the two elves before me. Silence stretched between them until Ezrin grinned a practically toothless grin and let out a belly laugh. Lilja joined in with a chuckle—and I had never been more confused in my whole life.

"Come down here, dear, and give this old man a hug, or have ye' forgot ye' manners?" Ezrin feigned seriousness again.

Lilja jumped down off her horse gracefully, her fine clothes now rumpled from riding for hours. Much taller than the man, she leaned down almost awkwardly, pulling the older man into a bear hug. Her lanky arms reaching nearly all the way around his chubby hunched form. Ezrin gave her a tight squeeze and looked up at me. Lady neighed softly.

"Hello to you. What is your name, young lady? I usually see another crew with Lilja. She must have singled you out for your good looks," he said as he chuckled. His light eyes were bright, contrasting with his dark, aged skin.

I grinned at him, sending him a wink as I dismounted. I held out my hand to curtsy, introducing myself. His hands—calloused from years of work—enveloped mine, which he gave a small kiss.

"Pleasant manners. This one is much better than the last group I saw you with. Those boys always started so many fights between each other, especially Kallan."

I raised my eyebrow at Lilja; Ezrin melted her strong façade.

"We should get to my house and out of the open. Jaz will be happy to see you, Lilja. She'll be ecstatic to see you made a new friend." He winked as he walked down the road without his cart.

"Wait, what about the cart?" I asked.

"Oh, the other boys will grab it for me when they finish up filling theirs. We help each other out around these parts," Ezrin said.

As we walked, Lilja explained our adventure to get her. Instead of jumping into the conversation, I looked around at the surrounding fields. The land was flattened, small streams set between each field for irrigation. We soon found ourselves at a small cottage, similar in size to the cottage I had built. It seemed like ages ago, but in reality, maybe a few months had passed. My world had changed so quickly, but even so, the crowd that I had surrounded myself with felt safe.

Ezrin opened the door, hollering, "Honey, I'm home."

"It's about time, you little old man. I told yer before and I'll tell yer again. Yer cannot be out the whole day, yer not a spring chic'en no more. What if ye' fell out there who'd be picking ye'r butt up? Hm? The birds would be once they got hungry," an older woman said from the other room. Ezrin grumbled something about not being old, as the woman, who I presumed was Jaz, walked around the corner.

She paused mid-walk as she spotted us. Lilja gave her a sheepish grin, rubbing the back of her neck. "Hello Jazzy, nice to see you again."

"Ezrin Michael, maybe warn me next time that we are getting visitors. Perhaps before I rip into ye' old hide for doin' shit, ye' ain't supposed to do no more." Jaz warned, as she wiped her flour covered hands on her apron. "Now Lilja, darling, come give ol' Jazzy a hug," she cooed.

Already in motion, she grabbed at Liljas' tall frame, pulling her face down to hers and giving Lilja a wet kiss on the cheek. "Now Lilja, who is your pretty friend, ye' girlfriend?"

I made a strangled noise in the back of my throat. Jaz gave me a strange look but said nothing, leading us into the kitchen area. A fire was going in the brick oven built into the corner, and dough covered half of the table. Jaz gave us an abashed look, apologizing for the mess. Ezrin stepped away from our gathering, tugging up a rug just out of the kitchen area. I watched him intently, out of curiosity, as he pulled away three loose boards. He exposed a large sack, grunting he yanked it up and let the contents clatter on the ground.

"These are the items you asked for, your highness, everything should be here. I was very discreet in obtaining them. I hope we satisfied you with the aliases." Ezrin's hands shook as he grabbed a small box from the bag. He opened it to revealed two small scrolls. Lilja grabbed both of them. Her eyes skimmed the contents of each scroll, nodding almost as if to herself as she handed it to me.

I read through the paper. It was about someone named Zaria. A young Elf from the coast of Llidan, whose family had been murdered by pirates. I looked up from reading to Lilja, "Who's Zaria?"

"It's your new identity for the time being," Lilja looked up from her own paper. "For the time being, my new name is Ophelee. I am the Lady of Niyian. Are the rest of our clothes in the sack, Ezrin? Do you have a proper dagger?"

Ezrin nodded, handing the large bag over. I grabbed it, peering inside. The clothes were neatly folded and tied with ribbon. I pulled them out, inspecting them and unwrapping a few dresses and shirts for various events.

"I put a handful of coins in each of your purses, enough to last for a while if you are smart about how you use them." Ezrin's gruff voice filled the air. "I've made arrangements for you to rent an apartment towards the middle of the capital. Now, it's not nice like the Castle of Valdis, but it's comfortable and is in the middle of everything. You'll be able to come and go there as you please. I've already talked to the landlady. She won't bother you. She thinks you are on your honeymoon."

"Thank you, Ezrin, truly. We wouldn't have been able to do this without you." Lilja grabbed the older elves' wrinkled hands, giving them a squeeze.

"Honeymoon?" My mouth was agape in surprise.

Lilja gave me a grin. "Oh yeah, I forgot to tell you. In the Kingdom of Ardour, we are newlyweds."

17

The Beginning of What?

I stared at her. My mind raced as my mind processed what that could mean.

"It's just pretend until we get out of Ardour, don't look so stressed. I'm *not* that bad to be married too—well, at least, I think. I've never been married, so I guess I can consider this practice." Lilja grinned.

Her smile, however, didn't reach her eyes. She looked anxious, like she was worried I was going to go running for the hills.

A slow smile spread across my face as I pictured us "married" in Ardour's capital. "I can't wait to be married!" My voice projected more than expected, resulting in a surprised look from both Jaz and Ezrin.

Liljas' eyes searched my face for hesitation. She must have found none because, this time her smile hit her eyes. Making her beautiful, brown eyes disappear from her cheekbones. She reached into her pocket, grabbing a small box from it. Lilja examined the contents, closing it with a resounding *thunk*. She flipped the velvet box open once more, getting down on one knee, with the contents now facing me. A ring looked at me, as if it was piercing into my soul. A small blue stone sat in the center and bronze delicate tree limbs wrapped around the gem holding in place.

I gasped as she continued. "Elowen Alwyn, would you do me the utmost pleasure of being my wife for this adventure?"

My cheeks reddened. *For a fake marriage, this feels remarkably real.* Lilja looked so happy, gazing up at me from the ground, her hands steady as they outstretched the ring to me. I nodded, afraid that my voice would fail me if I tried to speak the words *I do*. Lilja grabbed the ring and discarded the box by throwing it at the grinning Jaz. I allowed her to slip it on my finger. I admired the craftsmanship up close. The details of the ring were remarkable. The smiths back home could never get this much on such a small ring.

Lilja must've read my facial features, because she said, "The elves blessed with earth magic can craft objects from the earth."

"It's beautiful." I looked at the ring on my finger.

"Thanks. I figured I'd make it something plant-related since you're into plants." Lilja said, as she ran her fingers through her hair.

I looked up from the ring, zeroing in on her face. "You made this?" I flung my hand that donned the ring in her direction, as if showing her was going to change her answer.

"Yes," she said, walking closer, leaning into me. "I couldn't have just any ring mark what's mine."

My face reddened at her comment, and my mouth opening slightly. Lilja looked at me and laughed. Jaz and Ezrin joined in as my face was still deepening to a color similar to blood.

I huffed, not liking the fact that people were laughing at me. Lilja sobered when she saw my expression flipping from glee to annoyance.

"Alright, alright, I apologize for laughing at you, but you should have seen your face."

She grabbed the bag that had been disregarded on the ground. We piled the items in the bag, along with snacks from Jaz and Ezrin.

Bidding our goodbyes, we departed from their small cottage and continued on towards the Capital of Ardour.

Road by road, we got closer and closer to the Capital. Passing small towns as we traveled, we spread the woes of our backstories and the new marriage between us. Children ran with our horses as we rode through the towns.

"What is going to happen when we get to the capital? How is being undercover going to find us information about the blight?" I said, as we passed the bend of the road we were currently on.

"People have loose tongues when they think you think the same way." Lilja pulled a piece of jerky from her bag and munching on it. Her usual short hair had got long, since I had first met her, further disguising Lilja, Queen of Valdis.

Keres had truly been doing her part in transferring information between all of us. Armand, Aidan, and Cassia had all found their way to the Capital before us. Our route was much longer, and the stays in the villages had delayed us significantly. We left a trail of people who "know" us in our wake.

"According to this map, we should reach the Capital tonight if we aren't delayed," the map crinkled with Lady's movements. My legs and nether bits were sore from the constant riding. I groaned.

Lilja glanced at me, "What?"

"I want off this horse," I said, earning a neigh from Lady. "No offense, Lady." I patted her neck affectionately. "I'm sore and want a bed."

Lilja rolled her eyes. "Or a warm bath."

"Yes," I said, daydreaming of a nice, hot bath.

Lilja laughed, and I frowned, sticking my tongue out in her direction. "For someone who lived in a cottage before you came here, you sure like to be pampered."

"As you know, madam, I didn't always live in a small cottage. Plus, I am a tad high maintenance," I said. When I was with her, laughing came easier, and the weight on my chest lessened by what seemed like a minute amount each day.

"Just a tad?" She hummed to herself, riding closer to me, our legs nearly touching.

"Yes, *just* a tad, Lilja" I pushed Lady to get ahead of Lilja and to get to the top of the hill.

I gasped as I looked across the fields as my eyes laid on the castle walls of the Capital. The gray stone nearly sparkled as the sun hit it, giving off a cold glow. Lilja sped up her horse to stall next to me, giving the castle a hard gaze.

I looked at her, grinning. "First one there gets the first bath!"

I pushed into Lady's side, making her go into full run. The wind whipped through my hair, the air stinging my eyes and making them tear up. Lilja shouted a war cry and bounded past me, giving me a quick, smug look. I pushed Lady harder, grinning, running nearly neck and neck with Lilja. The castle loomed closer and closer as we raced. Farmers were working in the fields as we got closer, guards stationed at each large cart of food. Two donkeys were at each cart, ready to pull the loads of food behind the castle wall.

The guards stared at the two women racing, saying nothing. Stopping at the entrance, not wanting to run over a random person in the street, I waited for Lilja to catch up, unsure of how to proceed in this bustling city. People were everywhere. They set multiple temporary shops up at the entrance to scam overwhelmed people. Lilja halted next to me, looking around, assessing what each shop held and what the temporary shops sold. She dismounted, walking up to a man selling leather work.

"Hello, my wife and I are new here and I was wonderin' if you could tell us how to get to the center square." Her voice was sweet, not like her usual brazen voice that made people question if they knew what they were talking about. The man folded his hands politely, resting them on his oversized belly, smiling.

"Well, yes, I can direct ya' to get there. All ya' need to do is take a left at the end of the road and continue going straight away. Stop when ya' see the herbalist shop and turn to the right. There yer' goin' to see a big round area of shops and lil' apartments. That'll be the center of the city." His accent was thick; I could barely understand him. Lilja must've, as she was nodding enthusiastically at what the man said.

Silently I prayed that not everyone in the Capital spoke like that. She thanked him, slipping him a coin for his help. His large rough hands snatched it quickly, bowing his head in thanks. We walked through the cobblestone roads. Storefronts were busy and decorated for fall. I couldn't help but feel welcomed to the Capital. Lilja gripped the rein of her horse, her knuckles white. I gave her a small smile, knowing she would talk to me about it later. As we passed the herbalist shop, I couldn't help but peer inside. Shelves lined one side and jars of various sizes filled them.

Plants lined the window, making it nearly impossible to see anything else. A weathered-looking man worked the counter. Lilja spoke, breaking my concentration.

"Come on, I see our apartment from here." Her voice was eager; her eyes told a different story. They looked unbelievably tired. I hustled, pulling Lady to the stables behind the apartment building. I handed the reins to the stable boy, starting for the back door.

Lilja grabbed at my empty hand, whispering in my ear. "Go with it," as we walked inside, our fingers interlocked. The doorbell jangled as we walked in. The elderly lady at the counter peered down at us through the top of her large, thick spectacles; her facial features brightened as she saw us.

"Well hello dears, so lovely to see you. I suppose you are my new tenants for the apartment on the top floor. You ladies are the ones beginning your honeymoon. How exciting." She clapped, excitement in her voice, making me grin back at her.

"So nice to see such young people get married and start their journeys with their fated ones."

Fated? What does that mean? I made a mental note to ask Lilja about what that meant later. Lilja smiled brightly at the older lady, holding up my hand and giving it a small kiss.

"It sure is." Her voice was light. She spoke at a slightly higher pitch than normal.

"Great," she said, clapping her hands again. "Let me get your keys. The apartment is furnished, so ya don't need to worry about that. The neighbors below you are never home. Ya don't need to be worried about being too noisy, if ya know what I mean." She chuckled, sending a wink our way. I blushed; Lilja squeezed my hand and giggled.

The old lady, named Galen, kept talking up the three flights. Lilja continued to giggle at what she said, keeping things pleasant. My mind was racing with the future. How long was this charade going to go? Was I able to continue with being "married"? Was it right to do this? *What would Belle say? Wait—Belle is dead. She's gone. The life I knew is gone. This is my life now.* The sound of the key jangling broke me out of my thoughts in the lock. The door creaked open, revealing a small living area.

"I bought the plants you requested and placed them by the windows so they could get some light. I think they add a lovely touch to the room. You guys must have wonderful taste. Let me know if you need help to move any of the furniture around. I'm sure I can get a hold of my grandson to help. Have a good day, girls," she shut the door behind her with a resounding *thunk*. Lilja sighed, dropping the bag she held onto the floor. She pulled her hair into a low ponytail, barely able to do so.

After waiting to hear the Galen's shuffling feet hit the first floor, Lilja began talking.

THE BEGINNING OF WHAT?

"We start a life here, Zaria." I flinched as she said my new name. "We make *friends*, we talk to people, we find out what they have heard about the blight. Most importantly of all, we never tell anyone the truth. We lie and we stick to the story we create. You are from Llidan, and I am from a prominent family on Niyian." She balled her fist. Anger rolled off her in waves as she stood in our temporary home.

"We will stay here, stay until we find the answer to this blight infecting my land—"

"Our land," I walked up to her, pulling her face down to be level with mine. "We find the cure for our land and our people." I leaned forward, giving her a small, tender kiss. She pulled away, nodding.

"Together, we will find the reason this kingdom can stay so healthy, so happy. That way my—our people can once again prosper like in my father's age."

We stood looking at each other. It was as if the world had stopped. Held on pause, on pause long enough for me to know that this—whatever *this* was—was what I wanted. I wanted her and a world I felt safe in. If we could do this, I knew that I belonged in this realm. Human or not.

18

Morally Grey

We settled into the apartment over the next couple of days. Our basic tasks included going to the market each day and talking to people. I loathed the second part.

I found myself in the center of the market after a short walk. People screamed at anyone who would listen, trying to sell their goods and services to potential customers.

Lilja was behind me holding a basket. A ribbon held her hair.

"Well hello, pretty little lady; can I interest you in some fine cloth? You'd be able to sew a great many things with it."

The man walked close to me, nearly taking up my path to continue in the market. Lilja stepped behind me, so close she could have pressed up against me.

"We are fine. She doesn't want any of your fabric," she said, using her normal voice. I looked up at her surprised, *why was she breaking character?*

The man walked away, grumbling about young people. The crowd huddled towards one stand, a man our age stood selling newspapers. He stood yelling, "News! News from the Capital!"

Lilja and I walked over to the screaming man, buying a newspaper.

It read: *VALDIS SUSPECTED OF MOVING MILITARY MEMBERS IN MOUNTAINS: Please report any suspicious persons to the closest authorities.*

Blight kills thousands in Valdis, the cause of how and why the infection mutated is unknown.

Pirates have disappeared off the coast of Llidan. Their Mayor claims the glory of scaring them off!

Lilja's face was passive as she read the paper, her eyes skimming over everything at least twice, her eyes betraying her genuine emotions. She was worried. The surrounding crowd began whispering to each other, some worried about the blight. Some talked about war with Valdis. We hustled back to the apartment after buying food for the day.

My chest was tight. I took a deep breath. Lilja paced the living area, her hand on her chin as she frantically began thinking of the future. "We need to speed this plan up. We've been here for weeks and have heard nothing substantial about the blight. Playing the good girls just isn't cutting it. We need to go underground."

"What do you mean, go underground? How is that going to help?" I asked her.

"We need to talk to the people in the underbelly, where people are always under the influence." Lilja walked to the cabinet, grabbing scissors. "Right now, the most important thing is to get rid of this gods-forsaken hair." She grabbed her shoulder-length hair, peering into a mirror, and began cutting.

I stood there frozen in horror as she hacked away her long black hair. Her eyes were hard as she looked at her reflection, keeping eye contact with herself as she snipped. "People here sit on their ass all day. While *my* people suffer from a sickness that kills almost everyone who gets it. Ardour *has* to have a way they are keeping everyone so healthy. Tonight we get closer to the upper circle. Brothels are prominent fixtures. High-profile people go there every night to decompress. This is where we strike." She spun to look at me, her hair uneven, the sides nearly clipped to the base and the top kept long.

"Okay, Lilja." I gently grabbed the scissors she gripped; her knuckles were white.

Lilja stilled as I began fixing the hair she had just cut. We were so close to each other. I pointed to the empty chair in the living room, instructing her to sit. My chest constricted as I sat on her lap, still trying to fix the hair. Her eyes softened as she stared at me. Her hands rested on my hips.

Snipping the rest of the stray hairs, I tossed the scissors onto the ground. I pulled Lilja into a tight hug. "We will find out what is going on here, I promise."

I searched her eyes and looked down at her full lips, then back into her eyes. I leaned down, capturing her bottom lip, lightly sucking on it. My heart pounded as I moved to kiss down her neck. She breathed erratically; her hands squeezed my soft sides.

My shaking hands went to her trousers, attempting to undo the buttons holding them up.

A hand stopped me. "No."

I looked up, surprised. "Did I do something wrong?" I asked, trying to get off her.

"No, no, it's not that," she said, reaching out to my hands. "I want our first time to be *us*. Not as Ophelee and Zaria. I want it to be as Lilja and Ellie."

Her voice was soft, as if attempting not to scare away a wild animal. My heart melted at her words, and tears sprung to my eyes as she spoke. I nodded, not trusting my voice. She brought my hand to her lips, kissing it.

"Let's get ready for tonight." Her eyes were stern. "It's important that you stay by me and don't leave my sight tonight."

Lilja put together probably the worst outfit I had ever seen. It was revealing and looked downright grubby. We left the apartment right after the sun set letting the streetlamps light our way as we traveled up to the upper circle. The buildings got nicer and nicer as we traveled, stopping only for the carriages to pass. A few people stood talking and smoking outside a large maroon building. Their smoke entered my lungs, making me cough. Lilja gripped my hand. While we slipped inside the looming building, as the men outside stared at us. Their eyes burned holes into my back as the door shut. Loud music emanating from a band in the corner.

Men and women filled the smoky room. Few of them were very obvious workers of the night. Most wore little to no clothing, both men and the women. My eyes widened. I looked at the ground, alarmed. What were we supposed to find here?

"Awww, look, the chubby little mouse is bashful." A male voice boomed behind me. His friends giggled at the comment.

Lilja sucked in a breath.

"Must be her first night here. She even brought her big sister." The men behind him giggled again. His eyes were pink; the power of liquor had overtaken him and his common sense.

"Come here, chubby mouse, let me show you a good time."

He grabbed at my arm, stumbling as he did so, his clammy hands bruising my forearm. Lilja moved quickly, grabbing the man's hand and twisting it. He yelped, cursing at her as the men behind him didn't move.

"It would do you well to not touch her again." Her voice had a deadly edge to it. "Now be on your way, and we will be on ours."

She threw his arm down. It hung down at an awkward angle. He opened and then closed his mouth as he thought better of it. The men behind him backed out of the door, dragging the intoxicated man out of the building.

My eyes were wide as a woman approached us, her hips swaying side to side as if she was doing a mating dance. "I am the owner of this establishment. I can't have you being rough with my customers. With that being said, I can't have the customers messing up my girls either. So I suppose I should thank you. Who are you?" She smacked her lips together like a cow chewing cud. "What are ye' trying to do? Wanna work here?" She grabbed a mug off of a tray held by a less-than-clothed individual.

Lilja sent me a side look. "I'm trying to start a job as a lady of the night. My friend here wants to be a waitress."

A WHAT? My brain swirled with questions, my eyes widened as I stared at the women before me.

"Oh, how fabulous! I could always use new workers. I can see you are prepared to help, but is your friend?" she asked Lilja, giving me a look as if I couldn't hear her.

Unable to voice any pertinent thoughts that were going to make me sound intelligent, all I managed was a mere nod to the brothel owner. *Could I do this? Could Lilja do this?*

"That settles it. Dedra! Get yer sorry ass over here." Her voice cut through the noise of the band and people in the room. A girl smaller than me ran to attention. Tiny and nearly all bones, her brown hair flounced as she bounded towards us with fear in her eyes.

"Yes, ma'am, what do you need, ma'am?" Her high-pitched voice was barely audibly, her eyes downcast.

"You take—wait, I never asked yer name," she looked at me expectantly.

"Oh—ah, my name is Zaria, ma'am." *What have I got myself into?*

"Well, you take this Zaria lady and teach her the ways of waitressing. And you—" She pointed her plump finger at me. "—don't give her no trouble—or you're out. Understand?"

"Yes," *I can already tell this woman was going to be a joy to work with.*

Dedra grabbed my hand, making me jump, dragging to behind the bar.

"First thing first, don't let the customers touch for free. Second rule is, if you spill a drink, you buy it—no exceptions. Third, don't fall in love with the customers, even if you sleep with them and they seem nice. It's a trap. They might have some money, but not enough money." By Dedra's tone, I could tell she knew what she was talking about from experience.

Lilja disappeared into another room with the owner. I craned my neck to keep track of her, but lost her as the curtain swished closed. Dedra explained how to make drinks and take money, all the while simultaneously pushing me out onto the floor. The men were outrageously loud. Music flowed through the room.

My heart beat hard in my chest as I walked through the floor handing out drinks. Dedra had given me a small purse with change, which I placed on my hip. Most of the men were in fancy upper circle clothes, some had medals and specific-colored patches neatly attached.

"Hey there, lil' bunny, why don't ye' bring some of those drinks to me?" A drunken voice slurred behind me. Carefully, I walked to him, trying not to allow the mugs to clink together.

He grabbed the mug, while putting coins on the tray. "As I was saying, men. This," he said, waving his hands in the air, "will all eventually go away. Think about it, this blight can't kill everyone. Even if it kills some people, it's just thinning out the weak."

I rolled my eyes, trying to will this man to be quiet. I moved away from the group, which was now in deep discussion.

"Well, you heard about the conspiracy. It was all planned by the gods to get rid of the Valdisians."

I held my breath, trying to push down the anger rising in my throat. *The gods, the gods don't want this. They want me to stop this. Someone else is causing this bullshit.* Some men grumbled in agreement to the man speaking, some made a face but said nothing.

"I heard it's all because of the water nymphs, that's why the mages couldn't help the Valdisians in the beginning," another man said, his face red and the whites of his eyes a pink color.

If my fake Elven ears could perk up any farther than they already were, they'd spot me for eavesdropping. Instead, I forced myself to walk a circle in the room, still handing drinks out.

"Water nymphs have gone extinct, no one has seen any in hundreds of years," the original man said, his voice rambunctious. With his glass now empty, I eagerly walked over to him, offering another full mug of beer.

"Why thank you, lil' bunny, such excellent service." As he spoke, he wrapped his hands around my waist, pulling me down and onto his lap.

I squeaked, my face burning with embarrassment, eliciting a wave of laughs from the men around the table.

Dedra said from the bar, "Aislen! That's going to cost you, y'know. Girls don't sit for free."

His hand roamed my waist, the other was on my thigh. My skin crawled, bile rose in my throat. He tightened his grip while I squirmed. "I wouldn't do that, bunny. You're gonna get me all excited." I halted my movement, realization hitting me.

I looked down at my tray, careful to make eye contact with the men around the table. Not wanting people to pay attention to me, I wished I could cease to exist and melt into the floor.

"The water nymphs aren't extinct, merely in hiding. I heard they hide up in the Sald Forest."

"That place is haunted. Nobody goes there."

"Exactly, you dense pig head. That's why they hide there. My Da told me he saw one."

"Well, your Da is about as blind as the brothel owner. He can't see two feet in front of him."

"My Da can see, y-you-you prick." The man's voice shook with rising anger. "In his younger years, he had the best vision ever."

"Well, I think your Da is full of pig shit," said the man whose lap I sat on.

Next thing I saw was a mug flying right in my direction. The rough hands holding me captive pushed me towards the ground. The tray I was holding tumbled out of my grasp as I hit the floor, the mugs shattering, spilling the beer.

The two men lunged at each other, throwing punches, both eager to pummel each other. Dedra ran up to the scene, grabbing my shoulders, pulling me up to my feet.

"Gentlemen, unless you want me to burn off the very thing that will continue what I'm sure is a great, prosperous lineage I suggest you take this fight outside—and Aislen, you still need to pay for my employee's time," the brothel owner said from the open curtain, where she and Lilja had disappeared to earlier.

Lilja stood behind her, in less clothing than before, with stain on her lips and powder on her eyelids. Her face was emotionless, but her eyes gave away her feelings. She read the room, her gaze going from me to the men who were previously fighting. Coming to some dark conclusion on her own.

The men each grumbled something unsavory about the brothel owner, but sat back down. Dedra began picking up the pieces of the mugs on the ground. I bent over to help. Careful not to cut myself on the exposed pieces of glass, I tried to listen to the men talk.

"I'm telling ye' regardless of what you think about my Da, the water nymphs aren't extinct and they are hiding in the Sald Forest."

I looked up at Lilja. She was talking to a tall, with dark hair and dark eyes. Patches and pins lined the jacket he wore. I assumed they symbolized his status. Her hand was on his arm. She laughed at something he said. He had a pipe in his hand. Taking a long drag, he passed it to her. My heart beat faster as I saw it meet her lips. She held the smoke, puffing it out in a shape of a circle on the man's face.

He grinned at her and whispered something in her ear. If it was anyone else watching the interaction with them, they wouldn't have noticed the way she stiffened at his words. Pushing whatever reservations she had about the man down deep, Lilja gave a sly grin, grabbing the man's hand and walking behind the curtain.

"Oh, don't ye' worry about her. The madam makes sure the customers are nice," Dedra said to me as if she could read my thoughts. I looked at her in horror as we finished cleaning. *Are they going to do what I think they were going to do?*

My breathing came in quick. *I can't—I can't let her do this. I can't let her do this for her kingdom, or anything else.* My vision tunneled as I threw the glass away in a bin. My heart beat faster and faster as the band in the corner continued to play, as if to hide the noise coming from the back room.

Dedra raised an eyebrow at me as anxious sweat ran down my face. "Are ye' alright?"

I gulped, managing to say, "Yes. I-I'm going to see if they need any help in the back."

Dedra stilled a bit and looked at me with her hands on her hips. "Aye, Lilja wanted this job, girl, and you have a job as a waitress. It ain't none of yer business of what is happening in that room, unless you plan on making it a three-way thing. Which will up the price for the customer, you can ask if he wants another girl or if he wants to switch but if the answer is no, that means no, ye' hear, we might not be high-class people but we have morals."

I nodded in agreement. She had to be saved from herself. *I can't let her do this.* Forcing myself to go at a normal pace, I walked to the curtain, pulling it aside to reveal the unexpected.

19

Scrambled

Lilja stood naked before the man with dark hair; his hair was messed up as if fingers had run through it. His shirt was off, revealing a toned body. Ropes attached his hands to the bed. His mouth was gagged, his dark eyes widened with fear as Lilja stood before him. I held in a gasp as I gazed at her bare back for the first time. Scars littered her back; a few were brutal, jagged marks. They appeared to be purposeful, as if torture was involved. Each scar appeared shiny in the current light. A knife glinted in her hands. *Where did she get that from?*

My entrance to the room went unnoticed.

"Tell me what you know about the blight." Lilja's voice was low as she spoke to him. She held the tip of the knife to his throat. She grappled at the gag pulling it out of his mouth, roughly.

"I-I don't know anything. You're crazy." The sound of the band nearly drowned him out.

"How has Ardour prospered so well as Valdis is getting weakened by the blight?" Lilja pushed the knife tip further, puncturing the first few layers of skin on his neck. A bead of blood formed on the tip, trailing over his Adam's apple and down his chest.

"Wait, please! I have a wife! I don't know anything!"

Lilja didn't let up on the knife while she began talking again, "You're never going to see your wife again if you don't answer my questions. What does the military know about the blight?"

I stood in horror as Lilja interrogated the vulnerable man before her, "I-I don't." He stopped talking as the knife moved, pointing over his thigh, gently, if you could call it that. Lilja pressed the tip into his skin, drawing more blood.

"It's some spell," he said, his voice high with fear.

Lilja lifted the knife out of his thigh, twirling it in her hands. "What do you mean, spell?" she asked, placing a hand on his shoulders, her fingers digging into him.

"There is someone handing out orders to select a few military members, in secret, via crow."

"Who is handing out these orders?" She pressed on.

"Ow! I-I don't know, a bird gets sent out, with instructions. If we refuse, we disappear! I swear! That's all I know, no, please let me go!" He jerked his body around, trying to break free of the bed sheets tying him to the bed.

"Jemp, you know you've helped me a lot. You truly have, but I can't let you leave this room." Lilja clambered onto the bed and behind the man, her knife on his throat. She was prepared to end this man's life. Finally, they noticed me.

His eyes pleaded with me. "Please help me, she's a spy!"

"I...I." My voice died out in my throat as I made eye contact with her. "Maybe we should let him go, as long as he promises to not tell anyone." *Is this the right way to do this?*

Jemp attempted to nod his head in agreement with my words. His movement halted, with Lilja tightening his grip on his hair. "Zaria, we can't let him go. As soon as we do, the first thing he is going to do is run to his boss. We can't let one man live over the lives of many."

Her voice was hard, unmoving.

"I won't, I promise!" His veins throbbed in his neck; his face was red as he strained against the bed sheets.

"We can take him with us! I heard guys talking in the front room. They know where the water nymphs are hiding!" I spoke quickly, desperately trying to talk her off the ledge of killing this man.

"What?" Jemp asked.

Lilja thought for a second, letting her grip on the knife loosen for a second. "Okay, but we get rid of him once we get there, and if you—" She pointed the blade into him again, making another bead of blood fall down his neck. He winced. "Try anything, I will send you back to the gods—early."

Lilja hopped off the bed, snatching her discarded clothes from the ground, clutching her shirt to her chest. She handed me the dagger, grabbing her discarded clothes on the ground to get dressed.

Jemp looked around the room, trying to ignore the woman who had just wanted to kill him. "Thank you," he said. He stared at the dagger in my hands. Following his gaze to the blade in my hand, I stared at the blood on it—his blood.

Lilja spit in the water basin that was in the room. Splashing clean water on her face from the pitcher next to it. The powder rolled off her face in lines. With a discarded sheet, she furiously rubbed the ruined look off.

Lilja grabbed the blade from my hand gently, now fully dressed. Walking forward to the man, she wiped the blood on his pant leg. "Now, I am going to untie you, but if you try to run, I will throw this dagger in your back. Do you understand?"

He nodded, and she slipped the blade underneath the fabric holding him onto the bed. She cut upwards to free him. He rubbed his red bruised wrists with his hand and untied his other hand himself. Lilja threw his shirt at him.

"What now?" I asked, worried about the people in the other room somehow hearing us.

Lilja walked up to me, talking lowly, just to me, "We take him with us and find the water nymphs, maybe they know something about the blight. Where did the men say the nymphs were located?"

"They are hiding in a forest. I think it's called Sald Forest?"

Lilja pulled away from me, her face paling.

"What? What's wrong with that place? The men said it was haunted."

"It is," she said with a gulp.

We forced Jemp to walk between us. I led and Lilja was in the back as we slipped out of the brothel. The men from earlier were still talking in hushed tones. None of them looked up as we slipped past them. The cold autumn air was crisp as we stepped out into the night.

My revealing clothes did very little to cover my chilled skin. I shivered as we hauled Jemp into an alleyway. I blindfolded him at the same time that Lilja bound his hands. He grunted as she tightened them, the cloth she used digging into his skin.

"Where are we going?" he demanded, his voice loud in the quiet night air.

"Be quiet," Lilja hissed at him. "If we get caught because of your loud ass, it will be the end of you."

After what seemed like hours, we made it to the apartment building. The old lady who greeted us on our first day sat sleeping in the chair behind the lobby desk. *Does she just stay in that chair all day?* Her glasses almost falling off as they sat precariously on the tip of her nose. Lilja held Jemp from behind, her hands gripping his biceps so tightly that I was sure it'd leave bruises.

"How are we going to get him up the flights of stairs?" I said, my eyes on the sleeping figure at the desk.

Lilja looked back at me, her earlier facade melting away, giving me a smirk. She swiveled the muscular man around, squatting as she threw him over her shoulder with a grunt. Jemp yelped as she carried him up the steps with ease. I unlocked the door. It swung open with a *thunk*. Lilja placed Jemp down as ceremoniously as a whale walking on land.

I undid his blindfold. He squinted at our temporary home, waiting for his eyes to adjust to the dark room. Lilja struck a match, lighting a candle, carrying it over to the table in the room's corner. Unfurling the map on the table, she bent over it, the light of the flame highlighting the curve of her muscles.

The last couple of weeks of a well-balanced diet had done her well. Her form—which had been almost too skinny—had filled out. Her womanly figure showed her strength. Every part of her body showed the diligence the queen had towards keeping her body for battle.

Pointing to the map, she called me over. Her finger lay on a large patch of land, a lake surrounded by trees. The map's drawings suggested it was on a higher elevation than the one we currently sat at. Sald Forest had a plethora of rivers flowing out of it, spreading into the continent like the tendrils of a spider web.

"This is where we are going. We leave tonight." Lilja's voice was hard, the hair on her arms was raised.

I raised my eyebrow at her. It was unusual for her fear to manifest outwards. "Why is the Sald Forest considered haunted?" I asked her.

Jemp whirled his head to stare at us.

"We're actually going to the Sald Forest? Do you have a death wish?" Fear dripped from his words; his eyes were wide in shock.

Lilja gave me a look. "People who go to Sald Forest rarely come out. If they come out, they cannot assimilate back into the world. Their brains are scrambled—"

"They are more than just scrambled. The elves who come out of that forest can't even remember their own names," Jemp interjected, his voice distant.

"We have to go. The water nymphs disappeared the same time the blight showed up. They have to know something about it. We don't have a choice." Lilja searched my eyes for a protest against the idea. Not seeing one, she began throwing items from our life in the Capital in a bag, along with clothes and other supplies. Our "house" began to look as bare as when we first moved in.

The sun had just risen above the buildings as we dropped the keys off at the lobby desk. The older elf still snored, slumped over in her chair. I rummaged in my pocket, pulling coins out; I dumped them on the quickly written note that stated we wouldn't be back and to sell all the belongings that remained.

We grabbed our horses from stables, Lilja laid Jemp on his stomach over the sides of her saddle. We rode north and out of the Capital just as people rose to complete the tasks of everyday life. I looked back at the Capital as we left. The city where Lilja and I had gotten to play pretend got smaller and smaller as we raced towards the hopeful answer to the blight that was decimating the land Lilja grew up in. While I hadn't fully explored Valdis, her people—my friend—pushed down the fear in my throat. For them I would do this, I would save them.

20

Sald Forest

A small village came into view as we travelled. The sun stood in the center of the sky. Dark circles sat on top of Liljas' usual pale skin. I cringed to think about what my face looked like. Jemp upgraded his original situation of being hung over the saddle like a fresh kill. He now walked beside Lady, his hands bound and tied to Lilja's saddle.

"Let's stop here for a few hours, sleep for the rest of the day, and travel the whole way in the dark. We all will need our rest for the upcoming days, so let's get to work." Lilja said with a yawn and a stretch.

Silently, I thanked the gods, unsure if I could have kept going after working all throughout the night. A village called Hellow sat alongside the river, with large docks on either side. Men and women both worked on the side of the river, systematically pulling nets out of the water. The village was small, and the end of the village houses were visible, even from where we were on the path as we neared the edge of the town's limits. The men and women working by the water paid us little to no mind, singing a song to help synchronize their work.

Just before we entered the village limits, we stopped, allowing the horses to graze off the grass beside the road. I got off of Lady with a huff, stretching my joints, which were screaming from sitting in the saddle all day.

"Where are we going to sleep? I don't see an inn." Jemp plopped down on the ground, wheezing. Dark hair plastered to his face, sweat glistened on his brow and soaked his shirt.

"Zaria and I are going to sleep in a tent by the river." Internally, I sighed as Lilja spoke. *How long were we going to keep up the personas?*

"What about me?" Jemp scooted away from us, as far as the rope tied to Liljas' horse would allow.

"Don't worry, I'm not planning on killing you. Well, unless you try to do something stupid." Lilja dismounted.

I threw the tent pack on the ground, unrolling it. Lilja sighed, her eyes closed. Strain showed on her face, sweat beaded on her hairline as a tent made of clay erupted from the earth.

I looked at her in surprise as she grabbed Jemp by the collar of his shirt and threw him in— "WAIT!" Jemp squirmed against her hold.

Lilja crossed her arms looking at him, "what do you need?"

"What if I have to pee?" he asked, attempting to look as meek as possible.

"Well, if you have to pee, go pee. I made your house for the night out of dirt." Lilja said in a hollow, snarky tone.

He gasped as her muscular arms threw him in, grunting as she put the door up. She built the door like bars, allowing air to flow in. I raised my eyebrow and gave her a look. "Are you really going to make him soil himself if nature calls?"

With her back to him, she grinned at me, mouthing *no*. "Only if he pisses me off." We went to work, setting up the rest of the temporary camp. All the while, Jemp complained loudly. His feet hurt—he was cramped—he needed to pee.

Lilja groaned, plopping down on the ground, stretching her feet towards the fire. "Ugh, my feet are killing me. I'm entirely too old to be doing all-nighters sober."

"Ma'am, aren't you young by the standards of elves?" I joined her, stretching dramatically on the blanket placed down earlier.

"You talk as if you are also not an elf." Jemp wrapped his fingers around the sturdy clay bars. His eyes were wide with curiosity.

Shit, I thought to myself. "Ha, I'm about as Elven as they get." I looked to Lilja for help, panic clear in my body language.

"What do you want to eat, Zaria?" Lilja interrupted my feeble attempt to diffuse the situation I got myself into. I looked at her, giving her a grateful smile, silently thanking her for the question.

"We have jerky and I suppose we can find something in town to buy." She rummaged through her bag. Lilja threw jerky at Jemp. He snatched it from the air with ease.

"No, the less attention we cause for ourselves, the better, plus I doubt they will take kindly to us kidnapping mister military over there." I nodded my head towards Jemp.

Lilja nodded in understanding, and then crawled into the small tent we set up. "Come on, you can eat later. Come cuddle."

I rolled my eyes but listened, allowing her to pull me into a warm hug. Her arms snaked around my body.

"I don't want to hear any gay shit going on in there. If I do I'm going to sing, so unless you want to be serenaded by my lovely voice…" Jemp trailed off as I laughed. Lilja soon joined in the laughter, dramatically kissing my cheeks as I trailed off into blissful sleep.

I awoke to the sounds of crickets and an owl hooting into the night air. Lilja stirred next to me, still asleep. I yawned, crawling out of the tent, and stretching. Jemp slept slumped into his temporary clay jail, asleep. I broke down our camp, taking advantage of the quiet. Lilja stirred as I smothered the rest of the fire. She took a deep breath, returning the clay jail back into the earth. Jemp's sleeping body slumped into the ground with a thump. He groaned. Turning his back onto the ground, he zeroed his eyes on Lilja.

"Was that really necessary? Couldn't you just wake me up before you made me kiss the ground?" He struggled to get up, still bound at the hands. I walked over to him, looping my arm under his armpit, hauling him up with a grunt.

"Well, you didn't seem to mind it when L—Ophelee was kissing on me earlier before we went to bed," I said back.

Silently, I cursed myself for almost slipping up. Jemp didn't appear to notice. He stiffened under my touch, mumbling thanks as I finished righting him. After we put the tent away, we were on our way, traveling north to Sald Forest.

As we traveled, the land changed to less and less farmland, becoming more undeveloped. Hours passed. The road we were traveling on transformed from paved brick to dirt, the path becoming narrow, only allowing for one horse at a time. Dense vegetation covered each side of the path. The sound of animals dwindled.

The vegetation appeared to be varying shades of green and blue hues, unlike anything from the Human Realm. We approached a clearing as we rode on. A wall of trees lined the horizon, marking the entrance to Sald Forest. Stars sprinkled throughout the sky, the moon once again full, illuminating the space before us. Sitting up, I peered around the clearing that was empty save for us three. The air felt heavy as fog settled; the land filled with uneasiness.

Hm, this forest is awfully welcoming, I thought as we pushed forward. I shot Lilja an uneasy glance.

"Stay close, guys. For the first time in a while, I-I don't have a plan."

Jemp looked at her, alarmed— Lilja's statement alarmed even this man who we had not known for a while.

"How does this forest scramble the minds of those who enter?" My voice wavered slightly as anxiety crept into my chest.

"It's said the trees here whisper to the people who enter, feeding on the doubt they have—" Lilja said as Jemp interrupted.

"There are supposed to be monsters that live here, making people disappear. The previous victims haunt the forest. They have been witnessed in multiple sightings from people passing by." His voice was low as he spoke, as if the monster he spoke of was going to come and attack. Jemp looked around, clutching his hands together, his knuckles white with strain.

We moved forward, two old trees woven together marking our point of entry. I sucked in my breath as we dismounted, walking through them, holding onto a myth my mother told me. She used to say that holding your breath means demons cannot enter you. The forest was dark, the leaves and the tall branches from the trees blocking out nearly all the light the moon tried to provide for us. Moss grew underfoot. The only evidence of a path through was a game path created by an animal, the moss worn away to nothing.

The forest was quiet, save for our footsteps, eerily so. Jemp walked right next to Lady on the other side of me, as if he was using my horse as a shield for whatever upcoming dangers awaited us. Lilja was at the front, her shoulders tensed, ready to strike at anything that came our way.

A branch broke. I paused just long enough to look around. Jemp and Lilja kept going. I sped up again with a slight jog to catch back up. "Did you hear that?" I asked Lilja, trying to keep my voice low. She gave a slight nod but said nothing as we continued.

Another branch crunched underfoot, Lady neighed nervously, stomping her hooves. Lilja looked back at her, alarmed. I patted Lady's neck, attempting to calm her. Lady looked at me as if she was trying to tell me something. Tentatively we continued, each step feeling like one step closer to the truth.

"Untie me if we get caught. I-I'll have no way to defend myself,"

Jemp pleaded, his eyes darting around the forest.

I looked at Lilja expectantly.

"We will protect you." Lilja stared ahead, not sparing Jemp a look.

"Plus, there is no guarantee that you won't turn on us as soon as we take your bindings off."

She was right, but so was he. The forest was unpredictable. My heartbeat echoed in my ears. I half expected Lilja to hear it as it bumped hard in my chest. *Something is here, something is here, SOMETHING IS CLOSE*, my inner voice screamed out at me. Lilja halted, walking back to me as if she could hear my thoughts.

She stayed silent, but her face portrayed an unasked question of *what's close?*

I mouthed, *I don't know.* "Something doesn't feel right."

The sound of rustling erupted from the left, then a growl.

We froze, waiting. I turned my head towards the sound. Darkness met me. *Something is close, something is here, watch out,* my inner voice yelled again just as a large Ossory wolf lunged at us. A scream crawled up my throat involuntarily. I stumbled back, running into Lady. She jumped up on her hind legs. Jemp let out a yelp, falling on his butt.

Lilja unsheathed her sword from her hip, swinging it at the beast. Its eyes were blue, almost human-like. I lunged towards Jemp, hauling his ass back up to standing. *He's going to die if I leave him tied up*, I thought to myself as my shaky hands were already untying him as Lilja fought the beast before us. I looked at him as the last knot came undone, pleading with him not to kill us as I had just freed him. His panicked eyes met mine, and he nodded, rubbing his bruised wrists.

For a moment I thought he was grabbing my hands in appreciation as I had just made his chance of survival greater. Instead, he gripped my wrists roughly, swinging my whole body towards the fight. I let out a curse at him. Jemp grinned at me as he turned around and disappeared into the dark forest at night. My body hit the ground. I rolled to a stop against a tree trunk. I gasped as all the air from my lungs escaped.

Faintly, I could hear my name being called. I stared at the top of the tree I was under, dazed. Once there was a sufficient amount of air in my lungs, I sat up, my head swimming. Lilja continued to fight. The Ossory wolf was mutilated. Blood dripped down the side of its fur. Lilja was covered in scrapes, and the trousers she wore had a rip exposing her pale skin to the night.

She swung again. The wolf backed up its butt in my direction. I froze as it inched closer to me, my fight-or-flight instincts disappearing in the circling air, as if the tree I leaned on was begging me to stay with it. *Stay with us forever,* it seemed to whisper. The beast—no longer wanting to fight with Lilja—turned. Unfortunately, I was now in its path.

21

Murder?

For a split second, it was as if time had frozen as the wolf registered I was in front of it. Its eyes were angry and hurt. Its breathing was heavy, the chilly air turning its exhales into steam, so close I could smell it.

Lilja yelled from behind the beast, "Run!"

My senses finally came back to me. I scrambled up, wincing at the splinters in my back from the tree. I spared her a second glance as I ran into the night. The only sounds in the forest was my heavy breathing as I got farther and farther from the wolf. *I am getting really tired of running for my life.*

Curved tree trunks butted out in every direction, making my run for it a precarious one. I ran through them like a serpent slithering through tall grass in a swamp. The wolf's breathy pants were coming closer and closer. With the tree's large, broad leaves in the way, the moon's light couldn't get through. Fog permeated the trees, making visibility slim. Heavy footsteps thundered after me, crunching on the leafy debris that blanketed the forest floor. The wolf's shadow began to creep up on me as if Runen the god of death had reared his head to take me with him. I glanced behind my shoulder as the wolf snarled, jumping over the curved trunks with ease as it came after me, its prey. Lilja's footsteps followed us as I ran; her steps sounded desperate, a series of curses trailing out of her mouth.

Branches and bushes cut into me, slicing my skin, the moss underfoot slippery with dew. Looking around, desperately searching for somewhere to hide from this beast. "Watch out!" Lilja said as a rock flew in my direction, I assumed, narrowly missing the wolf. I crouched instantly, still moving, trying to keep up my speed before straightening back out. Lilja cursed behind me, as a *thunk* sounded. I turned, alarmed, just in time to see the wolf's body hurdle towards me. Lilja let out a scream.

The Ossory wolf fell with a thud in front of my feet as it whimpered, attempting to scramble up. I peered out into the dark, mysterious forest; curtains of moss hung off the trees, blocking my view of Lilja. The beast stood up as I wasted precious seconds. Its fur color was unrecognizable; it stood covered in blood and mud. Slobber dripped down its snarling monstrous grin, launching itself at me.

Instinct took over. I lifted my arms up in an *x*, trying to cover my throat. Its teeth came down with a sickening crunch. My skin hung oddly off my arm, and blood poured freely down my arm.

I let out a blood-curdling scream as it lifted its head and my body at the same time. *Why, why was I so useless? Lilja is risking her life and I am over here dying.*

"*Lilja!*" I screamed out into the night sky as the wolf dragged me. Its spit ran down my arm, as if it was salivating for the chance to eat me. *Why wasn't it eating me, already?*

My eyes grew heavy as the blood began to leave my body in copious amounts. The smell of iron filled my nostrils as the blood dripped, mixing with the musty wet dog scent of its fur. Twigs and rocks scratched at my legs as they dragged on the damp earth. My feeble attempt to kick myself out of the beast's mouth went ignored. Weakly,

I smacked its face, attempting to poke out its eye.

It grunted at me as if to say not to do that anymore. I could have sworn it rolled its eyes at me. Anxiety shot through me as I wondered if wolves played with their food before killing it. The world seemed to tilt as we continued to what I assumed was its den. *I'm dying,* I thought as the world swirled into darkness as my eyes fluttered closed.

Pain. All I felt was pain. I attempted to scream out to voice my discomfort, but no sound rippled through my lips. I struggled to open my eyes, but it was as if I glued them shut.

"Did you have to break her arm, Cerious?" a feminine voice said. "What is the king going to say?"

"She's lost too much blood." A frantic voice said in a hushed tone. "Is she going to die? Shit, the king is going to kill us. He just said to bring them to him, not to kill them."

"The other one was much easier to catch. He barely put up a fight after he pushed the fat one to me." His voice was sheepish, like a child who got caught stealing candy.

A thump resonated in the room, followed by an "ow" from who I assume was Cerious.

"Where is the other girl?" said the original feminine voice.

"I knocked her out. She's in the other room." The frantic voice said their tone, calmer than before. A warm hand pushed my hair out of my face, snagging it on my prosthetic ear, pulling it with the strands of hair. A gasp erupted from her mouth as the fake elf ear tip fell to the ground.

"She's fucking human?" Cerious demanded.

"Shit, she will not heal like us. If we don't do something, she's going to die!"

"We have to get the queen, she can heal her!" The frantic voice called out, now more frantic and alarmed than before. Scrambling sounds moved through the room, a door closing.

"Oh, little human. I'm sorry this has happened to you. Things just got out of hand," the feminine voice said as they put a warm rag on my head as I drifted back out of consciousness.

I did not know how much time had passed since I was last conscious. It must have been only a few minutes before the door slammed open. A scrawny young man and a tall, pale woman stepped through the threshold. I squinted at them, my eyes attempting to make sense out of the dimmed room.

Lilja, where's Lilja? I twisted my head around, scanning the room for her. My head swam with the movement.

"What did you three do?" The pale woman kneeled down beside the bed. Her eyes went wide with surprise as she saw my ears. She quickly attempted to make her face neutral. She winced at the rough bandage my kidnappers used to wrap my wounds. Blood had already begun seeping through the white bandage and onto the blanket covering the bed.

"Where is—" I croaked out, my voice hoarse from screaming.

"Shush, don't talk right now." The pale woman interrupted me. Her thin fingers gently began unwrapping my arm, prodding the spot where the bone had jutted out, almost protruding from my skin.

Her fingers were blue. *I must be hallucinating.* Swirls traveled up her exposed arms. My head was swimming as I followed the lines. "I-I need Lilja. I-I-I'm so tired." I yawned, my eyelids heavy. "Lilja, I'm so cold."

Lilja, Lilja, where are you? I th-think I'm dying, my mind wanders, even my inner voice failing to make sense of the situation I found myself in.

"Stay awake, sweetie," the pale lady said.

A crash erupted from the other side of the room, following with some grunts. The long-haired man's body launched through the door. He hit the wall with a thud, sliding down onto the floor with a grunt. Everyone paused for a second, and shouting erupted as Lilja limped into the room. Her chest moved up and down rapidly, breathing hard, her knuckles bleeding and her body bruised from the fight.

She zeroed in on me, her face softening. Lilja stumbled over to me, the tip of her sword dragging on the ground. She cupped my face, leaning down, tears streaming down her cheeks, pulling away as she scanned my wounds, her skin white with fear. *What are you scared of?* I thought as she pointed her knife at the pale woman kneeling before me.

"What are you doing to her?" she said, the sword wavering with exhaustion.

"Oh, put that away, young elf. I do not wish to hurt her. My subjects only meant to bring you to a meeting with the king. His subjects did not mean for things to get so out of hand, right, Cerious, darling?"

The pale woman narrowed her eyes at the long-haired man as he nodded furiously.

"Intentions mean nothing if she is still laying there in a pool of her own blood."

"Fear not, I am a water mage. I will heal her. However, only if you stand down, Queen Lilja of Valdis." The pale woman's voice was soft, however, even behind the warm tone there was a double-edge sword behind it.

Lilja faltered, wavering slightly as her true identity was exposed, thanks to my incoherent mumbles. The water mage looked at me as I lay on the cot, bleeding.

"This may hurt, my child, for I am not accustomed to healing humans." She grabbed my injured arm with one hand, placing the palm of her other hand on my forehead.

I sucked in a breath as her brown eyes began shining white; her hands were so cold to the touch that they burned uncomfortably on my fragile skin. My muscles and bone shifted without my permission. My skin stitched itself together, the bone moving back into place. A scream rang out of the room. I was unaware if it was me or someone else watching this horror unfold. Wood slivers from Jemp's betrayal popped out of my back one by one. Scratches from the branches and twigs that ate at my skin disappeared.

My blood rushed to my ear with a dull roar, my pain subsiding with it. Lilja gave a breath of relief, her color coming back to her skin. She dabbed the sweat on my brow with a rag, discarding the sword in her hands. Tentatively, she kissed my forehead.

"I'm sorry," I said with tears threatening to fall. "I let your name slip."

Lilja laughed, kissing my forehead again. "Ellie, you almost died and you're apologizing to me."

"While this is beautiful to watch, the king still awaits your audience." The water mage wiped her hands on a discarded piece of cloth.

"How did he know we were here? Where's Jemp? Who are you?" Lilja asked.

After my healing, her body appeared to be reinvigorated, and I leaned on her for support. While the wounds on the outside of my body were healed, the blood I'd lost wasn't back yet. The room still swirled with every movement, and my eyes focused and unfocused as we began walking with the mysterious water mage. Skillfully, she ignored our questions, giving us an unnecessary tour of our surroundings.

The night sky slowly began to give way to the morning light's orange and pink tones. The sound of rushing water blissfully filled the air, making it impossible for small talk. We were on the outside of a castle, in a semi-outside covered hallway. I assumed it was for the hot, damp air to move freely throughout the building without it getting stuffy. Green vines covered the arches, and large waterfalls faced the side, misting our faces, making the cobblestone floor slick, moss growing in some spaces.

Creatures floated by; they had green skin flowers and leaves sprouted from their hair. Lilja stared at them, her eyes wide with surprise. She mouthed to me *"forest nymph."* The water mage walked in front of us and the three elves responsible for us being there walked behind us. I scowled. *I can't help feeling like a prisoner,* I thought. Lilja tightened her grip on me as two large doors opened, revealing the throne room.

Stained glass filled one side of the room, and colored streams of light decorated the ground. On the other was a large tapestry depicting water nymphs and a creature I assumed was a forest nymph. Opposite of the door lay two large chairs; a dark-skinned man occupied one. Tight curls hung down to his shoulders, streaks of gray revealed his age, and his eyes were green like sea foam. "Hello travelers, the animals have talked much about your adventure."

"The animals?" I asked, unable to hold my tongue. "Your highness," I said, straightening up, standing on my own.

"Ah yes, you are unfamiliar with the abilities of the water and forest nymphs, since we have been in hiding for 400 years. Longer than both of you have been alive, I might add. I see you have already met my beautiful wife, Pelicia." His voice was loud and deep, resonating in the room with an echo.

"Elowen Alwyn, a human in the Elven Realm, you have caused a commotion with my people. For you and your team have killed two of us."

Pelicia walked up to the throne, giving the king a kiss, taking her seat beside them and putting her hand on his thigh. Lilja and I both looked at each other. *Two people? We haven't killed anyone... have we?*

The king looked at us in disgust, scoffing, turning his head to the side, his gaze upon Pelicia. "They do not even know what I speak of," he snarled.

"Dear, they are unaware of our abilities. Their team was defending themselves. After all, Jalen and Kemil did attack." Pelicia gripped her husband's thigh tighter.

I racked my brain for hints of what they were talking about. Two people? Abilities? Lilja mumbled to herself under breath behind me, and then stepped forward.

Bowing low, she said, "I'm under the impression you speak about the Ossory Wolves by Delias Inn?"

"Yes, so you know you murdered my people. See, Pelicia, and you think we should save them," the king grumbled, banging his wooden staff on the ground.

Murdered? The wolves, those monsters we killed, were people? I killed someone?

22

A Deal with a Nymph

I stumbled back a few steps, enough to garner a look from Lilja. The king gave me a sickening grin, nodding as if to himself. "Ah, so you truly did not know of your manslaughter against our kind?"

I shook my head at a loss for words. Lilja's voice chimed into the silence that had settled on to the room. "Your highness, if we had known the wolves were citizens of Sald Forest, things would have ended differently. Perhaps we could have found an alternate way to deal with the strike. However, they attacked us without provocation. With that in mind, the upper circle should know then that it is the two individuals' fault they were slain."

An audience had begun to build in the room, the upper circle began streaming into the room. Curiosity rolled off of them in waves, each of them eager and noisy to see how this interaction would play out.

A gasp erupted from the crowd, followed by shouts of outrage. The king rubbed his chin. *"Silence,"* he said, his voice echoing in the stone room, effectively silencing the crowd.

Pelicia spoke out, her voice soft yet projecting through the crowd with ease. "Unfortunately, it is true, citizens of Sald. Jalen and Kamil spent far too long in their spiritual forms. The animalistic desire was too much to ignore. For lack of better words, they went savage." Another murmur rolled through the crowd, silenced by a raised hand from the king. "I am sure we are all saddened by the loss of Jalen and Kamil. We have already handed the punishment out," Pelicia said.

I fought the urge to raise an eyebrow at her statement. *Punishment? We didn't walk to the king for an audience with him, we walked into a courtroom. Where we were the bad guys.*

"We have come to talk to the community of water and forest nymphs that have dwelled here for the last 400 years," I said, attempting to keep the crowd from turning into a mob situation.

Lilja nodded at my comment. "Yes, we have. We believe they may have some insight into a situation we are researching."

"You come searching for answers for the blight," the king said.

"Yes, the blight has been ravaging my kingdom for far too long. It is high time we find the cure for it. As I'm sure you know, the blight has mutated, not only infecting plants but people as well." Lilja's voice was loud, her intentions clear. She would not leave without seeing and speaking to the nymphs face to face.

The crowd seemed unfazed by the information of the blight. Pelicia was the first to move.

"Creatures of the upper circle, I can assure you these people have come here with good intentions. You're dismissed," Pelicia said. I could have sworn she added *imbeciles* under her breath. Upper circle members filtered out quickly, a few of them mumbling loudly.

"Let me show you where they congregate. Theatrics aren't really my thing." Pelicia pinched the bridge of her nose as the last of them filtered and left.

"No, really, I couldn't tell," the king said, a grin resting on his face.

Lilja and I both looked at each other in surprise.

"Sorry about all that. The upper circle here is a pain in my ass. They truly think they have a say in the law. I apologize for the altercation last night. Our intentions were just to scare you a little. Missed the mark a bit—"

"A bit? I nearly died," I said.

There was a pause. "True, but you didn't. My beautiful wife saved you. My connections in the rest of the world failed to mention that you were human. If you truly were an elf, you would not have been captured so easily. Humans are frail."

Internally, I rolled my eyes. *Really, this was his reasoning, that I was frail?*

"Queen Lilja and Elowen, let's go before my husband ruins the mood." Pelicia stood from her throne, her long blue dress shimmering as the colored lights from the stained glass reflected on the fabric.

The king's hand tightened on his staff as we crossed into the hallway. "We have lived in this forest for hundreds of years. Seems odd that we finally get outsiders in the castle."

"What about the people who have set foot in the forest and whose mind has become scrambled?" Lilja asked, walking beside me.

Pelicia descended the spiral steps at the end of the hall, her voice echoing off the stone. "The people who come here with bad intentions are the ones who come out scrambled, others who have *disappeared* into Sald Forest have stayed on their own free will."

"Where is Jemp?" I asked, as the realization of his absence hit me. Lilja stiffened beside me but said nothing as she waited for Pelicia to answer.

"Oh, the young elf who betrayed you? Sald Forest does not take kindly to people that only try to save themselves, by killing others in the process. In addition to that crime, which is punishable by a stay in the Forest Nymph Prison, he attempted to murder one of the gardeners for their plow horse. Undoubtedly trying to flee back to Ardour. Don't worry, the king and I have already handed out his sentence. His trial was not as pretend as yours, believe me," she said.

The sun had illuminated the once-dark forest we entered. It was full of life. Large animals meandered through game paths; a large stag passed in front of our path with no urgency. Flowers and vines decorated the large antlers on its head with grace.

The sound of rushing water increased as we encroached on a large lake that their castle overlooked. Waterfalls cascaded down the mountainside, and large rocks pushed through the surface of the water, creating a resting area for water nymphs, who sunbathed on the mossy rocks. Lilja looked at me, grinning, her smile reaching her eyes with child-like excitement.

The water nymphs all appeared different, few of them with the lower half of a large fish. Others were blue in skin tone, their hair appearing drenched. Their clothes were tattered and lacked color, as if they were sun-bleached.

Pelicia walked in front of us, holding up her inked hands in the air, gathering the nymphs' attention.

"Nymphs! The queen and her—" she said, giving me a sideways glance. "Her friend has gotten word that you may know something about the blight."

The nymphs began whispering among themselves. I gave Lilja a worried glance. Pelicia turned her attention to us, speaking lowly, "The nymphs are not citizens of Sald Forest, merely visitors. Who have become visitors for far too long. They are mysterious creatures, ones obsessed with riddles and secrets. Be careful when you speak to them, one wrong word and they can have you ensnared in their hold."

Pelicia attempted to keep her face light and void of the emotions in her words, careful to hide her warning from the nymphs a few feet away.

Lilja nodded, her hand absentmindedly grabbing onto the hilt of the sword she wore on her hip. My head pounded with anxiety as Pelicia walked away, her gown billowing in the wind as did so. I gulped, taking in a big breath of air as we walked forward. The nymphs halted their conversation and murmurs as we neared. All of their eyes were on us with anticipation.

"Answers 400 years lost may be. Curious seek now when answers sooner could be saved," a voice rasped out, sounding gurgled as if they had drowned. The talking water nymph moved forward, their skin lighter than the rest.

I paused for a moment, trying to decipher what they meant. "We are seeking answers for the blight as new information has come to light. We hope to solve the problem that is plaguing the Kingdom of Valdis." Lilja nodded at my statement as she stared at the speaking water nymph.

"My name you know not, yet big price answer for manners no, *her friend*," her bluish tint lips spoke out, echoing in my ears. I winced at the jumble of words she spit out at me, trying to decipher them in my head as Lilja spoke from beside me.

"My companion's name is Elowen. We would like to know why you came to congregate in Sald Forest."

The nymphs looked at each other murmuring amongst themselves and spoke, "Congregate not trapped, yes."

Trapped? Pelicia said nothing about them being trapped here.

"Who trapped you here?" Lilja took a step forward.

"Forced threat."

"Forced threat by who?" Lilja pushed her hands into fists at her side. I could feel her anger rising as I stood behind her.

"Darkness in a skin. Creatures of evil congregate around chomping. Evil are we aye, but worse things them around. Destruction is wish. Wish entire world gone, want to rise. Rule and rise." Her cryptic, echoing voice reverberated in my ears. Lilja and I were silent as we dissected the words the nymph gave us.

"Someone is threatening to hurt all the nymphs if you don't stay here?" I asked.

She gave us a silent nod.

"The person who is doing this is evil and dark creatures are his companions?" Lilja's voice rang out.

Another nod.

"Who is this person? Are they the reason for the blight?" I questioned, stepping forward to be beside Lilja.

"Know not who. Blight, yes." She walked towards us, leaving wet footprints in her wake.

"What did he do to start the blight? How do we stop it? It's killing people faster than before!" I all but shouted at the nymphs. Lilja's hand snuck over to grasp mine, attempting to calm my erratic breathing.

The nymph nodded solemnly, "Threat cannot."

"They have forbidden you from telling us about it?" Lilja said slowly.

Another nod. "Show can," she hissed out. "Price needed."

I took a step back. Price? *Price for what?*

"How can you show us?" Lilja said, standing her ground like an unmoving rock.

"Vision," the nymph replied as if it was the easiest answer in the world.

"What is your price? Do you want gold? Land? Title? I am a queen. I can give you nearly anything you can desire. Show me the vision and I will reward you, I assure you." Lilja spoke urgently, her voice showing how eager she was to get the answer for the blight that was killing her people.

A cackle escaped the nymph's blue lips. "Show you cannot. Her I show." She pointed her spindly finger at me.

My heartbeat in my chest painfully, as if my heart was constricted to limited space. "What is your price?" My voice was barely above a whisper. I didn't trust it to go any louder, fearing it would crack and show the fear I felt rising in my throat.

"Scared rightfully, wish I do not see again." The water nymphs' speaker paced, though whether in fear or thoughtfulness, I didn't know. She looked at me up and down, settling on my left hand.

She wants my hand? "Token is want, love."

"You want my ring?" I looked down at the intricate ring that sat perfectly on my hand. The blue stone sparkled in the rising sunlight. I gave Lilja a pained look. Her face was hard, her near perfect *mask* back into place.

But this was just for being undercover. I'm not sure this falls under the love token category. I thought, as Lilja mumbled something under her breath. *But it was my ring.* I winced as the other pained thought crossed my mind. I held out my hand to the nymph before me. Greedily, she grabbed at it. I winced as she twisted it off of my plump fingers, roughly.

She held it up to the light, watching it sparkle before putting it on a strand of her hair, tying it into place. "Show me," I said, still watching my ring swing in the nymph's hair.

"In water must go, show on land cannot," the nymph said. Grabbing onto my now bare hand, she began pulling me into the water.

"Wait!" Lilja shouted. "You never said you had to take her into the water to show her! She's human. She can't breathe underwater like you!"

"Asked never, you did," nymph said, shrugging her shoulders. "Die she won't, unless wants to," she said, turning to me to grin, her mouth full of sharp pointy teeth resembling a shark.

Lilja grabbed onto my hand. "We can find another way. You don't have to do this."

"Yes, I do." I said, jerking my hand from her grasp. "We don't have a choice. I can't have more people die because we delayed finding answers." I gave her a small smile, trying to reassure her. "Sorry about the ring," I blurted out as the nymph pulled me deeper into the water. It was now up to my waist. I shivered as a breeze pulled through the treetops and over the water, as if it were urging me to accept the vision the nymph was trying to show me.

"I—" Lilja said as my head went under water.

23

The Past Held in a Rock

I gasped as I went under the frigid water, air bubbles escaping my mouth, fighting their way to the surface. The water nymph swam farther and farther down with incredible speed. Her skin became translucent, almost invisible in the water. As if she was becoming water herself. My lungs burned as I struggled to fight the urge to breathe in the murky water. The temptation to inhale the water like air grew stronger with each swimming stroke of my body.

Visibility at the bottom of the lake was minimal, the movement we created disturbing the surrounding sediment, making it flow with us as she pulled me along. My heart beat uncomfortably in my chest. *I can't—I can't breathe*, I thought. Without being able to fight the urge any longer, I let out another gasp of air, inhaling the water unconsciously. I gagged, the pounding in my chest feeling impossibly loud. The nymph slowed, turning towards me. As if she could feel my body betraying me.

Stupid girl, her voice said in my head. She pulled me closer, grabbing onto my face. Her lips were suddenly on mine, blowing air into my lungs.

My eyes widened with surprise as she pulled away. *Yes, projecting thoughts in your head I can. Communication water important is, nymphs a lot talk. Name is Sylp.*

Turning away from me, she began pulling me once again towards a large mouth cave. Plants grew around the side, stones piled on the lake floor as if for a path. They had stacked stones upon each other into pillars guiding our way into the cave. Sylp began pushing me forward into the darkness of the cave.

Sylp banged her fist on the side of the cave, making the rocks rumble and light up in reply. The cave lit up, revealing paintings covering every available surface. The paintings depicted the past of the water nymphs.

Place is sacred, Sylp said. As I looked at the wall with wonder. Sylp grabbed a glowing rock, rubbing the sediment and algae off of it. The rock was the size of my palm. In any ordinary circumstance, it would look like a normal rock. But it gave off a ghoulish green glow.

Past will show, this will. Sylp swam near me again, grabbing my neck to once again put her lips on mine. She blew another lung full of air into my mouth, grabbing my hand, placing it on the stone.

The stone glowed brighter once my skin contacted it, fading everything to black. Suddenly lights passed us repeatedly, as if the sun was setting in rapid ascension.

Going backwards, the world is. Sylp projected into my head as we stood side by side, our hands still on the glowing rock.

Stay silent and do not touch, past see us cannot. Hear can, she said, placing the rock down. Sylp pulled us out of the cave, towards the surface.

This would be a good time for me to know how to swim, I thought as she pulled me along. I gasped as I hit the surface, the fresh air welcoming itself into my lungs like an old friend.

"Along come, Elowen. Time not have we," Sylp hissed.

I looked back at the rock where Lilja was standing 400 years later.

My heart ached as I wondered what she had been trying to say as Sylp had pulled me under the water.

Sylp swam away from me, beckoning me to follow her as I struggled to keep afloat. My arms felt as if they were rocks weighing me down.

"Wait." My voice was barely above a whisper; I was afraid for the ghosts of the past to hear my plea.

Sylp paused, looking back at my struggling form.

"I can't swim," I said.

Sylp scoffed, swimming back for me, mumbling something about humans being a useless pound of flesh. *In my case, a few more pounds than necessary,* I thought as she dragged me along like a puppy. I huffed a sigh of relief as I crawled on to dry land.

Dry land. Sylp stood up, lending her hand to me, helping me up. I gave her a grateful smile.

I followed behind her. She began walking deeper and deeper into the forest. The land before us was nearly unrecognizable from the present day. Sald Castle, which now stood behind us, looked grand and fresh. Moss had yet to grow on the sides of the wall facing the waterfall it fed the lake with. The Sald Forest still appeared old, however, a few of the trees appeared young. Their skinny trunks tried to reach for the sunlight that filtered through the leaves of the older trees. We walked in silence as we continued. Sylp looked around nervously as we went.

We followed a river branching off from the lake. The water was clear, revealing the riverbed. Fish and other small animals rustled in the water towards the lake for more shelter. *Shelter from what?* Shouts interrupted the otherwise quiet forest. Sylp and I looked at each other in alarm, running towards the shouts.

Sylp and I ran into the clearing where we were met with Elven men and creatures of the night. Their colossal forms were at the other end of the clearing by the mouth of the river. They wore matching uniforms, resembling Jemp's clothes when we captured him. Two men held a water nymph by the arms. He was battered and bruised. Sylp's face was tight, a tear sliding down their slim face. It was clear this person was from Sylps' past. Someone they were close to.

An Elven man resembling the age of my father yelled at him. His face was hardened with age and anger. He pointed his finger in the water nymph's face. His shouts were indiscernible because of how far away we were. The water nymph shouted something back, spitting in the Elven commander's face.

The commander paused long enough to realize what the nymph did. He pulled his sword from his sheath, making a quick swipe, effectively detaching the nymph's head from his body. Sylp's tears fell off her face in rapid succession, one after another. I grabbed her hand in a poor attempt to calm her.

We hurried towards the murder scene, and their voices became clear as we got closer.

"Gather all the nymphs you can find. If they want to play hero, they can die like the scum they are!"

The commander's voice was as rough as he looked. A single gray streak ran through his hair. Wrinkles had started at the corner of his eyes. His black beard was short and orderly; a few gray hairs sprouted from it. In any normal circumstance, he would have been a prime specimen of what some straight women and gay men felt was attractive. Well, if he hadn't been a murderer.

Sylp avoided looking at the two pieces of what used to be a water nymph, pointing her knobby finger towards the commander, who now was speaking to a dark creature, its skin gray. The hair sprouting from their head was a mixture of coarse hair and feathers sticking out haphazardly.

"Take this," the commander said, pushing a jar into the dark creature's hand. "You know your orders."

The creature nodded, grunting as various shaped black feathers sprouted from his arms. His leg bowed, claws sticking out where his toes were previously. The jar previously in his hand was now on the ground, where he grabbed it with his feet.

He flapped his wings, taking to the sky, the wind from his powerful take off flattening the plants around where he stood. The commander looked towards where we stood. I froze out of instinct. *He can't see us,* I reminded myself as he walked towards us.

His eyes squinted towards whatever took his attention away from his plan at hand. A guard called for the commander; a young water nymph stood beside him. The guard gripped the young nymph's arm. "I could only find this one, my lord. The others must be hiding like cowards."

"Papa," the young girl shouted at the dead nymph's body. She pulled away from the guard, dropping to the headless body before her.

"Yes, I killed your papa," the commander spat at the child, giving her a crazed grin. "I'm going to do the same to your kind if you get in the way. Now, where are the rest of you hiding?"

The young nymph shrunk down before squaring her shoulders and standing up. Her short form, compared to the commander's large one, was almost comical. The tiny fists that once hung limply at her sides were in fists. She lunged at the man, letting out a war cry. The commander merely laughed, throwing her to the ground, face to face with the her father's discarded head. She let out a scream, rolling away from it.

"Enough!" he shouted at the young girl, silencing her. "Mohan! Where are you?"

As he finished, his shadow seemed to rise out of the ground, materializing into a fully formed man. The sparse hair on his head resulted in a bad comb-over. He was all bones, lanky. Mohan tapped his knobby fingers together, his pale skin virtually translucent in the sunlight.

"Yes, my Lord?" his voice squeaked out, as he bowed before him.

"If this nymph won't tell me where the rest of them are, I need you to create a spell. I can't have them leaving this cursed place and telling the world of my plans. If they won't come out so I can kill them, I need them to stay here and not be able to tell anyone. Do you understand!?" The loudness of his voice carrying to the treetops, scaring the birds previously roosting in them.

"Y-y-yes, my lord, certainly, my lord," Mohan said as he slipped into the shadows again. The ground rumbled, and the young water nymph hacked a hard, chest racking cough. As it subsided, a blue light erupted from her mouth, flying in the air.

Hundreds of lights appeared from the treetops, presumably where the other nymphs hid, frozen in fear. Mohan rose from the shadows with a scepter in his hand. He lifted the scepter, attracting the blue balls of light, which zeroed in on it, rushing for it, flying into the tip before disappearing.

"It is done, my lord. They can no longer speak of this interaction ever again," he said with a low bow.

"Adequate. Now all that's left is to pour this into the river that feeds Valdis. It'll spread slowly, much like the bottle I handed to the Alti creature. Soon, the two kingdoms will fall and I will be the one to pick up the pieces."

The commander unscrewed the cap of the bottle and began pouring the black liquid into the water. I watched in horror as the black liquid dispersed into the water, becoming undetectable as it flowed toward Valdis.

Sylp grabbed my hand, pulling me back towards the lake once more, "Go must. Surface body your needs," she said.

The commander's head whipped in our direction, and Sylp turned abruptly, spinning me around. She all but dragged me towards the lake, until I ran beside her, making it back to the lake in record time.

Sylp pulled me into the water, dragging me under.

The water was freezing as we swam to the sacred cave and reached the rock Sylp had placed there earlier. She turned around, putting her mouth back on mine, blowing air back into my depleted lungs. The rock grew as both of our hands were on it, the lights in the cave brightening and darkening each second.

I blinked as the cave was once again back to normal. The rock in Sylp's hand was bland, no longer glowing.

Come, surface now, her voice projected into my head. The water was already clear from our earlier disturbance, making the bottom of the lake more visible. I looked around at our surroundings.

The cave sat next to large boulders with chains wrapped around them. Bones were scattered around the rocks. Looking at the other side of the cave exterior, I came face to face with the punishment the king and queen had placed on Jemp. His body floated in the water with grace, his ankle tied to the boulder with the chain. I let out a squeak of surprise; the bubbles escaping my mouth with an eagerness as Sylp tugged on me.

She tossed me onto the shore as we neared the surface. When we reached it, I took a deep breath, trying to get fresh air into my lungs. Nausea hit me. I rolled onto my side, coughing up lake water.

Lilja ran for me, pulling the hair out of my face. I looked at Sylp, raising an eyebrow. *Why was I throwing up lake water? I didn't even swallow any down there,* I thought.

"When gone, seep in water." Sylp gave a shrug. "Why had hurry we."

"Gone? Gone where you were supposed to show her something and come straight back. You were gone for hours," Lilja said.

"It's okay, Lilja, she showed me the past. Your suspicions were true. The people behind this were wearing Ardour clothing. They have to be the ones behind this!"

"We have to contact the others. It's time the rest of the group find out what we know." Lilja's voice was firm, her face determined. *I wonder what the others have found out?*

Lilja grabbed at my hand, pulling me off to the side. "Let's set up camp by the lake. I don't feel all that comfortable staying in a castle where all the upper circle wants our blood."

I nodded, pouting at her comment while looking at the castle. A warm bed was what I wanted.

"Plus, I feel uncomfortable letting anyone know how we contact Keres. The technique could be used to our disadvantage, if it's discovered." I raised my eyebrow at her comment. How were we supposed to contact Keres? Before this point, Lilja had only contacted her late at night, after I had already fallen asleep.

We set up camp. Lilja pulled together a fire. Glowing beetles lit the sky, each blinking themselves into existence. The lake reflected the lights of the castle as the sun set, becoming a mirror.

Lilja sat cross-legged by the fire, her hunched form energetically scribbling on a scrap piece of paper. Concentration covered her face like a veil. *This isn't what I thought a queen would be like. Nor did I ever think I was going to be in front of an Elven queen.* My inner monologue scoffed.

"Alright," she said, looking around, "we found this while back when we were kids. Armand, Keres and I found a book detailing fire magic in the castle library, a book that should remain lost. However, this spell is actually useful and doesn't cause damage. All you have to do is draw this symbol on a piece of paper and say the phrase correctly." Her voice was excited yet hushed, like a child talking about their favorite book.

Gingerly, she placed the corner of the scrap paper on the fire, allowing it to catch on fire. Lilja pulled it back. We both watched as the fire engulfed the paper hungrily.

"Seek the one I wish. With darkness comes light. Keres Genteen, answer the call of the flame," Lilja said, enunciating each word with precision, as she dropped the remaining paper and the flame devoured the rest of it.

Her eyes trained on the flame. The world seemed to die down around us. The beautiful scenery that once surrounded us was now replaced with darkness, as if someone had simply placed a black shawl over the forest. A form built in the fire, a silhouette of Keres' head.

"Finally, someone calls. I've grown quite tired of watching Cassia play upper circle for Ardour. If I have to watch her flirt with one more upper circle lady for gossip, I am going to go insane," Keres' silhouette said. Lilja laughed in response.

"We haven't talked to each other in months and I don't even get a hello," Lilja said.

"Hi," Keres said.

"Elowen and I have found something. I think it is time to get everyone back together. I need you to call out to the boys and Cassia. We need to make a plan to strike. The Ardourians are a part of the blight. Maybe even more so than I suspected. I thought the reconnaissance mission was the proper way to go. Easy in, easy out to fix the mess my parents made, but I fear we may have to go to war to get what we need to survive."

Keres face sobered as Lilja finished speaking, and the faint outline of her face reflected a deep frown. "Understood. Where is your current location?" she said, straight to the point. Her earlier complaints disappeared.

"Sald Forest," I said, "in the center."

Keres' mouth gaped open. "I can tell you guys have quite the story to tell. I'll contact everyone. Stay safe." Keres form vanished from the fire, causing it to die down to embers. We had a lot to explain.

24

Disobeying a Direct Order

Kallan POV

Sweat ran into my eyes, making them burn as the hot autumn sun beat down on the sparring ground. I breathed heavily as the next strike came at me. "Again!" the general called out from the edge of the sparring ring.

Armand grunted as our swords connected with each other. "Is that all you got?" he said, panting, pushing back on my blade, making me stumble back.

"Are you going to fight like preteens or men? I didn't realize training had turned into a social hour!" The general's voice boomed around the room. The other men, who were also training, sniggered in response.

"Shape up! There are only a handful of you here. If you are not up to par, I will kick you soft asses out! Do *not* tempt me with a good time."

Does he have to shout for everything? I thought to myself. Armand rolled his eyes in my direction. I fought the urge to smirk at him.

"*Enough!* Why don't you stop here? Take the rest of the day to learn how to stop being such a soft ass. I *expect* mean and robust training tomorrow. Do not leave the training house tonight. If another one of you disappears, I swear I'll whip the rest of your hides so hard your ancestors will feel it."

The other men dismissed Armand, and I continued to train. Lilja and the rest were risking their lives and here we were play-fighting, I thought grimly. Time passed quickly as we fought.

"This is getting old." Armand said as he took another hit from my blade.

I nodded in reply, throwing my sword down, wanting to fight the attitude out of my body. We grappled with each other. Armand grabbed at my leg, hurdling his body weight into me, pushing me into the dirt floor of the courtyard.

Armand stood up, grinning, he held his hand out to me. "You are supposed to get me on the ground, Kal. You can't let me win every time."

"How do you know I let you win? Maybe I'm just remarkably bad at fighting? We both know I'm much more adept with a bow," I said. I brushed the dirt off my clothes, looking around. We made the training house our home for the past few weeks. Built out of large cut wood, the construction has a temporary feel to it, the surrounding buildings were made of stone.

"What's the plan tonight? Do you know who is taking the other house members?" Armand's voice was low even though we stood in an empty courtyard. I shook my head, grabbing my discarded training sword and hanging it up.

"I have no idea who is—" My words died in my throat as shouting started at the entrance.

"I need help over here," one of the younger soldiers said as his lanky form struggled to carry Tengsin's battered form.

Armand and I rushed to him.

"What happened?" I looked at the boy before me, who hadn't yet quite grown into his body.

DISOBEYING A DIRECT ORDER

"I-I don't know, I sn-snuck out to see my girl and saw him by the creek." His voice cracked as he said, "I swear that's all I know."

I looked down at Tengsin; his usual golden skin was replaced with an ashy look. His nose was crooked and stab marks littered his torso.

"Is he breathing?" Armand looked around nervously.

Fuck, this is going to garner more attention from us than I want, I thought.

I put my ear down to his bloodied chest. "He's breathing—but barely. Armand, grab his legs. We have to get him to the infirmary." I looped my arms around his limp shoulders, and his head lolled to the side. Tengsin groaned as we hurriedly began our path to the infirmary.

"Kid, go get the physician and the general," Armand said as he struggled to keep up with me.

I kicked open the infirmary door, laying him on the cot. "Tengsin, can you hear me? What happened to you?" I called out to him. He groaned in reply, opening his swollen, puffy eyes slowly. I put my hand over the most prominent stab wound. His body was caked in mud from the creek.

"Ugh," he wheezed out as a cough racked his ruined frame. "I couldn't, I-I can't, I'm sorry I can't," he said, tears welling. His eyes darted back and forth, searching the room.

"What in the holy gods happened?" The general's voice boomed as he and the physician entered the room.

Physician Jenx rushed to Tengsin, checking him over and checking his pulse. My hand still covered the major entry point. "Move, son, I need room to check him over and bandage him."

I pulled away as Tengsin's blood covered my hands. Armand's face was hard as we made eye contact. *He's only been missing for a few days.* A few days prior, he was in peak physical health. The scrawny kid who found him stood in the doorway as if he was ready to run out.

The general stalked over to him, grabbing him by the ear.

"What did you do, boy," he said, pinching him harder.

"I did nothing. I found him by the creek," he said, his face bright red.

The general tossed the young teen out of the room. "We will talk about this later, Druim. You two—" He narrowed his eyes. "—out. Do not speak of this again."

Armand and I looked at each other, and then back at the general, nodding. We were definitely going to speak of it later.

We exited the room and went down the hall far enough away from the room to not be heard. "What the fuck is that about?" Armand said in a hushed tone, his burly form towering over my lean one.

"He's the fourth one since we showed up, the only one to have reappeared. We have not seen or heard from the other three since they disappeared," I said as I paced in the hallway.

Armand nodded. "What do these disappearances have to do with us? Lilja has instructed us to find out what the military knows of the blight. So far, all we've done is play fight in the combat ring like teenagers."

I placed my hand on his shoulder, looking up at him. "I don't know if this has something to do with the blight or not. But it is our duty to find out why these members keep disappearing. The only way we can rule out if this has anything to do with the blight is to find out who keeps taking them."

The infirmary door creeped open as the general and the physician slipped out, deep in conversation. I pulled Armand's huge form and me behind the corner. The physician spoke something to the general, shaking his head. The general's face was full of sorrow as they followed each other down the steps. Armand and I gave each other a look and rushed to the infirmary, only to find a dead Tengsin in the cot.

Tengsin's battered body laid limply, his blood-red eyes open, staring vacantly at the ceiling.

"What the fuck happened?" Armand said, wide-eyed.

I gave Armand a look. How was I supposed to know?

Reaching over his body, I closed his eyes. His body was already cold. "Let's go, Armand. We need to follow them."

I stalked out into the empty hallway and down the step, Armand close on my heels. Carefully, I skipped the squeaking spots on the steps, wary of garnering the attention of our target. The two older men were deep in conversation as they passed through the courtyard and out into the street.

"Quick! Follow them!" I said, already going out onto the street.

We ran after them, into the busy street. The military training building was located to the left of the city. Busy workers packed the streets, coming and going to work after their lunch breaks. Tall factories loomed over the training facility, each one more depressing than the next.

The general's tall form made following him easy. Armand and I walked slowly behind the older men, attempting to look like we not were following him. With surprising ease, the two men traveled through the streets, turning multiple times as if they were worried about being followed. *Well, I mean they were right to worry,* I thought sarcastically.

We slowed down as the men in front of us turned into a large building. The outside was nothing special. It was devoid of any personality as it sat in between two colorful apartments.

I held out my arm to stop Armand, who was busy perusing the selection of young elves walking through the streets.

"Wait," I said, grabbing him.

He stumbled into my arm, looking at me in surprise before straightening up. Armand instantly began looking for entry points other than the front door.

The windows were all shut, except one. I hurried towards it,

Armand quickly following behind me. I leaned against the wall, trying to listen to the conversation inside. Armand sat underneath the window, pretending to be a bum by grabbing a discarded bottle from the ground.

"I just don't understand. Why would you kill him? He was more than likely going to succumb to his wounds. Now his blood is on your hand, Anthin." I could tell from the voice that it was the physician. I inched closer to the window, the physician's voice becoming hushed towards the end.

"Jenx," the general said in a warning tone, "you shall address me as General. You don't even have the clearance to know my name, let alone speak it. This boy should have been dead from the start. He disobeyed a direct order. The only thing on my hand is that the men I instructed to kill him didn't succeed. Dammit Jenx, a good soldier follows orders from the top no matter what. There is a bigger ploy on the horizon, bigger than you could fathom. The blight has been changing over the last couple of months, not because of some damn mutations. It's changing because we are making it change!"

Jenx was silent for a moment, before letting out a quiet, "How?"

"The higher ups find people to enhance the spell's potency. If they can't, or refuse, they disappear." As shock coursed through his body, I assumed, a wave of anger rocked through me. I balled my hands into fists. *People—my friends and family—are dying because of some Elven-made disease?*

I resisted the urge to propel myself into the window and kill them both. A frown formed on my face. *I can't kill them yet, I can't. Death is too good for them. We have to get this message to Keres. Then I am going to torture these monsters into telling me what they know.* Armand and I rushed back to the training house and up to the room we shared.

Once we reached our room, Armand lit the candle. His face was red and void of expression, his anger clear in his eyes.

With shaking hands, I drew the sigil on the paper, speaking the words: "Seek the one I wish. With darkness comes light. Keres Genteen answer the call of the flame."

25

Just a Little Chat

Kallan POV

Keres' head flittered into the small candle flame, adding light to the quickly darkening room. The sun was setting into the golden hour. "Kal! Thank the gods, I was nearly done getting ready to conjure to you. Lilja and Elowen have found something."

"What did they find?" Armand grabbed onto my shoulder, looking over me to the flame.

"Get off of me, you oversized oaf. What did our favorite little lesbians find?"

Keres scoffed at our playful banter. "They found that the Ardourians are behind the blight. War is on our horizon."

Armand gave the flame a hard look. "The men we overheard just solidified that."

My mind raced with the information. I felt worry building itself into an ugly little ball in my subconscious. I pushed it back. Now was not the time to worry. If we were truly going to go to war against the Ardourians, we had to have no fear. The last 400 years had been kinder to them than to us. The blight had caused famine and poverty

JUST A LITTLE CHAT

to ravage our kingdom, leaving morale low. The number or men and women available to fight in a war was even lower.

"That's the thing, they aren't even in the city anymore—" Keres began.

"They aren't in the city?" I said, interrupting her. My breath making the candle flicker, dangerously close to being blown out. "What do you mean, they aren't in the city anymore?" My voice was low and strained. "That was the plan."

"I know that was the plan, dumbass. Obviously, the plan changed. They found a lead, and they took it. It would have been better if they had told me first, but they are safe."

"Where are they, then?" Armand said, confusion clear in his voice.

"For whatever reason, those two are in the Sald Fore—"

"They are in Sald Forest!" Armand said. I turned, giving him a dark look, willing him to shut up in my mind.

"Yes, they are. I don't know why or how they even got there and didn't die. Especially with Elle being a human." Her voice trailed off as she contained whatever else she wanted to say in her head.

I rolled my eyes, knowing her comment was only because she was jealous of how close Elowen was becoming to Lilja, our queen.

"We will head over first light tomorrow. I have some unfinished business to attend to here," I said. *I hope to gods those men are still in that building.*

"Whatever your business is, make sure you hurry. Li—the queen makes it sound as if it is urgent that we get to the forest. We must be reunited again; we are stronger together." She said as Armand extinguished the candle flame.

"What was that for?" I gaped at him.

His eyes were dark, his hands balled into fists. "My little sister gets too caught up in the details. We need to find out what the general knows about the blight."

A wave of anger rolled off of him in waves. It surprised me. Armand was usually the man to make some sort of tactical plan. He didn't rush into things. His dark hair was messy, as if he had just been running his fingers through it.

"Kal, if we don't find out what he knows, then a lot more people could die! Being calm will not cut it," he said, as if he could read what I was thinking.

"Calm down, Armand. I was about to suggest we pay the big bad general a visit."

Armand's body expression visibly calmed as I spoke, "now pack your shit and let's visit general when he is sleeping. There is a space under the canal we can take him. Nobody will hear us."

While we waited for the sun to set, we packed our necessities again. I left anything we had to buy for the training house in disarray. *This is definitely not going to pass room inspections tomorrow.*

"At least we will be gone before room inspections," Armand barked out as if he read my mind again. I rolled my eyes, grinning as I grabbed my roll of knives, slipping the ties into my belt. *This is going to be a long night*, I thought as we walked out of the door and into the dark hallway.

The courtyard's light filtered through the railings that lined the sides, dimly illuminating the hallway. We crept to the general's room; the space underneath his door was dark. *He must be asleep.* I held my breath as I twisted the nob, nodding at Armand as I did so. As soft snores hit my ears, I breathed a sigh of relief. I held up three fingers.

This was just going to be like that situation in Nyrim. I prayed

Armand would know what I wanted to do, as I lunged for the sleeping form's head. In a swift motion, I grabbed the sheet covering his body, stuffing it into his snoring mouth. Armand grabbed his legs, tying them together with a rope—*wait, where did he grab the rope?* I shrugged the thought off as I grinned at him.

"You remembered—"

"Of course I remembered what happened in Nyrim, Kallan. That was the best raid we had," Armand whispered.

The general's eyes were wide as he looked at our shadowy forms in alarm. He garbled something as I hit him over the head with a candle holder from his bedside, knocking him unconscious.

"Alright, let's go! We need to figure out what this soft ass knows and then get to the rest of the team." I grinned at Armand as I spoke. This was going to be fun.

"Uh, Kal, we have a problem," Armand said as he looked down at the general's sleeping form. I cringed as I realized the general's sleeping form was also a naked form. I rolled my eyes looking at the ceiling, sighing. Gods what did I do to deserve this? *I guess the times I bothered Lilja finally caught up to me, epic karma.*

"It doesn't matter." I let out another sigh. "I guess he won't be the only one bleeding tonight. I think I can already feel my eyeballs being wounded from just glancing at him."

Armand laughed as we carried the sleeping body out into the hallway. I gave a quick glance around, seeing nobody as we walked down the steps and into the night air. The smells from the factories were the only thing on the streets as we hurried down into the alleyway.

The alley was littered with trash and wreaked of urine. The ladder to go down to the canal's walkway was at the end. "How do you know about this place?" Armand said, his voice echoing into the empty air.

"Will you shut up, Armand? Hold him while I climb down." I grinned at him as I dropped my end of the general.

"Why do I have to carry him? He's naked."

"Look at the broad shoulders you have. You have the most muscles. Plus, you have air powers. Just make him lighter." I gave him a pout and flexed at him as I made it to the bottom.

"Yeah, yeah, if you keep at it, I'm going to throw this man straight in your face. I'll be sure to aim the waist at your mouth." He retorted as he turned to climb down the ladder, the general's head hitting the rungs as he descended.

"Did you have to make sure he hit his head all the way down?" I said with a raised eyebrow.

"Yes, yes, I did."

"Well, we need him coherent, not concussed," I said.

Armand paused as if that thought suddenly hit him, lowering his own head slightly. "Oh, yeah. Sorry." He grinned, using his free hand to run it through his hair again.

"We're close to the hiding spot—and before you ask again, I went on a few adventures these past few weeks, looking for potential routes to escape if the need ever arose."

"Ah, my route was over the roofs. I tested it out a few times, very practical. Just not when it rains," he said with an attempt at a shrug. The shrug was difficult with the dead weight on one side of his shoulder."I thought you didn't like enclosed spaces?" Armand asked quietly, as if not wanting to spook me. His voice was the only sound permeating the air around us.

My hand paused at the door, the scar on my face twitched. An aching memory washed over my vision like an oncoming wave.

That cave.

The skirmish between Ardour and Valdis.

Caught behind enemy lines.

That man, the faceless man.

I shrugged my shoulders, as if shaking off the memory of Lleaven. A memory better off forgotten.

"Not ones I get to choose."

I yanked the door open. It creaked with protest. The moisture constantly attacking it had taken its toll, the hinges rusted slowly eroding the metal away. I winced, as it nearly came unattached from the wall.

The room was dank and smelled of mold. It was empty save for a few boxes and a chair. "Armand, set him down in the chair. I'll light the torches." My voice echoed in the small room.

With the torches now lit, the lights illuminated the room, solidifying the fact that Ardourians don't come down here much. I shut the door to the outside. His screams should not wake the rest of the kingdom.

I looked at Armand as he finished securing the general into the chair. "Wake him. We need to find out this information in any way possible."

Armand nodded grimly. Neither one of us enjoyed torture, per se. In this situation, there was too much to gain. If we didn't, more people could die, people we loved.

Armand reached into his pocket, pulling out a smelling stick and putting it under general's nose. The general's eyes widened as he whipped his head around to take in his surroundings. Finally he settled on Armand and me, frowning, the gag still in place in his mouth.

"Now, I'm going to remove this and you are going to shut yer trap and not peep out a sound unless you're answering a question. Do you understand me?" I pointed my index finger in his face, my face void of expression.

He nodded. I ripped the gag out of his mouth. He opened and closed his mouth, his jaw probably sore from being open for so long.

"What in the gods name do you think you are doing, boys? This is treas—" he said. I quickly stuffed the gag back into his mouth.

I spoke again, gripping his shoulder tightly, my voice barely above a whisper. "I told you not to speak unless spoken to. Now, unless you want to lose a finger because of your own insolence, it would do you well to shut the hell up."

He nodded again, the gravity of the situation finally weighing down on him. He squirmed in his chair.

This really was going to be a long night.

26

Body Dump

Kallan POV

I grabbed a small blade from my bag. The metal gleamed with excitement as the light of the flame hit. Armand's arms were crossed as he leaned against the wall. The general continued to squirm in his chair fruitlessly. He opened his mouth to say something but thought better of it and said nothing.

Smart choice, dumbass. Don't tempt me with a good time. I settled the blade on his exposed thigh. The blade hovered over his skin, a breath away from cutting him. He stilled, fear making him freeze into place. "Now, General. What were you and the physician speaking about? Who is causing the blight to happen?"

The general stared at me, looking me up and down as he tried to figure out why I knew about such things. "I don't know what you are talking about," he said, trying not to trip over his words.

"Don't lie! We followed you to that building. We heard you explain to the physician what Ardour was doing." Armand's voiced boomed in the room, the sound ricocheting into my ears. I cringed. Armand pushed himself off the wall and gripped onto the general's wrist.

"You two boys are into something you can't comprehend. Queen

Alieta will hear about this," spit flew out of his mouth as he spoke.

Armand whipped his hand in the air, smacking him in the face, knocking it to the side. "If you don't tell us what we want to know, I am going to make killing you a pleasure. The guards won't even know who they find when they find your body in the canal."

"I'd be less concerned about your queen and be more worried about my queen." A smug smile played on my lips.

The general's pale face darkened with rage, "You are Valdisians! You two sorry saps of military men. It could only make sense that you are Valdisians."

I pushed the blade that hovered over his skin into his leg. "You and I know that Armand and I were your best students."

He gritted his teeth.

"Now, what do the Ardourians have to do with the blight?" I twisted the knife into his leg. Blood pooled from the wound and trickled down his leg.

"Ow, you son of a bitch! Why don't you go back to where you came from and die like the rest of the Valdisians?" The aged, wrinkled skin on his face contorted into anger, transforming into a smug look.

I reached back and punched him in the face; his face whipped to the side. In one fluid motion, I pulled the blade down, leaving a deep gash about the length of my hand in its path. The general let out a gargled scream, the previous blow having knocked a tooth from his mouth. Blood and spit came from his mouth like foam from a crazed dog.

I pulled away, the knife still in my hand, his blood making my hand sickly slick. My stomach churned at the sight. How long could he keep this up? *I need answers.* Armand grabbed the general's hand, clutching his fingers.

"Now, we are going to play a little game. You answer a question, and if I think you are telling the truth. I might, just might, not break one of your fingers. If you don't answer my question, or if I think you're lying. I'm going to do this—" as he jerked his finger back. The bone made a sickening crunch as it did so. Armand released his finger. It hung at an awkward angle.

The general screamed in reply, his face beat red. He nodded in reply. "Now, General, who is behind the blight?" Armand asked, his forehead glistened with sweat. If anyone else saw him, they would assume it was from heaving the general's wrinkled form down here. I knew better. He was anxious. Torturing came with a price. A mental price and a physical one, nights of torture haunt the dreams of the next night. A shiver ran down my spine as the general spat to the side, blood coating his teeth.

"The royals."

Armand and I looked at each other and then back at the general. I gripped the man's unbroken finger. "How are they causing the blight?"

The older man's breath was ragged. His chest heaved up and down. The blood from his thigh flowed freely. *That might have been too large of a cut.* "Magic," he wheezed out.

"Magic? How can magic be the reason behind this?" I racked my brain for knowledge of elemental magics. *How can magic cause this? Magic is just earth, fire, air, and water.*

"Olken elv—"

"They are extinct. They have been extinct for thousands of years. Their dark magic is gone like themselves," Armand said. I twisted the finger in my hand, the feeling of the bone snapping nearly making me gag.

"Agh, stop, please. I promise they aren't extinct, they went north! The royals have made a deal with them. I've told you all I know. Please. Please, just stop hurting me. Just let me go. I won't tell anyone what has transpired over the night."

"What do the Ardourian Royals gain from killing off the Valdisians?" Armand hit his fist against the wall, making the general jump.

"I-I don't know, no…no! Don't!" He shook his head as Armand grabbed it.

"Wait!" the general's gargled voice shouted. "They want Valdis, they want you to fall! Ardour has plans for expansion. More power! We will get it. One by one, Valdisians are dying, soon it'll be the masses. Valdis will soon be a land of bodies, just like the military did to that damn town to the north, Lleaven! That's when we will take over, killing off the ones that survived one by one!"

Armand and I shared a look, I gave him a slight nod. Armand understood twisting. With a snap, the room was filled with a deadly silence, the weight of the information settling on us like a wave of death.

I shook myself out of the trance we both seemed to be in and began untying the shell of what used to be the general. The dead weight of the body slumped against me. I grunted, finishing untying the other wrist. I slung the body over my shoulder.

"What are you doing with the body?" Armand's hard facade was gone, his voice now coming out with a bit of doubt.

"I am going to toss the body into the canal." My voice strained with the effort of carrying the dead weight over my shoulder.

I tried to ignore the feeling of his bare skin pressed against my clothing. Internally, I reprimanded myself for ending up in this situation. Armand pulled the door open for me. *I should have just become a painter like my brother,* my inner voice chastised.

"No, I don't have a better idea," he said.

I searched our surroundings, plopped the body on the edge of the canal. The moon offered little light. I walked over to the wall. Due to age or weather, it had crumbled, and slabs of concrete had broken off and lay haphazardly on the ground. I reached for a slab slightly larger than the size of my hand. I pounded it onto the face of what used to be the general, with a grunt.

"What are you doing?" Armand looked around searching for witnesses, his eyes darted back and forth.

"We have to make sure the people who find him don't know who he is," I stressed. The blood that had splattered on my face was already drying.

"Once we're done here, we have to ride for Sald Forest and tell Lilja what we found." I rolled the unrecognizable man into the filthy canal water, grimacing. I rubbed the crusted blood off of my face, using my shirt, and started for the ladder.

I glanced back at Armand, who stood staring at the lifeless form floating away to gods knew where.

I walked back to the edge of the canal where Armand stood, putting my hand on his broad shoulder. He jerked away from my touch, leaning over heaving the contents of his stomach into the water.

A few seconds passed before he finally stood up, his normal dark complexion a few shades paler. "I hate having to do shit like this, even if he fucking deserves it." He looked back over to the slowly disappearing body in the water.

"Hey, it had to be done. The kingdom relies on us finding the answers, Lilja needs us. Let's go."

Lilja POV

I watched Elowen's form toss and turn in the dim light the moon provided. The sounds of night animals and bugs filled the air, giving the world a peaceful feeling. It had been a few days since Keres had sent word to the team. *Everyone should be nearly here.* From what Elle had told me from her travel to the past, the Ardourians were behind the blight. *How, though? Is it some kind of sickness cooked up by the royal physician? Why? What do the Ardourians gain from killing off the mass of my people?*

I got up, pushing the blanket that shrouded me from the crisp night air into Elowen, who greedily wrapped herself in the covers, keeping a hold of them like a little troll in the stories Mama had once told me. I grinned at the memory as I walked out into the night and into the water. The crescent-shaped moon reflected on the still pond. The water nymphs were asleep for the night down below the depths of the water. Probably in the cave Elle had told me about.

    I settled on a rock, the surface cold to the touch. I squirmed as I got comfortable, waiting for what the gods wanted to bring for the day. For whatever they threw my way, I was going to be ready for it. This world was my home, my kingdom was the most important thing. It was my responsibility to keep my people safe and happy. I glanced back at the tent where Elle was sleeping. Maybe the *second* most important.

27

Telling a Secret

Elowen POV

"Everyone should be on their way, your highness. Kallan and Armand also have information on the blight."

Lilja sat in a chair in front of the large tent Lady Pelicia had gifted to us. She stated that while she understood our reasoning behind staying away from the castle, she couldn't live with it if a queen and her partner slept on the ground in a small tent. The very next day, we found a large tent being put up by their servants, rather begrudgingly.

Lilja's hand was on her chin, her thin legs crossed over at the knee. "What did they find, Keres?" she asked the dark-haired girl before us.

I leaned on the chair, standing next to Lilja. Our relationship has been strained the last few nights, ever since Sylp and I went in the water together.

Keres shrugged, shifting her weight to the other leg, like Lilja, she had filled out since our time in Valdis. The well-balanced diet from Ardour's food had given her a chance to get a healthy glow. I prayed soon they would all be able to keep that look. I was still full of weight, but it seemed to shift in other places versus just my stomach. The extra weight seemed to go to my legs and my butt. All the physical exercise and fighting for my life had pushed the weight elsewhere as muscles.

"They were uncomfortable with sharing at that time. I-I keep trying to contact them. But I can't get through. They are riding hard and fast here for the team to regroup." She stared at Cassia, who danced with a forest nymph. She giggled like a young child would. Her eyes were fixed on the flowers and moss flowing off the nymph's head like an enormous hat.

Keres looked nervous. Her eyes flitted around, looking at things randomly and then back at Lilja.

"What is it, Keres? You look like you are about to die of an anxiety attack." Lilja sat up straight and pushed herself off the chair. She strode to Keres, grabbing onto her shoulder. A red blush rushed to Keres' cheeks at the contact.

"When Cassia and I were at the castle, I couldn't help but feel watched. When Cassia would come to me with information on the court, there would always be someone around a corner. I-I worry it might've compromised us."

"Were you followed?" I asked, as they turned their attention to me.

Her hands balled into fists at my question. "No, of course not. We followed the training we were giving in Valdis, but I'm nervous. That's all."

"Keres," Lilja said in a warning tone. "She isn't accusing you. It was merely a question, a valid one at that."

"Have you spoken with Aidan at all?" I asked, worrying about my pacifist journaling friend.

Keres nodded, replying, "Yes, he has been up to his neck in books and scrolls in the library. When we last spoke, he was in some village on the way here. I believe it was called Hellow."

Lilja and I looked at each other. That was the town Jemp, Lilja and I

TELLING A SECRET

had passed through just a few days prior to coming here. "How many days have passed since your conversation with Aidan?"

Keres cocked her head to the side at my question as if she was trying to recollect the memory.

"How many days, Keres?" Lilja asked, a hint of annoyance in her voice.

"A few days ago? Honestly, I don't remember; there's been too many things happening as of late." Keres played with her hair as she spoke, twirling it around her finger.

Lilja rubbed her hand down her face roughly, sighing. "Did you at least tell him not to kill the Ossory wolf who will guide him here to the castle?"

"Shit, I knew there was something that I forgot to tell him. I mean, Aidan isn't the best fighter anymore. He likes books more than a sword. He's been like this since Llidan—"

"Do not talk about Llidan, you weren't even there, Keres." Lilja warned.

Where my persona was from? What happened in Llidan? I lifted an eyebrow but said nothing. Keres folded her arms, looking to the side.

"Your highness," a small servant said as he ran towards us. The servant couldn't have been over twelve. He still hadn't grown into his enormous feet and large hands. He panted as he made it to us. His hands were on his knees as he struggled to regain his breath.

"What is it?" Keres asked of the boy as he straightened up.

"A man," he coughed, "a man has shown up in the clearing. Cerious is fighting with him!"

I whipped my head at Keres, giving her a dark look. *How could she forget to tell him about the giant wolf?*

"Shit," Lilja mumbled under her breath. She ran to the tent, grabbing her knife. "Boy, which direction?"

The kid stood dazed at the command. "Dammit, boy, which

direction? Before Cerious kills Aidan!" The kid pointed his finger to the south. Without a second command, she took off running. The dagger I had for my time in the Elven Realm sat heavy on my hip as I bolted after her. The forest path that lay before us became rougher as we ran down it. Its intended to deter any travelers from finding the center of Sald Forest.

Fog was rolling into the foliage, signaling to us that the clearing we entered before was nearing. Branches whipped at my exposed skin as I came to a screeching halt at the edge of the clearing.

Cerious stood in wolf form, snarling at Aidan. His glasses stood cockeyed on his face. The books and supplies he had on his person strewn about the ground as he held his sword towards the beast. I lifted an eyebrow. *This is the first time I've seen him use his sword.*

Aidan's blonde hair was wet with sweat. His chest moved up and down with ferocity as Cerious lunged at him again.

"Wait!" I screamed, running towards him. Cerious faltered slightly, tuning towards Lilja, and I, ducking his head down, growling. The Elven emotion veiled behind the wolf, threatening to take over his eyes.

"Pup, unless you want to be turned into water nymph food, I suggest you shift back or whatever you call it and turn your ass back to human. Otherwise, if you touch my Ellie, it will make dismembering you very pleasurable." Lilja enunciated her words loudly, her intentions clear.

"Wait, for your Ellie?" Aidan asked, still trying to catch his breath.

I gave her a look before walking over to Aidan. The wolf whimpered. Bones snapped and shifted underneath his skin. The fur fell off in tufts, revealing the Elven skin underneath. Cerious' curly hair took shape on his head first, the other features coming in slowly. We watched in horror as his naked body lay on the clearing form, whimpering. He glared at us, getting up brushing his body off. He turned towards the castle huffing and took off.

I peeled my eyes away from him to look at Aidan. His eyes were downcast at the knife in his hand. Aidan's chest still rose and fell rapidly with each breath; he abruptly discarded the knife as he looked up at me. Anxiety was present in his eyes; I gave him a small smile, pulling him into a hug.

He faltered before returning the affection by enveloping me in his burly arms. My head went into the crook of his neck. "I missed you, Aidan."

Liljas' long arms wrapped around the both of us.

"Lilja darling, the next time you ask me to go on another secret mission. I'm saying no," Aidan said.

Lilja rolled her eyes, pulling away to give Aidan a once over. His face was still a tad gaunt. The time in the library had not given him ample opportunity to eat, apparently.

"You said that last time. You still came on this mission, didn't ya? What did you do on your half of the mission, turn into the undead? Gods, it doesn't even look like you've seen sunlight since we split up," Lilja said.

"Hey, I'll have you know, your highness, that I was diligently looking up books and scrolls on the blight," he said with a huff. His frown turned into a grin, his pearly whites shining ear to ear.

"So, Elowen, how did Lilja tell you guys are fated?"

"Fated?" I cocked my head to the side. "What do you mean, fated?"

Aidan clapped his hands excitedly. "You know, soulmates."

"Soulmates? What are you going on about? We only dated for the mission. It wasn't real, Aidan."

I looked at Lilja, who was pale.

"This is a joke, right? There's no such thing as soulmates. Right?" I pushed as my gaze switched over to Lilja and then to Aidan.

"Ooh, she didn't know?" Aidan asked. "Shit."

Lilja's face was flushed. She tensed, glaring at us both before answering. "Yeah, *shit* is right, you dumbass."

28

Fated?

My heart raced as I stared at my two friends. Lilja looked visibly stressed. Aidan stared at the forest behind me as if it had grown legs and walked away. Maybe it had. This forest seemed to have a mind of its own.

"Elowen, fated elves are very lucky. Many elves don't meet their fated spouse. If by some chance they do, they meet them well into the years of life. We are extremely lucky to have found each other at such a young age."

"We? How is there a *we*, Lilja? I'm still a human." Blood rushed to my cheeks.

"You." I pointed my finger at Aidan. "How long have you known?"

Aidan's face was pale as he picked up the books and papers that were strewn around the clearing. "What?" He pushed up his glasses, that teetered on the edge of his nose.

"How long—"

"Oh—ah, we've known for—"

"*We*? Everyone knows besides me?" I could feel the anger building in the pit of my stomach. I looked at Lilja; she stood looking at her feet. Aidan held his mouth open for a second, realizing the mistake of his wording.

"Elle—I was meaning to tell you; I just didn't know how to—"

"Don't you *Elle* me, how did you know I am your fated or soulmate or whatever? I don't know if you forgot, but I'm a human and you are an elf." Tears sprang to my eyes. *Am I just a joke to everyone here? I thought—I thought we were friends. Friends are supposed to be honest with one another. I thought—I thought we were going to be something. Are humans just a toy for elves to play with their emotions?*

"Elowen, we aren't trying to play with your emotions," Lilja said.

Did I say that out loud? My heart beat fast in my chest as we stood in the clearing. It was as if Lilja and I were the only two people in the world. Silence filled the clearing. The only sounds were our heartbeats as we stood staring at each other.

"Truly. I-I just didn't know when was the right time to tell you." Anxiousness coated her usual calm and confident tone. "And no, you didn't say that out loud—elves and I guess human/elf pairs can hear each other's thoughts if they are projected correctly. You accidentally do—"

"You *read* my thoughts!" Anger seemed to roll off of me as I spoke.

"No—well, I mean, I guess technically...I did. But you literally project those thoughts in my head. How am I supposed to ignore them?" Her voice rose above a normal speaking tone.

Oh, so she wants to yell? I can yell.

"What? I am not yelling right now." She crossed her arms, her pale face turning red.

"Get out of my head!"

"Stop projecting it into mine and I will!" She took a step forward. Out of instinct, I took a step back.

She halted, holding up her hands, as if trying to say, *I won't hurt you.*

"How long?"

"How long, what?" She asked, her voice wavered with uncertainty.

"How long have you known that we were fated? How do you even know that we are fated?" Words seemed to fly out of my mouth at a mile a minute as anxiety took over.

"Since you came and passed out on the mainland," her voice was firm as we stood in the clearing; Aidan had made himself sparse.

"How do you know? I'm human, after all." I tried to keep the distaste out of my words. *How could someone be fated to me? Me? The gods must have a cruel sense of humor to stick someone with me.*

"When you first meet the person, you are fated with, the universe seems to light up. Color where they never existed showed up, i-it was like getting fresh eyes to the universe. It was like a breath of fresh air. Like it was the first breath of air I took in years. I-I let my duty consume me for so long. Even then I wasn't sure if you were truly my fated because you're human. B-but when I picked up your battered body, I felt it."

"Felt what?" My heart slowed in my chest. My breath evened out as I watched the once-stoic Lilja tell me the emotions she kept hidden from me for so long.

"It's hard to explain. Every time I touch you, it's like a gentle shock. Warmth spreads through my body like wildfire, burning the insecurities I have. Nearly overwhelming, it's the strongest when we are apart or hurt. When we first made it to the castle, I—" Her voice hollowed out, overwhelmed with emotions. Tears were now present in her eyes, and my heart broke slightly. I took a step forward, trying to close the gap between us.

"I thought you were dying. I felt your heartbeat in your chest slow. As the coldness spread throughout your body, and your voice—" a sob broke through her voice. "Your voice was screaming in my head, yelling for me, and then it was like a whisper. A little voice telling me to find you and hold you."

I took another step forward, sufficiently closing the gap between us, wrapping my arms around her tall frame. Aidan's figure was nowhere to be found.

"Hey, I'm alive. Aren't I? That's in the past."

"I told the team as soon as I knew for sure, the second day you were here. The night you woke up screaming from the past, when I wrapped my arms around you, I knew. I knew you were meant to be my counterpart."

I looked up at her, my chin resting on her chest. "But, I'm a human, Lilja. I don't have the lifespan you have. Before you know it, I'm going to be gone from this world. I-I don't think I want to put you through that."

Lilja stiffened underneath my touch. Silence stretched on for a moment. "The world will right itself. I know these things. Don't worry about that for right now. Let's just focus on the now."

She placed her hands on my shoulder and pushed herself gently away from me to look me in the eye.

"I didn't tell you because I wanted to manipulate you. I didn't know the right time or place. My mission keeps thrusting my friends and I into these dangerous situations, and I've never been as nervous as I was to tell you we are fated. I didn't know how'd you react. You might try to run away. I couldn't let you run through the Elven countryside unprotected. If people were to find out that I found my fated, they would stop at nothing to find you and possibly kill you for the connection you have with me." Lilja's eyes darkened with anger as she spoke. "I guess what I'm trying to tell you with this is I'm sorry. I want to do this right. Usually when fated elves find their counterpart, they propose. So, Elowen Alwyn..." She got down on one knee, pulling out the same ring box from Jaz's house. She flicked it open, revealing the same ring as before. *How did she get that back?*

"Will you marry—" she began again.

"Wait! I-I don't know, Lilja, I don't know if I'm ready for that." I took a step back. My heart beat in my eardrums, blood rushed to my face.

Pain flickered her face before she could neutralize her features. Quickly, she plucked the ring out of the box, grabbing my hand and pushing onto my ring finger.

"That's okay, you—you don't have to be ready right now. Just keep it on your finger until you know the answer, once you know what you want. Just let me know." She pulled my hand up to her mouth and gave it a small kiss. Letting my hand fall, she grabbed my face and kissed my forehead.

She searched my eyes for the answer she wanted and then walked back into the forest that housed the castle. I watched her figure as she disappeared into the trees. Not once did she look back. The weight of my ring felt like it was going to cleave my heart in two. I fell to my knees as a sob broke out of my mouth, clutching my ringed hand.

Why? Why would the gods do this to me? Why would they make me feel like this? So soon? I don't deserve this. Lilja has gone through enough. She doesn't need to watch the person she is fated to die so soon. She doesn't deserve this.

Another sob escaped my mouth as I lay on the ground, staring at the clouds that passed by. I held my hand up to the blue sky, watching as the stone sparkled under the sunlight. The weight of the future pushed itself on me as I waited for the unknown.

29

Child-like Glee

The clouds passed the sky, as if their greater purpose in life was to play tag with the sun. I groaned and the tears dried on my face, making the path they took feeling crusted. *Why, why am I like this? Why must I feel everything so deeply? Must I fall so fast and so hard for a tall, mysterious woman I feel like I know nothing about?*

The forest clearing was quiet, other than the animals that called it home and the distant laughs of forest nymphs. *Kallan and Armand should arrive soon,* I thought to myself, sitting up. Blood rushed in my ears with the sudden movement as I gazed at the tree line. A small nymph ran through the trees, pausing to look at me. She glanced away from me, giggling. I wiped the snot off my face, smiling.

"Hello," I said, trying to hide my emotions from the young nymph.

"Ewwo," the little voice called out, their body partly hidden behind the trees. They grinned; their teeth white. A stark contrast to the light green skin that appeared in patches on their pale skin.

I gave them a small wave. They giggled again and held up a small hand. A four-finger wave. *That's new,* I thought as the small nymph cautiously inched out from behind the tree.

The young nymph had a thin dress on, the edges tattered from age

CHILD-LIKE GLEE

and hard play. Moss had eaten away at the dress, leaving patches of holes and green soft moss in its wake. Their blond hair was carelessly put up with twigs. Plants and flowers seemed to grow from their scalp, adorning their head like a beautiful arrangement.

"Where is your mamma, young nymph? You are too young to be far from her," I said, trying to keep my voice light. The little nymph just stared at me for a moment until an enormous grin filled her face. With a giggle and a shrug, the nymph turned around and ran off.

I rolled my eyes and bound after them. The light filtered through the trees, giving everything a green hue. The child ran in front of me, moving with incredible speed for someone with such small legs. They let out a loud, playful laugh, using their hands to climb up a large, old tree. Its branches appeared to weep, as most of them pointed downward in a wave motion.

I laughed along with the child. "Hey, now that isn't fair." I pouted at them dramatically. They peered over the enormous trunk to stare down at me. I stuck my tongue out defiantly. They screamed with excitement and giggled again.

"Pway!" the little one squealed.

"Sure little one, let's play. Find your mamma." I held out my arms to them. The ring on my finger flashed as a small patch of sunlight hit it.

"Come on, come down so I can carry you."

"Noooo, play instead." The little one rolled from the edge of the limb away from view.

"We can still play, we can play—" My voice faltered as I racked my brain for something a small child would enjoy. "Hey, I know, let's play *tell me your name and I will tell you mine!*"

"My name is Erun Thurn. I am fifteen years old." Erun looked down at me from the limb. "Yer turn. Yer turn," they said, tapping the bark.

"My name is Elowen. You, my little one, can call me Elle."

"Ewwe," Erun said, as if they were testing how it rolled off the tongue.

"Do you wanna play tag?" I asked Erun. *Surely they will run straight to their house or mom, right?*

"Tag?" Erun cocked her head to the side, scratching at her head.

I closed my eyes and sighed internally. *How does this child not know what tag is?*

"Yes, tag. I chase you while you try to run away." I raised an eyebrow at my response. *That's the best you can do to describe tag,* my inner monologue retorted.

"Oh, wanna play grab the water nymph."

"Grab the water nymph?" I raised an eyebrow at her.

"Yes!" With a squeal, they jumped from the top branch with grace. My heart palpitated as their slight form seemed to meet the ground unscathed.

"I be the water nymph. You can't catch me!" Erun said before bolting deeper into the forest.

I grinned as I ran after them. The birds seem to chortle at us as we bounded through the forest. Flowers were growing in patches at the bottom of trees, each one unique from the other. Bugs buzzed through the area, trying to find a place to perch. Erun ran, jumping over fallen trees and small puddles. I laughed as I ran for them, the glee of play coming back to me like a child. Erun paused abruptly. The laughing had stopped as a familiar voice called out.

"Elowen, so nice of you to play with my child. Thank you for playing with my mischievous little Erun."

Lilja POV

I stared at the body of water before me. The water was still other than a few occasional ripples made from a water bug. I looked around, sighing. *Elowen should have made it back by now. She is probably with Aidan. They seem rather close to each other. Probably trauma bonding or something like that.*

I groaned as I got up. The discomfort from the last few weeks of sleeping on the ground had finally seeped into my bones. Keres had popped up her smaller tent next to Elle's and my tent to take a nap. I rolled my eyes; she was always the one to take the opportunity for a quick snooze. A few forest nymphs meandered their way near our camp, still transfixing Cassia. She seemed delighted to talk to them about gods knows what.

The nymph seemed content to listen to whatever Cassia was saying, even allowing her to touch the flowers and vines growing out of her head. *Pretty docile beings.*

Aidan strode his way towards me. A small notebook in his hand, the glasses on his face threatening to fall off as they were on a balancing act on the tip of his nose. I fought the urge to punch him in the face as he neared me.

"What do you want, Aidan?" I pinched the bridge of my nose, feeling a stress headache coming on.

"I just wanted to say sorry about earlier. I just thought when you said *your Elle*, you meant you had told her about the whole being fated thing." He rushed out the words without pause.

"This is your fault. However, I should have told her when I first found out." I looked over the lake, avoiding eye contact with him.

"Where is Elowen? I wanted to apologize to her too. Is she in your tent?" As he already shuffled towards the large tent in the growing campground.

"Wait, I thought she was with you." I jogged up to Aidan, instinctually grabbing on to his shoulder. He flinched under the contact, shrugging away from the touch.

"Sorry, Elowen was with you, right?" I asked, fighting my voice to not raise an octave.

"No, I thought she would be mad at me for hiding the truth from her.

So I gave her space." His eyes widened as he understood the severity of the situation.

I turned, not saying anything to Aidan as I ran back towards the clearing. *Should I try the mind link we share? No—it might freak her out even more to know that I can talk in her head,* I thought grimly as I took the path we took forty-five minutes prior. Aidan ran after me, using one of his arms to block the onslaught of branches, trying to cut his face.

I took a labored breath as I entered the clearing ground from the earlier fight between Aidan and the Ossory wolf. The pushed down grass was the only remnant of anyone being here. I turned, stalking up to Aidan who was a few feet away from me, grabbing the top collar of his shirt.

"If anything happens to Elowen because of this, it will be your head on the chopping block." *Did she leave because of me? Was she taken?* My heart ached as I thought of the possibilities.

Aidan's eyes widened with fear, gulping as I began looking for tracks.

30

The Mother of All

Lilja POV

Aidan and I followed the trail of broken twigs and branches silently. Anger rolled off of me like a tsunami. I clenched my fist as doubt grew in my head. *Did she run away? Away from me? Was she captured? By the Ardourians? Keres said that Cassia and she were being watched.*

Thoughts of the unknown swirled in my head as I found footprints. The footprints were small, each little toe was clearly indented into the mud. I looked up, staring at the old tree in front of it.

"Whoever these footprints belong to must have climbed the tree to scout for something. Or someone." Aidan's voice cut through the forest silence like a hot knife. I turned my eyes, sending figurative daggers in his direction.

"Wow, Aidan. Thank you for the wonderful deduction. I never would have found that out on my own," I said.

"Hey, I was just saying what I was thinking. They must have been watching Elowen walk away from the clearing. Maybe she got confused in the fight you guys had?"

"Ugh, we didn't have a fight. Even if it was a fight, this is all your fault." I searched the ground for more footprints. On the other side of the tree was a larger set of prints, clearly Elowen's. She must have been hiding from whoever was chasing her and they crawled up the tree to get the jump on her. My heart sank.

"This wouldn't be my fault if you had just told her you were fated. You knew she was gay—"

"No, I didn't know for sure. I *assumed*. You know what people say about assuming, right?" My tone was sharper than I intended, but I kept my stance. This mess we were in was his fault.

He winced at my tone. My words assaulted him like hail. "It makes an ass out of you and me," he said, peering down at the fresh prints a few lengths away from the tree.

Aidan pointed to the ground. "The assailant must be after Elle."

Again, obviously. I bit my tongue to not make another smart response. We rushed through the dense overgrowth. The footprints were spread apart in long strides. *The assailant was small. What were they? Some type of nymph species I wracked my brain for the history lessons drilled into me from my endless number of tutors. Drawing a blank,* I cursed myself for not paying enough attention in class.

"Do you know of any small species that would fit these footprints? Clearly, they are some sort of humanoid creature based on these footprints." We followed the tracks. Elowen's and the assailant were practically on top of each other. *Must have been a close run. Why do humans run so slowly? How is she supposed to run away properly when she is a whole other species?*

"Do you think she ran away from us? Maybe she found someone to take her back to the Human Realm."

His words hit me like daggers, impaling my heart and my emotions. I winced, not saying anything. *Gods, I need a drink after this.* I roughly ran my fingers through the longer part of my hair, rubbing my hand down my face.

A scream called out, cutting through the thick dark trees of Sald Forest.

"Elowen!" I bounded through the forest. Years of strategy flew out the window as I bounded after my fated. My Elowen. Aidan followed immediately after. My eyes were on the ground, watching the tracks before me. One after another, I pushed myself, willing the ground underneath me to obey my will. The trees blurred past me, leaving Aidan struggling to catch up.

The ground underneath my feet faltered, sending me flying forward.

"Now Lilja, while I appreciate an entrance. The going-to-war look is rather unnecessary," a familiar voice called out.

I rolled forward in a somersault, attempting to cover my face from kissing the ground. I whipped my head around, finding nothing except trees, jumping up. My chest moved up and down rapidly, the use of my gift leaving me winded.

"Where's Elowen?" I called out as Aidan caught up. He raised his eyebrow at me, yelling into the forest. The leaves on the trees absorbed my words; my yelling fell on deaf ears.

"What are you doing? Why did you stop?" Aidan asked, alarm obvious in voice.

"Somebody spoke, ugh, their voice! It was so familiar, I-I can't place it," I searched through the trees, frantically.

Elowen POV

The scream died in my throat as I stared at the rooted lady. She stood before me, her roots transformed, trading the dark wood for dark skin. The long twigs on her head, replaced with long dreads reaching her waist. I stumbled backwards, tripping over a rock, sending me on my butt. I winced as I contacted the ground. Sticks and small rocks dug into my skin.

"Fear not, Elowen Alwyn. I do not wish to hurt you, but to warn you." She extended her still-altering hand to me. I stared at it for a moment, watching the roots shift and become skin. I grabbed hold of it, trying to ignore the movement in my palm.

"Is the little nymph your daughter or was play time a ploy to just get me alone?" I spoke as I crossed my arms, scanning the trees for a trap. *She won't even need a trap; she'd kill me with the snap of her fingers.*

"It was not a complete lie. Erun is, in fact, my daughter. I am the mother of all forest nymphs. The creator of all things nature—give me a moment," she said, disappearing into the air.

I stared at the vacant space she'd just stood in with shock. Erun stood behind it, looking not at all shocked by what occurred. She played with the mud created by her "mom."

The rooted lady reappeared as soon as she came, showing up to the right of where she had been. On each side was a confused-looking Aidan and an angry Lilja. Her arms were crossed and her hair had fallen into her eyes, making it appear something physical must have happened.

My heart felt like it faltered as I gazed upon my fated. I looked away as the pain welling in my chest threatened to fall out of my eyes.

Liljas' face was tight with worry as she looked me up and down. While she didn't speak in my head, her eyes told another story. *Are you okay?* They seemed to ask.

"Anyway, before I was interrupted, I am the one who creates all living plant—"

"I thought the gods did that," my arms still crossed. Lilja's presence called to my heart, commanding it to beat erratically in my chest.

Aidan scoffed. Lilja sucked in a breath.

"I am a demigod, you insolent girl. I am here to help you, not be insulted about my lineage by your feigned ignorance. The Ardourians are close. Day by day, they grow closer to finding out you have been spying on them."

"How do you know such things?" Lilja's voice was loud, with an edge to it. Sharp enough to cut anyone who got too close.

"Little queen, I have roots extending the whole content. One just has to know to listen to what they have to say. How do you think the oracle could see into the near future, how Elowen took a quick peek at the bloodshed to come? Hm? Me, that's how, for I am Darach, the mother of all forest nymphs and the creator of plants." The words rolled off her tongue with the ease of someone full of themselves.

"What do you gain from helping us? Why warn us about the Ardourians? Elowen has already seen the past. We know the Ardourians are the ones behind the attack." Lilja cut straight to the point. *Why would she help us? What does she gain from helping us?*

"Like I have pointed out, my roots allow me to see into what can be. The future as it stands is grave. If you do not gather your troops before the season changes, the blight will ravage your country beyond a few thousand dead. Your friends—well—grave." Darach's tone was dark, her face just as upsetting. "While I do not have the luxury of helping in the fight to set things right, I can give hints when deemed appropriate."

"That's what you call a hint?" I looked at her with disdain.

"You merely said we were going to die, and the Ardourians are close. How does that get us any closer to a cure for the blight?"

"If you don't go to war with the Ardourians, you won't be able to save Valdis." Her words hung heavy in the air as her body disappeared along with her young child. Aidan, Lilja and I stared at each other in shock.

Till seasons' change? That's a few mere weeks away.

31

Before the Seasons Change

Elowen POV

"How in the gods' hell are we supposed to gather forces that quickly?" The earlier uneasiness from Lilja's presence was gone, replaced with anger and fear.

Lilja and Aidan stayed silent for a moment. Lilja ran her steady hand through her black hair.

"The forces are already gathered—" Lilja said.

"Wait, what do you mean the forces have been gathered? I thought you disbanded the military on Ebbon Mountain after rumors swirled in Ardour?" My voice shook as I spoke. Were we going to die? Was Lilja going to die? My chest tightened at the thought. I winced at the uncomfortable feeling.

"I merely told the men and women to disperse on the mountain and hide the supplies. That way, when it was time to strike, we'd have the supplies and the hands," she said, calmly for a queen ready to start a war with another kingdom.

She would do anything for her kingdom, the voice in my head said. *Kill people, sleep—wait, did I even check on her? Is she okay? I never even asked.*

"Kallan and Armand should be there by now. We need to make preparations. By the end of the next month, we will be at war." Lilja's voice was stern. Hate and anger built inside her as she stood before me.

Lilja POV

I was angry—so angry. My world threatened. My kingdom threatened. By what? A fucking blight, a mere sickness of a damn plant. A blight threatened to take my kingdom, my friends and family are being threatened from existence. Unless what? *Unless I cause a war that might decide the fate of my kingdom.*

Elowen's sad eyes watched me, as if she could hear the thoughts that I locked in my head. *I could share these thoughts with her, but does she want to be my fated?* I couldn't make that decision for her. She had to decide that she wanted it. Consent was everything. I couldn't force her into anything. I couldn't live with that.

"Let's get back to camp. We need to notify the others," I said, my voice hollow of emotion—a skill I learned a long time ago. Aidan opened his mouth as if to say something, but didn't. We rushed back to the lake. Keres, Cassia, and the boys were laughing and hugging. Their faces were full of joy as they embraced.

My face was grim as I walked forward. Armand and Keres embraced each other begrudgingly. However, the siblings gazed at each other with warmth. *Why does this happen to me, today? Today is supposed to be joyous. For the first time in our lifetimes, my team is healthy and well fed.*

"I would say, gentleman, but we both know neither of you are." A grin spread across my face. Regardless of the situation, I was glad to see my family.

"Come on Lil, is that any way to treat us? Oof, I am wounded. Your brutality astounds me." Armand clapped his hand on my shoulder.

I winced as it made contact, still smiling. Even with the history we held between all of us, the things we had to do to keep our kingdom safe were immense. These individuals before me had my back. *They would go to war with me,* I thought grimly.

"I know I'm a gentleman. But I can't speak the same as the oaf next to me," Kallan said, interrupting the depressing thoughts in my head.

His black hair tousled, as if he had run his hands through it multiple times. Muscles had covered his arms and legs before our separation. However, with a well-balanced diet, my dearest friend had become a well-defined man. *The ladies of the court would think the same.* My inner voice sang gleefully for him.

How different from the young stable hand boy I met when we were kids.

"You know I might just believe, but *just*," Elowen said in her usual soft tone. The anger and fear in her voice earlier gone, as if nothing bothered her. Deep down, I knew it was still with her. The forced smile she gave everyone was to just hide the sadness that ate at her, bit by bit. My heart tugged at the idea of a time when she wouldn't be present in my world.

Elowen walked over to Kallan and gave him a peck on the cheek. While Armand balked at her.

"I'll have you know, Miss Alwyn, that I have not once looked at your ass. I can't say the same for Kallan." Armand crossed his arms playfully, leaning his cheek down for Elowen to kiss. Elowen laughed, giving Armand a dramatic kiss on the cheek.

"I'm sorry to interrupt this beautiful moment, but we need to talk." My voice was low, the severity of the situation weighing down on me. Everyone turned their attention to me, the joy of being back together squashed by my tone.

I looked around the area of the lake we were in. The nymphs were lounging. Not a single castle goer was present, save for a few servants cutting shrubs into place. "Let's all meet in my tent."

Everyone gathered their items and entered the tent silently. The mood was significantly dampened. "We have received word that the Ardourians are close. War will happen before the seasons change."

The group before me looked unsurprised at my announcement. Kallan squirmed on the pillow he sat on. "Before we left Ardour, Armand and I interrogated the general of the training ground. Quite a few trainees went missing during our time. On one of our last nights, we found one of those young men. Barely clinging to life. The general then murdered him at the training ground. The general said—" Kallan paused his explanation for a second while taking a breath.

Armand's tired voice interjected. "Long story short, the general claimed that Olken Elves are back."

The room exploded into uproar save for Elowen, who remained quiet. I held up a hand to silence my dear friends. "Explain. What did the general specifically say?" *Gods, this is giving me a headache.*

Kallan began explaining again, with a much more concise version ending with a huff.

"What is an Olken elf?" Elowen's soft voice called out.

"The Olken elves are thought to be extinct. However, they differ from us and are more dangerous. Some of the ancient texts even suggest they were demigods sent from the underworld. Their powers were—*are*—dark magic. Different from the earthly powers we possess," Aidan said, the history lesson flowing from his mouth as if he were a scholar.

"A few of them took on animal body parts, instead of their Elven one—"

"Like the Ossory wolf?" Elowen asked.

Aidan raised an eyebrow, the question clear.

"I'll tell you later." My mind was scrambling trying to connect how the Ossory wolves were a part of the Olken elves.

"They must be descendants," Elowen said, her face pale.

I walked over to her, squeezing her shoulder slightly, towering over her seated form. "Hey, don't worry, the Ossory wolf here won't hurt us. He works for the king and queen of Sald."

"No, it-it's not that. The man who took the vial had feathers. H-he turned into a bird. He had gray skin! He had to be an Olken elf!" Elowen hit the table with her fist, surprising me.

"Why didn't you tell me before?" I fought the anger that fought to spill out.

She shrunk under my touch. "I-I didn't know the connection. Like the Ossory wolves, I thought they were special. I didn't know they were evil."

"Wait, if these elves were so powerful, how did they go extinct?" Cassia asked, dispelling the situation between me and Elowen.

Aidan looked upward as if trying to search through the plethora of information stored in his head. "They traveled over the north mountains and never returned. Many people assumed the dry heat got to them, or some distant civilization took them out."

I paced what little space I had left in my tent. "This information does nothing to help us. Aidan, I need you to send word to the troops. They need to congregate again. This time we will attack Ardour. No more spy work. They have the answers, and if they don't want to give it up willingly, I will take it from Queen Alieta's cold, dead hands."

Slowly, the heads around the circle nodded grimly. War was something no one enjoyed, death was never something to sing about. However, we needed to be free of the grip Ardour had on us.

32

For a Favor

Elowen POV

"I'll send out scouts to my second-in-command. He'll be more than pleased to hear that this cursed war is happening." Aidan's voice was rough, showing that he was anything but happy with the threat of war looming over our heads.

We all nodded in response. Liljas' face was grim.

"Is Valdis capable of taking on Ardour?" My timid opinion flew out of my mouth before I could censor it. All heads whipped towards me in surprise.

"I-I just mean, the Ardourians have been well fed and trained their whole lives." The unspoken words hung in the air. *The Valdisians haven't been.* The people before me were courageous. But they lacked the strength that came from having a nutritional diet their whole life. On the other hand, the Ardourians were basically bred to fight.

Lilja sighed, looking at the top of the canvas tent. "We are currently eight thousand strong. The men and women in my fleet have trained since they were young children to gain the right to fight in the Valdis army. While we haven't gained muscle mass like Ardourians, we make that up with courage and ingenuity." For a moment, she looked down at me. "It's true, unfortunately, that we don't have the numbers that Ardour has."

The room was silent. Keres stared out of the flap of the tent, gazing at the green foliage growing in the tree line.

"Why not ask the people of Sald to join the fight?" Keres finally said.

Kallan snorted. "You'd have a better time trying to get the nymphs to help you."

"That may not be a bad idea. Why not ask both? Water nymphs can swim up rivers and scout the land before we get there. Elves think all the nymphs are extinct. Why not use that to our advantage?" The words flew out of my mouth with ease as I saw the scenario in my head.

"Forest nymphs can morph into trees and travel through the roots. We could really use that to our advantage." Cassia pulled back her curly red hair from her face.

"Nymphs have a price for the help they give, and a request of that magnitude will have an enormous cost." Kallan crossed his arms.

Lilja balanced on the back legs of her chair, precariously. "The Ardourians placed a spell on the nymphs. They're trapped here."

"Hm, we could speak to Darach. She is their creator. She's bound to have some thoughts about getting rid of the spell that binds them here." Aidan finished cleaning the smudges off his glasses, looking at us as he spoke.

"Every time we have come in contact with her, she finds us. How on earth are we supposed to find her?" My question hung in the air until Armand spoke up.

"When we were younger, our mother would tell us stories about a hero who contacted a god by praying every day—"

"Brother, we do not have the luxury of hoping Darach will come immediately from one prayer."

"As I was saying, sister, the hero of the story, made an offering into a fire. I'm sure if we made an offering large enough, she'd come. How could she resist?" Armand finished, waiting for a reaction.

Aidan flipped through his journal, his finger following his writing, reading out loud. "After our first meet up with our lovely demigod acquaintance, I researched her in Ardour's library. One book spoke of an old tale. In exchange for a wish, a young Elven woman gave a lock of her hair to Darach."

"What does Darach want with a lock of hair?" Lilja settled the four legs of her chair back on the ground, leaning onto the table.

"The book said she used them to grow trees in her garden. A piece of the person's soul comes with it, diminishing their life force." Aidan gulped as he finished the passage in his journal.

Silence spread across the table. I shifted in my seat uncomfortably. "We have to. Darach might be our only hope."

We went to work, making the fire outside our tent larger. Servants catered our dinner to us as we worked, but it went untouched. Cassia rolled the cart of food over to the fire, sending it in with a prayer. Lilja pulled her knife from her belt, cutting a chunk of hair from her head. Her face somber as she handed the blade to me.

One by one, we all cut a locket of hair, clenching onto them. "Darach, we call on you the Mother of Nymphs—" Lilja held my hand, cutting off circulation to my fingers as she spoke.

"Well hello, what an unexpected surprise. I'm not even dressed. It has been a while since I've been summoned. To be summoned by a queen. What an honor." Darach stepped out of the clearing. A bathrobe hung limply around her otherwise naked form. She looked almost human, her long wooden braids put up in a silk bonnet.

I bowed low. "We apologize for the unexpected house call, Darach." Lilja bowed to Darach. "We would like to ask you for your help—"

Darach clapped her hands, a grin growing on her masked face. "Ooh a favor! How exciting! Do go on!"

"The Ardourians have put a spell on your children. We would like to help them, with your aid," Lilja said.

"What do you offer for my help? With my children stuck in Sald Forest, they are safe. I cannot assure their safety out in the world." She eyed the hair in our hands hungrily, licking her lips.

I held out my hand, my lock of hair encased in it. "I hear you like growing your garden; would you like to grow your orchard?"

"You realize this would shorten your lifespan, making a permanent hole in your soul? Elowen, darling, if you're not careful, you could die. The price might be too high. Are you willing to pay that price?" Darach eyed me curiously.

Without looking at Lilja, I nodded, a lump forming in my throat. "Yes, I am—we are—sure."

She snapped her fingers, and a velvet bag appeared in my hand. I placed my hair inside, handing it around in a circle to my friends. The air in my lungs felt like it was emptying. I coughed, and my friends joined me.

Darach grinned at our coughing fit, snapping the bag back into her hands. I covered my mouth, pulling away my hand to reveal blood splattered on my pale skin. "My darling elves, a year is what I have taken from you. I have been gracious, for stopping the war will benefit us both."

Lilja wiped the blood from my hand with the bottom of her shirt. Her forehead creased with worry. "Why would you ask for the hair if this will benefit you?"

"You already had the lock cut. How could I not ask for it? The spell is simple. Take this flower to release my children. A pretty little thing from my garden, a drop of the queen's and Elowen's blood, paint it onto a piece of bark. Drop it into the lake. With that, the spell will break."

"Why Lilja's and my blood, specifically? I am only human." My voice was empty of emotion. *A year? A year off my life.* How many would I have left?

"My darling Elowen, you are fated to help Valdis defeat Ardour. You are quite literally fated to Lilja for life, and the blood of a fated couple holds special magic. A powerful magic, something that cannot just be conjured. You'll paint your blood onto the bark because I have created this whole forest—it's a piece of me—and that piece of nature will call on my power to help the curse break. Keep in mind, my children are not dense. It'd be a good idea to bind them to help you before you release them into the world."

Without allowing us to ask questions, she disappeared, only leaving the flower in her wake. I closed my mouth, the question I had dying on my lips.

We stared at each other. Lilja walked over to the spot Darach stood, reaching down grabbing the flower.

"Kallan and Cassia, I need you to ask Queen Pelicia if we can recruit the people who want to fight. The blight affects all of us, Sald Forest included." Lilja said, as she looped her fingers through mine, and my ring twisted with the movement.

"We will speak with Sylp, the leader of the water nymphs. Hopefully, we can reach some type of agreement with the nymphs. Keres, I need you to scout out a suitable area for a temporary training ground. We need to get back in shape," Lilja said, dismissing the team. The sun beat down on us as we walked towards the lake in silence.

My heart pulsed in my throat, threatening to pop out. "How will we bind them to us? What if they wish to remain in Sald? After all, they are safer here."

Lilja stroked her thumb on the back of my hand gently. "I'm not sure, but whatever it is, we will face it together," Lilja said.

She grabbed an empty bowl from our sacrificed dinner, tearing off the petals. Using a small piece of firewood, she rubbed the flower into a paste. She looked at me expectantly, taking her knife, poking her finger, and sending a small drop of blood into the bowl. I did the same. Once finished, we headed towards the lake.

Sald Lake before us was crystal clear. The water nymphs were careful not to disturb the sediment at the bottom. The large ceremonial cave, barely visible at the bottom. To the right of the castle, most of the water nymphs lounged. The waterfall misted them, giving their bodies a shimmer as the sun hit the speckles of water.

"Sylp," I called out over the water. "May we speak to you in private?" I asked as she lounged on the wet rocks.

She stared at us for a moment and nodded, pushing herself off the rock. Her clothes and hair were thoroughly soaked; her blue skin seemed to reflect the sunlight as she approached. I raised my eyebrow, looking down at my finger and then back to her. My ring was still tied to her hair, sparkling as the sun hit it. *Lilja remade it?*

"Yes, Queen Lilja and Lady Elowen." Internally I rolled my eyes as she spoke. We did not need theatrics at a time like this.

"We would like to ask the esteemed race of forest and water nymphs to join us in the upcoming war against Ardour. Darach has warned us that the war will hit us before the changing of season." I struggled to not marvel at Lilja as she spoke with such eloquent ease.

Sylp raised an eyebrow, hissing low with disgust. "Stuck here, we are. Leave man will kill us," Sylp said as if the words refused to obey her wish of coming out of her mouth. "Elven dark magic, find us will."

"I will assure you the Olken elves will have no idea we are making a pact. Once Ardour is underneath our power, we will push back the Olkens to wherever they have been hiding for the last thousands of years," Lilja said, not wanting to spook the nymph before us.

I walked forward, slowly, tentatively putting my hand on her shoulder. "What happened to your father was wrong. He died saving his people and saving you. Don't let his sacrifice be in vain because of fear. The blight won't pick sides. The magic sickness that ravages Valdis will get here. When it does, it won't hesitate to infect you too."

Tears sprang to her eyes as I finished speaking. Then, in an instant, they were gone; the tears were replaced with hard resolve.

"Fight cannot. Bound land here. Told before to you. Incompetent are human." Sylp looked at me and then at Lilja.

I squared my shoulders. "We have spoken to Darach, striking a deal with her to help release you from your prison. But only if you agree to help us first."

Lilja pulled the bark out from behind her, the sigil already dried on it.

Sylp stared at it, her hand twitched at her side. As if she wanted to reach out and grab the spell from her. "Fight in war will. However, over when require will favor need." Lilja stilled next to me.

"What type of favor do you require, Sylp?" Liljas' voice was cautious. She eyed the dripping women before us, warily.

"Know not yet, moment in will know," Sylp shrugged as she spoke, as if that were the most logical answer.

I glanced at Lilja and mulled the answer over. We *needed* this, Lilja needed this. I twisted the ring on my finger anxiously. Sylp's eyes traveled to the movement.

"Yes, it's a deal." The words felt like a hollow reply as I extended my hand out to her. Her icy hand sent a shiver down my spine as she contacted my forearm. Pain spread throughout the surface of my arm. I gritted my teeth in response, willing myself not to cry out. Her hand revealed an intricate scar, not much longer than my ring finger, as she pulled away. The scar was three lines resembling waves.

"What is that?" Lilja's voice was sharp with anger.

"Bind is, word is permanent. Word carried out not die will," Sylp said.

"I'll *die* if I don't follow through with my word?"

"Correct, human young."

I grabbed Liljas' hand and pulled her back roughly as she lounged for the nymph before us.

"That was never part of the deal! You didn't think to mention this before we agreed?" Lilja screamed, her voice garnering the attention from the nymphs still sunbathing on the rocks in front of us.

Sylp shrugged again. "Asked never. Not fear, if you complete on plan our agreement through. The scar binds us." She held up her hand revealing a mirror scar on her wrist.

"She's right, we never asked, Lilja. Drop it. I don't intend for us to go back on my word, anyway. So it's fine," I stressed to Lilja, still gripping onto her tall frame. "You don't intend to go back on yours. Finish the spell, Lilja."

I eyed the scar warily; they placed it right above the brand from my previous life. Sylp retreated, taking her place among the rocks.

Lilja searched my eyes for any doubt she thought I harbored about the idea and pulled me into a tight hug. "You shouldn't have done that. You're now bound to them. I'm sorry—I didn't realize the practice of binding your word to your lifeline was real. The nymphs have been gone for so long that I thought most of the stories surrounding them were false. From what I've read, the spell will physically manifest itself until it is over." Her usual calm demeanor was replaced with a stressed-out version.

"Hey." I placed my hand on her cheek. "It'll be okay, I promise."

Lilja sucked in a breath before chucking the bark into the water. For a moment, nothing happened, long enough for me to wonder if we did it right. Bubbles exploded from the lake, sending out a green wave of color into the lake. The color washed over the nymphs in front of us all took a collective gasp, smiling. A few laughed, uncharacteristically giddy, as if a weight had been lifted off their shoulders.

"It is done. Please begin traveling to the countryside. Stay unseen and unheard. It is important your presence goes unnoticed for as long as possible. Keep an eye out on the Ardour military. It is important to find every detail they know." Lilja held up her hands, projecting her voice as far as possible.

The nymphs jumped in the water. With the spell broken they were free to travel out of Sald through the water. The sound of splashes filled my ears as Lilja turned to me. She cupped my face, "Elowen, it is imperative that when Sylp calls on you, you go to her. There is no expiration date on this type of spell, it doesn't fade. You must complete whatever she asks of you, no matter the task. Your life depends on it. Now let's go find where Keres placed the temporary camp."

My mind raced as I pulled her away from the nymphs, following what already seemed to be a mass of servants doing the bidding of Keres.

"Why did the binding include the scar?" I asked as I traced it with my finger, sending a shiver down my spine. *One more scar on my body wouldn't hurt me more than any of the other ones.*

"From what I have heard and read, the scar is to serve as a physical representation of the binding. Quite honestly, I thought it just sounded like a scare tactic. Because depending on who is involved in the spell, the scar could be anywhere and be anything." Lilja squeezed my hand, before pulling it up to kiss the back of it.

At least it's not on my face.

"Let's head over to the training ground, I'm sure it's almost done." I said, attempting to keep things light, not wanting my worry to transfer over to her.

I watched in awe as large carts were being pulled by ponies into the clearing I had visited in the past, where Sylp's father was murdered. The area used to be covered with flowers, but now was covered with grass. Dead limbs were strewn at the edges of the trees. Keres stood in the center of the clearing, her eyes closed with concentration.

We stared at her for a moment as she sent out a controlled burst of flame, burning off a large portion of grass. Opening her eyes, she stumbled forward, the use of her powers sapping the energy from her. Lilja rushed to catch her friend. "Oof, I got you. What did you do that for?"

"I wanted to make a space for sparring." Keres leaned into Lilja, breathing heavily.

"You could have just had the servants cut the grass." Lilja rolled her eyes.

"Where's the fun in that? We need to train now, not when the servants find time to trim the clearing down." Keres coughed, righting herself.

Servants began breaking off the long branches of the decaying fallen trees at the end of the clearing, strategically placing them around the perimeter of the burnt ground.

"I have Aidan grabbing supplies from the castle. They should finish the training ground by the end of the night. Honestly, we could even start sparring now, if we wanted to." Keres finished her sentence with a huff, sitting on a limb lining the sparring ground.

"I don't think you'll do much sparring in that state." Aidan's glasses were finally placed where they were supposed to be. His tunic appeared to be pressed and tucked in.

I raised my eyebrow. "Well, don't you look presentable?"

"I'm going to take that as a compliment. It's rather hard to look nice when we are constantly traveling over the countryside." Aidan pushed his hair back, the locks perfectly placed until Kallan reached up behind him and ruffled it.

"You know, I think it looks much better like this." Kallan snorted.

Armand attempted to stifle a laugh from beside him with a cough.

"At least you didn't have to stand in front of a crowd imploring them to help for the good of the world. A few of them downright laughed at us. Idiotically saying that the blight is fake. These elves have not been past the fog of this forest for hundreds of years. They can take that ignorance and shove it up their asses." Kallan crossed his arms, glaring at Lilja, as if asking, *why would you make me do this?*

"I see regardless of whether in human or Elven society, some people are still simpleminded." I rolled my eyes.

"Did anyone join in the fight?" Lilja said as a party of approximately 200 strong walked through the trees. Pelicia and her husband were at the front.

"These courageous elves have joined the fight. The blight will soon affect all of us. They have agreed to train and fight to your command, Queen Lilja of Valdis." Pelicia's voice floated over the noisy crowd easily.

Lilja nodded in their direction, overcome with emotions. "Thank you for joining the fight. With your help, the blight will soon be behind us." Her voice was full of love and admiration for the people standing before me.

They ranged in different shades of colors and sizes. Some were old, some were young. The clothing they wore ranged from fine to peasant. Regardless of the garbs on their bodies, these men, women, and everything in between wanting to fight for what was right.

The rest of the day happened in a blur, consisting of training. Aidan and Kallan took up the bulk of my teaching. Having never truly thrown a punch in my life, they had a long road before I was self-sufficient in a fight.

I huffed myself down beside the fire. Nighttime seemed to come quickly. My body was bruised from the day's events. *I was going to be sore in the morning.* My inner voice groaned at me in protest. The fire crackled, the light from it casting shadows over the team surrounding the rest of the space around the flame.

33

Found Family

"Cassia, how did you come to meet Lilja and the team?" I looked at her, realizing she was the only one whose story I didn't know. Cassia's dark skin seemed to glow with the light of the fire, her hair matching the light it gave off.

"Oh, I'm actually the newest member of the group. I only met Lilja and the rest of the group around—how long has it been? Hmm, probably around twenty-five years ago—"

"Twenty-five years?!" I exclaimed, looking at Cassia with wide eyes.

"I mean, come on, Elle. Everyone else has known me for over a hundred years," Lilja said back to me as she traced invisible swirls onto my thigh closest to her, sending shivers up my spine.

"Oh yeah, I forget that you guys are literally hundreds of years older than me," I said, earning groans from the elves around the fire.

"Gods, you make us sound so old," Keres said.

"Well—"

"No, I don't want to hear it." Lilja nudged my side slightly.

"Anyway," Cassia said, "I grew up in Havn poor and orphaned, my biological parents killed in the war between Valdis and Ardour. The nuns that raised me kicked me out when I became an adult—"

"War? I thought we were just now potentially getting into a war with Ardour. There was one before this?" I snuggled into Lilja more. Her body heat radiated off her comfortably, keeping me warm.

"My parents went to war with Ardour almost 200 years ago, following an assassination attempt against them. Ardour was the obvious perpetrator. They killed the king and queen of Ardour in the battle," Lilja said, as if reading from a textbook.

"Anyway, as I was saying before Lilja's history lesson, when the nuns kicked me out, I had nowhere to go. No money to my name. I decided to work on a ship. Havn is the hub of all exports and imports into the country. So it wasn't hard to get a job. On a trip to the mainland, the ship I was working on got attacked by pirates. They enslaved everyone who survived the attack on board, including me. Eventually, I got sick of people pushing me around, so I pushed back, killing the captain. Unbeknownst to me, if you kill the captain of the pirate ship, you become the captain."

"You were a pirate?" I looked at Cassia and then went back to Lilja. *A pirate? Is Lilja a pirate?* I racked my brain trying to put all the pieces together. "So what kind of deal did she want?" I sat forward, slightly, out of excitement.

"Yes, for a few years, Lilja and the rest of us were pirates. However, I was with my crew and she was with them. As for the deal: Lilja wanted help, and I was a well-known pirate. She came to find me."

"Well known? You *were* the pirate of the sea," Kallan said, bolstering his friend.

"If you were so well known, then why did you leave your boat?" I asked.

"Ah, that is because I saved Liljas' life from the Llidan troops and she offered me a spot on her crew. It the day of a terrible storm—"

Cassia POV

The wind whipped at my curly hair as another wave came onto the ship assaulting the poor crew present. Few crew members let out a yelp as the wave threw them around on the deck. Ropes tied to their waist were the only thing keeping them on the boat as they worked to keep us afloat. Rain pelted me as I stood at the helm. I grunted, trying to turn the wheel.

My second pulled hard on the slick wood next to me. With his help, it would bend to our will, moving ever so slightly.

"Captain!" Mink, my third mate, called out from the bird's nest. I looked at him, squinting as he pointed towards the horizon. I looked around at my crew as the waves came at us in horror. This wave was huge, easily the height of a castle.

I grabbed Mink, pulling him to the mast, bear hugging us both to it, before the wave smashed into us. Chaos surrounded us; thumps and a loud resounding crack filled my ears. Water pushed against my body, screaming I gripped onto the mast, holding Mink with me, willing the earthly properties in the wood to keep us safe.

My crew was in a flurry of activity. The center mast laid broken in half on the deck. Its sail lay on the deck like a rag forgotten by someone cleaning up their summer home. "Roll up that cloth! Don't let the water take it!" They scrambled for it, my command enough for them to haul ass.

"If you let the water take that sail, I'll let the water take your ass with it! Do not tempt me!" I pulled the wheel again. My eyes searched the horizon. We had to find the eye.

"There!" Mink pointed off to the left. Sunlight showed through the clouds, blessed sunlight. We pulled at the helm, turning the ship, who creaked in protest. The tide was in our favor as we pushed forward. They rolled the sail up into the pieces of the broken mast.

Calmness hit us as we emerged into the eye. Sunlight beat on us as we cheered for the minor victory of staying alive. I grabbed at the small telescope on my belt, putting it to my eyes, and I scanned the horizon. Dark clouds still covered a majority of the sky. I gasped as a dark ship loomed into view. I looked up from the telescope as another ship made its way here. The ship was larger than my own.

Its coloring was black with dark maroon, the gun ports painted yellow. My heart fluttered with fear and anger as the black flag went up, the white symbols clear—pirates.

"Grab ye' weapons, crew! I believe we are about to meet some friends!" I hollered at my crew as I unsheathed the sword from my hip.

She gained on us fast and the wind seemed to will her forward to us. Before we knew it, the large ship sat next to us in the open water. *With our own ship crippled, we are defenseless to run away,* I thought.

With my sword unsheathed, I grabbed the large horn to amplify my voice. "We are not looking for a fight. But if you wish to fight, we will put you into the sea!" My crew roared with war cries as I spoke. We watched the captain climb the ropes on the side of her ship, skinny thing. Muscles shone through the dark clothes she wore as she stared at us, a grin on her face.

"I think your boat said no more fights," she pointed out, laughing at us.

"My ship is just having a bit of a moment, is all. I would be more worried about your crew having something similar if we get into a fight." I said. I wasn't afraid of her. While her ship was larger, we made up for the lack of size in people. My crew were the best out in the open waters. Trained and well paid, a family on water.

She scoffed, searching my eyes for an answer. To the question only she knew. "I am not here to fight you Cassia Castor of Havn, I am here to strike a deal."

I raised my eyebrow toward her in shock. *How does she know my name? What kind of deal does she want?*

"Wait, why were you on a boat looking for Cassia?" I asked Lilja.

"Um, well, with Valdis being starved out by the blight, we had to resort to less favorable ways to feed my subjects." Lilja spoke slowly, as if saying the sentence slower would lessen the implication behind her words.

"You stole from people?" I scooted away from her slightly, her missing hand on my leg leaving me feeling cold and empty.

"We pillaged, slightly." She raised an eyebrow at my sudden move away from her.

She pushed on speaking, the rest of the crew silent other than the crackling of the fire. "It's not like we had much of a choice, Elle. The choice was to take from people who are more fortunate and give it to my people or watch my people starve to death, or even resolve themselves into obtaining food in a less savory way. Like attacking our own people."

I fought the urge to say something. It was wrong. People died because of it, but Valdis needed the help. "How did the food you gathered from Llidan go into the people of Valdis?"

Lilja looked around at the faces surrounding the fire before answering. "We dropped it off at food banks. We didn't want anyone to know that we are the ones donating the food. It would raise too many questions. They'd distribute the food and keep their mouths shut. My people don't care where the food has come from, as long as it is safe to eat."

I merely nodded. This was one of those gray areas where not one way was the right way. People were getting hurt. She had minimized that. *There was no better way, I suppose.* I scooted back to her, welcoming her warm touch again before my gaze landed on

Aidan, who was getting up, stretching, "I don't know about you guys, but I am exhausted. Let's get to bed."

We all nodded in response. I was tired. Following Lilja to the tent, I plopped down, curling myself into the blanket next to her. I sighed contently, closing my eyes, letting sleep overtake me.

34

The Skin Weaver

Sun filtered into the tent, giving Lilja a soft glow as I awoke. I groaned as I sat up. The bruises that had occurred the night before littered my body; my muscles strained from the physical exercise. Lilja rolled over, putting an arm over her eyes, still asleep.

I leaned over, giving her a small kiss on the lips to wake her. "Wake up, my sleep queen. We have lots to do today," I said.

Lilja groaned in response, pulling me down and rolling us over so she was on top. She smiled before leaning down and kissing my forehead. "Let's just hide away for the day. Let's just stay in this tent and forget that the world is happening outside of this sanctuary."

"I wish we could," I said, cupping her face in my hand.

"Wakey wakey eggs and bakey!" Kallan shouted outside our tent, smacking the outside before busting in.

"Well, what were you guys doing?" He grinned, his hands on his hips. Looking like a disappointed parent, Lilja looked down at me, rolling her eyes before getting up.

"We were just speaking about hiding away for the day before you rudely interrupted us." she said, before taking off the shirt she slept in, throwing it at Kallan before grabbing a clean one to put on. Kallan rolled his eyes before turning around, unaffected by her nudity. My cheeks turned red for her. Lilja looked down, noticing the blush.

"Don't worry about me traumatizing him with my breasts. This man has seen me naked plenty of times," she said before she flipped off the back of Kallan's head.

"Yes, it's rather unfortunate, not much to look at. If I say so myself," he announced, still looking at the entrance of the tent.

"Hey!" Lilja threw another item of clothing at the man.

"Get out, so Elowen can get from underneath those covers. I don't think she wants you in the same tent as she changes. We will be out in a minute." Lilja pushed Kallan out of the tent. I got dressed quickly, not wanting him to pop back in for us taking too long. As I emerged from the tent, a flurry of activity happened. People carted weapons and supplies to the training area in the clearing.

Pelicia walked up to us, her long dress from the other day replaced with a new green dress. The blue swirls on her arms seemed to glow against the color contrast. I fought the urge to stare at them. Lilja looped her fingers with mine, the ring on my finger moving slightly with the movement.

The rest of the team was already awake and moving, the sun still rising slowly from its meeting with the earth. It gave everything a warm, lazy light. I fought the urge to yawn. *Fuck, I need coffee.* Clangs of metal filled the air. *How are people already training? I'm barely awake.*

"Alright, let's get you started on physical fighting. You need to hold your own in a fight," Aidan called out while jogging up to us.

"I don't know, Aidan. I'm not comfortable teaching Elowen how to fight. She shouldn't be on the front line," Kallan cut into the conversation.

"See it this way, if she is somehow captured by enemy lines, do you want her to be defenseless?" Lilja said, crossing her arms.

"Well—no. I guess not, but she is a human, Lilja. They are fragile creatures," he said.

"It's settled. We will train Elowen until she can hold her own in a fight. Or at least not die long enough for one of us to save her," Lilja said, the tone in her voice making it sound final. They all nodded, reservations gone, Aidan already pulling me into the ring. His burly frame seemed to dwarf me.

Slowly, we practiced, first how to throw a punch and then how to wrestle. Sweat beaded on my forehead, running into my eyes. I squinted at the burly figure coming at me. I twisted to the left, missing the full force behind it. His arm hit mine, making me stagger, the bone snapping in the process.

I gritted my teeth, tears pricking my eyes.

"Fuck," Lilja said as she walked over to me.

Aidan's face said it all. It was broken. "Man, I'm sorry, Elle. Truly, I didn't mean to I-I'm sorry," he said, exasperated. Gingerly, Lilja prodded at my arm. Her fingers barely touched me, her face pained.

"Aidan, go get Pelicia. She can heal her quickly!" Lilja commanded.

Aidan stalled slightly, his eyes flitting from me to Lilja. "*Now*, that's an order from your queen."

Her command was enough to yank him out of whatever trance he was in. Turning, he ran towards the large tent placed in the back of the clearing.

"I'm fine Lilja, it's just a bruise or something. Pelicia will heal me and then we can go back to training." I gritted my teeth, trying to ignore the tears threatening to spill over my eyelids.

"Elowen," she said. "It's definitely broken, Elle." Lilja walked me to the tent, where Aidan and Pelicia stood.

They were in deep conversation as we approached. I cradled my arm as we followed her to a cot.

"I'm really sorry, Elle," Aidan said, searching my eyes for any hatred.

"Don't worry about it, Aidan, you didn't mean it. I'm just a terrible student so far." I winced at the jolting movement.

"Everyone other than Elowen, out. I can't work with all of you yapping over here. Even if Elowen has a broken arm, I will heal it, so get out of my tent," Pelicia said, uncaring if she was talking to a queen or not.

Lilja gave me a long look, mouthing *I'll be waiting,* before walking away.

Pelicia clicked her tongue in disapproval. "What are we going to do with you, little human?"

Her blue-stained fingers grabbed onto my army, gently. "This may hurt a bit," she said, grabbing a thick leather strap of fabric with her free hand.

"Here, bite down on this. Queen Lilja would be rather displeased if I let you bite off your tongue. That is something I can't fix, just like some of the other ailments." The leather taste seemed to permeate my tongue as I closed my eyes.

The bone under my skin shifted. I bit into the leather strap, the skin around the area crawled with the sensation of movement. Almost like warm water rushing over the affected area. I sighed as the sensation stopped, the pain now gone.

"What things can't you heal?" I asked, blinking as the sensation subsided along with the pain.

"Hm, oh. Water mages cannot heal people with serious illnesses or from the brink of death; we can only do that if we want to deal with the consequences of it afterwards." Pelicia spoke as she washed her hands off in the white water basin on the table.

"What type of consequences?" I probed as I stood up.

"If we don't have some sort of protection stone or charm, the illness or injury could inflict itself upon us. In other terms, I would die. Water mages are a dying breed. I cannot reproduce the same way other elves can. If I were to die, the power within me would find another host. Or die out completely. I have not seen another water mage in years. I fear they are all gone, save for myself. The only other way to make more would be for Pavati, the goddess of rivers to create more mages. But I fear she is gone, she hasn't been seen for a hundred or so years." Pelicia looked up from her hands, pain clear in her voice.

I grabbed her hands. They were cold to my touch. "I'm sure there are other mages, Queen Pelicia. We just have to find them. I'm sure they will come out after the war is over, or maybe Pavati will come out of hiding."

She stared at me for a moment before motioning for me to leave the tent. "Thank you, Elowen, for the kind words. I hope they are just hiding because of this terrible blight. Water mages find it hard to be around people who are sick and hurt. We can feel the pain as if we are the ones getting hurt."

"Elowen! Thank the gods you're okay! I was so worried." Lilja said, rushing towards me, Aidan hot on her heels.

"I'm fine, really. Queen Pelicia healed me right up and I'm ready to go back to training." I smiled reassuringly at them both.

"I don't know, Elle. I really didn't consider how fragile humans could be. Maybe we should just show you something like archery or how to use a dagger properly," Aidan said as he stretched.

Lilja sighed, staring up at the sky as if she was looking for answers written in the clouds. "Honey, I just really don't want to see you get hurt again. Maybe it wouldn't be such a bad idea?"

"How am I going to pick up archery in a few weeks? The war will start before winter," I said, trying to keep my voice low.

"It is impossible to be an expert at it. However, you can learn to hit a target. We need archers anyway. One more will benefit us. I can't worry about you being on the front lines next to me when we are fighting," Lilja responded, reaching for my face.

"But I want to be with you," I all but whined. I would not be good at fighting, but I didn't want to be away from her.

"Elle, just agree with me, please. I can't focus on you and the fight. You are just too valuable to me." Lilja said. "I promise, once you are taught to fight properly, you can be at my side for the rest of your life." She cringed at the end.

"I—okay." I looked down at my feet.

With the conversation over, Lilja led me to the archers. Cassia was the leader. The rest of the day was filled with new instructions like how to hold the bow and how to nock an arrow.

Days passed. The others filled my days with training. They placed special attention on the people with earthly abilities. They were supposed to be the first line of defense.

Aidan, while not happy about it, was placed as the head of the group, ordered by Lilja to train them into fighting as a team, as if they were all limbs of the same person. Preparations were made to travel back to Ebbon Mountains to regroup with the military men and women who traveled with us when I first joined Lilja.

35

The Enemy

"Are you sure you will be okay by yourself?" I asked the tall, burly man in front of me. His glasses glinted in the morning sun.

"Yes, Elowen. Plus, if I take you away from Lilja, she'll tan my hide," Aidan grumbled. I raised my eyebrow, knowing full well Aidan and I would cause way too much trouble together. Aidan reached out for a hug, my head at his chest.

"Take care of yourself, big guy. I know fighting isn't something you want to do." He cocked his head to the side as if to stop the conversation, but I pushed on. "I know you don't want to talk about why, and I can respect that. Just know I am here when you are ready to talk." I rushed through the sentence, not wanting to make him more uncomfortable.

"Elowen, it's time to go. Lilja and the rest of us are ready." Kallan spoke from the top of his horse. I nodded. Kallan reached down to shake hands with Aidan, grabbing onto his forearm.

"Be safe brother, we will meet again," Kallan said, his voice hard, as if trying to manifest his next meeting with Aidan.

Kallan rode beside me as I walked across the grass beneath my feet, wet with dew. "What is Aidan supposed to do alone with these new members? Why can't he just come with us?" I asked Kallan as we continued to where Lilja was standing.

She wore one of her usual black shirts; her hair hung down just past the tips of her ears.

"He will stay here and train them more. People with elemental powers are indispensable to our war against Ardour. They will be the first line of defense. As the Ardourians are fumbling to regroup from their attack, we will come in and make them yield to us." Kallan said as we reached Lilja.

"What if they don't yield?" I looked at Kallan, his face grim.

"We have other ways of making the problem disappear if they refuse," he said, tight lipped.

"Are you ready to leave, Elle?" Lilja interrupted our conversation. "We need to head back to Ebbon Mountain. It'll take a few days. The sooner we get there, the better." She ran her fingers through her hair, a thing she only did when she was nervous.

"Yes," I said anxiously, twisting my ring around my finger. *I don't want anyone to get hurt.*

Grabbing Lady's reign from her, I mounted her saddle, which was cold to the touch. *The seasons are changing faster than I realized.* Wagons and carts pulled up beside us. Cassia, Keres, and Armand soon joined us at the front of the group of people. Keres appeared to have just rolled out of bed. Her black hair was pulled up into a ponytail, bags clear under her eyes.

"How is an army traipsing through the countryside going to make it across without raising eyebrows?" I asked Lilja and the rest of them.

"We are going undercover," Armand sang as he rustled in the bag on his saddlebag, pulling out a hat.

"Your version of going undercover is wearing a hat?" I gaped.

"We are traveling under the pseudonym of Lady Pelicia's court. A rich heiress traveling to the Kingdom of Valdis to help the needy," Lilja said, not looking up from the map.

"Lady Pelicia—" I said.

"It is the only way this plan will work. You'll need a water mage to heal the injured, of course," Queen Pelicia said as she rode to meet us. A large carriage followed shortly behind. It was a dark maroon in color with carved wood lining it.

"That will be our cover," Lilja said as she rolled up the map, placing it inside her boot.

"Alright, everyone listen up! We will begin riding out. Queen Pelicia will now be Lady Pelicia, a rich noble trying to send aid to Valdis. For now, hide your weapons and act like members of the court," Armand said, the hat he pulled out of his bag now on his head. I fought back the urge to laugh at the feather sticking out of his cap. A few people in the crowd voiced agreement; others merely nodded mutely.

Lilja pulled ahead with her horse, becoming the leader of the group leaving Sald Forest. The morning fog was thicker than usual. Visibility was low as we began the two-day trip to the mountain.

We traveled quietly, attempting to keep the noise to a minimum, not wanting to attract more attention to ourselves. Scenes changed quickly; greenery replaced trees. Village houses soon replaced the castle of Sald Forest.

I twisted the ring on my finger; the motion was calming to me. I smiled at Lilja as she eyed me. "What?"

"Can't I just look at you?" she asked.

"Nope," I popped the *p* sound.

"Maybe I thought you looked cute wearing my ring," she said smugly, looking at my hand and back to my eyes.

"Wait, *your* ring?" Armand all but yelled as he urged himself up at us.

"Let me see! Are you engaged?" Cassia said, next to me. Her brown eyes nearly bulged out of their sockets.

"No—" I said.

"Yes—" Lilja interjected at the same time.

"It's complicated," I finished saying, cringing as the faces surrounding us fell into confused ones.

"But you're fated to each other," Cassia whined, slumping her shoulders. As if the world was going to end from my statement.

"Why did everyone know before me?" I said. *Now it was my turn to whine.*

"It was obvious, if you ask me, as soon as Lilja said you slept in her bed. She's let no one do that before; she's always been a one-night stand kind of queen." Keres pulled back her reins to be even with me.

I looked at Lilja and for the first ever time, a blush spread on her cheek. I grinned at her, my chest swelling with love as I blew her a kiss, obnoxiously. The group surrounding us giggled at the sight.

"That type of information should not be shared with the class, Keres." Lilja turned away from us.

"Aww, come on Lil, don't be like that, we're just giving you shit," Armand said, cackling, his horse neighing as if it were laughing too.

We continued to ride towards the mountain, its shadow looming at us. Immense clouds congregated at the tips of the three larger mountains. Each of them was majestic in their own right.

Lilja must have tracked my eyes. "When I was a child, my parents used to say that the largest of the Mountains of Ebbon were the homes of the most important gods. I used to think my mother was just telling me to scare me into listening to her. She'd always say if we weren't good she was going to send me there," she said while laughing softly. "Although they may very well live there, I never thought in this lifetime I would meet a god, and so far I've met Darach," Lilja said, her eyes scanning the road.

The path in front of us was flat, a large river flowed through the land lazily. Shrubs stuck onto sides of rocks, growing out of control. It was clear this land was unkempt and uncultivated. My chest released a small bit of tension it held, as I realized no one would see us here.

"Let's set up camp here for the night," Lilja said to the rest of the men and women traveling with us.

It was well past noon already. The sun began reaching for the land, yearningly. I could hear sighs from the back, people ready to drop the bags where they stood. The carriage rode up beside us, the maroon color appearing almost black in the remaining light of the day. Pelicia pulled open the door, stepping out stretching out her arms. "Finally, I am exhausted."

Keres gave her a look but refrained from saying anything as she got off her horse. Everyone followed suit, dismounting, pulling out their blankets for the night. The sky was clear, and we were in a hurry, with no time to put out tents.

Lilja handed out orders, pulling out the map from the side of her boot. "Armand, pull together a group of ten individuals adept at hunting. We should get some soup going on a fire. Kallan, I need you to pick a few people from the group to stand watch for the night. This land is flat, meaning anyone can see our flames from miles away. Elowen and Cassia, I want you to search the vegetation. See if you can't gather herbs that will aid the future injured and sick. I imagine we will have quite a few by the end. The more supplies we have, the better. We cannot just rely on Queen Pelicia for everything. Odds are she will hit her limit sooner than we expected. The stones she carries can only be used so many times before they break." She scrawled on the corner of the map, rolling it up, and with a whistle she held out her arm.

A small messenger bird flew from the crowd, its white wings reflecting orange as the sun began its descent. "This message is to notify Aidan that we have made it to the halfway point." Lilja spoke as she tied the tiny letter to the bird, lifting her arm into the air so it could take off.

Cassia and I hurried, with the light waning. We could only gather a few small handfuls of herbs. Silently, I cursed myself. *This war has been imminent for months. Why haven't I been gathering this whole time?*

My eyes strained as I searched the ground for plants, many of them becoming nearly black. The plants melded together as the light disappeared.

"Alright, Elle, let's get back to camp. We can't see anything in this light, plus my back is killing me." Cassia stretched as she stood up straight. I nodded, looking around. The land surrounding us was fairly flat. The only bumps were large blackthorn bushes and a few trees. My eyes followed the mountain line as we walked back to camp. Its shadow loomed over us. Even from miles away, the large trees were visible at the base of the mountain.

A small flicker sat next to a tree. I pointed towards it. "What is that?" I said to Cassia. Even though the flame was far enough away, there was no way the inhabitants could hear us.

Cassia followed my finger, crouching down slightly, out of instinct. "It must be another traveler. We will tell Kallan and the other night watchers to monitor it. If we can see them, they can see us."

We made it back to camp without an issue. The large moon fully replaced the sun. It illuminated the camp we had set up beautifully. A blue hue covered each sleeping form.

"Kallan," I whispered out to the dark form sitting on top of a carriage.

His sword gleamed dangerously as he slid the sharpening stone over it.. The metal on stone sound made me squirm uncomfortably.

"If you are here to tell me about the fire to the west. I already see it. The other night watchers are monitoring anything suspicious." The metal sound halted as he peered down at us. Beside him, Cassia's cloak was pulled over her face, curly strands of hair spilled out erratically.

"Good night, Kallan." I pulled away from the carriage.

Lilja sat next to one of the small fires laid out throughout the camp. Each one was just large enough for a pot to cook food. The smell of simmering food greeted my nose, making my stomach grumble in response.

"We found little, Lilja. We can keep looking on the way to the mountains tomorrow," I said as I watched the food boil in the broth.

"That's okay. I didn't expect you to find much with the light disappearing, but something is better than nothing." Lilja spoke as she mixed the pot's contents, ladling it into the small cups she had placed beside her.

Lilja handed me the cup, sighing as she leaned back on one of her arms, sipping the contents. We ate in comfortable silence. The ring on my finger sat contently, a reminder of a life I could have, if only I would reach for it.

"The late autumn sun really is beating pretty hard, huh," Armand grumbled as he took a swig of water from his canteen.

"Yeah, unfortunately, this heat will be replaced by the cold air," I said. Sweat rolled down my temple, stinging my eyes.

Leaves rustled in the wind, the previously green leaves now shades of yellow and orange. Few of them filtered down into the forest floor as we passed, making room for the new buds in spring.

The night was uneventful. When we awoke early in the morning, they snuffed the fire on the mountainside out. Whoever had been there for the night already moved on.

"How much longer?" Keres fanned herself with a small fan.

"Half a day's ride. We barely rode today. Why are you so tired?" Lilja rode ahead of us, her voice barely discernible.

"I got little sleep last night." The circles under her eyes are nearly as prominent as Liljas' hair.

"Does this have anything to do with the hunter I saw enter your tent last night after coming back from the forest?" Armand questioned.

Cassia raised her eyebrow, smirking. "I bet bunnies aren't the only thing he killed last night."

"Ew, Cassia. I definitely do not want to hear about my twin's sex life," Armand said, making a gagging motion with his finger pointing in his mouth.

I laughed while someone else whistled and a breeze swept by my face. My face fell as Liljas horse neighed, panicked by something. I turned and saw that blood covered her horse and an arrow stuck out of its front leg. It reared back, throwing Lilja off. She scrambled, attempting to get out of the way as her horse struggled to regain its balance, falling to the right.

"Gather, protect the Qu—the heiress," Armand's voice boomed over the chaos that bloomed. The carriage halted. The subjects of Sald Forest gathered weapons and stood at attention in front of the carriage as thugs leapt from their hiding spots in the trees. With a war cry, they stumbled down the hillside as another wave of arrows rained down on us.

"Lil—" I shouted as an arrow grazed the side of my arm. Blood welled up at the wound almost immediately. I cried out in pain, forcing Lady to push forward. She gave a nervous neigh but obeyed my wish.

Lilja was behind her horse, looking over its injured frame for the shooter in the woods. "Elowen, go! Go hide! I will find you!" she said as someone ran in front of her with an ax in his dyed red hands. With astonishing speed, she grabbed a dagger from her hip, throwing it at the assailant. The blade found its way home in the man's shoulder.

I snatched my bow that laid tied to Lady's hip and began firing off into the armed burglars farther away. A few of them met their marks.

"Men, fight with honor! These foes are more important than we thought." A man held up Armand's cloak from his bag, the Valdis insignia glowing on it.

"I bet they have a mighty enormous price on their heads!" someone else shouted. War cries erupt from either side as we attacked each other mercilessly.

"Elowen, get back." Lilja smacked Lady's ass, sending her to gallop off to the edge of the road. I aimed my bow at one of the men, the tip bouncing as Lady shifted beneath me. Taking a deep breath, I let the arrow fly. It struck its target, sending his body backwards, hitting the carriage, and leaving a dark red smear as the attacker fell to the ground.

A silence fell over the party of men and women I traveled with. My eyes scanned the crowd, looking for more men to bury my arrows in. *I did it,* I thought. My heart raced in my chest, the adrenaline still pumping through my veins. With a shaky hand, I dismounted from Lady, wincing as the movement stretched my wound on my arm.

I stumbled over to her, ignoring the men and women who lay dead at my feet, their blood soaking the ground as I walk, making every step a wet one.

"Lilja," I croaked out. The horse's dead carcass still pinned her leg.

She looked tired and mad; her hair was messed up as if she'd spent the whole time running her hand through it.

"Lilja, are you okay?" I placed my hand on her cheek.

She flinched under my touch. A flip must have switched as I began trying to pull the horse off. With a grunt, the earth underneath the horse pushed up, shifting the horse enough for her to get out from under it.

"I told you to stay—" Lilja's voice was hard.

Kallan's voice boomed over hers. "There is one more!"

Frantically, everyone moved. Lilja stood up, holding onto the side of her dead horse to steady herself. "Cassia, shoot him, before he can send that hawk out!" Lilja said, with a nod and with not even a fraction of a second of deliberation, Cassia pulled back on her beautifully made bow.

Armand, Kallan, and Keres bounded after the man as he raced to exit the forest. His bird bobbed on his shoulder as he did so. With an exhale, Cassia sent the arrow flying just as the man twisted behind a tree, as if he could tell the arrow was released.

"Fuck," Cassia and Lilja said at the same time as the man released his bird into the air. With a flick of hid hand, he used his powers to push it high above an arrow's range.

Kallan caught up with the man a second later, using his dagger to slit the man's throat.

"Lilja, what did that man just send out?" I held my hand to her. The wound on my arm was still bleeding.

"A warning to the queen, I imagine." She looked at me for the first time since the attack. "Elowen, you're hurt." She walked towards me, her hand gently grabbing onto my arm so she could get a better look at it. "Why didn't you tell me before?"

"We were busy." I shrugged my shoulders.

Lilja clicked her tongue in response, as if she was a disappointed mother. "Let's get you healed up," she said as she led me through the crowd to Pelicia, who stood in the middle of the wounded. Blood stained her dress.

"Let her heal them first. I can wait," I told Lilja as I watched Pelicia work. She was amazing. With a simple breath, she healed wounds almost immediately. Pelicia clutched the stone hanging from her neck. I assumed it helped give her power. It was a blue stone, ornately placed in a gold setting.

Pelicia finished in a matter of minutes. The people dispersed quickly to gather the supplies back up.

"Queen Pelicia, can you please heal Elowen? She had a rather unfortunate meeting with an arrow," Lilja said to Pelicia. Her voice held no room for negotiation.

"Of course, your highness." Pelicia grabbed onto my arm gently, and with a small tingle, the wound was gone.

I glanced up at Lilja's face; her lips were thin as she pondered over our next move.

36

You Will Always Be Enough

"We need to make it to camp as fast as possible. The men aren't in the military, but money makes people talk. I imagine there is a high reward for anyone going against the crown, especially seeing a Valdis insignia. The insignia here alone means war. The gods are with us today because I do not think they knew who we were. All the crown will know is that the Valdis army is here." Lilja hoisted herself onto an extra horse. We had killed its original owner in the attack.

"Our element of surprise is gone. How are we supposed to conquer Ardour without it?" Kallan spoke as he hitched a small cart to a donkey. His moral was low; he felt personally responsible for the robbers discovering us.

Lilja spoke with confidence as she sat on her new white horse. "With the added members to our army, I am confident we have a chance. Sald Forest has already taught them how to fight, at least the basics. I will send word to Cann Village and Ebbon City. They both understand the risk of the blight, it is mutating, and it's spreading fast. If we try, we could die, yes, it's true. But if we don't find the truth about the blight, then all of our people will die."

A silence spread throughout the group as we moved. The survival of the my new home hung on the balance of Lilja and her army, making Ardour tell us about the cure. I straightened up my back as I sat on Lady.

Home. This place was home. I peeked out of the corner of my eye to look at Lilja. She sat stoically in her saddle, her hair placed again as if she brushed through it. My gods, she was beautiful. The Elven Realm wasn't my home, she was. The light to my dark, the reasoning behind my inner thoughts.

I twisted the ring on my finger, and the weight of it seemed diminished. It no longer felt like I was going behind Belle's back. It no longer felt like I was moving too fast. This—this was right. This was supposed to be. We were fated. Not only by the romantic standards of the Elven culture, but by the gods as well.

My heart beat quickly in my chest as I realized I was ready for this; I thought as I gazed at the ring that sat on my finger. The sun shimmered as if it knew that I wanted it. As if it said, *finally you want me.*

I pulled Lady's reins to the side, guiding her towards Lilja's horse.

"Lilja," I said.

While keeping her eyes on the path ahead, she made a noise in her throat.

"I've given this a lot of thought, and I'm sorry it's taken this long for the answer. But I was worried. I feared the unknown. All of this is new to me—"

"Say what you need to say," she said as she interjected my unintentional tangent.

"Yes." I looked at her anxiously.

She raised an eyebrow at me, her face blank. "What?"

"Yes, I—I will marry you."

A grin grew on her face, ear to ear. She held out her hand, grabbing mine, placing one small kiss on my knuckles.

It was impossible to get an embrace right now, as we rode harder towards the camp. Anyone could find their way through. As the horses climbed up the path, the air got colder and thinner. Snow appeared in patches and soon covered the area in totality. I shivered, rubbing my arms to get warm.

"Here," Kallan extended his arm out. In his hand was a dark green cloak, nearly identical to the one Cassia always wore.

"Where did you get this?" My frozen fingers snatched the thick cloak from him. At this point, I didn't care whose it was as long as it kept me warm.

"Lilja knows how often you lose yours, so she asked me to carry a couple for you. B-but don't tell her I told you. She told me not to tell, and only to give them to you when you need them." Kallan appeared stressed from just spilling the secret.

I smiled at him warmly. "Don't worry, your secret's safe with me." I put my finger to my lips, dramatically earning a groan from him.

"We've made it," Lilja announced from the front. She somehow always made it to the front of the line. I peered ahead of her. The camp before us was large, and thoroughly set up to survive the blistering cold. Fire pits were set up periodically around the camp and a large temporary shelter built as a mess hall. A large tent was over to the side. The rest were modestly sized for two people to sleep in.

A tall man briskly walked towards us. He appeared older, nearly my father's age. However, with elves' ages working so differently than my own, I did not know how old he actually was. "Good afternoon, your highness, the ride must have been very difficult these past few months."

"Yes, yes, we have much to discuss, Ledgin. The past few months have been hard. But I am happy to announce that Elowen Alwyn has accepted my proposal to become my wife." Lilja beckoned me to come forward.

I inched forward nervously, all eyes on me. Gasps went through the crowd, Kallan and the rest of the group whooped excitedly. "You know what that means, ladies and gents, a *party* is in our future," Armand clapped his hands.

Ledgin looked surprised. His mouth hanging open, he pulled himself together slightly, coughing as if to hide his surprise. "How wonderful, Queen Lilja. I am so glad you found your life partner! Please come to the mess tent so we may discuss the party we shall hold in your honor, and of the upcoming war with Ardour. Tensions are high because a few—not I—feel like it has taken too long to come to this point—"

"Silence, Ledgin, you are coming very close to treason." Kallan placed his hand on the hilt of the sword that lay on his belt.

Ledgin quickly closed his mouth and then opened it again to speak. "I assure you, your highness, I do not mean to sound treasonous. The men and women here are eager to fight and win the war against Ardour."

"Only fools are eager to create a war that will kill thousands. Even if the war results in us finding the cure to the blight, death will be unnecessary." Lilja dismounted. Coming over to my side, she waited for me to, giving my hand a squeeze as we entered the mess hall.

She absentmindedly rubbed her thumb over my hand. They did not beautifully construct the mess hall, but it was expertly built to resist the cold weather. Armand had shown the newly recruited troops where they set up their tents. Men and women who were already stationed here peeked around and greet the newcomers.

Cassia came up to me, clapping her hands. "You said yes," she shrieked. Her body seemed to vibrate with energy. Keres stood behind her, excited.

"Yes," I beamed.

"Cassia and I made bets on when you were going to say yes. You took so long, we bet you'd say yes immediately." Keres stomped her feet playfully.

Armand slung his arm over my shoulder. "Kallan and I won. We bet you'd have to think about being tied down to Lilja." He rubbed his fingers together to symbolize money.

Kallan pulled out his coin purse, shaking it for effect. "Pay up, ladies. Just don't tell Lilja we bet on this. She'd have our hides." His eyes flitted across the room.

My eyes widened as I watched Lilja walk up behind Kallan, placing a hand on his shoulder. "Kallan, stop harassing my future wife, your queen. We need to go over the business at hand."

Queen? My inner thoughts screamed at me, Say what? I mean, I guess it makes sense. I just never thought about it that way before. My heart beat in my chest; sweat coated my palms. *I need air.* I scrambled to exit the mess hall. Word had spread fast, it appeared. People moved like I had the plague—a few bowed. Plastering a fake strained smile on my face, I urged myself forward. *I can't look weak. I have to be strong, like Lilja.*

I rubbed my scar on my arm. My stomach churned as if it was trying to make butter. It felt like my heartbeat was in my eyes. I breathed a sigh of relief as the cold air hit my face. I leaned against the building. People still talked inside, their voices leaking out of the door that sat ajar.

In out. In out. In out. My inner voice commanded me as I tried to breathe. I slid against the wood wall, my clothes catching on the unfinished wood. The world swayed as I did so, my body weight becoming too much to hold up.

"Elowen." Lilja rushed towards me, crouching down. "Hey hey, it's okay. Breathe baby, what happened?" She pulled me into a hug.

I took a big breath in her scent filled my nostrils. Minutes passed; my heart beat threatening to come out earlier now subsided.

"I'm sorry," I breathed out. "I-I-I just got overwhelmed. I j-just needed a minute." My head is still on her chest.

"It's okay, Elle, I just got worried when I didn't see you. It felt like I could feel your panic. I knew I had to find you." She caressed my head. "I have to go to a meeting to discuss the evidence against Ardour and discuss the next step. Why don't you go to our tent and lay down for a bit? I'll come afterwards and we can go to bed for the night. Cassia and Armand insisted on planning a small engagement party for us. It will happen tomorrow," she said, overloading me with details as she tried to distract me from my panic attack.

The energy from my body was gone, and I nodded, not saying anything. "I can't tell who actually wants to throw this party. I suspect that Armand only wants to get drunk. Cassia presumably *really* wants to. She has been begging since she saw the ring on your finger." Lilja held out her hand, helping me stand.

She pulled me towards the larger tent that sat over to the side, separate from the rest of the tents. I didn't mind that it pulled away us from the camp; at least it would be quiet.

We walked into the tent together. Three servants were inside, placing furniture and uncovering larger items. "Your highness," one said, causing the others to turn towards us and bow in unison.

"Please leave us. We can finish the rest." Lilja's voice had a type of finality to it, not allowing for any back talk. They all nodded in agreement and scrambled out, their faces pale.

"Man, you must have quite the authority around here. They looked downright terrified," I said.

"Hmm, they did, didn't they? Well, I have to keep up my barbarian persona. As you know, I have to look very tough to rule a kingdom," she taunted as I pulled off the sheets covering the desk and then the same to the bed. The dust on the sheets was minimal, so I folded them and laid them off to the side. Flopping down on the bed, I sighed as the fabrics seemed to wrap around me. Lilja laughed at my reaction, grabbing another blanket to cover me.

"Go to bed, my little sleepy girl. Once this meeting is over, I'll come and join you." She tucked me in, kissing me on my forehead.

"I love you," I said as she turned to walk away from me.

She paused and turned around, a small smile on her lips, "I love you too."

After that, she disappeared into the world, as I succumbed to the darkness of sleep.

The clearing stood ahead of me; water cut through it lazily. The military men were back; their shouting met my ears. My heart beat in my chest as my eyes locked with Lilja. She was on her knees, her hands tied behind her back, a rough-looking hand placed on each shoulder, forcing her down.

"Men!" the man's voice called out.

"We must take down Valdis with a crushing force! We must not show mercy! To be swift in decimating them means to kill the queen, if you can call her that." He spit off to the side. In his hands was the same blade used to kill Sylp's father.

Shouts of agreement erupted from the crowd. *Oh, my god. These men are monsters.* Without a second thought, I bolted towards them.

"Stop!" I screamed, my voice cracking with the ferocious use of my vocal cords.

Nobody acknowledged my presence as I became closer and closer to them.

"Please, don't!" I sobbed as he held the blade up high, swinging down with force. The wet sound of flesh filled my ears with silence.

I stumbled, my face meeting the ground hard, in pain. Pain was all I felt. My heart felt like it was the one being cut in half. A scream erupted from my mouth as I struggled to get up. *I had to get to her. I had to save her.*

She's dead. She's dead. It's all my fault, if only I had been an elf.

"Elowen, baby. Wake up!" Lilja shook me.

My eyes flung open as I sat up. I buried myself in her arms. Sobs crawling their way out of my mouth, tears began after. "I-I thought you were dead." I blubbered. "I saw you die," I wailed into her arms.

"Shh, baby, I'm very much alive. See?" She pulled away so I could look at her face.

"I couldn't save you. I was too slow. Useless. I am just a useless human." I pulled myself back into Lilja's embrace.

"Elowen, you are not useless. Regardless of whether you were born an elf or a human, I love you the same. It was a nightmare, nothing more, baby. Now please stop crying before you wake the whole camp. It's roughly two in the morning," Lilja said in a whisper as she stroked my back.

She held me until my sobs turned to sniffles, pulling me down. Lilja squeezed me to her side, covering us up. I laid there until her breaths began slow and deep. My head rested on her chest as I waited for sleep to overcome me.

I waited and waited for sleep to come. It never did. Before I knew it, the sun filtered into the thinner parts of the tent's fabric. I slid myself from Lilja's sleepy death grip and grabbed my cold clothes from my pack, slipping it on. A shiver ran up my spine as I gave one last look at Lilja and walked out into the world.

I pulled my cloak close to my face; the wind biting at my face as I walked to the mess hall. It was early enough that only a handful of people were lingering, grabbing food and drinks off of a long line of food still being set up by the servants. I meandered to the table, grabbing a plate and a cup from the end. I gave the servant across from the table a nod and a small thanks.

With my plate filled and my glass full of coffee, I meandered my way to an empty table. I sat sipping my coffee.

"Well someone looks like shit. What, did you and Lilja toss the sheets around for a few rounds?" a voice from behind me said. I choked on my coffee. I turned my head, coming face to face with Kallan.

"What? No, I-I just didn't sleep well last night." I said in between coughs, trying to clear my airways of the coffee I inhaled.

"Sure, you know I heard some other men say they heard screaming off to that side—" Kallan wiggled his eyebrows as he sat down. He piled his plate high with the vegetables and meat.

"Kallan, leave my future wife alone," Lilja warned as she sat down next to me with only a coffee in hand. My face burned at her comment as the others filed in.

"I am so excited for tonight," Cassia squealed as she sat down, her hands full of papers and food. "I already have so many plans." She rolled out one paper on the table.

"Whatever you plan, Cassia, will be great." I forced a smile at the elves who surrounded me. *I am happy,* I told myself as everyone continued talking obliviously to me, forcing my smile. Partially listening, I caught words like "streamers," "lights," "food," and "fancy clothes."

"Even though it's short notice, I am sure I can find a dress for you to wear, Elowen, as long as you want to." Lilja gave me puppy dog eyes, probably as she imagined me in some type of revealing outfit.

"Of course, my queen, anything for you," I said.

Kallan scoffed from across from me, mimicking me.

"You're marrying her, you don't need to be so formal," Keres all but cooed.

"Alright, once we are all done eating, grab your weapons and let's head to the training ground," Lilja said, not allowing for anyone to continue the earlier conversation.

"But Lil, who is supposed to decorate for the party?" Cassia whined, her lower lip protruding into a pout.

"Alright, everyone else other than Cassia goes to the training ground. We all need to brush up on our skills, especially Elowen. Even though she seems quite natural at archery already. Cassia, I don't care how you make people help you decorate. Just make sure it gets done." Lilja got up, handing her plate and cup to eager servants ready to please a queen.

Once breakfast was over, we headed to the camp's training ground, which were littered with shades of brown and dark red, as mud and even blood discolored the snow.

"Kallan, please teach Elowen more about knife fighting and archery. We only have a short time until war will be upon us. I might not like the idea of Elowen fighting, but I dislike the idea of her being helpless more." Lilja grabbed onto his forearm, patting him affectionately on the shoulder.

"I will teach her to the best of my ability," he gave a quick bow. He motioned for me to follow him to a large building off to the side. Heat seemed to radiate from it. The distant sound of clanging metal hung in the air like electricity. Smoke billowed out of the chimney on the edge of the roof.

"What is this place?" I asked as I followed Kallan as I craned my neck around his thin, yet muscular, frame.

"This is the forge. Lilja asked me to order a few daggers for you. They will be yours, so please take care of them. They can be the difference between life or death," he said as we entered the building. Heat stifled the room as a large, gray-haired man slung a hammer on to what appeared to be a sword.

"Reid! My kind gentleman, I have a guest for you to meet!" Kallan all but screamed over the clanging. The older man barely paused as he clanged the metal again. We stood there for a moment, unsure if he heard us or not.

"Surely he heard you," I said as I leaned over to Kallan just as another clang occurred. I jumped slightly, my nerves unhappy to be in a place with so much unwelcome noise.

"Of course I heard him," Reid shouted as he threw the hammer onto another table. Reaching for a pair of tongs, he gently grabbed the sword, placing it back into the flame. Sweat rolled off the man before us freely. He was nearly the size of Kallan. His wide shoulders and burly arms led me to the conclusion that he had been doing this for a while.

"I can't very well ruin a sword because one of the queen's men wants to introduce me to his girlfriend. And before you ask Kallan, I will not be taking any ring orders. I have far too much to do," he huffed.

Kallan crossed his arms. "Elowen is not my girlfriend, Reid. I do not think Queen Lilja would appreciate you talking about her future wife like that."

Reid opened his mouth and then closed it, reminding me of a fish. I stifled a giggle unsuccessfully, gaining a look from both of them.

"Well, are you here to pick up the daggers her highness had you make?" Reid said, probably trying to further the conversation away from the fact that he'd insulted me.

"Of course we are. I am trying to further the future queen's training. Without the proper tools, it will prove quite difficult." Kallan was enjoying getting his way.

Reid moved with ease for a man of his age—well, for old he looked in human years. He opened a large chest; the insides shone with a metallic gleam. Daggers were strapped to the lid with thick leather bands. His fingers danced across them, grabbing onto two of the same sized ones and one smaller one.

He turned his back to us. "These are some of my best work. Make sure you teach her well, Sir Kallan."

I looked across the room; a desk sat on the far side of the room. Papers were strewn on top of it and pinned to the board.

"May I?" I motioned towards the desk. Reid said nothing as he handed the daggers to Kallan. With using his silence towards me as a *yes*, I ventured to the desk, stifling a yawn. Each paper was drawn on blueprints for some type of weapon. "Are these your design?" I held up a completed sketch.

"Ah yes, those are the new designs for the fight. I am planning on having them approved by one general so I can employ some men to help. I am not as muscular as I used to be and an extra set of hands would be beneficial," Reid said as he used a towel to rub the sweat off of his neck.

"They look brilliant. I am sure they will say yes," I said as I handed Kallan the paper.

Reid stuck out his chest in pride, a grin spreading across his face.

"These look like they could be of some use to us in the fight against the Ardourians. Let me know if the other generals give you any trouble. While it appears Elowen could spend the whole day looking at your blueprints, we really must be off. Lilja will tan my hide and hers if we don't get to training." Kallan reached into his pocket, pulling out a few gold coins and depositing them into Reid's oversized hands.

Reid nodded, bidding us goodbye as we traveled out of his building and to an area of dummies.

"This is where you can stab someone. If you want them down, they will go down hard." Kallan pointed to the back of the dummy's neck.

The whole day went like that—the groin, the neck, and even the armpit could lead to a bloody death if you knew where to stab. A few hours passed into learning how to roll with my bow slung across my shoulder and how to roll with it in my hands. Followed closely with knife work, sparring with small daggers, a few strapped to my thigh, the other (a dull one) placed in between my breasts.

They were plain looking, none of them beautiful. Lightweight, silver, and well balanced. Sleek killing points for whoever poor sap I had to stab.

I followed his instructions closely; his skill was at the master level.

"Elowen, Kallan, let's call it a night. We need to get some rest and get ready for the party," Lilja called out across from the yard.

I sighed, slumping my shoulders. My muscles were sore from the exercise. My heart, however, fluttered for our engagement party.

Lilja and I walked together to her—our tent. My daggers remained strapped to each thigh, the blunt one placed in between my breasts.

"Thank you for the daggers," I said as I went inside the tent. They placed a new item off to the right, a tub.

"Of course, Ellie, I can't expect you to defend yourself if you don't have the tools. I hope Reid wasn't too much of an ass. He is a grumpy old man. Older than my grandfather if he were still alive," Lilja said as she took off layers of clothing.

Her tunic clung to her sweat-coated torso, fresh bruises filled her pale skin. A servant had already filled the tub with water. It must have been filled recently as the steam still billowed out of it like fog in the early morning. I watched open mouthed as she undressed, lowering herself into the water.

"Are you just going to stare at me while I wash, or are you going to come in here with me?" Lilja said.

"Um, yeah sure." My voice betrayed my nervousness.

My hands shook as I scrambled to take off my tunic and my pants. I swung my leg off to the side, slinging the pants across the room. I stood there exposed; the air hit my skin, making goose bumps appear. Self-conscious, I crossed my arms, hiding my breasts.

"You are beautiful, Elle. Come here. Let's get washed up and take a nap. When we awake, our engagement party will begin," she said.

I lowered myself into the tub, the water almost too hot for comfort. She used the soap on my back, rubbing it in to make a lather. I fought back the urge to moan as she hit the spots that were sore from training. She moved down to my sides, pulling me closer. My back hit her front, sloshing the water onto the floor of the tent. A giggle erupted from my throat.

"Is this okay?" She cupped water into my hair.

"Hm? Oh yes, please continue," I said as she lathered soap into my thick hair.

She chuckled. "I thought you might like that."

We continued to wash comfortably, laughing like children. Soon the bath was over and she pulled me into the bed. The sheets clung to us as we covered up the small amount of water that lay on our skin and seemed to grip onto the blankets.

Soon her breaths were long and even.

I was soon asleep as well, exhaustion from the sleepless night prior taking me over.

"Elowen, honey, it's time to get up. Our party starts in a few hours." My eyes flung open, my chest beat erratically, startled at being woken up dead asleep. The tent was dark. Lilja remedied it by striking a match, illuminating a handful of candles on the desk.

The flames wiggled the breeze from the tents opening, causing a shiver to run down my spine.

"Your highness, I have brought the clothes you had made. May I enter?" a young, anxious voice called out from outside the tent.

Lilja looked at me and then back to the space the young boy occupied. "Just a moment," Lilja called out as she threw the blanket back over the top of my naked frame. She wrapped the sheet around me like a toga.

"Just come in and place the clothing on the desk, and do not lift your eyes off the ground. We are slightly less presentable at the moment," she said, looking at me, grinning, sending me a wink. My cheeks burned with embarrassment or love. I couldn't tell. Presumably both.

The young boy walked into the tent with two large boxes in his oversized hands. It was apparent by the size of them he was not done growing. With his eyes on the ground, he hastened to the illuminated desk and placed the pale covered boxes on it. With a lower bow than he was already doing to keep his eyes on the ground, he scrambled out of the tent.

Giggling as I watched his awkward form leave, I rose from the bed, walking to the desk. "I thought you said you were going to find a dress, not get one made," I said as I peered down at the delicate boxes wrapped in satin ribbon.

"Of course I was going to have something made. Don't worry, I didn't burn anyone out. I had this made weeks ago, as soon as I proposed the first time," Lilja said.

"Wait, did you mean when you proposed to me at Jaz's house? When I thought you were proposing for a cover in Ardour?" I asked.

"Well, yes," she said as if it made all the sense in the world. "I was quite confident you'd come around and marry me. I just had to wait it out. After all, who could resist all of this?" She gestured to her body.

I rolled my eyes, looking away, back to the boxes, unsure if I should open them. "They are yours. You can open them." With shaking fingers, I undid the tie on the ribbon, opening the box to reveal a dark blue fabric. Gold designs occupied the bottom of the dress. Pulling it out of the book, I shook it out, unfolding it in all its glory. It was floor length, the sleeves made to cascade down my arms. Little fabric flowers were sewn in the sleeves, creating depth.

"Do you like it?" Lilja asked. "I picked the shade because I thought it would complement your eyes and skin color. I hope it suits your taste."

I hugged the dress to my chest, turning to her. "I love it, it's perfect," I said as I planted a small peck on her lips. Placing my dress on the bed, I opened the second box to reveal a petticoat and a pair of shoes. They were flats and impractical for winter.

"Sorry about the shoes. I didn't predict you would take so long. Must be pretty rusty in the ways of complimenting women. I should practice on you more, if you'd allow it," she said.

I fought the urge to roll my eyes as I put the clothes on. "Will you tie up the corset for me?" I asked as I held the dress to my breasts. Without a word, Lilja tied the back up tight enough to highlight my waist, but not too much that I couldn't breathe. I adjusted the petticoat on my waist. Holding her hand, I slipped on the flats.

Lilja dressed instead of dress, she chose a black pair of pants and a white loose button up. Using a balm on the desk, she slicked back her hair. Running a brush through my hair, I pulled it up, putting a decorative pin through it.

"Alright, let's go," Lilja said as I looped my arm into hers.

"Do I look okay?" I asked as we walked outside. Lanterns illuminated our path to the mess hall.

"Of course you look gorgeous," she said as she leaned down, kissing my forehead. "Cassia went all out, didn't she?" Lilja said, a hint of surprise in her voice.

"Did you expect anything less from her?" I said, laughing.

"No, I guess not." She laughed as thick snowflakes floated to the earth.

A band blared in the mess hall. Barrels stood out front with flames welcoming us inside; two guards stood beside them, snow coating the tops of their hats.

With a smile and a slight bow, they pushed the large doors open. Decorations and laughter filled our senses. Cassia ran up to us, her dark skin complimented with flowers tied into her red hair.

"Finally," she squealed. "I was wondering when you were going to show up! You look beautiful!" Cassia said as she grabbed my hands, jumping up and down.

I grinned, bowing to her dramatically. "Why thank you, my lady."

"Madam, you wound me. You would bow to someone other than your betrothed. Ugh, my heart," Lilja said beside me, grabbing onto my waist pulling me to the dance floor.

I laughed, allowing her to guide me into the mass of joyous people. Servants walked through the crowd with food on wooden platters. Lilja grinned at me, leaning down to kiss my forehead.

"You look completely breathtaking." Lilja said in my ear as the band began another song.

The music seemed to take us away from the crowd and melody. It was intoxicating and swept off my feet the rest of the night.

"May I have this dance?" Kallan asked as he extended his hand out to me. His hair was slicked back, and his usual outfit replaced with a refined military uniform.

"Of course," I curtseyed. He grinned at me, pulling me to the outer rim of the dance floor. "I don't know how to dance to this," I said as I listened to the beginning few notes.

"Just follow my lead." He winked at me.

Awkwardly, I made it through the song without making a complete fool of myself.

"May I have your attention?" Lilja spoke from the front of the room, her feet planted on top of a table.

"First, I want to thank everyone for being here tonight, for our engagement party. Second, I want to thank Elowen for allowing me to be her fiancée. Now please, let's get back to the party!" She spoke as she held a glass high in the air, taking a long swig of it before jumping down to the floor.

Lilja stalked towards me with all eyes on us as we did so. The crowd seemed hungry for a peek at us.

"You, madam, are exquisite," Lilja said as she caught up to me.

"As are you, my queen?" I said.

"While I know this party is for us, do you mind if we sneak back to our tent? I am rather people'd out at the moment." Her eyes pleaded with me, her lower lip protruding.

"I thought you'd never ask," I said, already pulling her towards the door.

"Kallan and Armand—Aidan shall be here tomorrow. A group meeting will happen with all of our generals. Please make sure some of the other higher-ups are awake in the morning. For now though, make sure no one disturbs us in our tent." Lilja said to them as we passed them.

They nodded, looking around for the generals.

***

Back in our tent, the corset was the first thing to come off. Lilja's nimble fingers worked swiftly as they undid the tie, leaving goose bumps in their path.

"I love you Elowen Alwyn, elf or human. To me, you will always be enough." Lilja said, her lips crashing onto mine, leaving me breathless. I hugged her.

I was enough for someone. I, Elowen, was enough for her, an Elven queen. *Maybe I could be happy...*

37

Attack, Explode, Kidnap

I blinked my morning into existence; the blankets tangled around my body like the arms of a squid, holding me in a toasty cocoon, keeping my body warm and leaving my face cold. I reached for Lilja, my fingertips meeting nothing but cold space. I yawned, stretching, hitting a paper where Lilja should be.

I left to have a small meeting with a few of the generals before the large one later this afternoon. My apologies for not waking you when I left. I just thought you'd need your beauty sleep over the next couple of days. Please reset the ear tips before the meeting. One is nearly off. I don't want to alarm the arriving generals. Unfortunately, a few can be rather behind in the times. I can't afford to have a mutiny.
    By the way, you snore rather charmingly.
    Love,
    Lilja

My face burned as I read the last sentence. *I most definitely do not snore.*
    The start of the morning was slow. As I emerged from the tent, all

ATTACK, EXPLODE, KIDNAP

the party goers were still asleep, or were miserably sobering up with their morning tasks.

Tentatively, I sipped the coffee in my hand. The mess hall was abuzz with movement. Servants are still cleaning from the party. With my free hand, I grabbed one of the coffee cakes on the table; I took a bite of the sweet treat crumbling off into my mouth.

"Good morning, Elowen. Today is going to be a rather long day. Most of the meetings will extend a few hours a piece. I would make sure to eat the coffee cake instead of having all the crumbs land in your lap." Kallan crunched on an apple, its juices spraying.

I mimicked him with the coffee cake still in my mouth, letting even more crumbs fall out. "Yes, I know. Lilja left me a note before she left for earlier meetings. What time is the first one? Are the generals going to accept me being there? Obviously, I am not a general or a part of the military in any sort of form. I'm essentially a mascot," I said, exasperated, slumping in my seat.

Kallan patted my hand. "That's not true, Elle, you are a valuable member of this team. Plus, you aren't too bad with that bow either. We know you haven't lived as long as us, but soon you will learn these things. Lilja does not expect you to know everything right away. You will learn as you go, and the best way for that to happen is to immerse you in the action. It's better than any book."

Kallan handed me the other apple he had in his free hand. "Eat up. We have a few hours before the first meeting, and I want to get some training in for you."

I nodded, demolishing the apple. "Okay, just let me grab the bow and the daggers from the tent."

Kallan looked at me with narrow eyes. "You should carry them with you at all times, especially during times of war. Go get them and meet me on the training ring."

I grimaced at his sharp words. He was right. *I should have them on me*, my inner monologue scolded me. I ran back to our tent, grabbing my daggers. *He's right.*

I hustled to the training ground, trying to not let anyone hear my rough breathing as I did so. Even with all the activity of walking throughout the countryside, I was still incredibly out of shape. I thought back to my father scolding me for being larger and curvier than most of the women in our city: *"You should look more like your mother. She was stick thin when I met her."*

I cringed at the words haunting me from my memories. I never minded the extra weight surrounding my body. It was comforting the weight. Each beautiful curve held a story of my life, a beautiful silhouette of my memories.

We came across the cleared ground quickly. The ground had been stamped flat. "You ready?" Kallan asked as he clasped a leather holster at his waist. Knife handles littered the front of it, each appeared ready to kill.

"Yeah, of course." I put myself in a ready stance, my daggers in each hand.

"Whoa there, Elle, instead of practicing with the real thing, perhaps we should train with something safer," he said as he reached down into his bag, pulling out two wooden replicas of my daggers. They felt lighter in my hands. He had smoothed the wood down to a fine polish.

"Okay," I said, embarrassed I didn't think of it.

We went at each other intensely. Kallan showed me where to grab and where to throw a punch. We grappled with each other; he flipped me to the ground, knocking the wind out of me. I squinted at his tall form above me.

"Was that absolutely necessary?" I said, trying to breathe in air into my deflated lungs.

"If I am to train you how to fight, we need to fight for real. Even if it means having you knocked on your back a few times." Kallan loomed over me, extending me his hand.

"You two!" Armand said. "The meeting starts in ten minutes! Let's go!"

The young general spoke, his hands balled into fists on the table. "We have no other choice! The troops must gather by the end of the week. If the prophecy Darach gave is correct, they will attack before winter. While snow already covers the mountain, the countryside has to be attacked by its wintry foe."

"The cold air has already ravaged the towns at night. It's a sign," an older general said, nearly shouting.

Lilja banged her fist on the table. "Quiet! You have not given me a minute to speak, since I have sat my royal ass in my chair! If you won't listen to what I have to say, then undoubtedly we will all fail."

A hush filled the tent. I fought the urge to raise an eyebrow at her booming voice. *That's new.*

Lilja spoke to the group of men, women, and people surrounding the wooden table. "The troops will follow us down the mountainside, grabbing whatever supplies and food we can. Make sure they only harm the people that fight back."

"We should take a small team to infiltrate the castle, while the main mass of the army pillages the countryside. It would be the perfect distraction," Kallan said.

"Yes! Because while the Ardourian military fights the main mass of Valdis army, we will infiltrate the castle, capturing the queen, to torture her for information." Aidan nodded. Blood ran down his head.

Everyone turned to him. *When did he sneak in?*

"What happened to you?" Armand asked beside me, his voice laced with concern.

"They attacked the Sald Forest team halfway up the mountain. We were able to fight them off with no casualties," Aidan said, his chest puffed out with pride.

"I'm glad you made it here alive. I trust you weren't—" Lilja said as a scream pierced the air.

"What was that?" Cassia stood up from her seat as the sound of metal clanging together filled the air.

"We are being attacked." Armand stood up from his chair. He went for the tent flap; smoke billowed underneath. I looked towards Lilja, my eyes wide as the world stood still, as red and orange filled my vision. Heat blasted towards us—an explosion.

Suddenly my body was in the air, the force of it toppled everyone in the tent. The world faded into black.

The constant sound of ringing deafened my ears. Muffled shouts and screams filled the air. Tears sprang to my eyes, but whether it was from pain or something else, I didn't know. I searched the room for Lilja slowly, my neck hot. My shirt clung to my chest; it was wet.

The explosion had turned the table we sat at earlier over; the legs jutted out in my direction. Lilja lay underneath the left brace, her body pressed against the underside of the table like a fly on glass. Kallan stood over her body, cradling her.

Screams erupted throughout the room. I didn't know whose voice belonged to who.

I opened my mouth to scream for Lilja, but the only sound that came out was a groan. Hands grabbed at me. Weakly, I lashed out, trying to kick off the person touching me.

"Get yer hands off of her."

I looked up, my head bobbing without control as I gazed at the person touching me. I couldn't remember his name. But he was a high-ranking official, the one who greeted us on our first day.

Snow crunched below me as he dragged me out of the remnants of the tent. The cloth sides were long gone from the fire.

"I said *stop!*" a voice said.

I watched, terrified, as a sword sliced through his chest and up into his chin. With his eyes wide, he opened his mouth to say something. Although the only sound that came out was the gurgle of blood. With a wet squelch, they pulled the sword from his chest. His body slumped to the side, dropping me.

"Grab her," the voice ordered again. Whether it was from pain or from shock. The world faded away into nothingness, again.

38

Just a Toy

I had no idea how long I was out for. When I came to, water dripped from my face as I sat tied to a chair, the water a murky brown color, making me question its origin. My stomach flopped at the idea. I pushed down the thought. The room was dark; the gray rock that built the room glistened with moisture. The air was damp. When I took a deep breath, a sharp pain stabbed at my lungs.

I looked down at my body. My shirt was filthy. Blood encased the fabric, drying on it. Leaving the cloth to hang stiffly on me.

The door rattled, as whoever was on the other side unlocked the door.

"Look who finally woke up. Now you can answer a few of my questions, girl," an aged voice called out. The darkness of the room seemed to surround him, the shadows cursing him to appear faceless.

"I know nothing," I said to the silhouette before me. By his stature, it was apparent he used a cane. His silhouette was slightly bent over as he walked into the room.

His feet dragged against the stone flooring, making the tap of the cane sound aggressive. "How did you make it to the Elven Realm?" He pounded the cane on the ground.

JUST A TOY

A guard slipped into the room with a large trunk. The elderly men nodded at him as he placed it on the ground, leaving promptly.

The repetition of his footsteps and cane set me on edge. My heartbeat felt as if it was in my throat, threatening to spill out onto the floor if I spoke. "I was shipwrecked here," I stammered out as I watched him flip the old, weathered box open. The contents gleamed dangerously. Few of the tools were rusty.

"Shipwrecked from where?" He singled out a small blade from the box, shifting it in his hand as if he was testing the weight of it.

My inner voice fought with me. *Do I divulge the location of my cottage? Does it even matter? It isn't your home,* my inner voice shot back.

"Answer me, girl, or I will make you wish you had." He shook the blade back and forth. It appeared to glow with devilish delight.

I turned my head to the side, not willing to look at the man to hide my resolve that grew in my heart. "I'm from the Human Realm, in a town called Mallert."

Silence stretched for a few moments, too long, as the older man likely wracked his brain for information about the Human Realm, a realm he had never been to before.

"How did you become friends with the Queen of Valdis?" he questioned me, gently dragging the back of the blade on my head. The older man walked around me as he did so, pausing once he came face to face with me once again.

He grabbed my chin, forcing me to look upon his weathered features. Hair that once had been another color was now completely gray. Skin that had once been firm and elastic now hung uncomfortably around the eyes and at the jawline. Magic swirled around his face, leaving his face void of any defining characteristics.

I closed my eyes at the mention of Lilja, as tears threatened to spill out onto my cheeks. My inner voice seemed to yell at me: *He can't know how much she means to use. He'll use me as a pawn. A game piece to get back at her.* I took a deep breath, allowing the moist air to fill my lungs to calm my racing heart.

I met him face-to-face. As I opened my eyes, he searched them for answers. "How do you know the Queen of Valdis?" He pushed the blade into my cheek. Heat spread through that side of my face as blood welled at the injury.

I scrambled for a reasonable answer. "The queen's men found me," I said. My voice was wavering as I thought of Lilja. "They took me to her. They promised me a way back home. Back to my realm." A sob broke through as I spewed lies at the man interrogating me. "But they lied. They kept me, dragging me along on this quest of theirs." I winced, trying to seem spiteful.

"If they kept you as a slave, why were you in the military tent we attacked? Why risk classified information by speaking it in front of someone who could run away at any moment?"

"Because she wanted to keep me as a pet."

Another sob broke through my body as I thought about Lilja being held by Kallan. *Was she even alive?*

"If you were a pet, then why did you have this ring?" he asked as he held up my engagement ring in his meaty hands.

"It was a gift from my mother," I said, trying to hide my authentic emotion. "Give it back," I lunged at him, the ties holding me to the chair biting into my wrists and ankles.

"No, I quite like it. Maybe I will give it to my niece. She always did like dainty things. Why did you have these daggers strapped to your thighs? Most importantly, why did you have one in between your breasts? I can't imagine Queen Lilja was daft enough to allow you to carry a weapon." He pushed the tip of the blade into my thigh. It pierced through the trousers on my leg and into my soft flesh.

I gritted my teeth, trying to ignore the pain radiating through my leg.

"Tough one, aye. Not for long," he said, grinning, a gleam of satisfaction in his eye.

"How. Do. You. Know. Lilja?" He gritted his teeth, spit flying into my face with each syllable rolling off his tongue. His breath smelled like alcohol and pipe.

I turned my head in disgust. A wetness traveled down my leg, pooling in the chair.

"Why hide the fact that you are a feeble human?"

"Queen Lilja was ashamed of keeping me as her plaything…" I said, not willing to break.

"You. Are. Lying. I don't know what you are lying for but you are. I'm not sure who you are or what your plan is, but you need to tell me—if you want to live, you'll tell me." He bent over the chest, pulling a pair of clamps out. For an elderly man, he walked towards me quickly, his eyes trained on my fingernails.

I curled them into a fist as a response. "No, please don't." My heart beat erratically, sweat stung at my tear streaked eyes.

"Give me the truth!" He shook his head.

"I am!" My stomach did somersaults in my abdomen. *I can't let him know the truth. Lilja is my fated. I have to protect her.*

"You will!" His free hand he grabbed my middle finger, grabbing onto my nail, pulling it free from its fleshy bed. I writhed in pain. A shiver ran up my body as I stifled a scream in my mouth. "If you want to act like an elf so badly, I am going to make you look like one."

His hand grabbed the tip of one of my ears as he jerked my head to the side. He leaned to the side, grabbing the knife from the chest and slicing my ear. I jerked in response to the pain, a cry escaping my lips.

"Stop." Tears rolled down my cheeks. "I am telling you the truth, I am—was—the queen's plaything. Nothing more, nothing less. Please, just let me go." A sob wracked through me.

"You are not telling me the truth! I know it. There is no other reason for you to be in that tent. I will ask you one more time, who are you to the queen? Are the humans rallying behind her to overthrow Ardour?"

"The queen never told me anything. She was careful to not speak about the war in front of me. She thought I could be a spy. I swear, it is all I know." I hiccuped, my head swimming from blood loss. "Please, just let me go."

"Wrong answer, girl, I will make you regret not telling me the truth." He grabbed my other ear, slicing a piece off, much like the other. His eyes gleamed with darkness, holding the mangled piece of my ear.

My head hung to my chest. My strength felt like it was leaving as fast as the blood welled at my various wounds. *This is it. I'm dying. I'm sorry, Lilja. If you are alive, I didn't tell them.*

My eyes fluttered closed as a chill set over my body. *It's so cold.* A bang occurred somewhere in the distance. My essence felt like it was trying to fly away from my physical form. I blinked, staring down at my lifeless body. A tether held me to it. Mindlessly, I tugged at it. The room was blurry, all shapes in nonsensical blobs of color. *No, not yet.* Someone in my head said. *Please don't leave yet, you must live.*

Another blur of color entered the room, as I tried to climb down the rope holding me to my body as the darkness behind me tried to swallow. I cried out in frustration, my happy ending gone. *Lilja, she's dead, she's gone and now I'm going to die a weak human.* Hands grabbed at my body, hot, almost burning to the touch

I screamed, but no sound escaped as something tugged me back to my body. I blinked as a weathered water mage sat beside me, her body blessed with wrinkles of old age. She gasped, her hand to her chest, clutching a shattered necklace. "She is back from the brink of death, your highness. I cannot heal her wounds. The stone is shattered."

"Thank you, Bruama, you may leave. I can take it from here," a high, feminine voice called out. "Uncle, that is enough. Killing the only informant we have is unwise. I believe she would have already told you the information she had, especially after you mutilated her so. Poor thing nearly died from fright."

The slender hands of my rescuer quickly unstrapped my arms and legs from the chair. Roughly scooping my form up, she grunted.

"I see Lilja has a taste for the larger women," the lady chuckled. With no strength left in my body, all I could do was lay limply as she held me bridal style.

"Oh, uncle, it would be unwise to go behind my back again, especially if you want to keep your head." The woman glowered as she turned for the door.

The man sputtered, "Of course, your highness. I meant no disrespect. I was only thinking of the kingdom." Out of the corner of my eye, I watched as the elderly man's face turned beet red. He bowed at the tall woman who seemed to hold me easily.

She said nothing as she carried me throughout the vast castle. The only sounds present were my fast-paced breathing and her footsteps. Soon we found ourselves in front of a large wooden door. While the design was plain, it was not a door to a cell. She adjusted me, only holding me with one arm, just long enough to open the door.

Placing me down on the small cot, a little less than gently, she turned, not facing me. "A physician will be over to bandage your wounds. Do not give them trouble or I will tell them to let you die of infection."

I gulped, nodding my head. My eyes fluttered closed once more.

I awoke to murmuring voices and gentle hands tugging on my ears. "Hold still, human, if you squirm, it will only make it worse." I halted, moving as the soft hands worked on my ear, a whimper escaping my lips.

The room was cream colored, ornate trim covered the borders of the wall, revealing the opulence of the owner. I eyed the deep-voiced physician cautiously. He had dark short hair. It was just long enough to brush the tips of his eyelids. Tattoos covered his skin, dark swirls circled his forearms and traveled into the rolled-up sleeves of his bottom up.

"Do you like what you see, human?" he asked, a superficial smirk on his face. The young elf on the other side of my head scoffed.

I recoiled, wincing at the movement, my head swimming. "No. I was trying to decide if I could take you in a fight."

He tipped his head back and laughed. "Well, you certainly have a backbone. I suppose you'd have to have one to be interrogated by Daveed."

His trained eyes were on my ear as he gently put a salve on top. The result was instant numbness that spread throughout the area, creeping to my cheek.

"Sit up so we can work properly. Odds are if you are to stay in your current position, one of your ears will be crooked." I sat up, wincing as the scabs forming on my body tugged uncomfortably.

"I cannot make your ear look like a human's. The damage is irreversible. The salve will make it numb until I finish sewing. Your ears will end up looking like an elf's, much better than a human's."

"What are your names?" I asked, trying to ignore the tugging sensation as both of them began sewing the tattered remains of my ears back together.

"My name is Pima, human," the younger physician said.

"My name is Orus. Now stop talking. It makes you move too much," Orus said.

I fought the urge to roll my eyes in response, wondering why they were helping me. They certainly didn't seem to want to help me.

They worked rapidly, wrapping up my ears to protect them from air and dirt. Before I could protest, they grabbed shears from a tray and cut away my shirt from my body. A shiver ran down my spine as the air hit my bare waist. Goosebumps spread throughout, stopping just below my wrapped breast. They stitched the wound, rubbing it with salve. With each stitch, the blood clotted and slowed. Streaks of bruising had already spread around the wound. *That will definitely hurt in the morning.*

"Why are you both working so hard to sew me up painlessly? What does that woman want with me?"

Orus stood up from the chair, stretching, ignoring my question. He poured a cup of tea; steam rose from it lazily. "Drink this. I will answer questions later. After they have answered the questions from the front."

"What is it?"

"Something to make you more comfortable and help promote healing. Just drink it." He held the cup up to me as Pima cut the trousers I wore. I raised an eyebrow, sniffing the liquid apprehensively. Lavender, feverfew, and something else I couldn't pinpoint. The aromatic smell was enough to make me crinkle my nose.

Orus, noticing my disgust, rolled his eyes. "Drink it. The taste is much more palpable than the smell."

I sipped the overly sweet tea, feeling it slide down and settle uneasily in my stomach. I leaned back, allowing the herbs to take effect.

When I blinked, I awoke to a large canopy bed. Yellow fabric hung from the top, cascading down to the floor. I sat up slowly, the stitching on my wounds protesting as I did so. I looked around, taking in my surroundings.

Where am I? I swung my legs over the bed. My head pounded as I stood. Unsteadily, I grabbed onto the dresser beside the bed, my body still weak from the injuries I sustained. The memories from the attack and the interrogation rush back to me. I shook my head as if to push away the result of painful memories picked away at my sanity.

Making it to the vanity, I look at myself in the mirror. My usual full baby face I had once struggled to lose now looked hollow; dark circles gripped at my eyes. Bruises kissed at my skin. I pulled up the nightgown I wore, trying not to worry about who put it on me. The cut below my ribs was covered. Fresh blood had bloomed on the white sterile padding. My thighs appeared the worst. The small stab marks Daveed carved into me littered them like trash on the beach after a storm.

Dark bruises circled the entry points of the stitches. I limped to the window, peering outside. The sky was sunny, the snow below reflected it, making the kingdom shine. Mother nature was apparently not understanding my mood. The rock wall seemed to go down forever.

"I hope you weren't planning on jumping. It would be quite the descent." I whirled around, the motion sending me crashing to the ground.

"Who are you?" I asked the tall, muscular woman before me. Her straight hair was brown and down to her waist. It was the same woman who had saved me from Daveed. I crossed my arms, attempting to make myself look as menacing as possible.

"Who are you?" I asked, trying to ignore the pounding in my head.

She stared at me for a moment. "You've spent all this time with the late Queen Lilja and never figured out what I looked like?"

"Late?" I asked, not waiting to see if she had anything else to say.

"Ah, yes. You don't know, do you? I suspect the Queen of Valdis is dead, little pet."

39

Suspected Dead

I fought the urge to dissolve into the floor, blinking back tears. I stared at the tall women before me. "Suspect?"

"Yes, she's presumed dead. My spies have yet to see Lilja since the attack. I assume her inner circle is keeping her death a secret. To keep morale high for the war, which they will inevitably lose."

I tried to keep my pain out of my face. "You never answer my question. Who are you?"

"I am Queen Alieta of Ardour, little pet. Lilja might have enjoyed keeping you as a pet." Alieta walked near me. Her fingertips brushed against my chin, and I fought the urge to pull away. "But I would take little joy in keeping an animal with such a short lifespan." Alieta pulled away from me, peering out over the bustling city. "Stay in my good graces. I will find you a way home to the Human Realm."

I took a step backwards as her unexpected words spilled from her mouth. "Why? Not that I don't appreciate your hospitality," I said. "I just don't understand why you would help me."

"Ah, I see. Unlike my uncle, I recognize the innocence in people. Valdis is a cold kingdom, just like their queen. Lilja saw an opportunity with you and chose you as a pet. She might even have acted like she cared for you. But I assure you it is all a sham. She's coldhearted. Incapable of showing affection to something so weak as a human."

Her face was void of any emotion other than disgust.

I tried to not let the words she spat out affect my emotions. *She's beating you.* My inner voice warned me, *she's testing you. She wants to see who you are. Is Lilja truly gone?*

"So I'm to stay in this room until you decide to let me go back to the Human Realm? Like a caged animal?" I asked, unable to hold back the myriad of emotions running through my heart.

"Yes, my caged animal. I will have a maid come to your room every day to bring you food and to take you on a walk, for exercise. Once a week you will have dinner with me, if you behave. If I find you are being unruly to my employees, I will have you thrown in the dungeon. Is that understood?"

I nodded slowly, unable to think of anything else to contribute to her statement. She smiled back to me as if she was content with my mute answer. Alieta turned her back to me as she left the room. The lock mechanism clanked back into place. I slid to the ground, ignoring the pain in my stitches as sobs broke free of my chest as I heard the queen's footsteps fade down the hall.

The cold tile underneath me sent an icy shiver up my spine as tears ran down my cheeks. *What is the point? What was the point of all of this?* my inner voice shouted at the gods. *Why must you ruin everything? I had something. Something good.* Absentmindedly, my fingers went to where my ring hand been, only to notice it was gone.

I stared at the ceiling, attempting to use my grief to glare through the roof, at the gods. They deserved to see my pain, to feel uncomfortable.

I wasn't sure how long I laid on the floor—long enough to watch the shadows stretch and consume a better half of the room. My tears dried on my cheeks.

A quiet knock echoed in the room. Without waiting for a response, the door creaked open. A small elf maid walked in. I turned my head in her direction. If it surprised her to see me on the ground, she gave no indication.

"My lady, it is improper to lay on the ground. Even in your current condition. Did you fall?" Her voice was flat, reminiscent of the neighbors south of me growing up. They always acted so uninterested in my family because we were at a less financial standing.

I croaked out a *yes*, unwilling to let her know how hurt I was. She approached me; each footstep clinked on the ground deliberately. "I am going to pick you up by the shoulders, to sit you up. It is up to you to stand. If you feel you cannot, I will have to fetch someone else to assist. I lack the strength to pick someone up of your size."

I rolled my eyes, fighting the urge to mock her. She looped her arms under my arms, helping me sit up. Blood rushed in my ears, making them throb. I stood up, trudging to the bed.

With me on the bed, the Elven maid nodded, satisfied. She pushed in a small cart with a domed platter from the hallway. Walking up to me, she grabbed a small folded tray from underneath the bed. I scooted back; she plopped the tray on the bed bitterly. *As if she should be doing something better than serving me, the pet of the royals,* I thought. Placing the plate on the tray, she took the lid off, leaving the room. I eyed the food cautiously. The plate comprised a fruit and typical breakfast fare.

I pushed the meal away, ignoring my grumbling stomach. Not listening to the food calling to me, I pulled the blankets up and over my head. *There's no point. No point to this,* I thought as I waited for sleep to take me once again.

When I awoke again, the sky was dark. Warily, I set up in bed. The tray of food was gone. I waited, listening to the quiet groans of the old castle shift in the night. Waiting for her, for her voice to call to me. *Lilja,* I thought, not daring to speak out loud—in case they had spies listening into my room.

Lilja, baby, please. If you are alive, please answer. Please, I-I need you. I feel like I just found you, found my happiness. My family. I can't lose it so soon. I can't lose you, so please, if you are alive, send me a sign. Anything, please.

Tears ran down my cheeks as another round of sobs broke through the silence. The silence not only in the room but also in my mind. Was she truly gone?

I must have cried myself to sleep, because when I awoke again, light was streaming through the yellow fabric of the canopy bed. The door opened, revealing Orus. He carried a small medicine bag. The contents clanked as he strode towards me.

"How are you healing, my lady?" His eyebrow raised as he looked me up and down.

I looked down at myself, the clothes I had donned for the past two days wrinkled. My hair hung dully at my sides, tangled. I could only guess what my face looked like, bruised to all hell.

"I'm fine," I responded mechanically.

Orus hummed in response, not saying anything as he sat on the side of the bed. He reached for my ears, undoing the bandage. He cleaned the wound and re-bandaged it. "Take your shirt off so I can assess the wound on your ribs."

I squeaked in surprise but listened. Unsteadily, I undid the buttons on my blouse. I gripped my chest as he clicked his tongue disapprovingly at the dried blood on my bandage. "You broke open a stitch."

He pulled away the bandage. I peeked down at it. Dried blood covered my skin. Most of the stitches looked perfect. A few hung limply, unraveled next to the wound.

"I will have to sew it back, I hope you know. And I do not have a numbing salve, but that's what you deserve. No doubt you were trying to do too much." He rummaged in his bag, pulling out a small sewing kit. I hissed in response as he poked the needle into my skin.

Once he finished sewing, he re-wrapped the wound. "Now let me see how the wounds on your legs are healing." I nodded, revealing my thighs. Bruises circled each wound.

"At least these look good. Make sure you are resting. You popping your stitches will accomplish nothing other than letting infection in." With his work finished, he left, leaving me alone in my thoughts.

Time crawled by. The maid brought food without saying a word. She deposited it on the tray again. I got up, ignoring the platter of food, meandering to the window to peer outside. The wind rustled through my tangled hair. People moved outside, trying to get out of the blistering cold. Gardeners and guards circled the yard like vultures.

I pulled myself up on the seat and leaned my head on the half-closed window.

Days ticked by. The routine became clear. The maid, whose name I still don't know, brought food twice a day. I barely touched any of it, my appetite gone. Orus or Pima entered and changed the bandages that littered my body. I spent my days looking out the window, out into the freedom I couldn't have.

40

Resolved Feelings

Miss stuck up the maid walked through the door abruptly. The items on her cart rattled with protest at such sudden movements. "The queen has instructed me to prepare you for brunch with her," she said.

"Well, you can tell your queen I have no interest in accompanying her to brunch. I am quite content to sit here," I said, turning my head to look back out of the window.

She placed her hand on her hip. "It was not a request. I am to prepare you. Brunch is in two hours. With the looks of you, it'll take every minute of those two hours to get you ready. From the smell of you, it's like you haven't taken a bath the entire time. Plus, your hair looks greasy enough to lotion your whole body. You look like a matted dog. If you are intent on disagreeing with me, I can have the queen come up here herself and set you straight. I doubt you want to go through that."

I remained looking out the window, debating if I should even retort anything back to the stubborn maid.

I slipped off the window seat, turning to look at her. "Do what you will," I motioned to the rest of me. The maid nodded, grinning evilly.

The next hour and a half was tortuous.

Two male butlers wheeled in a large steaming tub of water. I gritted my teeth as the hot water stung my skin. "It's too hot." I glared at her.

"It's cleaning you. Stop complaining. We need to get the grime off of you somehow." She lathered my hair in soap. She moved to roughly scrubbing my skin, allowing the soap in my hair to soak.

With the bath now done, she shooed me to the bed. I shivered as the air hit me. She grabbed bottles off of the cart, painting my fingernails and toenails a blue tint. While those dried, she walked to the wardrobe that I hadn't bothered to open this whole time. It was packed with dresses, each one a different color and style. Shoes littered the bottom of the cabinet. I raised an eyebrow at it. *Why in the world is that thing so packed? Why does the queen care what I wear?*

She pulled out a white dress—blue embroidery littered the ruffled sleeves and bottoms—long with a corset. I groaned internally—I did not want to wear that.

"Oh, don't even complain; it is improper to not wear one. I'm not sure of the current fashion in the Human Realm, but I can assure you this is the right way here. Now get up so we can get your wound re-wrapped and you dressed."

I obeyed, ignoring the pulsing pain on my side as she tied me into the corset. After clothes, she turned to torturing me by brushing through my unkempt hair. She roughly undid knots as she ran the brush through my hair and then put my long hair into an updo, curling random strands to hang gently at the sides of my face. I gazed into the mirror, looking at my strange body. I was nearly unrecognizable, my cheeks gaunt from not eating. My eyes held onto dark bags from the nightmares that plagued me.

My ears were the most foreign. Orus had done a good job of stitching them back together. A faint pink line traveled up to my now pointed ear. My hair was dull and lifeless, even though she had just washed it. The maid moved to my face, powdered it, and added rouge to my lips, giving them a pink color.

She pulled away, cracking a small smile. "Finally, you look halfway presentable." The maid glanced up at the clock. The hand read 9:45.

"Just in time, too. Now you will follow me and say nothing to anyone unless you are spoken to," she said firmly, giving me a pair of flats.

"I feel like a doll." I looked at myself in the mirror.

"This is the clothing the queen has provided to you. This is what she wants you to look like. Now follow me." Without another word, the maid turned and walked out into the hallway.

I paused at the threshold between the hallway and the room I had called my cell for weeks. *Please Lilja, if you are truly still out there, give me strength,* I projected into the void as I closed my eyes tightly. Taking a deep breath, I watched the retreating form of the maid down the hall.

I hurried to her. The hallway was flawless, beautifully decorated with paintings and statues. I couldn't help but shiver as a foreboding feeling came over me. The feeling of being watched.

The maid walked hastily as I struggled to keep up. Her lips were tightly sealed, as they always were.

Leading me down a winding staircase, we soon found ourselves outside in a large and closed-off greenhouse. They set a table up in the middle of large, manicured rose bushes. Even though the weather outside was blisteringly cold, inside here it was warm. It was a wonder that something like this was possible. On the table there was a small spread of breakfast food.

"Good morning, Elowen, how nice you are to join me. I would say that you look beautiful today, but I'd be lying. Have you been eating?" the queen commented, coming from behind a large bush in the greenhouse.

"Why does it matter to you?" I looked down at the impractical flats on my feet.

"It matters to me because you are my guest for the time being." The queen raised her eyebrow, looking me up and down.

"I've been eating enough." My stomach betrayed me by rumbling. Feeling the blood rush to my head, I looked off to the side, pretending to look at the miscellaneous flowers growing in bed before me.

"Cailin, have you been adequately feeding my guest?" The queen stood with her arms crossed, her eyes slit in the maid's direction.

So that's her name, I thought.

Cailin shifted her weight on her feet, her eyes cast downwards. "Yes, your highness. She chooses not to eat. When I leave the plate, she does not eat, every time I come to take away the plate, it is always un—"

"Why did you not bring this to my attention?"

"I did not think a small matter of a woman starving herself would concern you. My apologies. I seemed to have misread what she meant to you." Cailin's face was red with embarrassment or anger. I didn't know.

"You may leave us. I'll have someone call for you when Elowen will be taken back to her room. Oh Cailin, in the future it would be wise of you to make sure you notify me if Elowen seems to have this problem again. Do you understand?" The queen's face was hard, her lips in a tight line.

Cailin nodded and gave a small curtsey and scrambled out of the room. The confidence she had earlier was gone, now replaced with fear.

The queen turned towards me, smiling, the rage on her face gone, replaced with a smile. I couldn't help but notice the anger still held in her eyes.

"Please sit and eat, Elowen. It will do you no good to starve to death. Do not give Lilja the satisfaction of breaking you," the queen said quietly, as if I was going to dissolve into tears.

"Have you heard anything from the front? Is she truly gone?" I asked as I sat at the table. She pushed in my chair and then went to her own, crossing her fingers together.

"There has not been an official report of a funeral, but there has not been a report of her being alive either. Fear not if she is alive. I will not let her take you back. You will not go back to being her pet."

I paused, putting food on my plate, to look her in the eyes. "Thank you, my queen. I can't help but feel like your pet now. I fear that I have switched from one master to another."

I attempted to smile through the pain I felt in my heart. *Is she truly gone?*

"It would bring me indescribable joy to be free," I said, my voice cracking at the end.

"Do not feel like a pet here, Elowen. After all, you are my guest. Think of it as a protection from the Kingdom of Valdis. You are your own person. As long as you do what I ask, you are free. Elowen, you may call me Alieta," Alieta said, nodding towards me as she held up a cup of tea as a toast.

"Thank you, Alieta, for not letting people control me." I sipped the tea, the heat of the hot liquid falling down into my empty stomach.

With my stomach uncomfortably full, I sat as Alieta had another servant fetch Cailin. As we waited, Alieta showed me around the greenhouse.

"Your greenhouse is exquisite," I said, attempting to fill the awkward silence between us.

"I'm so glad you think so. You may ask Cailin to bring you down here from time to time. I apologize for the emotional trauma this realm has put you through. The physical trauma alone is enough to break some people." Alieta sucked in a breath. "It just goes to show how strong you are."

Strong? How was I strong? I'm letting this woman keep me as a plaything. Even though Alieta was a few feet away, I still felt impossibly close to the women responsible for Lilja's death. Taking a step back, I gazed at the tall tree in the center of the greenhouse. It was apparent that the tree had seen many winters. Its thick trunk was nearly the size of the door frame. Its tall branches fanned over the ceiling, giving the space beneath it a dark shadow.

"My great-grandfather had this tree planted for his wife. She loved gardening so much that he had this whole greenhouse added on to the castle," Alieta said.

"I am here, your highness."

I accepted Cailin's presence gratefully. Time with Alieta made me feel uncomfortable. *Why is she so nice? What does she want?*

"Finally. I was wondering when you were going to show up," Alieta said, already walking away and out of the greenhouse.

She paused, turning towards us, giving a slight bow. "Thank you for spending time with me today, Elowen. You humble me."

Cailin led me back to my room, saying nothing as she locked me back in it, leaving me to my thoughts. I took off the makeup from brunch, not wanting a reminder of the day. I dove underneath the warm inviting blankets of my bed after slipping the corset and dress off.

Wishing nothing more than to be in Liljas' warm arms, tears pricked to my eyes as I drifted off to sleep.

"Queen Elowen, do you want tea cakes at the ceremony today?" the elderly butler asked as I sat down at my desk.

"What ceremony?" I looked around at the room. Books lined the built-in shelves.

Where am I?

"Have you truly forgotten what day it is? It's the opening ceremony for the new garden. All the kingdom will be present. It's the largest ceremony we've had since the great war. Peace and prosperity have finally blessed this land thanks to you and the rest of the brave souls that fought." She proudly puffed out her chest.

"Oh yes, of course," I said, trying not to look too confused. "I'm not sure how I forgot today's date. My apologies for the confusion. Tea cakes will be fine for the ceremony, be sure to add drinks as well. Today is certainly a joyous day." I shooed away the elderly lady.

What is going on?

With the servant gone, I went to the window. It was apparent I was in a castle. An enormous wall separated the royal yard with rows of busy business streets and houses.

"It's beautiful, isn't it?" Darach's voice called out from behind me. I whirled around to be face to face with her rooted form.

"What is this?" I demanded.

"Your potential future. This is Valdis. Or what could be Valdis if you defeat the people responsible for the blight. These people have an opportunity for a happy ending. They won't if you don't stop feeling sorry for yourself. Is starving really the way you want to go?" She crossed her arms.

"Why are you just contacting me now? It's been weeks since the attack. I haven't spoken to anybody since then. Ardour suspects Lilja

RESOLVED FEELINGS

is dead. What else am I supposed to do? I'm just a human. I'm not immortal and I don't have any special powers. What am I supposed to do to stop the blight?"

Darach's voice echoed in my head. "You can find the source for this damn infection. You are at the castle, the castle in which the original plan was to infiltrate. Don't you see? You are instrumental in finding the cure for it. Elowen, I thought you were smarter than this, but evidently not. Get Ardour's queen to trust you. It is obvious she has taken a liking to you. Use that to your advantage. The people of Valdis deserve to be happy. As Lilja's fated, it is your responsibility to make that happen. Regardless of whether she is alive or not."

I blinked, sitting up straight in bed. My thoughts ran rampant in my head. *What the fuck did I just dream? Was it a dream? Was it truly Darach? She doesn't even know if Lilja's alive.*

I clutched my chest, trying to calm my racing heartbeat. *She's right, of course she is.* Lilja loved me enough and trusted me enough to help run her kingdom. The food from brunch rolled in my stomach uncomfortably as anxiety sent a shiver running down my spine. I rubbed the scar on my arm anxiously with my palm.

I can't let her down. I can't. She deserved more—more than just me. More than just some random human girl fated to her.

I clambered out of bed, sitting in front of the makeup mirror. My hair was in disarray, the bags under my eyes dark with the lack of sleep.

"No," I whispered to my reflection. "She wanted me. Lilja loved me. She trusted me enough to welcome me onto her team. I can and will show Valdis that her trust was not ill fated. Ardour will rue the day they let me live, because in the end Valdis will be prosperous." I thought back to the vision Darach had just given me.

I clasped my hands together, looking at the ceiling. "Don't worry, Lilja, I will find the cause of blight and I will find the cure. Even if it's the last thing I'll do."

THE END

Afterword

I was tired. Tired of reading books that never reflected me. Tired of pretending like books were (insert y/n) fanfictions. Where I could insert whoever I wanted into a book.

I read a book at the peak of the pandemic and thought it would be phenomenal as a LGBTQ+ version. This is how this story came to be. A fever dream of staying up in the middle of the night writing a chapter a week. Sometimes with everything sprawled onto my breakfast bar and sometimes tucked next to my pretty wife as she snores in my ear. While I tried to come up with the next great fight scene.

As cringey as it would sound, an online writing platform played a huge part in this book. My faithful hundred readers pushed me to keep writing, so if you are reading this, thank you.

Thank you to everyone who has listened to me prater on about my book and thank you to my friends who pushed me towards success.

God's and Goddesses

Here are all the titles and names of all the Gods and Goddesses. Not all of these beings will appear in this book. It is just a way for you to get a taste of what is to come.

Niamh- Goddess of the Sun

Esmersey- Goddess of the Moon
  Their three Children

Athren-God of Seasons

Darach-Goddess of the Nymphs
  Darach's and Riand's Children

  - Arclavian (First ever Forest Nymph)
  - Easian (First ever Water Nymph)
  - Gairen (First ever Siren)

Hesper-Goddess of night
  Hesper's Children

  - Endri God of Vision/Dreaming (Non-binary)
  - Runen God of Death

Mabilia- God of the Fated.

Pavati- Goddess of Rivers

Riand- God of the Sea

Arlo- God of the Earth

Printed in the USA
CPSIA information can be obtained
at www.ICGtesting.com
LVHW052019170924
791344LV00001B/62